EMBRACE
THE NIGHT

Books by Crystal Jordan

CARNAL DESIRES

ON THE PROWL

UNTAMED

PRIMAL HEAT

EMBRACE THE NIGHT

SEXY BEAST V
(with Kate Douglas and Vonna Harper)

SEXY BEAST 9
(with Vonna Harper and Lisa Renee Jones)

UNDER THE COVERS
(with Lorie O'Clare and P.J. Mellor)

Published by Kensington Publishing Corporation

EMBRACE THE NIGHT

CRYSTAL JORDAN

APHRODISIA

KENSINGTON PUBLISHING CORP.

www.kensingtonbooks.com

APHRODISIA BOOKS are published by

Kensington Publishing Corp.
119 West 40th Street
New York, NY 10018

All Kensington titles, imprints, and distributed lines are available at special quantity discounts for bulk purchases for sales promotion, premiums, fund-raising, and educational, or institutional use.

Special book excerpts or customized printings can also be created to fit specific needs. For details, write or phone the office of the Kensington Special Sales Manager: Kensington Publishing Corp., 119 West 40th Street, New York, NY 10018. Attn. Special Sales Department. Phone: 1-800-221-2647.

Aphrodisia and the A logo Reg. U.S. Pat. & TM Off.

ISBN-13: 978-0-7582-3831-3
ISBN-10: 0-7582-3831-2

First Kensington Trade Paperback Printing: June 2011

10 9 8 7 6 5 4 3 2 1

Printed in the United States of America

Acknowledgments

This book is special. No, really. It is. This is the first book I ever started to write, quite a few years ago. At the time, it was a comedy. At the time, I had no idea what I was doing when it came to writing a story. I labored through many, many drafts of this book, and finally realized I didn't have the chops to do the characters justice. Frustrated, I put it aside and thought I'd never come back to it.

But this book is special. These characters are special. Merck and Chloe and Alex wouldn't stop popping up in the back of my mind, reminding me that their story was still untold.

So, I dragged it out one day and dusted it off. I started reading, and it was even more awful than I remembered. I had to scrap everything, except the characters and the basic bones of the story. It went from comedy to dark and sexy. And my editor, John Scognamiglio, was his usual awesome self, bought the book, and gave these characters a chance to have their story finished. Finally.

There are so many others who have helped me get where I am with my writing, and helped me get this book to where it is. This acknowledgments page wouldn't be doing what it's supposed to if I didn't give them a nod for all they've done for me.

There is my best friend, Michal, and my boyfriend, Frank. My two favorite partners in crime. Then there are the other authors who've prodded, cajoled, encouraged, or otherwise kicked my ass into meeting my deadlines: Kate Pearce, Loribelle Hunt, Dayna Hart, R. G. Alexander, Eden Bradley, Karen Erickson, Robin L. Rotham, Patti O'Shea, Rhiannon Leith, Elaina Huntley, Lilli Feisty, and Gemma Halliday. And, of course, my Grams.

Thank you all for being part of this story with me. My story as a writer.

I

Gods, but she needed this.

Chloe's body arched beneath the heavy, muscular form of the most talented warlock she'd ever fucked. And he wasn't even inside her yet.

A low moan slipped from her throat when Merek's hands closed over her breasts. His thumbs chafed her nipples, and a little smile kicked up the side of his full lips and crinkled the corners of his gray eyes as he watched the tips of her breasts tighten for him. Little bolts of lightning flickered around the warlock's hands and up his forearms. The shocks hit her flesh, sizzling her nerve endings. She jolted, but a flood of moisture slicked her pussy. *More.* Gods, she craved more.

Sinking one hand into his dark blond hair, she urged his head down. A chuckle rumbled from his chest while he obliged her. His hot tongue swirled around each nipple in turn, sucking them deep into his mouth. When that same electrical current pulsed from his tongue to her breast, she writhed helplessly, a scream ripping from her.

"You like that, don't you, Chloe?" He glanced up at her, his gaze gleaming with silver light. His teeth scraped over her nipple when she didn't answer. She jerked against his hold on her, her thoughts scattering into incoherency. "Don't you, sweetheart?"

"Y-yes, Merek." A shiver rippled over her skin as his tongue soothed the sting his teeth had left. "Oh, gods, yes. I like it."

Her nails scored his back, raking down his flesh. He shuddered over her, groaning. His hips bucked against hers. She could feel his long, hard cock sliding over her naked flesh. His dick was already damp with pre-cum, but he didn't try to enter her. She wanted him deep inside her. Now.

Parting her thighs, she wrapped her legs around his flanks and lifted herself into him, rubbing the lips of her wet pussy on his cock. His white teeth flashed in a pirate's grin, his gaze heavy-lidded. She arched her body into him, enjoying the pleasure that flashed in his gaze as she watched him watch her twist on his sheets, the fabric warm and smooth against her back. He angled his hips and ground himself against her clit, but still didn't slide that long cock into her. Instead, he eased his weight away from her a bit.

"No, don't go," she whispered, shoving her fingers into his silky hair and dragging him back down to her breast. Her heart pounded so loudly in her ears, it drowned out the ragged sound of their breathing.

He batted at her nipple with his tongue, shoving the tight tip against the roof of his mouth. Her nails dug into his scalp, and he grunted, biting down on the beaded crest in retaliation. Her breath froze in her lungs, her body jerking under the lash of too many sensations overloading every nerve at once. "*Merek. Merek, please!*"

He released her breast, blowing a cool stream of air onto her damp flesh. "I like it when you beg."

It felt so fucking good, she thought she might die. Still, she needed *more*. She needed to lose herself in the scorching heat of this moment with this man. "P-please."

Those tiny sparks of lightning arced from his fingertips as he stroked them down her ribs, her stomach, and into the thatch of hair between her legs. The first touch of his hand on her clit made her sob with need. Excitement twisted like a wild thing inside her, and she had to grit her teeth to keep from screaming again when his callused finger penetrated her sex. He flicked his digits over her slick folds, diving into her soaking pussy. He hummed low in his throat. "So wet for me. I'm going to love fucking your tight little pussy."

"Yes. I want that." Her head rolled on the pillow, sweat gathering at her temples to slip down her skin as her muscles shook in reaction to all he was doing to her, in anticipation of all he *would* do to her. "Hurry."

"Not just yet." The pad of his thumb stroked her clit in time with his plunging digits. He worked her at a fast, punishing rhythm that made her twist in his embrace, a low keen of need spilling from her lips. She was so close, her inner muscles clenching on his fingers with every hard push into her body, tingles skipping and racing down her skin, but she knew he wouldn't let her go over the edge into orgasm until he decided. He was the master of this game, of that she had no doubt. The mere thought made her burn. It was exactly why she'd picked him for the night.

She sucked in a deep breath, trying to calm herself, but it only drew in the heady smell of sex and the rich, masculine scent of *him*. Heat and magic flared deep within her, spells she was barely conscious of casting. If he was going to drive her crazy with lust, then turnabout was fair play.

Golden light poured from her fingers as she slid them down his skin, over the flexing muscles of his chest, his arms. He went still, a great shudder racking his big body as the spell worked on him, transferring her searing pleasure to him. It would feel like flames were licking at his flesh. He groaned, and she watched his control strip away—just as she had wanted. A tiny smile curved her mouth.

"Such a talented little witch." He parted the lips of her sex with one hand and guided his cock to her entrance with the other. A hard thrust drove him hilt-deep into her, and she choked at the exquisite stretch. Gods, he was so big it was painful to take all of him, but she didn't care. She wanted this too badly to stop now. She bit her bottom lip and closed her eyes to savor the sensation.

"Mmm. I think that's my job." His tongue slid along her lower lip, sucking it into his mouth. The feel of his hard cock within her, the pleasure-pain of his thick shaft stretching her, almost made the gentle sweetness of his kiss overwhelm her. The man could *kiss,* his taste honey-spiced. He was already inside her, and his lips and teeth and tongue seduced her, coaxed her into an even wilder response, made her grow even wetter, her nipples bead tighter, her nails dig into his back as she slanted her mouth under his. His hands cupped her breasts, his fingers rubbing her nipples. She moaned against his lips.

Undulating her hips beneath him, she wrapped her legs tighter around his waist and broke the kiss, gasping at each hot plunge of his flesh into hers. Her eyes pinched closed as she dragged in the musky scent of sex and man. "This feels so . . ."

"Fucking good," he finished for her. His hands moved to close around her knees, pulling her legs farther apart to allow him to drive as deep as possible. His thrusts were hard, but too slow to shove her over the edge.

Shivers raced over her skin, every muscle in her body trembling with insipient need, with dark, unspeakable magic. It pulsed from her to him in sharp stabs of lust, making them both groan. "Hurry, Merek."

"And end this so soon? No way in hell." But his hands gripped her hips tightly enough to leave bruises, his fingers sending waves of that same overwhelming power, silver lightning flashing between them to sting her flesh. It was too much and not enough all at once. A spasm clenched her sex, and she cried out at the sensation. He gritted his teeth over a harsh sound of need.

Squeezing his cock with her inner walls, she tried to increase that consuming ecstasy. He groaned, his thrusts picking up speed and force, just the way she wanted. Her nails sank into the heavy muscles of his chest, and she tugged at the light smattering of curls there. "That's perfect, Merek. Just like that. You feel so good inside me."

"*Gods,* Chloe." Those gray eyes closed, and he swallowed hard. His breathing was nothing more than ragged panting, his powerful body arching between her thighs as he pushed them both to the edge of sanity.

They moved together seamlessly, magic building around them, flowing through them as their power cycled back and forth, feeding the need. The raw, stark sensuality of it shook her from deep within. It was perfect, just as she said. Too perfect. Shuddering away from that thought, she focused on the physical, carnal reality of sex. The scent of him, the feel of his flexing muscles against her skin, the creak of the mattress beneath them, the gasps of air that escaped their lungs as they moved faster and faster. The fire and magic that heated her blood, made her heart pound until she could feel nothing else, think of nothing else.

"Oh, gods, yes." She clenched her jaw to hold off the orgasm building within her. As much as she wanted it, she also wanted to savor every second of this experience.

He chuckled, the sound rough with unspent lust. Slipping his hand between them, he rubbed his knuckle over her swollen clit and took the choice to linger away from her. "Come for me."

"Merek!" She shattered, her body bowing in a tight arc, and

she lifted him with her as she convulsed around his cock. Her pussy gripped him tight, relaxed, and gripped again, milking him until she was sobbing with the force of it and he was groaning with his own orgasm. He slammed deep, shuddering over her as he came, his fierce expression emptying as he collapsed on top of her.

Slowly, she went limp, utter contentment sapping her will to move. His weight crushed her into the mattress, and she ran a hand down his sweat-dampened side before letting it drop. With a soft groan and a final thrust of his still semihard erection inside her, he managed to leverage himself off of her and onto the bed next to her. He hooked an arm around her waist and dragged her up against him, running his palm down her body, cupping her breast, tweaking her nipple, swirling a finger around her navel, and finally slipping between her legs to settle over her sensitized clit.

A low moan tore from her throat, shivers raising goose bumps on her flesh. She'd been so right. This was exactly what she'd needed. For one night, she'd needed to forget everyone and everything in her life and just *feel*. She'd needed to be touched, to have a man's hands slide over her skin.

She'd needed to be fucked.

"Mmmph." Something heavy landed on Chloe's stomach, jerking her out of the erotic dream, the erotic *memory*. Her heart thundered, sweat slid down her face, and her lungs heaved in a desperate bid for air. Icy fear and hot lust warred for dominance inside her as the fantasy gave way to reality. She shuddered, her fingers balling in soft cotton sheets. Her familiar's eyes glowed in the low lighting of the lamp she'd left on, a freakish little alien head peering down at her. Ophelia blinked, her whiskers twitching. Chloe groaned, shoved the Siamese cat off her belly, and flopped over to bury her face in the pillow. "*Gods.*"

How many times was she going to have that dream? How often did she have to relive that wild night? It had happened two months ago, and hardly a night had passed that she *hadn't* had the dream.

Maybe she just needed to get laid. Get that night out of her system. She moaned into her pillow, squeezing her thighs together as a lingering throb of desire went through her. That was how she'd ended up having that night in the first place, by telling herself she needed to get laid, to get her cheating ex out of her system.

That had gone *so* well for her.

She'd gone out to Sanguine, her favorite Magickals-only private club, scoped out every species of hotty the Magickal community had to offer—elves, Fae, vampires, werewolves, warlocks. She had mentally debated the sexual gifts each species could bring to the table—bedroom, whatever—and then she'd seen *him*. After that, there'd been no contest. Chemistry was a bitch like that. She would know—she was a biochemist.

Sighing, she rolled over, kicked the sheet off of her, and forked her hands through her sweaty hair. Her body still burned, her sex aching with a need to be filled with more than just her vibrator. "Damn it."

Dwelling on her lack of a love life since her one-night stand wouldn't help her. And thinking about Damien-Raines-the scum-sucking-vampire who'd left her for a she-vamp he'd knocked up, which was where her shame spiral had started, wouldn't help her disposition at all. However, the fact that his ferret familiar was probably still hexed into an ugly lampshade made her lips quirk. Vampires sucked at casting spells. Damien had just sucked, period. Too bad it had taken her so long to figure that out.

She heaved herself out of bed and played soccer with Ophelia's sinuous body as she tried to twine herself around Chloe's legs while she walked. Tripping, she hit the swinging door to the kitchen and almost face-planted into the floor. "Damn it, Ophelia."

The cat sniffed, leaped up onto the counter, and flicked a delicate paw at her food bowl in an unmistakable feline demand. Chloe rolled her eyes and grumbled all the way to the cabinet that contained the outrageously expensive cat cuisine her familiar liked. Dumping the contents into the food dish, Chloe went about retrieving her own sustenance while the cat dug in.

Thirty seconds later, she had a steaming mug of coffee cradled between her palms. The first sip made her moan. "*Ahhh.*"

Bless the Normal human who'd invented the automatic coffeemaker. Magic did some awesome things, but sometimes Normal technology trumped all. She leaned against her counter and gazed out her kitchen window at the morning mist shrouding her Queen Anne Hill neighborhood and drifting out into downtown Seattle. The city lights were a pretty haze that streaked the skyline. Sunbeams began to pierce the fog, so she knew it would be a rare sunny day in the Emerald City. Yesterday had been wicked hot, too, but Chloe loved the brightness. She'd have to remember to go for a walk during lunch today.

Bon Jovi's "Bad Medicine" blared from her cell phone, jolting her from her reverie, and she jogged into her living room to grab it from the charger. Her best friend Tess's name popped up on the caller ID. Grinning, Chloe punched the button to answer. "Dr. Jones, I presume. What are you doing up at the ass crack of dawn this morning?"

"Still haven't slept from last night." A huge yawn fuzzed the phone line. "We're short-staffed so I pulled a double. Budget cuts."

"Ouch."

"Tell me about it." Tess worked as a pathologist for the FBI. The Normal side of the FBI. She was one of the most Normal humans Chloe had ever met. "I haven't put in hours this awful since my residency."

Along with werewolf Jaya Nemov, they'd become friends in med school, which was the only reason Chloe and Jaya had gotten close to anyone outside the Magickal community. Most Magickals didn't bother because it was just too hard to keep people in their lives who they had to constantly lie to about what they were.

Chloe knew she should probably ease out of her relationship with Tess, but when Jaya had died during a full moon Change, it emphasized to Chloe that a good friend was hard to come by, magic or no magic. Tess might never know the truth behind Jaya's death, but she'd still shared the loss of someone they both loved. So, Chloe kept her friend and did what she had to do to keep her secrets.

Then again, a part of her had always wondered if the reason she held on to Tess was because her long-dead mother had been a Normal. She grinned, and it wasn't nice. Her family was almost as horrified that she had befriended a Normal as they had been when her father had married one and bred a halfling.

Another yawn sounded through the phone, recapturing Chloe's attention. Her grin softened, and she cradled the phone closer to her ear. "So, you're calling because . . . you want to get together for dinner tonight and tell me more about the suckfest of budget cuts?"

Tess chuckled. "You're a mind reader."

"Sure. That's totally a plausible explanation, Doctor." Chloe inserted as much drawling derision into her voice as possible, and Tess laughed. Telepathy wasn't one of Chloe's magical skills, so it wasn't an outright lie, it just wasn't the whole truth. This time. A familiar twist of guilt knotted her insides, but she pushed it aside. Tess was Normal, Chloe was Magickal; there was nothing she could do about the need to prevaricate. "How about you meet me here around seven?"

"Perfect. See ya. I'm hitting the hay now." The call was punctuated with one final yawn from Tess before both women disconnected.

Chloe went to drop the phone in her purse and saw she'd missed a call about an hour before. There was a voice mail message waiting for her. She hadn't heard the phone ring, but then, why would her subconscious want her to wake up from a steamy episode of her regularly scheduled Merek dream?

She shoved a hand through her disheveled hair and pushed the reminder of her one-night warlock out of her mind. Flipping her cell over to speakerphone, she accessed her voice mail while she wandered into her bedroom to dress for work.

A deep, silken male voice emerged from her phone. "Chloe, it's Damien."

Chills crept down Chloe's spine and a hollow feeling settled in the pit of her stomach. The last person she expected to get a call from was Damien. Hell, the last person she *wanted* a phone call from was Damien. Shaking off that inane thought, Chloe zipped up her skirt and shoved her feet into a pair of ballet flats. While she walked into the bathroom to brush her teeth and hair, she hit the buttons to replay the message she hadn't really listened to.

"Chloe, it's Damien." A muffled thump sounded in the background of the call, but Damien hurried on. "I'm sorry to bother you at home. Don't erase this. . . . I need to talk to you about work. It's . . . It's important to the project. Call me back. Please." The call ended abruptly, as if someone had stabbed the *End* button with more force than necessary.

The *please* gave her pause. Damien never said please. Then again, he also never said *I'm sorry.* He was a vampire. They were, by definition, cold-blooded. They also tended to have superiority complexes and thought everyone, from other Magickal species to Normals, was so far beneath them they didn't even register on their radar. Sure, most of them would stoop to having a fling with a non-vampire, maybe one or two non-vampire friends, just for variety, but anything else was out of the question. They didn't mix.

Luckily, Chloe hadn't wanted more than that from Damien, but she had expected fidelity while they were together. Apparently, that had been beneath him, too. She sighed, disconnected the call, and slid her cell into her pocket.

The worst part about dating someone you worked with was when it ended badly. She'd learned that lesson the hard way. They were both team leads in pharmaceutical R & D for Desmodus Industries, but since those teams were working on the same project, they did see each other, though not that often. Thank the gods.

Shoving her arms into a jacket, she picked up her handbag and headed for the side door that lead to her detached garage. If the bloodsucker wanted to talk to her about work, he could do it when she got there.

She wasn't calling him back.

2

What a fucking mess.

Merek Kingston shoved his sunglasses up his nose and stepped away from the shattered window. His shoes crunched in the glass that littered the living room of the penthouse apartment. He swept the room in a glance. The woman's body lay crumpled near the entrance, her eyes blank and empty, her fangs still extended in a twisted snarl.

"Allesia Dawes. Thirty-five-year-old attorney. Vampire." Selina Grayson, his partner of three years, flipped her notebook closed before turning cool, dark eyes on the scene. At over four hundred years old, the slim elven woman had seen more than her share of death.

"Who's our guy down on the street?"

"Coroner's still scraping the charcoal off the pavement, but my best guess is the owner—" she consulted her notes again "—Damien Raines."

"Also a vampire." It wasn't a question. Even if the man hadn't charbroiled in the sun, the Vampire Conclave owned this high-rise, and everyone in it. It didn't take a genius to do the math on the kind of Magickals who might live here. He tipped his head toward the window and the street below. "Anyone down there see anything useful?"

"No. We have a few Normal gawkers, but the telepaths first on the scene say no one even saw anything worthy of a memory tweak, let alone anything that might help us."

Only certain Normals were permitted to know magic even existed. If a Normal married into a Magickal family. When officials were appointed or elected who had to interact with the Magickal branches in every governmental organization.

If those people no longer needed to know about magic, their memories could be adjusted. The All-Magickal Council made those decisions, and they were ruthless in upholding the nondisclosure laws. Merek was definitely in favor of those laws. They'd brought witch trials and vampire hunting to a virtual standstill a century or two ago, and that made everyone in Magickal law enforcement's job a whole lot easier.

Selina tucked her notebook into her jacket. "You get a read on the place yet?"

He grunted in response. Letting his eyes unfocus, he took in the room again, this time with his precognitive abilities. Power tugged in his chest, lifting the hair down his arms as it crackled in the air around him. He shuddered under the lash of magic that was almost painful.

The other officers in the room shifted away. Only Selina stayed near him while he "read" the room. Unlike the clairvoyant abilities of most Magickals, he was cursed with an overabundance of power. He could see the past, future, and present. A roaring sounded in his ears, ripping through his mind. Every historical event in Seattle tried to slam into him. Cold sweat broke out across his forehead, and his muscles shook from the onslaught. He pushed through the chaos and focused on just this building. Dark shadows of twisted memories layered over themselves in his mind as people raced in and out of the room in fast-forward. Then the walls crumbled into dust, and he stood midair over a city he didn't recognize. What he saw was the stuff of nightmares, the ragged end of humanity thousands of years in the future. Everything destroyed. Pulling back from the vision, he homed in on the room. The recent past.

Here he saw the door breaking wide, a man and woman fighting for survival. The woman begging while sinister shadows loomed over her. The man writhing and screaming in agony. Death. The images were smudged in his mind, without enough clarity to make out the perpetrators. Unusual, because he normally had visions clear enough to sear into his retinas.

Then a familiar face streaked through his mind. A woman with midnight hair and hazel eyes. She was nude, arched for him. The fire of his own desire made his skin feel as though it were too tight. Sweat beaded on his face as the woman whispered his name and reached for him. Irresistible. He wanted her. Always he wanted her. Craved her. His cock hardened to the point of pain, and a shudder racked his body. He groaned and pushed the image away. Not connected to this case. He'd seen her in his mind more times than he cared to admit, but she was a memory, not a vision. Chloe.

He became aware of reality by degrees, the smell of Selina's perfume, the chill wind blowing in from the window. A storm was coming, despite the brilliant sky. His hand lifted as though to touch the woman in his mind. He snorted and shook the visions away, dragging himself back to the task at hand, shoving away the gut-grinding punch of lust before he embarrassed himself. He didn't have time for a memory. He didn't even know her last name. Hadn't let himself look her up after she'd run out on their night together.

"You all right?" Selina's hand clamped over his shoulder, stronger than anyone would guess by looking at her. He sensed she used magic to tighten her grip.

He swiped a hand down his face. "Yeah. I can't get a fix on our perps."

"Anything? Male or female?"

"Nothing solid. Here's how it went down. Dawes answers the door, so someone had to knock. Maybe someone she knows, maybe not, but she opens the door for them. The perps force their way in, and things get ugly. They took their time with Raines—worked him over for hours, threatened his woman to get his cooperation. Raines eventually snaps, there's a struggle, Raines loses and takes a header out the window for some barbeque time on the way down to the street. That left the woman—"

"Medical examiner says it doesn't look like sexual assault." Selina dropped her hand from his shoulder.

"Not that I saw either," he agreed. His gut tightened before he finished telling his partner what he'd seen. "She was on her knees, begging, when she died."

"They wanted something from Raines, but they already knew it wasn't here." Her conclusion was obvious even without Merek's vision of Raines being questioned and tortured. The place was pristine. The only messes were the dead woman and a few pieces of furniture overturned in the struggle. There were none of the usual signs that the apartment had been tossed.

"Or maybe they didn't want a physical object. Maybe information." That felt right somehow, fit with his vision. His gaze swept the room again. "Still, do we know if anything was taken?"

"A patrolman is bringing the parents in for questioning. They might be able to identify anything obvious that's missing." Selina slid her hands into her pockets.

He sighed and scrubbed the back of his neck. His nerves jangled from too much caffeine and too little sleep, but that was standard operating procedure for his line of work. "Vampires killed in a Conclave-owned building. I'm guessing a prominent vamp family. This is going to be fun."

"Is that a premonition?" A rare grin tugged at her mouth.

"Call it a hunch." He mimicked her pose, shoved his hands in his pockets, and watched the crime scene analysts doing their job. Yeah, this was going to be a bitch of a case. He didn't even need the visions jockeying in the back of his mind to tell him that simple truth.

"Kingston, I don't know how you deal with that." She shook her head, her look half pitying and half respectful.

"The same way we all deal with our premonitions." Or, at least witches / warlocks, elves, and Fae. Vampires and were-wolves had other magical problems to contend with.

"Not all of us have it as bad as you."

A smile curved his lips, but it held no amusement. His gift was often more of a curse, but he'd found a way to make it useful. "Aren't I the lucky one?"

"Yeah. Lucky." She snorted and led the way out of the apartment. "Let's go talk to the parents."

Two uniformed officers escorted Chloe into the police department downtown, and though it bustled with people and energy, it felt cold to her. Sterile and ugly.

She tried not to tremble in reaction as the officers flanking her led her to a set of double doors that required pass cards to get through. They stepped into a short, wide hallway. One side held a high counter topped by metal bars. A plump, middle-aged woman sat behind the cage and gave them a pleasant smile. She motioned them toward another set of doors at the opposite end of the hall.

Chloe felt a short burst of magic flick from the woman's fingers as she waved them on. It flowed over her, made the hair on her arms stand on end. A test for magic? Only Magickals would be able to access this area of the police department. The woman gave her a polite nod. "Welcome to the West Precinct's Magickal Task Force Headquarters."

The doors in front of Chloe parted on their own, spilling them out into a frenetic office area. Uniformed police officers mingled with the occasional obvious werewolf or vampire. Some of the people in the room had a hard, scary edge to them. Criminals. Magic-wielding criminals. The flash of spells from a doorway and an angry shout sent a shiver down her spine.

She blinked and tried not to stare too closely at anyone. What was she doing here? An hour ago she'd been hip-deep in work, utterly absorbed in experimenting with their current round of formulas that she felt to her bones were *right*. They just needed to perfect their project, run more tests, and it would be ready. They were so close.

They. But there was one less to count among the *they* in their research team, wasn't there?

Damien was dead. Murdered, the officers had said. Damien. Murdered. Chloe still hadn't wrapped her mind around it. There was no love lost between them, for obvious reasons, but she hadn't wanted the man *dead*. The whole thing was surreal, and her thoughts skipped around in mad little circles. Who would want to kill a scientist? Chloe had an ugly suspicion she was at the MTF Headquarters because they wanted to ask her that very question. And they thought the answer might be *her*.

Then everything inside her froze, reality once again taking a nasty turn.

Gray eyes met hers from across the room. Magnetic, they pulled at her. Her dream from that morning, from so many mornings before that, flashed through her mind. It was him. Merek.

She didn't even have time to hope that he wouldn't recognize her, because the same involuntary heat that coursed through her body flickered in his gaze.

"Shit," she breathed.

The officer on her left stirred to alertness. "Something wrong, Dr. Standish?"

She swallowed a whimper when Merek started toward them, his long, muscular legs eating up the distance. Both the officers escorting her snapped to immediate attention. "Detective Kingston, sir."

His gaze never left her face. "Gentlemen. Dr. Standish."

A ripple of pure awareness went down her skin at his words. She wasn't even sure if it was because he knew her name or because he was close enough to *feel* the intensity of him, smell the faint musk of his scent, see the ebony ring around his silver irises. A lock of wheat blond hair fell over his forehead, but did nothing to soften the sharp angles of his face. He took another step forward, looming over her. His shoulders were huge, the heavy muscles of his torso tapering to his narrow waist and flanks. She sighed and felt a flush heat her cheeks, the warmth spreading through her body to make it throb. He was even sexier than on the night she'd met him. Gods, how was that even possible? How could she be here, in a police station, about to be questioned for the murder of her ex-lover, and still be fighting her attraction for the man?

Madness. Insanity.

This was why she'd crept out of his apartment and run like hell after their night together. Her reaction was too intense, pulled her in too deep, until she felt like she was drowning in it. And she had no desire to rescue herself, just to let herself go and hold on to him forever. That wasn't how she liked her affairs, but she couldn't deny her body liked him too much.

Crossing her arms over her chest, she hid the fact that her nipples had tightened to points. Merek's gaze followed the motion, the gleam in his eyes telling her he knew exactly what she'd done and why. She licked her lips, and he stared at them, his expression as hungry as it had been the last time he'd pulled her under him, mounting her to slide his cock into her wet sex.

She sucked in a deep breath, struggling for calm, and more of his tantalizing scent came to her. The buzz of the people around her, the hum of magic moving through the air, faded until there was nothing and no one but him. If she took a step forward, she'd be able to feel the heat of his body, two steps and she'd be in his arms again.

The officer on her right spoke, breaking through her daze. He gestured toward a hall off the main room. "We were just escorting Dr. Standish to—"

"I'll take it from here." A slim woman with a badge and a gun clipped to her belt walked up and nodded to the men. She glanced at Chloe. "I'm Detective Selina Grayson. If you'll follow me."

Merek blinked, and the fiery passion was gone, replaced by a remote, professional coldness that sliced through her like a razor blade. She shook herself, felt that same iciness stiffen her spine.

Forcing herself to think of something—*anything*—else, Chloe focused on Selina's face. What kind of Magickal was this woman? An elf, or maybe a fairy. She had the right bone structure for either race. Chloe tilted her head and narrowed her eyes, opening her senses a bit. Fae, witches, and elves all vibrated with magic, like the same song hummed in three different pitches. Vampires hissed like the low, ominous quiver of a rattlesnake's tail. Werewolves were a deep rumble, a subvocal growl that made prey freeze before a dangerous predator. The detective sounded more like an elf than a Fae, but sometimes it was difficult to tell.

Maybe other Magickals sensed it differently, but since Chloe's skills revolved around clairaudience, she *heard* the differences between the species. Someone with telemetry might have to touch to know. A clairvoyant or someone who sensed auras might be able to tell with a single glance. She'd never asked anyone else about it, but maybe she should. She wondered if any empirical studies had been done on the subject, and her mind began to ponder the scientific anomalies of divergent magical powers.

Selina cleared her throat, wrenching Chloe's wayward attention back to the present. "Dr. Standish, if you'll follow me. Now."

Flushing, she ignored the strange looks Merek and the officers gave her. Merek's presence flustered her more than it should. Turning, she scurried toward the hallway Selina indicated, escaping Merek and the feelings he generated within her with a mere look. Just as she had the night they'd met.

Twenty minutes later, Chloe stared down at a cracked Formica table until the ugly gold flecks began to blur before her eyes. Air-conditioning kicked on and cooled the already frigid room. Goose bumps raced over her skin, and she couldn't fight the chill with a spell because this room had been warded against the use of magic. It made her nerves jangle even more. This couldn't be happening. It could not be happening.

Even worse, she knew she focused on her physical discomfort, her impaired magical abilities, to stop herself from thinking about Detective Merek Kingston. Kingston. She hadn't known his last name, hadn't known he was a cop. She hadn't wanted to know. He was supposed to be a one-night lover, a memory that became hazy almost as soon as it was over. Instead, seeing him had demonstrated exactly how clear her memories of him were, how they'd been etched into her mind with stunning clarity.

One more ugly shock for the day.

"Dr. Standish?"

She jerked a bit when the door opened and Selina walked in. "Yes?"

"Thank you for waiting." Her brown hair swung in a layered bob around her sharply featured face, and her warm skin tone contrasted with the icy demeanor and cold, flat eyes. "I have a few questions for you."

"So I gathered when they asked me to come down here." Chloe's voice came out sounding almost normal, which surprised her. Nerves made her hands quake a bit, so she curled her fingers around the Styrofoam cup of coffee one of the officers had given her. Sitting in an interrogation room was intimidating as hell, even if she knew she hadn't done anything wrong.

Still, her belly looped a bit. Her heart pounded in slow, painful beats as she tried not to fidget or squirm. Damien had been murdered, but she hadn't done anything illegal, no matter what they might think. Turning his familiar into a lampshade might not have been totally aboveboard, but she hadn't killed anyone.

The slender woman slid into a chair across from her, settling a file folder on the table between them. She didn't look at Chloe for a few seconds, and while Chloe knew it was a ploy to set her more on edge—just as making her wait had been—she had to admit it worked.

The detective tucked a lock of hair behind her ear, and the barest hint of a point showed. Elf, just as Chloe had suspected. She might have allowed herself a momentary sense of victory, but the black ice of Selina's eyes sent pinpricks down Chloe's spine. "What can you tell me about your relationship with Dr. Raines?"

Chloe swallowed and didn't let her gaze waver. "We work together at Desmodus Industries. I mean . . . we *worked* together." She suppressed the urge to giggle nervously, that sense of pure unreality buzzing through her mind again. "Two months ago, we broke off a two-year-long relationship."

"Why?" Selina's gaze sharpened, and yet Chloe didn't think

she was startled by the information, just that she was judging every word and movement Chloe made.

She clenched her teeth, knowing the answer to this question wasn't going to get her out from under any suspicion. "He left me for another woman—a vampire. Last I heard, they were engaged, and she was pregnant."

"Do you know the woman's name?" The detective stroked her finger over the paperwork in front of her, and Chloe resisted the urge to try to angle for a look.

"No. I didn't ask." She took a breath, let it ease out, and tried to get a grip on her emotions, on the hollow feeling that opened in her belly. "I frankly didn't want to know. He wanted out of the relationship, and when I found out why, I was more than happy to see him go. I don't share."

"So you were angry." It wasn't a question.

"Yes, I was." She was careful to keep her tone reasonable, to not get defensive. She had done nothing wrong—they were just ruling her out as a suspect. "Understandably, I think. That doesn't mean I did anything to harm him."

"His fiancée, Allesia Dawes, was also murdered."

"Someone killed a pregnant woman?" For some reason, that stunned her even more than the idea that someone might have murdered Damien. Another level of surreal tilted her world off-axis.

Selina gave her a look that could only be described as pitying. "It isn't the first time, Dr. Standish."

"N-no, of course not." Chloe took a gulp of her coffee, just to have a solid grip on something real, and burned the inside of her mouth. She winced.

The detective leveled that blank, accusing stare on Chloe, and her heart skipped a beat, sweat slicking her palms. "Can you tell me where you were at five this morning?"

Chloe sighed, closing her eyes. "I was home, sleeping. Alone."

"I see."

She opened her eyes to meet Selina's gaze. "Am I going to be arrested?"

Those dark eyes were unblinking, and the detective's slim body appeared almost relaxed in her chair, but Chloe could feel the tension running through her. "Have you done anything I should arrest you for?"

Chloe clenched her jaw, stomping down on the unwarranted guilt that rolled through her. "No, I have not."

"Then you're not under arrest."

Yet. The word hung in the air, unspoken, but both women thought it.

"Well, that's a relief." Her voice was deadpan, because she knew for damn sure she was still under suspicion, if not arrest. Then something occurred to her, and she felt stupid for not having thought of it before. She reached for her purse. "Damien called me this morning around the time you're talking about. He left a message because, as I said, I was in bed, alone, sleeping."

Flipping on the speakerphone feature, she played the message for Selina, but could tell that the woman didn't think this ruled Chloe out of anything.

"We're going to want a copy of that message." The detective shifted in her seat, her gaze scanning the documents in front of her, and then she changed her line of questioning. "He mentioned a project. Can you tell me about the nature of your work with Dr. Raines?"

"We make up two of the three team leads involved in the Desmodus Werewolf Project." The breath eased from Chloe's lungs. This, at least, was something she could talk about without worrying. Her love life might be in constant shambles, but her career was impeccable.

Selina's body went rigid, her eyes rising to meet Chloe's, and for once her expression was unguarded. "The project to cure lycanthropy?"

"Not to cure it, to *control* it." All too eager to talk about anything but Damien's murder, Chloe started babbling. "At this time, wolves are compelled to Change with the full moon. Their magic fluctuates wildly with the lunar cycles. The result is an astronomical number of wolf deaths per year. As far as I know, there'd be no way to cure therianthropy, the magical disease that engenders the vampire and werewolf races. It changes their bodies on a molecular level. Regulating the worst side effects of those diseases is certainly possible, which is what I'm working on with Damien. *Was* working on."

Werewolves could shift at any time, and after enough years, it became easier for them to control, but a relatively low percentage of the population survived long enough for that. Full moon was the only time they were *forced* to shift. It was also the only time they could turn Normals into wolves, and without the older members of a pack to control the cubs and newly Changed, they rampaged at full moon, biting as many humans as they could. Wolves *and* vampires who turned humans without authorization were put to death for the crime and for possibly exposing Magickals to the whole world, but only werewolves dealt with a monthly rampage. The outcome of the lycanthropy project was important to so many people, but Chloe usually managed to focus on the research in front of her. More pressure didn't make the work go faster.

Selina was quiet for a long moment, obviously processing what she knew against what Chloe had told her. "You said two of *three* team leads."

How this was related to Damien and his fiancée's deaths, Chloe didn't know, but she was ready to tell this woman whatever she wanted to know in order to get out of this police station. And away from any chance of running into Merek again. "Yes, the third team is lead by Dr. Ivan Nemov. His wife died during the full moon Change several years ago. She was my best friend. Their son, Alex, is my godson."

"Sounds like this project is a personal crusade for you." The detective tapped her fingernail against the table, her brow creased in thought. Her gaze was no less cold when she looked at Chloe.

Again, Chloe fought the urge to fidget. She took a sip of the cooling coffee, tried a warming spell, and more disquiet crawled through her as she was reminded that no magic worked in this interrogation room. "It's very important to me, yes. It's an obsession for Ivan. It was an intellectual pursuit for Damien."

The table tapping continued, and Chloe heard it like an ominous drumbeat in her head. Selina's mouth worked for a moment before she spoke, as if this questioning had gone so far off track of what she'd expected that she wasn't entirely sure how to continue. "So, you all knew each other well. You're close to the Nemovs, dated Dr. Raines. . . . Did Desmodus Industries know about your relationships with the other scientists?"

"Yes, and before you ask, projects like this are top secret, subject to industrial espionage, and guarded like national treasures." Chloe sat up straight, her gaze narrowing. Security was something she took seriously with her work. Everything about her job, she took seriously. "No one working on the projects ever has all the pieces. You literally can't sell out the company if you don't have any secrets worth buying. In this case, I have one third of the information for the research-and-development stage of the drug."

"What, specifically, was your role?" Selina kept tapping her finger, and the noise danced over Chloe's ragged nerves.

"Can you stop that, please?" She gave the detective's hand a pointed look, and Selina froze, clenching her fingers into a fist. So, she hadn't noticed she'd been tapping. Chloe didn't know if that should reassure her or not. She sighed. "I'm a chemist, Detective Grayson. My specialty in the Normal world of science and medicine is biochemistry. My area of expertise in the Magickal world is potions, mixing chemicals, herbs, etcetera."

Selina hummed in her throat and looked like she wanted to start tapping again, but didn't. "I can see why they hired you for this project."

Might as well give her everything. Chloe didn't want to have to come back in for another round of questioning. In fact, if she never saw the inside of a police station again, it would be just fine with her. Sweat stuck her shirt to her back, and the frigid air-conditioning made an uncomfortable situation unbearable. She wanted out of here. "I came to Desmodus Industries with this project. Damien—Dr. Raines—and I both did."

Those dark eyes narrowed, considering. "That's very interesting. Desmodus is controlled by the Vampire Conclave."

Chloe shrugged. "Dr. Nemov and his wife were the foremost experts in the field of werewolf biophysics, and they'd been pushing their pack leaders to get more funding for their research for years. Dr. Jaya Nemov and I did our residency together, and when she died, I took an interest in her research. I went to Dr. Raines, who I was dating at the time, to see if he could convince his superiors that this would be a good project for them to take on."

What had always angered Chloe was that *she*, a witch, had been the one to push the project through. The pack leaders should have done something long ago, should have been *trying*, no matter how unsuccessfully, to find a treatment instead of accepting the terrible side effects of their disease as inevitable and unchangeable. The older wolves had the most control, of their magic and of their packs, and they'd spent so long embroiled in the vampire wars that they were comfortable with their isolationist politics. It was true they had a lot on their plates training their pack members how to use their magic, how to stay alive, but they were *leaders*. They—not Chloe or Ivan or Jaya— should have lead the way by reaching out for help from the other Magickal races.

Even if it wasn't the All-Magickal Council as a whole, they

could have gone to the Fae's Seelie Court, or the Elven Assembly, or the Witch Coven, or even to powerful individual families like the Standishes. Politically dangerous or not, Chloe had picked the Vampire Conclave for two reasons: they had the most money, and they had the technology and experience needed to work with Magickal diseases. Desmodus Industries had patented a serum vamps drank to manage their need to feed. They still sucked blood, but it helped them in a way that Chloe hoped her formula would help werewolves.

Selina frowned. "It seems odd that a vampire would be willing to go to bat for a werewolf project, even if he was sleeping with you."

Yeah, no kidding.

Chloe fought the urge to snort. It was like being hard-core conservative and screaming liberal in the Normal world. The two sides just never met. There was no common ground between them, and any ground they'd ever shared was blood-soaked from feuding. Except for the obvious abilities instilled by a Magickal virus, the cultures that had developed for each species were diametrically opposed.

The project Chloe had initiated was the first time, for as long as their very long records spanned, that they had set aside their differences for any reason. That someone working on the project had been murdered was bad for more than just Damien. If this project crumbled, it could put the two races at loggerheads. It would drag other races into the mix. It would just be bad for everyone. No, scratch *bad*, it would be catastrophic.

A sardonic smile curved her lips. "It wasn't the sex that convinced Damien. I appealed to his ego. Imagine not only the prestige of being on the team that broke through this formula, but the accolades afforded to someone making peacekeeping strides for the whole Magickal world."

The detective blinked. "Sounds too good to be true."

Chloe flicked dismissive fingers. "It's the same argument

Damien used to convince his superiors, to convince the Conclave. My aunt and I convinced the rest of the Council, including the werewolf pack leaders, to back the project."

"Your aunt." It was obvious Selina knew who Chloe was related to. Then again, you couldn't be Magickal in Seattle and
not know the Standish name. They'd helped settle Magickals in
America back in colonial days and had come West during the
gold rush. There'd been a Standish on the All-Magickal Council in this city since the day the Council was founded. "Mildred
Standish."

"Aunt Millie, yes. She's actually my great-great aunt, but she
doesn't like to be reminded of that." For the first time, Chloe
relaxed. No matter how bad this got, Millie would always be
there to help her. The Standish family stood together against
outsiders, and Millie led the local coven and represented the
witch race on the Council. She had more than enough clout to
fix any mess. A sigh eased past Chloe's lips, and she surrepti-
tiously wiped her clammy palms off on her skirt.

Selina's gaze swept over her again, assessing and reassessing.
"You're quite the mover and shaker."

"Coming from the Standish family has a lot of duties and
strings attached. Lots of expectation. But it also affords me in-
fluence most people my age wouldn't dream of having. The
least I can do is use it to try to help my friends, lobby for causes
I believe in. So I did." Her shoulder dipped in a shrug, a wry
grin curving her mouth. She waved a hand around the interrogation room. "And here I am."

"Here you are," Selina agreed.

"Son of a bitch," he breathed. Merek closed his eyes and
leaned his forehead against the glass of the two-way mirror in
the observation room. It had to be her. Of course, it had to be.
It wasn't his memory he'd seen in Raines's apartment, but a vision of the actual Chloe who had actually dated the vampire.

She'd been there before. He was damn grateful he hadn't "seen" her fucking the other man. His gut burned at the thought.

"What's up?" An FBI agent stood beside him, hands in pockets. Agent Rogers.

Merek already didn't like him. As soon as Selina was done, this asshole was yanking the case away from them. He was just seeing what Merek's partner could pull from their suspect. Why the FBI was interested, Merek didn't know. Likely, he would never know. It rankled, but he set that aside and refocused on the interrogation room.

The expression in those wide hazel eyes kicked him in the solar plexus. It was trapped, nervous, worried. Scared. He'd never wanted to see such vulnerability on her face. He'd seen her passionate, joyful, her eyes reflecting a wicked greed that made his blood heat to remember it. He didn't like seeing her afraid.

He cleared his throat and glanced away from Chloe to the man beside him. "I'm afraid I can't help in this situation."

"No?" The slight points to Rogers's ears declared him an elf, but the officious tone was pure red tape bureaucrat. One of Merek's least favorite kind of people. "Why is that, Detective Kingston?"

"I can't read her. It happens occasionally." It wasn't strictly true, but he'd be damned if he admitted anything to this pencil-pushing prick.

Because the truth was enough to break him out in cold sweat. The *only* people Merek couldn't read were those who would have the deepest impact on his life. Sometimes that meant a close friend or a lover . . . It had definitely included his wife and his parents. And look where that had landed all of them. In the morgue. Because when they'd been in danger, when it had really mattered, Merek hadn't been able to do shit to help them. He hadn't known about it, hadn't sensed a thing. His powers were fallow when it came to them—the only time his abilities could truly rest, the only time he didn't have to tightly leash his precognition.

A light knock sounded on the door to the observation room. Merek didn't even bother to look away from the scene before him. "Come on in, Cavalli."

"You know, having a creepy sense of who's nearby is supposed to be the purview of howlers and bloodsuckers." The tall vampire shut the door and settled his shoulder against the wall beside it, crossing his arms over his chest as he, too, watched Selina question Chloe.

Merek flicked his gaze over the other man and grinned. Cavalli was tall, taller than Merek's six foot three by at least an inch, maybe two. He was whipcord lean, dark haired, dark eyed, olive complexioned, and other than the soul patch decorating his chin, he looked like he'd just stepped out of a catalog for Armani. Or a corporate meeting for a Fortune 500 company. Family money. Vampire money. The kind of man that oozed centuries of charm, good breeding, good looks, excess income, and had women crawling all over him.

Merek arched an eyebrow. "Should I even bother to ask what brings you down to the pedestrian side of law enforcement?"

The vampire snorted. "What? Your precog doesn't tell you every little detail of why I'm here?"

Focusing on the other man, Merek tried to get a better bead on the situation. He might not be able to read Chloe, but Cavalli shouldn't be a problem. Images flashed in his mind, future events, past events, shadowy possibilities, crystal clear certainties. The threads that connected to Luca Cavalli's near future hit a blank wall, full stop. There didn't seem to be any getting around his inability to read Chloe's future. Merek rubbed his forehead and sighed. "This isn't just about Damien Raines's death."

"Got it in one."

"Do I even want to know what interest the FBI's Magickal Crimes Unit has in one little scientist?" He shot the vampire a narrow-eyed look.

Cavalli pushed away from the wall, opened the door, and waved an elegant hand at the pencil pusher. "Agent Rogers, thank you so much for looking in on this case for me, but I think my team can handle things from here."

An ugly flush mottled the little man's face, and his mouth moved stiffly when he spoke. "Of course, sir. Good luck."

Merek turned back to the interrogation room to hide his smirk. The bureaucrat didn't like when someone else pulled rank on him, did he? Served him right. Merek slid his hands in his pockets and rocked back on his heels as Cavalli shut the door behind the other agent. "So . . . care to share? Off the record, of course."

"Of course." The vampire grinned, and a bit of fang showed. "The murder was only the start of something we think is much bigger."

If it wasn't personal issues that motivated the murder, then it was professional. "Something about the werewolf project both of them are working on."

"Yes." Cavalli sighed and copied Merek's pose, hands in pockets, half his attention on Chloe's questioning and half on the conversation at hand. "I just got back from Desmodus Industries. The third lead in their project—Ivan Nemov—didn't show up to work today. He hasn't missed a single day for the entire length of the project—no vacation, not even a sick day."

Obsessed, just as Chloe had said. "That's more information than they gave us about anything."

"I'm a vampire." That elegant wave again. "They're owned by the Conclave."

Merek grunted. "What else?"

With a tired sigh, Cavalli shrugged. "Maybe nothing. Someone tried to hack your little scientist's project files . . . unsuccessfully, but that's apparently not unusual when a company is involved in multi-billion dollar research. My tech geniuses are impressed with Desmodus's encryption and security."

Which also fit with the information Chloe had revealed in her interview. "Why kill Dr. Raines if they're just wanting access to the research?"

"Hell if I know," Cavalli's voice roughened, showing a hint of the Italian accent of the vampire's homeland. "What I do know is that this is involved with Leonard Smith and his network."

The blood froze in Merek's veins, and the hair rose on the back of his neck. No one in Magickal law enforcement hadn't heard that name. The werewolf terrorist had been trying to start a revolution in pack politics—hell, *all* Magickal politics—for the better part of a century. Rumor was he had people planted in every Magickal branch of every government agency. With the number of times he'd slipped between their fingers, Merek wouldn't be surprised if that rumor were true.

And somehow, someway, Chloe was now involved with one of the most wanted men alive.

Merek's stomach did a slow pitch and roll. "Shit."

"Yeah, that was my thought, too." The fangs were fully bared this time, and pure predatory hunter flashed in the vampire's eyes.

"How does she figure into this?" Merek didn't want to ask the question, didn't want the answer. He'd thought of her too often in the last couple of months, and his mind absolutely rebelled at thinking she might be the only person left standing on the project's R & D team for a reason. A cop couldn't help but be a cynic, and while he knew the possibility was there, he damn well didn't want to consider it, which wasn't like him. He didn't like his knee-jerk reactions to this woman.

The vampire cast a glance in his direction, but he avoided it.

"We don't think she has any ties with Smith, if that's what you're asking. The woman is squeaky clean, and a Standish witch on top of that. More likely the connection is this missing Nemov werewolf. He's fanatical, spent every waking moment since his wife died trying to find a way to manage lycanthropy. His coworkers say he's constantly pushing things faster than their regulations can go, gets irate about red tape." Cavalli nodded toward Chloe. "As far as we know, she just happens to be working on a project that Smith wants to control."

"If they haven't *found* a treatment yet...*shit.*" They'd found a treatment or were close enough to it that someone—maybe Nemov—jumped the gun. Gods, but a treatment for lycanthropy. What werewolf wouldn't give damn near anything to be rid of the life-threatening aspects of the disease? And that was why Smith had to want it. With that drug, he could trump every leader of every pack on the planet, create total revolution or anarchy, if he wanted. The idea of rampaging werewolves unchecked by the packs and the All-Magickal Council sent a shudder through Merek. Smith could be more powerful than any one person should ever be.

"My techs have confirmed the company files were not accessed. Because Smith couldn't get the files, he appears to have gone the human route. So. We have to assume Smith got the information he wanted, what with Nemov unaccounted for and Raines dead.... Dr. Standish is the only thing standing between Smith and the lycanthropy treatment."

A hot burst of relief ran through Merek that he hadn't been fixating on someone who'd sell out to a terrorist cell, but the thought that she was the only one between Leonard Smith and what he wanted turned that hot burst to a frigid chill.

"We're putting her in protective custody, of course. The last thing we want is Smith getting his hands on her, but the fact that we know he wants her so badly could prove very useful to us. I'll exploit any advantage I can get." Cavalli ran a finger down his little soul patch. "One of my men—Peyton—is handling arrangements for her now."

"Good." But Merek didn't like it. He didn't like that this woman was disappearing from his life again, and especially when he knew she was in danger. Peyton he knew only by reputation, but Cavalli was good at his job, the best. Merek had crossed paths with him before, had been assigned to him once or twice when his precog skills came in handy to the FBI, and nothing he'd ever seen or heard had ever made him doubt the other man's abilities. He was legend.

And Merek still didn't want to let Chloe out of his sight.

The cell phone on Cavalli's belt vibrated, and he checked it. "That'll be Peyton. Keep an eye on her for twenty, maybe thirty minutes, and we'll get her out of your hair."

"She'll be in my office."

"Thanks. And don't tell her anything. That's my job." Cavalli waved over his shoulder, the phone already pressed to his ear as he spoke quietly to the person on the other end.

Merek heard muffled feminine conversation as Selina left Chloe at his office door and told her to go in and wait. His partner hadn't asked him why he'd wanted her to do so, and he was damn grateful. He didn't have an explanation. Cavalli could just as easily have picked Chloe up from the interrogation room, but Merek wanted a few minutes alone with her before she was gone again.

She came in, shut the door behind her, leaned back against it, closed her eyes, and sighed. Intense relief crossed her expression, and he felt the tiniest twinge of guilt that he was going to upset her, but he had some questions he wanted answered that had nothing to do with work. Starting with why she'd cast a deep sleep spell on him in order to sneak out of his bed. Anger he didn't want to feel burned in his gut at that, along with worry and ... fear ... for what she was about to be thrown into. A terrorist was after her, and there wasn't a damn thing he could do about it.

His jaw clenched, and he growled, "Hello again, Chloe."

She startled, her eyes flying open, and her gaze snapped to his face. The color fled her face in a quick rush. "Oh, fuck me."

"I tried that once, remember?" Steel edged his voice, and he realized exactly how pissed he'd been that she'd bailed on him. Denial. He didn't like that either. He was brutally honest with himself about everything. He had to be. Denial got people killed in his line of work. He sat back in his chair, laced his fingers over his flat belly, and stared at her. "You ran from me."

She twitched as if to dart for the door.

His eyes narrowed, and he tensed, ready to spring. "I wouldn't do it again. You won't like my reaction this time."

Chin lifted, she stared down her nose at him. "You didn't *have* a reaction last time. I haven't seen or heard from you since that night."

"Exactly. You wanted to go, and I let you. I didn't make an effort to find you, didn't invade your privacy, and we both know I'm in a position to do so." He flicked his fingers to indicate the teeming police department beyond the walls of his office. "But you've dropped back into my life, and now I know your name; I know what you do for a living; I know where you live. Isn't that interesting?"

"Not really." Now her chin jutted stubbornly, and something unholy lit within him at the challenge she presented. "Look, it's been a bad day. I'd like to go home now."

He arched one eyebrow. "My partner had to have told you that's not going to happen."

"Detective Grayson is your partner?" She swallowed, shifting her weight from foot to foot. She licked her lips, and he got hard, his body reacting as strongly as it had the first moment her gaze had met his. He wanted those lush lips moving under his, and something primitive snapped inside his chest.

Rising from his seat, he slowly stalked her across the small room, watching to see if she tried to bolt, ready to pounce, and almost relishing the thought of how that would force him to have his hands all over her. "Yes, she's my partner. I thought it best to excuse myself from questioning you. Conflict of interest."

"We had a one-night thing, so your *interest* was pretty limited." She tilted her head back to meet his gaze as he drew closer. Awareness flashed in those hazel depths, and he could feel his control stripping away. He wanted her. Gods, he'd never wanted a woman the way he wanted this one. He couldn't even remember wanting his wife with this kind of desperation, but he slammed the brakes on that guilt-ridden thought and any other about his dead spouse. He shoved away the past and focused on the present. Chloe.

His grin was just this side of feral. "Right, because when I have limited interest, I manage to stay hard all night long."

A flush stained her cheeks, and she sucked in a breath. "I don't know what this conversation is accomplishing. We were both looking to score that night. Touchdown."

Only he hadn't been looking to score that night. He'd gone to Sanguine to wash the bad taste of a shitty premonition out of his mouth. He definitely hadn't been trying to hook up with a woman who was blank to his clairvoyance. It wasn't a fluke either. No visions assaulted him in her presence. She was still unreadable. The reminder alone made his insides cramp. Being anywhere near someone like her was a mistake he'd sworn he'd never make again. Yet, here he was, hot and horny and angry because everything about her was beyond his control.

"Detective . . . Kingston, isn't it? I don't think—" She fumbled with the door handle behind her, and his fingers snapped around her wrist.

The feel of her soft, soft skin against his made him grit his teeth as his cock throbbed. Insanity. The way he responded to her, it was pure insanity. The lust that pulsed through him twisted with annoyance because she tried to escape him. Again. "Merek. You'll call me Merek. And you have an appointment with the FBI, Dr. Standish—*Chloe*—so you aren't going anywhere until they get here."

He planted his hands on either side of her, trapped her with his body, and leaned down to her level. He could feel her breath rush against his skin. She was panting, her breasts rising and falling. Her eyes looked glazed as her gaze moved over his features. "You're mad at me."

"Hell, yeah, I'm mad." He got right in her face, until his lips were no more than a hairsbreadth from hers. Gods, he wanted to kiss her, wanted to see if she was as good as he remembered. He snarled. "Two months later, and I haven't gotten the taste of you out of my mouth, the sound of your voice moaning my name out of my head—"

"Stop." Her breath caught, her eyes darkening with passion.

His laugh grated from his throat, a rusty sound of lust, self-derision, and rage. "I wish to hell I could, Chloe, but I can't. Can you?"

"I...I..."

"Tell me you never think about it." He moved one hand to let his fingers stroke over the inside of her wrist, and he felt her tremble. Good. "Tell me you walked away as cleanly as you're pretending. Tell me you don't remember clawing my back while I slid my cock inside you. Tell me you don't care that I made you scream and sob and sigh. Tell me—"

She dropped her purse to the floor, clapped her hands over his ears, and dragged his mouth down to hers, cutting him off.

Just like that, he had her pinned to the wall. His tongue was between her lips, and she struggled for control of the kiss, her tongue twining with his, her teeth nipping and sucking at his lower lip. Her breasts pressed to his chest, and he wanted his mouth on them too. Soon. He'd have her again soon.

He growled, picked her up, and turned away from the door. With a mere thought, he cast a spell to muffle the sound coming in and out of the room. He couldn't make out the voices and footsteps passing his door, and no one outside would hear what he and Chloe were doing.

He could make her scream, and no one would know.

A groan of pure satisfaction dragged from his throat. He set her down, backed her up against his desk, crowded her, bracketed her hips with his fingers, and held her in place. Her jaw set in an obstinate line, and her eyes narrowed. "This is crazy."

"Yeah. So?" His smile was more a baring of teeth, and he didn't care. "That didn't stop you from kissing me a second ago."

"Don't remind me." She wedged her palms between them and pushed at his chest. He fought another groan at just that nonsexual touch. Gods, but he loved her hands on him. It fed a craving that went far, far deeper than mere pleasure. Though the pleasure was undeniable, and his cock chafed against his fly. He leaned even closer to her, into those small, slender palms.

Her eyes widened when his erection prodded her belly, and he watched a flush race up her cheeks. She swallowed, her breasts rising as she dragged in a deep breath. Goose bumps rose on her arms, and she shivered. He grinned. "Cold, sugar?"

Her eyes flashed, magic sparking molten gold flecks in her irises. "You know damn well I'm not cold."

"That's a shame." He ran his hands down her back for just the enjoyment of feeling her heated skin under her blouse. "I would have offered to warm you."

She shoved harder against his chest. "Go fuck yourself, Kingston."

"But it's so much more fun to fuck you, Chloe."

She hissed at him, jerking her chin to the side. "I'm not in the mood. Let go of me."

"Not in the mood?" Anger shimmered through him. It pissed him off more than a little how she denied this *thing* between them, how she wanted to run. "Let's see if we can change that for you."

Her gaze snapped back to him. "Damn it, Mer—"

His mouth cut off her words, and he plunged his tongue between her lips. He'd heard enough; he wasn't interested in verbal games—he'd rather toy with her in other ways. Her breath caught, her nails curling in to dig into his chest. He wrapped his fingers around her wrists, twisting her arms behind her back to arch her body into his. Her breasts pressed against him, and they both groaned.

Shoving his thigh between hers, he rubbed his leg against her sex. The hot scent of her reached his nose, sweet and musky. He tilted his head, deepening the contact of their kiss. She wrenched at his hold on her, but couldn't break his grip, so she rotated her torso to move herself against him. The friction was going to drive him to madness or orgasm, he wasn't sure which.

Her hips snapped in infinitesimal jerks as she tried to work herself on his leg while her body was caught between his and the wide metal desk. She moaned a frustrated protest and bit his lip.

He shuddered, lust clouding his focus. Gods, she was the only person who had ever shredded his control like this. He broke the kiss, dipping forward to suck and bite his way down her throat. Her head fell back to give him greater access while she continued to wriggle against his grip. His breath bellowed out of his lungs, his blood boiling in his veins. He craved her so badly he wasn't sure he'd make it inside her before he came.

Working her skirt up to her waist, he cupped her smooth backside before he slipped his hands into her panties. She moaned, her hips still pumping in vain as she sought release. Easing her panties down her hips, he heaved himself away from her just enough to let them drop to the floor.

"Step out of them."

She whimpered and obeyed, pulling one foot free and kicking the scrap of lace across the room with her other foot. "Fuck me, now, Merek."

"Gods, yes," he groaned. He dropped to his knees, pulled one of her slim thighs over his shoulder to open her to his touch, and licked his way inside her slick, heated sex. Her muscles jerked, her body jolting at the contact. The taste of her cream on his tongue was intoxicating. Her fingers sank into his hair, tugging on the strands, her frantic, pleading gasps urging him on. He groaned against her clit, and she sobbed, twisting her fingers in his hair.

A wave of magic hit him from her, and he swayed backward, glad he was on his knees or he'd have been driven there by the lust that roared through him. Hot prickling skipped over his skin, red-hot embers dancing in the air around them.

Gods, he couldn't wait.

Shoving to his feet, he lifted her onto the desktop, thrusting paperwork out of his way. Her legs snapped around his waist, and she ground her pussy against him. He shuddered, unable to put together a single coherent thought. It should have worried him, but he was well beyond worry. Only the drive for orgasm mattered now.

He reached between them to rip open his fly, and she pressed her sex against his hand, seeking any kind of friction she could find. Her face was flushed with desire, her eyes heavy-lidded, and her breasts rose with each jerky pant she sucked into her lungs. She was the most beautiful thing he'd ever seen, and right here, right now, she was all his. The knowledge pushed him even closer to the tattered edge of his restraint.

"M-Merek, I need you." Her hands pulled him closer, her fingers balling in his shirt. "I need you inside me. Please. Right now. I need you."

His zipper gave way to his vicious wrench, and within seconds he had his cock deep within the slick sheath of her pussy. There was no slow possession this time. He rode her hard and groaned with every movement he made within her, her inner muscles milking his cock until he thought his skull would explode. "Chloe."

Her fingers moved to cup his jaw, and he dove forward to kiss her. He devoured her, drowning himself in the taste, scent, and feel of her. His hips bucked hard, and he fucked her with all the finesse of a teenager in the backseat of his daddy's car. She didn't seem to mind. Her hands tugged at his hair, her teeth nipped his lips, and her legs continued to wring his hips as she arched with him. She screamed and sobbed into his mouth, her slim body going rigid as she came for him.

The world around him dimmed as the last fetters on his control ripped away, and he plunged into her pussy again and again until he was roaring his orgasm, jetting his come deep into her hot, sleek sheath.

So long. So fucking long since he'd had this. It wasn't as good as he remembered.

It was better.

He dropped his forehead to hers, panting for breath, not one thought able to form in his mind. All he could do was rest against her, breathe in her sweet scent, and wait for reality to come back and bite him in the ass. It would sooner or later, he was sure.

Unfortunately, it was sooner.

The phone on his desk blared a ring that made them both flinch. His office phone. At work. In the police station. Reaching over, he plucked up the receiver. "Kingston."

Chloe wriggled beneath him, but he leaned more of his weight on her to keep her in place as Cavalli's smooth voice sounded in his ear. "Good, you're there. Is Dr. Standish with you or is Grayson still working her over?"

"No, I have her." He met her gaze, and she stilled, but his dick surged inside her. Her breath caught, and he clenched his jaw to stop a groan.

"Good. Peyton and I will be right there."

"Fine." He hung up the phone. His eyes closed, and he swore steadily under his breath, braced his arms on the desk beside her and pulled his cock from her body. They both moaned at the slide of flesh. "Fuck. How the hell did you do this to me, Chloe? I'm at *work.*"

A snort erupted from her as she sat up, slithered off the desk, and pushed her skirt down. A few spellwords, and any wrinkles smoothed from her clothes; her hair fell in perfect waves around her rosy cheeks. "I didn't *do* anything to you. You did the doing."

He grunted, but didn't argue. The same spell straightened his own clothes, and he shoved his fingers through his hair, then went to fetch her panties and purse from where they lay discarded on the floor. Fighting the urge to tuck her panties in his pocket, he handed her things to her.

A knock came on his door, and with a quick wave of his hand, he released the sound dampening spell and sent a quick whirlwind of air through his office to filter out the obvious scent of raw sex in the small room. If he could smell it, he had no doubt that a vampire and a werewolf would be able to.

He slid into his desk chair and scooped up the paperwork he and Chloe had scattered before raising his voice. "Come in."

Chloe took a seat opposite him and crossed her legs, which

drew his gaze and made it linger on her lithe, bare limbs. He wanted them around his waist, on his shoulders, anywhere as long as he could get inside her. He'd just had her, and he wanted her again. Still.

Fuck.

Swallowing the curse, he forced himself to focus on the men stepping into the room. Except for the blade-sharp edge that no operative could truly hide, there was little the two had in common. Luca's dark, exotic features contrasted with Peyton's all-American good looks. Sandy brown hair, blue eyes, tall and muscular physique, but not so much that it caught attention—the type of guy who could fade into the woodwork if he chose. His gaze swept the office, took in Chloe and Merek in a single glance. A chill went down Merek's spine, and he didn't doubt that with that single glance the werewolf could describe in minute detail everything he'd seen, smelled, or sensed about the room and the people occupying it.

A dangerous man.

It should have relieved Merek to hand Chloe over to competent agents, but it didn't. He clenched his jaw until it ached as he listened to Luca explain Chloe's situation to her, the need for her to give up her life, her family, her friends, her career because the knowledge she had in her head made her a risk to everyone she knew.

She grew paler and paler by the moment. Her eyes went wider and wider with shock, her fingers twisting the strap on her purse, and Merek's insides twisted right along with it. Those haunted hazel eyes turned to him for confirmation of this nightmare she'd found herself in, and he could only give her a single, sharp nod.

Gods, but he wanted to pull her into his arms and protect her from this. His fingers fisted on the arms of his chair listening to Cavalli's smooth voice lay out why she had to go into protective custody until they captured Leonard Smith—though

Merek noted the vampire failed to mention how many years they'd been unsuccessful in doing so, and that they might continue to be unsuccessful for years more. She might never reclaim the life she had now, might never see the people she loved again.

Every instinct told him not to let her go, to keep her with him, but he ignored them. The possessiveness wasn't something he should feel, and he shoved it aside.

Her dazed, terrified eyes met his just once more before she was pulled out the door, and he couldn't shake the feeling that if he let her go now, he'd lose her forever. She would be gone, ended. Dead. His gut clenched, twisted into a cold, hard knot.

The tension inside built and built until it snapped.

Cursing her, cursing himself, he grabbed his jacket and slammed out of his office. The captain would have his ass if he interfered with a case that was no longer under the MTF's jurisdiction. Hell, his partner would have his ass for fucking up like this, and that was a lot more dangerous than pissing off the captain. Neither thought slowed him down as he peeled out of the station to tail the FBI agents. Chloe.

He shoved a hand through his hair. "I have lost my fucking mind."

Worse, he'd lost control.

3

How had she ended up in this place? A few hours ago, she'd been at work in her pristine lab. An hour ago, she'd been a murder suspect. Now she was a victim in the making with a terrorist who wanted to do to her what he'd done to Damien. It just couldn't be real. She was dreaming. Having a nightmare. Having a psychotic break. Her research had finally driven her around the bend. Chloe stared blankly at her surroundings for a moment before anything even registered.

The safe house was small and dark, with a faint dankness in the air that said the Pacific Northwestern damp had set in and begun to rot the wood somewhere in the building. It was nothing like her beautiful, airy home.

She swallowed, already hating the gloom of this place. She wanted to go around and turn every lamp on. Instead, she glanced at the men who dominated the living room. Peyton's nostrils flared, the closest thing to emotion to cross his face in the hour since she'd met him. He didn't smile; he didn't talk much; he just looked over and summed her up in a coolly competent way that made her really, really glad they were on the same side.

What Peyton lacked in gregariousness, Luca Cavalli more than made up for. He had the gift of gab and had kept up a light stream of conversation she could tell was meant to put her at ease. It didn't work because she could also tell that, in his own way, he had summed her up and reacted accordingly as quickly as his werewolf agent had. She was being handled. She wasn't sure which method she liked less, but at the same time, she didn't feel threatened by either man.

Perhaps because Merek had given her that one tiny nod to let her know these people were telling her the truth, that she could trust them to look out for her.

At the same time, she knew she'd feel a lot safer if the detective were with her instead of the agents. She frowned, shook her head to clear it. She didn't know Merek Kingston any better than she knew these men. Sex was not the same thing as *knowing* someone. She'd had a lot of sex with Damien, and look where that had ended up.

The thought made something huge and horrible expand inside her chest. She couldn't breathe; she wanted to curl up and cry. Damien was dead, Ivan was gone, and her life was over. Her world had been shaken up and tossed out again like dice in a cup. She had no idea what was beyond the next roll.

"This is just temporary, until we get you transferred somewhere else." Luca's gaze met hers, and she guessed she was supposed to feel reassured. She would have if it had been Merek. She pushed that notion away. "Somewhere outside Seattle, but we will keep you safe."

Butterflies took wing in her belly, fluttering madly. She hoped that meant another big city. She didn't want to leave the people and the comforting brightness and energy that swirled around her when she was in a booming metropolis. She dragged in a breath. There was no need to worry about that now. They might ship her to New York or Atlanta or somewhere else just as frenetic.

"I understand. Thank you." She gave Luca the best smile she could manage. She understood they'd *try* to keep her safe, but whoever Leonard Smith was, she knew he'd already managed to break into a Conclave-owned apartment building and kill two full-grown vampires. That didn't say much for her chances, but she didn't voice that opinion aloud. Tempting fate just seemed like a bad idea at this point.

She stepped through the doorway from the small living room to the even smaller kitchen. Maybe looking around would make this all seem more real. At the moment, she felt like she was having an out-of-body experience. She was still moving around as if everything were normal, but her mind was floating about a foot above her body, looking down on some dream she wasn't quite attached to.

The tile was cracked on the floor, and the faucet dripped steadily into a big, old-fashioned enamel sink. A door on the wall adjacent to the entry she stood in led to what must be a backyard. It was half glass, and it wasn't until that moment that she noticed every window had the blinds closed so no one could see in. The place was ugly and worn down, but if it was safe, then she didn't care. She pulled in a calming breath. "Before I leave town there are some things I'm going to need."

Peyton spoke for the first time, his voice richer and mellower than she'd have expected. "It's best if you detach yourself from everything here."

"Trust me, you want my aunt to know I'm going into protective custody, or she will tear this city and then the rest of the world apart looking for me." Again, she didn't need to mention who her aunt was. Millie Standish was a byword in the Magickal community, and not just in Seattle. "Also, I need my familiar with me. I won't leave her behind."

Neither man looked happy, but both of them nodded their

agreement. Luca slid his hands into his pockets, his lips twitching ever so slightly. "I suppose I have the dubious honor of letting Mildred Standish know her niece's life is in danger. Wonderful."

"One of the perks of being the boss, boss." What could almost be called a smile crinkled the corners of Peyton's blue eyes. "We can send someone to gather your things for you, Dr. Standish. Make us a list."

"One more thing, and this one neither of you can do for me." Chloe twisted the strap of her purse between her fingers. "I need to call my godson and let him know what's going on. Unless . . . he's already in protective custody, too?"

"That would be Alex Nemov, correct?" Luca's shoulders rolled beneath his expensive shirt.

Peyton's gaze sharpened, cutting from her to Luca and back again. Something she couldn't quite decipher moved behind his eyes, but it was gone so fast she thought she might have imagined it. "Ivan Nemov's son. Werewolf."

"Yes, and now that his dad is missing, he's my responsibility." Being a godparent was a sacred vow in the Magickal world, reinforced by spells that bound a person to care for the child in his or her parents' absence. Or death. She locked her gaze with Luca, letting him know that this was nonnegotiable. She would never break her vow. "Alex *needs* to know what's going on. Maybe he knows where his dad went."

The big vampire sighed. "We've thought of that, and we're handling it."

She firmed her lips. "Well, it doesn't matter what you're handling. His sole remaining parent is off the grid, and that makes him my responsibility. If you haven't picked him up yet, then I need to. He interns with me at Desmodus after school. He'll know something is wrong when both his father and I aren't at work."

Luca looked her over as if deciding how much he was willing to tell her. "He didn't go to his internship today. In fact, when we tried to pick him up from school, he wasn't there."

Her heart stopped, literally skipped two whole beats as terror she'd never wanted to feel punched through her.

Oh, gods.

"Alex doesn't shirk his duties, which means he's missing, too." Cold dread gripped her belly, and she clutched her purse closer, fumbling for her cell phone.

"We can't know yet that anything has happened to Alex. We have agents still looking for him." The vampire gentled his voice, handling her again. This time she found it infuriating.

"Really?" She arched an incredulous eyebrow. "You know him well enough to know where to look?"

Irritation crossed Luca's too-handsome face, and she thought she saw a flash of fang when he answered her. "We spoke to his teachers, his friends—we found out his favorite hangouts. We have people waiting at those locations in case he shows up. We have other people out looking."

She snorted, sat down at the kitchen table, and continued digging around the bottom of her purse for her phone. Her heart still beat too hard, worry digging roots deep inside her. "One of his favorite hangouts is *my house*."

"Your house is already being watched. We're handling this, Dr. Standish. Try not to worry." Luca settled back against the cabinets and crossed his arms. Peyton propped his shoulder against the doorjamb to the living room. He just watched them both and said nothing.

"Yeah, I don't have a care in the world." Her hand closed around the hard plastic of her phone, and she yanked it out of her purse. Since neither man tried to stop her from making the call, she assumed that meant they were okay with it. Punching in the speed dial code for Alex's cell, she hunched her shoulders away from the agents. "Excuse me."

She didn't bother getting up and going into another room.

Vampires and werewolves both had exceptional hearing. If they wanted to hear her, she wouldn't be able to hide her conversation from them. The phone rang and rang, and her insides twisted tighter and tighter with each one. On the fifth ring, she knew it was about to kick over to voice mail, and her throat closed. What the hell was she supposed to leave on the message? Call me? Your dad's missing? Why weren't you at school or your internship? Are you okay? I love you, kiddo? She wanted to know all of those things, needed to say every single one of them.

"Chloe?" Alex's voice was rushed and breathless, the phone fuzzing with every quick exhalation.

She squeezed the phone so tightly the plastic squeaked. "Alex! Oh, gods!"

He wheezed out a laugh. "I'm okay. Don't worry."

"Too late. I'm worried." Her free hand clenched on the edge of the table until her knuckles whitened. "Where are you?"

"I'm being followed." The sentence was spoken so calmly and matter-of-factly that she blinked for a moment while his words processed. This just couldn't be happening. It couldn't.

"You're being followed? By who?"

"I'm not sure." What sounded like pounding footsteps echoed in the background of the call. "It's a male wolf, and he's been tracking me all day. My senses tell me he's a danger to me."

Now Luca straightened away from the counter, his gaze glinting. "We don't have any male wolf agents looking for him. Two female wolves, but Peyton's the only male wolf on my team."

"Who was that?" Alex's sharp question jerked her attention back to him. Right. Wolf-boy's hearing was just as sensitive as that of the agents before her.

"He's from the FBI." She swallowed, gripping the table so

hard it hurt her hand. "Alex, your dad's disappeared. The person tailing you might have something to do with it."

"Yeah, I went by the house, and it's been gone through by at least two groups of people. Lots of muddy scents, lots of bad vibes creeping down my spine. I've never had to deal with anything like this before, Chloe."

The vulnerability and tension in his tone scared the shit out of her. Alex was a rock-steady kid—mature, calm, and collected when most boys his age were prone to fly off the handle. If he was afraid, there was reason to be afraid. Her muscles trembled in reaction, but she forced herself to keep her composure. Alex needed her now. He was in danger.

Pulling in a deep breath, she let it ease out. "Okay. Okay. I need to know where you are. I'm going to send an FBI agent to get you. He's a vampire. His name is Luca Cavalli. Six foot four-ish, dark eyes, short black hair, little goatee on his chin. Good-looking, if you go for that type."

The boy's snort was almost a chuckle. "I don't, but I've got the idea."

Luca slanted her a narrow-eyed glance . . . because of the good-looking comment or because she was summarily sending him to fetch her godson? She didn't care so she ignored him to address Alex. "Where are you?"

A long pause came before the teen answered. "I'm at the corner of Denny and Westlake, but I can't stay in one place."

"That's fine." Luca nodded, already turning to walk toward the front door. Peyton stepped back to let him pass. "I can track him once I get his essence."

She arched her eyebrows. This was a Magickal skill she hadn't heard of. "His essence?"

"Blood." He glanced over his shoulder as he opened the door. His full lips quirked in a smile. "I can track the scent of his blood."

Alex's voice came through the phone. "That's fucking creepy."

Chloe snorted and shook her head. "Tell me about it."

"I'll see you soon."

"Yes, you will." Clutching the phone a little tighter, she forced herself to relax her hold on the table. Everything would be okay. She had to believe it because she couldn't bear the thought of anything happening to Jaya's son. "Be careful. I love you."

"I love you, too, Chloe." His voice cracked just a little before he hung up.

She looked to Luca, who was just about to step out the door. "Take care of him, and bring him back in one piece, is that clear?"

"Yes, ma'am."

"And don't call me ma'am."

For a moment, he appeared nonplussed, but then he shook his head and spun away in that eerily silent way only vampires could manage. A minute later, the sound of his car driving away faded into the deepening evening.

Peyton stood with his hands in his pockets, a cool expression on his face as he looked at her. Some instinct tickled the back of her mind and built until her shoulders twitched in discomfort. She dropped her phone back into her purse, trying to busy herself until the odd feeling faded.

It didn't fade. Instead it increased by the moment, some whisper-soft niggling growing to a harsh scream until she was all but shaking. She didn't know what it meant, what to do. Was it about Alex?

Danger. The word was clear as a clarion bell in her mind. Her gaze snapped to Peyton, but he wasn't looking at her anymore; he had tugged aside the blinds on the kitchen window to peer outside. Werewolves and vampires were both telepathic, but that hadn't sounded like his voice in her head.

"Peyton, is everything all right?"

He sighed, but didn't turn around. When he spoke, his tone was weary. "Everything is fine, Dr. Standish. Exactly according to plan."

"What plan?"

There was a knock on the backdoor before he could reply, and he went to open it. A small woman stood under the mellow glow of the porch light.

The instinct howled in Chloe's mind, the words becoming crystal clear. *Danger. danger. Danger! RUN!*

And then she knew what it was. Her usually dormant precognitive ability. She had clairaudience—and the voices in her head were warning her of oncoming peril. She didn't know what the danger was, but only a fool ignored her precognition. She lurched to her feet, staggered under the pain of what felt like unused muscles coming to life, and overturned her chair as she searched for a way out. There was only the backdoor and the door that led to the living room, both of which she'd have to get past Peyton to use.

They were on her before she could react. The woman hit her with a spell that left her stunned, the magic reverberating through Chloe the way only a Fae could make it.

Chloe barely managed to keep her feet under her, her body wanting to collapse under the force of violent, ugly magic. Her tongue felt awkward, too thick for her mouth as she looked at Peyton. Her voice was a mere breath of sound. "Why?"

He shook his head, what might have been regret flickering in his gaze before a hard mask settled over his features and his lips pulled back in a snarl to bare his wolf fangs. He reached her side with a speed that left her dizzy, and then he struck her with just the tips of his fingers, almost gently, and she lost consciousness.

She woke up bound to her chair by metal handcuffs and magical restraints. She didn't know how much time had passed. An hour. A minute.

All she did know was pain. It pounded through her in end-less, agonizing waves. Black spots swam before her eyes, and she prayed for death...or a return to unconsciousness, whichever came for her first, but they wouldn't let her rest, wouldn't let her pass out, wouldn't stop.

She told them everything, her every secret, every lie, every half-truth....She left nothing out; they wouldn't let her. And still it wasn't enough. If the spells would have allowed it, she'd have told them anything they wanted to hear. Anything. Even if it wasn't true. Just to make the pain stop.

Sweat slid in cold, sticky rivulets down her skin. It burned her eyes and blurred her vision. Every breath was a torturous rasp of air. Her head lolled on her shoulder, and she hadn't the energy left to lift it. The metal handcuffs were bronze, an allergy to all witches. They'd scorched her flesh, rubbed her wrists to ragged, bleeding patches of skin, but other than that, she was physically unharmed. It did little to ease the way she ached from the bones out.

Voices murmured around her, and she was no longer sure if it was Peyton and the Fae woman or the clairaudient voices in her mind. It didn't matter, but she clung to the question as if it were the key to saving what was left of her sanity. And maybe it was.

Another spell lanced through her, making her body arch away from the chair, rip against the restraints that bound her. A howl that wasn't quite human wrenched from deep within her. More pain. Her throat was already raw from all the talking, the begging. The screaming.

She knew she was losing it when his face appeared before her, the cynical gray eyes, the squared jaw, the lips just a little too full for his chiseled features.

"Merek," she breathed.

And then she knew no more.

* * *

They'd muffled the sound of her screams.

If Merek hadn't decided to get a better look at the house, he never would have peeked through a gap in the blinds to see her strapped to the chair. Arching, tears flowing down her cheeks, her mouth opened in what looked like a silent shriek.

He exploded through the door, past the warding spells that had been placed on the building, his rage and terror lending him extra power. The percussive boom of the ruptured spell shield made his ears ring, but his weapon was already up and leveled on the two Magickals looming over *his* woman.

The Fae had sweat pouring down her face, her breathing shallow and ragged. No doubt from the energy she'd spent torturing Chloe. His teeth bared, and he squeezed off a shot, aiming for her heart.

It never touched her.

Peyton looped his arm around the woman's waist, spinning her out of the bullet's path. Chloe's chair was knocked over, tumbling until it hit a wall. With a leap, the wolf had himself and the woman into the living room. Merek's next shot caught Peyton in the back, and he stumbled, a howl tearing loose. He hit the front door, ripping it off its hinges. Then he and the woman were gone, the werewolf's speed making it impossible for Merek to follow.

He might have attempted it, but it would have meant leaving Chloe alone. He couldn't do that. Holstering his weapon, he lifted both hands to cast a temporary warding spell over the house. No one less powerful than him could enter, and even then he would know his shield had been breached. His hands were shaking when he dropped them to his sides. A part of him stood back and wondered what the hell had happened to all his steely discipline when the fate of one slender woman could make his hands tremble.

Turning back toward the kitchen, he found Chloe struggling

against her bonds. He stroked a hand down her shoulder. "I've got it."

"Thanks," she grunted, going limp against the awkward position. "I . . . don't have the energy to cast a spell to get loose."

Her wrists were blackened, blistered, and oozing blood around the cuffs, so he knew they were made of bronze. As a warlock—a male witch—he was deathly allergic to the stuff, too. He was careful not to touch as he waved a hand to unlock them. His jaw locked as rage whipped through him. The bastards had used *bronze* on her.

The cuffs fell away, clattering against the linoleum. Then she was in his arms, her soft body pressed to his harder planes, and it felt so fine he almost groaned. Burying his face in the curve of her neck, he inhaled the scent of her. She was alive, and she was here. His brain was having trouble absorbing that reality. "Chloe."

Clinging to his neck with surprising strength, she dragged in great, shuddering breaths. They should get out of there in case Peyton came back to finish what he started, but Merek couldn't make himself let her go. Just another minute. He swallowed, pressure building behind his eyes.

She drew back until she could see his face, and the naked vulnerability there made his gut clench. "How did you . . . What are you doing here?"

"I followed you, but they were damn good about shaking someone tailing them." He stroked her ebony hair back from her face, the silky strands damp with sweat. "I'm sorry it took me so long to get here."

"You made it before I lost my mind. That's soon enough."

He winced at the bleak, utter certainty in her voice. From what he'd seen, she was right. They'd had every intention of ripping into her mind until there was nothing left. The darkness of those spells still lingered in the air, sent chills down his spine.

He pressed a kiss to her temple. "We need to get you out of here, sweetheart."

She nodded, pushing herself slowly to her feet. A soft chuckle bubbled out of her when he hovered, his hands outstretched to catch her like he would for a child just learning to walk. "I'll be fine, Merek. No permanent damage was done. Physically." She swallowed hard. "I'm really, really glad you're here."

He jerked her back into his arms, needing that contact. His heart hammered in his chest. Gods, what would he have done if he hadn't gotten here in time? Another loss he couldn't have prevented because of a blankness in his fucking precog *gift*.

She trembled against him, a violent shudder racking her body. "Oh, gods. I was sure I'd gone crazy when I saw you here."

"Sweetheart, I—"

He didn't get a chance to respond before she pressed her mouth to his. He stiffened, but her fingers shoved into his hair to hold him tight, and the feel of her lips against his registered over his shock. Then it was all over. His arms banded around her, pulling her closer. The fear and the need to confirm in the most basic, carnal way that she was safe and sound overruled his better judgment. She bit his lip, her movements as frantic as his, and he could taste the terror she'd been through, her need to forget.

One hand lifted to cradle her head, the silk of her hair spilling through his fingers. He tilted her face up and took control of the kiss. His tongue traced the seam of her lips until she parted them for him. He plunged into her mouth, the taste of her lush and female on his tongue. A low groan shook his chest, and he hauled her closer.

She twisted to get nearer, as desperate as he was to reassure herself that everything was all right. Her fingers skimmed down his arms, around his waist, over his ass, up his back, everywhere she could reach. Her touch had a predictable effect on his body. His cock went hard, his body ready and willing to give her anything she wanted.

Cupping the smooth curve of her buttocks in his hand, he lifted her into his body until he was right where he wanted to be—or as close as he could get when they were still dressed. He could feel the heat of her sex through their clothing as they rubbed against each other.

Releasing his grip on her hair, he let his hand drift down until he cradled her breast. Her tight nipple jabbed into his palm. He grunted in satisfaction at her eager response. He stroked the little nub with his fingers, pinching it, toying with it until she writhed against him. She whimpered and tried to climb him, her body straining against him, her leg wrapping around his to pull him closer.

It was all he could do not to back her against the nearest wall and take her.

Shuddering, he broke his mouth away from hers. "We can't."

"Why not?" Her palm slid between them to cup his cock and rub it through his pants.

"Gods," he groaned, and he couldn't keep the torment from his voice as he thrust against her hand before he forced himself to stillness. "Because I'm a big enough idiot to turn you down, but not a big enough asshole to take you up on your offer. And I really, really want to take you up on your offer."

"So take me up on it." Her breasts brushed against him with each panting breath, and her eyes were wild. "I'm offering. I'm not protesting. I want you."

He caught her fingers and removed them from his cock. Each digit was puffy and swollen from bronze damage. That brought a cold rush of reality in to chill his ardor. "We have to get out of here. We're not out of danger yet."

Her head tilted as if she was listening to something. Then she blinked, nodded, and dropped her hands. She stooped down to scoop up the scattered contents of her purse and hooked the bag over one shoulder. "Okay, let's go." She gave him a sturdy nod. "Luca went to get my godson, Alex, so we need to find them. If I wasn't *safe* in a safe house, they certainly aren't."

Dropping the shielding spell on the house, he led the way out, palming his pistol from its holster and keeping a death grip on her forearm, careful not to touch her chafed wrists. "Luca can take care of himself and your godson. I'd trust him with my life, unlike Peyton, who I didn't know. Right now, I'm taking you to the hospital."

"I'm just fine, thank you." She tugged at her arm, but he just hauled her along behind him. "Alex is—"

He spared her a bare glance. "I'd rather have a doctor confirm that. The kind of spells people use for that kind of questioning can have some nasty side effects. A doctor could take the edge off of those for you."

"I *am* a doctor."

"You're a medical researcher. You don't treat people. Even if you did, you don't have the energy to fix yourself, and I don't have the expertise to deal with bronze wounds." Pausing at the end of the garage, he peered around the corner to see if anyone was paying attention to this house. No one. At least, no one he could see or sense. They'd have to risk the run across the street to his car.

"If you—"

She broke off, stopping in her tracks as abruptly as if she'd hit a brick wall. "I can't go to the hospital yet. I need to go home."

"The hell you say. You're not running around after your godson, and you're not going home. We can call Luca on the way, but that's the best you're going to get." He palmed his keys before propelling her toward his vehicle. "Because you're *going to the hospital*, and that's final."

"Fine, Detective Control Freak." She snatched the keys from his hand and slid into the driver's seat, shutting and locking the door behind her. He blinked, but instead of standing there like an easy target while he tried to get her out of his seat, he loped around to the passenger side and climbed in. The woman had a knack for throwing him off balance that he didn't care for at all. She started the car. "I appreciate your saving me, but my life isn't the only important one. Put your seatbelt on."

He growled at her, but obeyed. "Your life is important enough."

She chirped the tires when she pulled away from the curb, quickly navigating Seattle traffic... and not going toward Harborview Medical Center with its Magickal ward that could treat her. "You want to tell me where you think you're going?"

"I don't *think* I'm going anywhere. I'm definitely going home. I *have* to go home." Those hazel eyes were wide with pleading. They both knew in her current condition he could overpower her easily if he wanted to. The thought of scaring or hurting her more than she already had been was too much for him. He stayed on his side of the car and fumed. If possible, her eyes went even wider. "I swear I'll go to the hospital without protest afterward."

He sighed and kept an eye out for a tail. "Chloe—"

"It'll take us—what?—an extra fifteen minutes? If I was going to drop dead, I would have done it by now. If you thought I was that bad off, you'd have called an ambulance instead of wanting to take me there yourself."

She was right; he wanted her checked out, but he didn't think she was *that* injured. He shifted in his seat to look at her. "There are people watching your house. And those people aren't necessarily the good guys. Hell, at this point, we don't even know who the good guys *are* except Cavalli."

They hit Lower Queen Anne and started working their way up the hill. Even though they were already on their way, she kept trying to reason with him, which he found both amusing and annoying. She shot him a grim look, her swollen fingers tapping lightly against the steering wheel. "I understand that, but here's how this is going to be. You can either let me go home now, and then take me to the hospital, or you can force me to go to the hospital and when I'm done there, I'll go home without you."

"If you think for a single fucking second I'm letting you out of my sight, you'd better think again." The glare he gave her was sulfuric, and his voice dropped to a dangerous softness that normally made grown men back up a couple of steps.

Chloe, of course, just sniffed, and her jaw took on a stubborn tilt. "You can go with me now, or you can let Luca drag me out of your sight again, in which case you won't even get to see if I make it home safely."

"Luca's not going to let you go home," he snarled, hating that she was right. When Cavalli showed up again, she was gone. His grip on his weapon went white-knuckled.

Her eyebrows arched. "He can't force me into protective custody, can he? I *can* walk away if I want to."

"Do it, and you'll be dead within twenty-four hours." His blood ran ice-cold at the mere thought, and he knew if he didn't have a hold of the gun, his hands would be shaking again. He'd already come so close to losing her. Too damn close. "Tell me what happened with Luca and Peyton. How did Cavalli end up running off to rescue your godson?"

She didn't even smile at his obvious concession and filled him in on everything that had gone down from the moment she'd left the police department until he'd come bursting into the safe house. Luca, Alex, Peyton, the Fae torturer. What Peyton and the Fae had to do with Leonard Smith, Merek didn't yet know, but he was going to find out. She'd just wound to a finish when she turned onto her street, which was awash with flashing lights from various law enforcement vehicles. He could pick out two patrol cars and what he'd guess were cars from some of Cavalli's FBI team.

Chloe left the car running and was already sliding out of the vehicle before it had rocked to a full stop. She probably figured he'd stop her if she waited. She was right. And he was pissed. He should have asked her *why* she wanted to go home so desperately instead of assuming it had something to do with traumatic shock. "Fuck."

He flipped on the blue light on his dash, shut down the engine, and caught up with Chloe before she'd reached the house. She didn't look at him. "I'm not going to apologize."

Getting a stranglehold on his temper, he had to remind himself of what she'd been through to stop himself from taking her over his knee and spanking her. "Do you know who broke into your house?"

"No, but I felt a breach to my warding spell, and Luca said he had people watching my house." She slid her hands deep inside her pockets in an obvious attempt to conceal her mangled wrists.

His fingers flexed on his gun before he forced himself to relax them. "Why didn't you let the authorities handle it then?"

"It could have been Alex." She shrugged. "He comes over a lot, but I've never given him a key. I should have. I will, actually."

He shook his head, trying to follow her train of thought. She might never get to come home again, and she was worried about giving someone else a key. He was more concerned about who was in her house right *now*. "Would Alex have led his pursuers to your home?"

One shoulder dipped in a little shrug. "I doubt it. He's a smart kid, but he's still a kid, and he's justifiably scared." She snorted, and he heard tears in the sound, but she glanced away from him, so he couldn't be sure. "Hell, I'm an adult, and *I'm* scared."

"You damn well should be scared."

"Thanks for the confirmation." Her tone was dry, and she arched a sardonic eyebrow.

They both stopped talking and pulled out ID as they approached the nearest officer, who Merek recognized as a rookie on the MTF. In seconds, they were cleared to go beyond the police barricade and approach the house. More cars with flashing lights rolled up, and the police officers did their best to move Chloe's neighbors as far from the scene as possible. The fewer Normals they had to perform memory spells on, the better. They'd have a telepath watching the crowd to see who noticed anything magical and snag them before they could talk.

Chloe ignored the ache in her limbs, the sting in her wrists, and the burn of sexual chemistry from Merek that apparently no amount of pain could fend off.

The closer they got to her house, the more secure she felt. It wasn't just that her home was somewhere familiar and safe for her, it was the bright lights of the police cars, the people and noise and hubbub. She wasn't trapped alone with terrorists who hurt her. Her heart tripped at the thought, her hands trembling so hard she had to clench them.

Every light in her house was on, just the way she left it. Just the way she always liked it. Bright and safe and surrounded by a city full of people. Cities never really slept. There was always something going on. Today's events had only reinforced a lifetime's understanding that there were monsters in the dark. She knew from experience just how scary and dangerous it could be.

Tess stood on her front porch, her hands raised above her head, but her posture was relaxed. Chloe couldn't hear what her friend was saying, but she watched her friend two-finger some identification out of her purse and hand it to the closest of the five officers surrounding the porch.

"Shit," Chloe sighed.

Merek squinted to see through the flashing lights and high beams. "What? You know that woman?"

"Yeah." Chloe tucked her hands even deeper into her pockets, not wanting her friend to see her damaged wrists. The fabric rubbing against her skin burned like acid, but an explanation was something she couldn't give. "My best friend, Tess Jones. She was supposed to meet me here at seven. We were supposed to have dinner."

He grunted and jerked his chin in her direction, but his gaze swept the area, taking in every detail of the street, the houses, the people, the cars. "She looks remarkably calm for someone with a whole lot of weapons pointed her way."

Chloe found herself following his example, discreetly checking everyone out. Her neighbors, she knew, but who else might be watching? Leonard Smith? More of his people? She usually liked being around a lot of people, but now it seemed just as dangerous as being isolated. Her belly cramped tight, and she stuffed the fear into the deepest corner of her soul, to be dealt with when she was in a safer place. "Tess's a pathologist for the FBI. The Normal side of it. She's a Normal."

"Ah. So, she doesn't know anything." He made it a statement, but Chloe could hear the question in his words. Had Chloe told her Normal friend anything? Had she broken Magickal law?

"No, she doesn't know anything." Chloe had wanted to tell the truth. Many, many times. But she'd never given in to the temptation. She licked her cracked lips, wincing as her body ached as if she had run a marathon. Or been worked over by a baseball bat. Now that the adrenaline was fading, she could feel every single twinge, every screaming echo of pain.

Merek's big hand closed around her elbow when she swayed on her feet, but the touch hurt so she tugged her arm away from him. "If you know who's here, we can take you to the hospital now. Don't you think so, Cavalli?"

"Not just yet." A low voice spoke from behind her, and she turned to see the vampire. A quiet and watchful Alex stood beside him, and relief so sharp she almost burst into tears sliced through her. He was safe and *here*. Thank the gods.

"You all right, Chloe?" His gaze searched her, his nostrils flaring as he caught her scent, using his senses to check her for damage.

Aside from the residual tension thrumming through her muscles, she wasn't sure how much, if anything, he could sense of what had happened to her. She hoped nothing. This was something she didn't want to talk about with anyone right now, maybe not ever. "I'm fine. You?"

"Never better." His young voice was flat, his face blank. It hurt to see him that way. Whatever he had seen, whatever he had been through today, had already done more harm to the boy than she liked. Her heart squeezed, but she let her mind cling to Alex rather than what she'd been through herself.

Cavalli caught up with me before the werewolves did, though it was a close call. Alex sent his private thoughts to her telepathically, a gift of only the werewolf and vampire races, so Chloe couldn't respond in public other than with a small nod of acknowledgment. She would definitely be talking to him about what happened and how he was really doing later, but this wasn't a good time for it.

"Hey, Detective? This woman says she's a friend of Dr. Standish's."

Chloe swung around to see a police officer with slightly pointed ears trailed by Tess. Keeping her hands firmly tucked in her pockets, Chloe nodded to them both. "Yeah, I know her."

"Thanks, Patterson." Merek jerked his chin at the onlookers gathered beyond the police line. "Let's get everyone cleared out of here."

The elf officer nodded, what looked almost like dazed awe on his face while he spoke to Merek. "You got it, sir."

The group stood in silence, each staring at the others for long, strained moments. Tess propped a hand on her hip, her body language resuming that lazy, casual pose that Chloe knew was a complete sham. Tess was unhappy, and they were all about to hear about it. "So. Does someone want to tell me *what the hell* is going on? I'm pretty sure my supervisor is not happy to have gotten a call from the police to confirm my identity. And his level of pissed off is nothing compared to mine. So, who wants to go first, hm? Alex? Chloe? Detective Whatever? Tall, Dark, and Agently?"

Luca lifted a sculpted brow. "You can tell I'm an agent just by looking?"

Tess flipped her sheet of long auburn hair over her shoulder, her gold eyes narrowed, and she wrinkled her pert nose. "You have that stench about you, yeah."

The big vampire's even white teeth flashed in a smile, his eyes lighting with challenge as he looked over Tess with slow, unmistakable deliberation. "And you are?"

Her lips twitched, but her gaze cooled as she gave him just as thorough a once-over. Her expression said she wasn't impressed with what she saw. "Dr. Tess Jones. You?"

"Special Agent Luca Cavalli. FBI." Taking a step toward her, he held his hand out for her to shake.

She sniffed dismissively. "Never heard of you."

"Good." His hand remained extended, a dare to see how she'd react. "My work isn't supposed to be broadcast on all stations."

Her amber eyes narrowed to slits, and she shoved her hand into his grip, giving two brisk pumps and pulling back. Or she tried to. Luca's fingers tightened, and he ran a thumb over the back of her hand. A visible shiver passed through her, and her eyes widened in what might have been alarm as she jerked her hand from his grasp.

Mating rituals for the vamp-human crossover. Chloe rolled her eyes. "Okay, focus, people. Seriously."

"Sorry, hon." Tess broke eye contact with Luca, and he scowled. Chloe tried not to grin. She'd bet he was trying a little vampiric mesmerizing on her friend, but the subtle stuff only worked on the weak-willed, and Tess was anything but weak, Normal or not.

"What happened, Chloe?" Alex's gaze locked on her, and he ignored everyone else.

"Later." She gave Tess a pointed look to remind Alex that they had a Normal in their midst, offered a weak smile, and nodded in Merek's direction. "Everyone, this is Detective Merek Kingston, Seattle PD."

She didn't mention he was on the Magickal Task Force—Alex would already have guessed, and Tess didn't need to know. A few more men joined their group, and the way they looked at Luca said he was speaking to them telepathically and that they were on his team.

Chloe shifted her weight to try to get more comfortable, but instead sent a sharp throb of agony ricocheting through her body. She bit her lip hard enough to draw blood, and when she finally refocused, she found that Luca had introduced the agents to everyone.

Alex shoved a hand through his dark hair and offered Merek and the new agents a solemn nod. His nostrils flared a bit as he caught their scent, his brilliant green gaze moving from one to the next as if marking their faces and scents in his memory. A few of the men shifted uncomfortably, and Chloe tried not to smirk.

A small smile crossed Luca's face, but before he could say

anything, Tess ignored all the law enforcement officials and made an impatient gesture at Chloe. "So. Forget the 'later' business. Tell us what happened. Why are all these people here? That's a hell of a lot bigger response than someone gets for setting off a home alarm." She waved a vague hand in Luca's direction. "FBI agents don't make house calls." She flapped the same hand at Merek. "Detectives aren't usually first responders either."

Chloe sighed, shifted on her sore feet—and why the hell were her *feet* sore?—and bit back a gasp of pain. As much as she wanted to be in denial about what had happened, her body was going to make that impossible very soon. "Damien and his fiancée were murdered. They thought I did it, then they realized Ivan was missing, and it may have had more to do with stuff at work."

Tess tilted her head, keen intelligence transforming her face from merely beautiful to stunning. "Industrial espionage?"

"Yeah." Chloe scrunched her shoulders in a short shrug that still managed to make pain shoot up her neck and down her back. She fisted her shaking hands in her pockets. Beads of sweat began to form under her hair. "You know how product development can be. That stuff is guarded like Fort Knox."

Tess took a step toward her, and it was all Chloe could do not to cringe away from possible physical contact. "If Damien and Ivan—"

"Yeah, I'm in danger." She tilted her head at the silent teen, who watched her far too closely for her peace of mind. "Alex, too, since they don't seem to have a problem hurting family members." Damien's pregnant fiancée came to mind, and Chloe's gorge rose. Yes, family members were definitely in danger, and she was suddenly grateful Aunt Millie kept a personal bodyguard.

"We'll take good care of them." Luca gave Tess his most engaging smile. She arched an eyebrow and gave him another dismissive sniff.

They'd take good care of her? Chloe snorted, tears burning her eyes. Yeah, right. She felt totally safe with the FBI. Merek's body was a rigid line of rage as he moved closer to wrap a protective arm around her waist, and she hated that she did feel safer, even if the touch hurt. A lot. Three sets of eyes took in the gesture. Luca's gaze narrowed, Tess's mouth quirked, and Alex's eyebrows rose.

A wave of exhaustion she couldn't hold off any longer crashed through her system. The entire day swirled through her mind, and the street in front of her cartwheeled before her eyes. She closed them tight and set her hand on Merek's brawny forearm. "Will you do something for me?"

"Anything." His warm breath brushed against her temple, and she shuddered.

"Keep an eye on my godson." She swallowed, feeling unconsciousness creeping in to claim her. She welcomed it, letting her breath sigh out. "And catch me."

Then her knees buckled, and she was caught, safe in his embrace.

4

"Water," she said softly.

Her desperate thirst, and the croaky sound of her own voice, startled her awake.

A straw touched her lips, and she sucked down the cool liquid until she was replete. She was shaking a little when she relaxed back, the intensity of her thirst a shock to her system. A soothing murmur of voices in her head told her all was well. It looked like now that her clairaudience had woken up, it wasn't going dormant again. Before now, she could have counted on one hand the number of times her precognition had piped up. Every Magickal had different skills he or she excelled at, and this had never been one of hers. The last time she'd had a clairaudient episode had been almost ten years ago when she'd almost been mugged by a couple of Fae. Unseelie asshats.

The internal whispering tapered off, and she managed to pry her eyes open, but her pupils recoiled at the sudden brightness. Jerking her head away from the harsh fluorescent overhead lights, she blinked away the spots whirling before her eyes.

A glance at the window told her it was nighttime. She

frowned. That felt . . . wrong. She felt like she'd been asleep for a while. Long enough for it to be daylight. "How long have I been out?"

"Almost twenty-four hours." Alex had his back to her, placing the empty plastic cup on a tray next to the wall. He took a deep breath, his ribs expanding. "Feeling better?"

Chloe wiggled her toes, flexing her muscles one at a time to test for pain. Everything seemed fine. She flicked her fingers, trying a small spell to check her magic. The glass Alex had just set down popped straight into the air and landed like a miniature party hat on his head.

"I'll take that as a yes." His tone was dry, but his pale eyes twinkled when he turned to face her again. He extended the claws on one hand, snagged the cup with the other, and set it to spinning like a top on one pointed talon. "So, yesterday was an interesting day."

"Yeah, about that."

"About that." He set the glass down, folded his arms, and leaned back against the wall, the look on his face far too serious for someone his age. The light reflected off the design on his T-shirt, a logo for some teen rock band. In some ways he was a typical boy, and in others, he was already a man.

At sixteen, he was six feet tall and growing. His young shoulders were already broad and muscular, his features were blade-sharp, and his black-brown hair and bronzed skin only made his pale, celery green eyes stand out in contrast. The kid was good-looking and going to be a lady-killer someday. Chloe almost felt sorry for the girls in his class. Almost.

His expression didn't waver under her scrutiny; it retained the same calm impassivity he'd perfected the day his mother had died. It was hard to remember the carefree boy he'd once been, but she did her best to remind him to have a little fun as often as she could.

This wasn't going to be one of the times she could remind him.

She sighed and sat up straighter in her hospital bed. "How much do you know already?"

"Dad's missing." Or dead like Damien, but neither of them voiced that thought. "Someone killed your ex-boyfriend and his fiancée. Someone—maybe the same someone—tried to hack into Desmodus Industries' servers looking for information on the lycanthropy project you're all working on." He angled a glance at her. "How am I doing so far?"

"Those are the highlights, as far as I know them." She closed her eyes at the emotionless little recitation, and crossed her arms. Her wrists were still puffy and a little red, but thankfully the major damage was gone. Normal technology rocked for some things, but magic was awesome for things like this. The Magickal doctors at Harborview were top-notch. Like most other public services, from law enforcement to education, major hospitals had private rooms for Magickals and medical professionals on call who had the skill to handle cases like hers.

"None of those highlights explains why you needed to be brought to a hospital. You were fine when I talked to you on the phone. The vibrations in your voice showed no real distress." He let his arms fall to his sides. "Merek and Luca seemed to be having a lot of private chats last night while the doctors were working on you. They left me to entertain Tess and made sure I couldn't overhear them. So. Something else happened, right?" His pale eyes lasered through her, incisive and demanding answers she didn't want to give. Still, she'd never lied to this boy, and she didn't want to start now. He'd know anyway. He was far too intelligent and had senses far too sensitive to not know when she was prevaricating. So, she didn't.

"One of the FBI agents worked for a terrorist named Leonard Smith. He wants the drug your dad, Damien, and I have been formulating." She met his gaze, but kept her face carefully blank. "After Luca went out to get you, the other agent brought in a Fae to try to pry information from me about my part in the werewolf project. She used spells. Dark spells. Black magic."

He swallowed audibly. "If Luca hadn't—"

"Don't even think that." She held her hand out for him to take, and after a moment's hesitation, he crossed the room to her. "None of this is your fault. Or my fault."

"But it might be my dad's fault." His strong fingers curled around hers, but his gaze held the awful pain of betrayal. His father could be a traitor to his entire race, to his son.

And Chloe couldn't take that pain away from him, because she knew it could be true, so she gave him the respect of honesty. "Maybe. That still doesn't make it *your* fault."

His chin jerked down in an abrupt nod, but he said nothing more.

She tried to smile, but knew it was probably a weak parody of the real thing. "You're going to stay with me until we find out what happened to Ivan."

His gaze snapped up to meet hers, blazing with relief he quickly hid. A small grin quirked his lips, and he gave an exaggerated sniff. "That's going to put a crimp in your social life."

That her godson smelled a man all over her would have made most women blush, but no one who'd made it through medical school could be a prude about the human body, and she wasn't dumb enough to think Alex had much innocence left in that department anyway. She just shrugged delicately, plucking at the thin blanket covering her legs. "You're my godson. You stay with me."

The grin widened a little. "Well. Okay. If you insist."

"Your enthusiasm bowls me over, kid." But she squeezed his hand.

A bark of laughter answered her. "I promise not to be too big a pain in the ass for you."

"You can be as big a pain in the ass as you want. I might hex you a little for it, but you're still staying with me no matter what." She held his gaze, making sure he could see, could *sense,* the depth of her sincerity. It was important that he knew he had someone, that he was wanted, especially after Ivan's blatant neglect since his mother's death. Jaya would roll in her grave if she knew, so Chloe hoped the afterlife kept that information from her friend.

"I love you, too, Chloe." He tightened his grip on her fingers, but gently, as if he knew his own strength and tempered it for her. He was such a good kid. He deserved better than he'd gotten.

She pressed her free hand to her heart and made her eyes go wide. "Aw, now that's what a girl likes to hear."

His white teeth flashed in a wicked grin that had to make the teenage girls pant, but he sobered quickly. "So, you were in protective custody, but...the FBI is done with you now that you gave all the project information to the bad guys, right? The terrorists don't want you anymore and you're safe?"

She swallowed, looked down at the blanket, ran her palm over the nubby surface, and worried a few loose strands between her fingers. "They didn't get any information from me. Not about the project, at least."

"What do you mean?" Merek suddenly loomed in the door, his expression thunderous. He seemed to take up all the space and oxygen as he stepped into the room, snapping the door closed as though the act required great precision. His gray eyes locked on her face.

She tried not to shrink back at the intensity of his gaze. Not because she was afraid of him, but because it took everything she had not to throw herself into the security of his embrace. The only secure place in the world that she knew of right now. Some part of her mind registered that the reason she'd slept so well the whole day before was that Merek had been there, holding her hand, murmuring quiet, soothing encouragement whenever her eyes cracked open. Her fingers flexed as she remembered the slight calluses on his palm.

No. She wouldn't let herself rely on anyone, *need* anyone. She'd been there and done that, and she wouldn't go back. She *could* handle whatever came her way. No matter how much it scared her. Clinging to him for comfort stopped now. She lifted her chin. "I meant exactly what I said, Detective. They didn't get any information from me about the Desmodus Werewolf Project."

"How is that possible?" He looked incredulous, but the expression softened to one of sympathy as if she were a small child in deep denial. "The spells they were using ... Sweetheart, there's no way you have the kind of training to withstand—"

She held up her hand, ignoring the fact that her hands and wrists still showed signs of what the terrorists had done to her. "I'm not talking about Magickal commando training to ward off black magic or torture spells or whatever. *My* training, *my* expertise, is in potions. I formulated a magic potion to erase certain portions of my memory that pertain to the specific details of this project." She let her hand drop to her lap. "If I go more than a week or two without taking it, it will wear off, but since work is basically a daily event, I have to take a counter potion every morning when I arrive at Desmodus."

His gaze sharpened. "Why would you do all that? Did you suspect—"

Again, she cut him off. "I didn't suspect a thing. For me, it's standard procedure, and it's approved by my superiors. If the potion wasn't so complex to create, they'd probably make it mandatory for all their employees. The projects I work on are subject to industrial espionage. We have people working round the clock on security—Magickal beings who are recruited from the special Magickal branches of the military and secret services."

"I know this." He folded his arms, towering over her from the end of the bed, his gaze still steely. "That doesn't explain why you were drugging yourself, Doctor."

She crossed her arms over her chest, mimicking his pose, then rolled her eyes when his gaze zeroed in on her breasts. "Would you want to be the one who gave up vital information on a project the *Vampire Conclave* has invested billions of dollars in developing?"

He shifted his stance, wincing. "No."

The Vampire Conclave was not a nice bunch of people. They didn't suffer fools, and Chloe didn't ever want them to think she was a fool they'd been suffering. She shuddered just considering the kinds of things they could do to her. Ruining her career would be just the start. "So, when the officers told me they'd have to bring me into MTF Headquarters for questioning and it might take a while, I took the potion. After everything else that happened, I'm more convinced than ever that it's safer for me and for Desmodus if I use my concoction. I can't tell anyone what I don't know, and when I'm not at work, I don't know enough to be a danger to the project."

Calculation flashed in his gray gaze. "Smith and his people don't know that."

"Obviously." She shrugged, still relieved that moving didn't hurt the way it had the night before. "And if they'd asked how to make the counter potion, they'd know how to make me remember. As it is, they got nothing they could use. Even if they did have the information on how to create my potion, they'd have to have someone with the same level of expertise as I have with potions."

He unfolded his arms and slipped his hands into his pockets. "How many people in the world are there who could do that?"

"Not many." She forked her fingers through her hair, wincing when she felt how stringy it was from dried sweat. Gods, she needed a shower. "The Conclave hires the best in their respective fields, so . . ."

"Yeah." He frowned, brows contracting. "Well, this is both good news and bad news."

"Yeah, they're going to keep coming after me thinking they just need to torture harder." Alex had drifted over to stand by the window, obviously hoping silence would keep him from being kicked out during the adult conversation, but now he made a strangled noise in the back of his throat. She closed her eyes, but forced herself to continue. "But if you circulate that I take a potion and *can't* remember no matter what they do, it'll just encourage them to find someone who can recreate my counter potion. If they just experimented on me until they got it right . . ."

Now it was Merek's turn to choke. "That's not a possibility we're going to consider."

She met his gaze, dared him to look away. "You may not, but you can bet your ass Luca would use it as a way to draw them out of hiding. That agent is ruthless under all the charm."

A muscle twitched in his jaw, but he said nothing to contradict her. Luca might be his colleague, but he obviously understood the cold-blooded core in the vampire. Chloe would rather not be his sacrificial lamb.

Alex interjected for the first time. His gaze was fixed on something out the window. "There are other ways they could get the information, even without you, Chloe."

"Well, yeah, they'd have to perform those kinds of spells on me when I'm at work or find a way to hack . . ." A horrible, ugly suspicion ripped through her mind. She focused on Alex, on the closed, composed features of his young face. "Alexei Mohinder Nemov, I think you have a lot of explaining to do."

His gaze didn't flicker; his voice was steady. "What should I explain, Chloe?"

"Tell me why they wanted to kidnap you." She sat up straight in bed, folding her arms, and arching an eyebrow. "Suddenly, I don't buy that they want to use you as bait for your father. You *know* something."

His lips twitched for just an instant. "How could I know anything?"

"How could you—" She cut herself off, unwilling to dance around the main question. "Damn it, Alex, did you hack into my files?"

He didn't blink, didn't show even a glimmer of remorse. "Yes."

"Fuck."

"This Smith guy would have to be really good to figure out it was me that accessed those files." His head cocked, eyebrows drawn together in consideration. "If he knows, it's a good bet Desmodus knows now, too. There goes my internship."

Like that was the most relevant conclusion he could have come to. Chloe let her head drop back. "Fuck."

Merek watched the conversation flying back and forth like a tennis match. "There had to be a lot of files. He probably doesn't remem—"

"He's a computer genius, Merek. He also has a photographic memory." She raised her head and rubbed a hand over her brow. "He remembers everything he saw in my files, so even if he has no idea what it means, he can sure as hell recreate the data for someone who does."

Or be forced to recreate it, though she didn't say that out loud and neither did he. Everything had just gotten a hell of a lot more complicated.

"Fuck."

She let her hand flop down. "You said it."

He opened his mouth to speak again, but the door swung wide, and Luca and Tess walked in the room, followed by an agent who'd been at Chloe's house the night before. Warlock, she'd guess. He didn't have the points to his ears that elves did, the odd energy that Fae did, or the animalistic edge that vamps and wolves had. The man nodded politely. "Ma'am. I'm Special Agent Jack Laramie."

"Chloe Standish. Don't call me ma'am." She stared at him harder, and he grinned back. He didn't have a hum of magic at all. Either he was the best she'd ever come across at hiding it or Luca had a Normal on his team.

"I come bearing gifts." Tess carried four paper cups tucked into a cardboard holder.

"Coffee." A moan that could only be described as orgasmic rolled from Chloe's throat. The scent of dark roast didn't quite mask the smell of Tess's lavender perfume as she stepped forward to set the tray on the bedside table with a flourish.

Tess grinned at Chloe's eagerly wiggling fingers, a demand for her cup. Being a smart woman and a good friend, Tess handed over the goods. "I know exactly what you mean. I need an IV drip to make up for the caffeine intake I *haven't* had today."

Nothing came between that woman and her coffee. She was worse than Chloe about it. The piping hot cup of java burned all the way down, and Chloe didn't care. She moaned again without a single shred of shame.

Merek and Alex accepted cups from Tess, and when Chloe met the detective's gray gaze, it glinted with carnal amusement. She flushed, remembering she'd moaned for him with the same amount of abandon. Then she also remembered how he'd shut her down the night before, and she blushed harder. Gods, she'd been a mess and probably looked like death warmed over and she'd *thrown herself at him.* She appreciated that he hadn't taken advantage of an injured woman, which said good things about his character, but in hindsight, she felt like an idiot. Poor man. What must he think of her? She sipped more of her coffee and refused to consider it.

That she was even worried about his opinion of her was telling, and she hated having to acknowledge that. It meant he mattered, and that scared her to death. She had enough problems right now, starting with terrorists and ending with a teenage hacker. Adding a man who *mattered* to her list was just foolish, especially when she was probably going to get towed off into protective custody for the gods knew how long.

She sighed, closed her eyes, and shook her head at her own stupidity. All those years of schooling should have knocked the dumb out of her, but apparently not.

When she opened her eyes again, all the males were gathered in one corner drinking coffee and talking. She wasn't sure she wanted to know what they might have to discuss with Alex, but she knew she'd find out soon enough. Tess was standing there staring at them with the strangest faraway expression on her face. She was also blushing, not something the straight-forward pathologist had ever done in Chloe's presence.

"Tess?"

Tess blinked and turned to meet her gaze. The blush deepened, and an embarrassed grin creased her lips, as if she'd been caught doing something naughty.

Covering an inappropriate whoop with a cough, Chloe grinned as the pieces fell into place. "Someone's getting laid. Finally."

The flush went straight to fluorescent red. "Shut up," Tess hissed. Her gaze flicked to the men again, and Chloe's eyebrows arched so high she wouldn't have been surprised if they met her hairline.

"So . . . which agent is it?"

Tess closed her eyes, swallowing a low moan. "Jesus."

"Well, there are only three adult options standing over there, and unless he's perfected time travel, I know Merek didn't have time to be with anyone last night but me." Actually, time travel was a magical impossibility, so unless he was pulling out some scientific technology she'd never heard of, her assumption was pretty safe. She checked the men again to make sure none of them were listening. They seemed intent on their own conversation. "So . . . which one?"

"Luca." Tess sighed, and the sound was more infatuated pleasure than resignation. "He calls me *'mia diletta.'* It means 'my delectable' in Italian. Or is it 'my delight'? I don't remember. Hell, I usually hate pet names. I've gone insane."

Yeah, and the fact that vampires fed during sex made the *delectable* pet name even funnier to anyone who knew the truth about Luca. Chloe wasn't laughing though. Cavalli was from a family that ruled the Vampire Conclave. His father sat on the All-Magickal Council with Aunt Millie. Likely he was playing with a human for a little variety in his sex life. Slumming with the Normal. Chloe wouldn't usually judge anyone on his or her love life, but the fact that the Normal in question was her best friend pissed her off. She didn't like that Tess might be a means of entertainment for a vampire, something to toy with and discard when it became boring. While Luca might be casual about burning up the sheets, Chloe *knew* Tess wasn't. Tess might not be head over heels for Luca, but she wouldn't sleep with a guy because he was handy and she was horny.

That was Chloe's forte. And it had landed her in hot water this time. She bit off a groan and focused on Tess again. This wasn't about Merek; this was about Luca. Chloe thought it might be a good idea to have a little chat with the vampire. Armed law enforcement officer or not, he wasn't going to mess with her best friend and not get a clear understanding of the consequences for breaking her heart, Normal or not.

Vampires, oy.

Maybe he had a familiar she could hex into a lampshade.

Voices rose from the men's corner, which drew Tess's and her attention to their conversation. For the first time, Luca's face wasn't a mask of amiable urbanity. His mouth was tight with irritation, his hard gaze locked on Alex. "That is a foolish decision, boy. You cannot—"

The teen wolf folded his arms, his voice unruffled as he swept the men with a look. "Gentlemen, I'm not interested in protective custody. I don't believe you can force me into it."

Agent Laramie arched an eyebrow. "With your father missing and your mother dead, you—"

Alex interrupted once more, his tone unchanged. "My parents designated Chloe as my godmother and custodian if anything happened to them before I turned eighteen. I've seen their will; I have copies of it. If Chloe wants me here, I'm not going anywhere."

"Chloe wants you here." She extended her hand, and the wolf came to take it. They presented a solid front against the agents. "I don't know what you're trying to pull here, gentlemen. Alex is neither a suspect nor bait to lure out his father, or whoever has his father." If Ivan was even alive. "Alex isn't going anywhere without me. He's staying where I can be certain he's safe, where I can *see* that he's safe."

The frustration on the men's faces would have been comical under any other circumstances, but she didn't feel very amused by any of this. She'd fight dirty to keep Alex if she had to. Even if she hadn't adored the boy, she owed that much to his mother's memory. She favored the men with the kind of look Aunt Millie had perfected a century ago. It meant anyone who disagreed could just get the hell out of her way.

"Alex is my responsibility. I'm his *godmother.* I took *unbreakable vows* when he was born." Unbreakable *magical* vows, at that. How many times did she have to say this before it got through? She spoke slowly and clearly, as if they had some kind of impairment. "I am his guardian. Anywhere he goes, I go, and vice versa. This is not negotiable."

"Those men were chasing him for a reason. He has something, knows something, or is somehow of value to Leonard

Smith. As are you. Together you're far too tempting a target for them." Luca ground the words out between his teeth. "The kid has a death warrant out on his life."

"If you're asking if I'm willing to die for him, then the answer is yes." Her fingers fisted in the blankets. "That's the end of the discussion."

"Not quite." A tiny whirlwind in a vintage Chanel suit swept into the room, the door whipping open so quickly, it was obvious to anyone with magical powers that she'd breached some sort of warding spell to get in.

The first real, wide smile of the day stretched Chloe's lips. "Aunt Millie!"

A short, broad middle-aged man in a nondescript black suit stepped in after Millie, closed the door behind them, and stood in front of it at soldierly attention. Millie's driver-cum-bodyguard, Philip Bakke. Chloe thought he might also be her aunt's lover, half her age or not, but had never had the nerve to pry into Millie's private life. Her aunt shared or she didn't.

"How did you know I was here?" And if her aunt had known she was in the hospital, why had it taken her so long to show up?

"I called her." The sentence echoed in three different voices— Alex's, Tess's, and Merek's.

Luca growled a low curse, and he met Merek's gaze, raised an eyebrow, but neither man spoke. Then again, what could either of them say? They'd both stepped outside the lines of professionalism recently. Merek wasn't involved in her case anymore, but banging her in his office had hardly been good conduct. Ditto Luca's banging of Tess the night before. Her connection to Chloe made her a connection to a case he was actively working on. That didn't leave either man much room to point fingers. Nothing they'd done was strictly unethical, but neither were they squeaky clean. Chloe had a feeling that was a rare occurrence for both of them. She wasn't sure whether to be impressed or not that she and Tess had apparently tempted them beyond reason.

In Merek's case, she was just glad, since she was just as tempted, if not more so. She was definitely more tempted than she wanted to be.

Millie's lips quirked in a grin. "My telephone was busy today." She offered a stately nod to Tess. "If you wouldn't mind, dear. Philip can drive you anywhere you need to go."

Tess looked as if she wanted to protest, but a pointed look from Millie was all it took to keep her silent. She turned to Chloe and hugged her tight. "Take care. Of you and Alex, you hear me? Call me if you need *anything*."

Tears stung Chloe's eyes, but she squeezed her best friend, praying this wasn't the last time she saw the redhead. "You know I will. To all of that. I love you, honey."

"I love you, too." With one final squeeze, Tess let her go and went to give Alex a quick hug before she nodded to Millie and then to Philip when he stepped aside and held the door open for her. "I have my car with me, but thanks for the offer."

She sent a last glance to Luca, but left without another word.

"Right," Millie said when the door shut, angling a look that was almost apologetic toward Chloe. "Much as I like Dr. Jones, Normals shouldn't hear Magickal business, so let's get on with this, shall we?"

"What are we getting on with, exactly?" Chloe met Merek and Alex's gazes, narrowing her eyes at them. "No one has told me anything."

Her aunt blinked. "But, Alex said he'd tell the FBI you're not going into protective custody."

Luca stepped forward and almost looked like he wanted to sweep a courtly bow to her aunt. "Ms. Standish, I can't begin to tell you how unwise that course of action would be. While I know it's difficult to understand how necessary it is to have your niece and her godson leave their lives behind, they are in grave danger, and that danger only worsens if they remain here as easy targets for the terrorist cell that wants them."

"Ah, I see." Millie's eyes twinkled with a glee that would give anyone who knew her pause. Chloe braced herself. "You mean, they'll be safer with you and your team?"

"Yes, they will be." He stroked his fingers down his goateed chin.

Millie tilted her head in apparent innocence, and Chloe almost groaned. "As safe as my niece was last night, when a trusted member of your team betrayed you and allowed her to be tortured for information? That safe, you mean?"

A muscle in Luca's jaw ticked, but he said nothing more.

"Let me be clear, Special Agent Cavalli." Millie dropped her act and gave the vampire the kind of look that had been making grown men cry for over a century. "Chloe and Alex are not going with you. Not now, not ever. I don't trust you to keep them safe, and I *will* be having words with your supervisor about what occurred last night. Since your father is as powerful as I am on the Council, I think it's safe to say you won't be fired, but a mistake was made, and it was made with a member of *my* family. I take that very personally."

"I understand." This time he did execute a short bow. "Ma'am."

"Good." She swept an imperious hand toward the door. "Then I suggest you leave now and take your lackey with you. Your supervisor—and, subsequently, *you*—are going to see just how unhappy this situation has made me. You should call your father and let him know he's going to need to go to bat for you on this."

"Of course." Jerking his chin at Agent Laramie, the vampire turned for the door. Philip opened it, not a single flicker of expression crossing his face. Before he exited, Luca paused for a closing salvo. "You may think I was mistaken in choosing one of my team members, but that should only emphasize how much danger Chloe and Alex are in."

"It does." Her chin dipped in a nod. "I've made alternative arrangements for them."

"Have you?" His eyes gleamed as they locked on Merek. The vampire pinned the warlock in place for a long moment. Then he huffed out a breath, and a wry smile flickered across his face. "With your clairvoyance, you have a better shot than anyone else I know of. Take care of them."

Merek winced before his face became an impenetrable mask. "I will."

The vampire opened his mouth to say more, but clamped it shut again and walked out, Laramie on his heels.

"Why are you still here?" Luca snarled at someone outside the room.

A throaty laugh floated through the doorway, and Tess's voice was soft but clear. "What? You think I couldn't guess she was going to kick you out, too? Even Special Agents aren't that special in Aunt Millie's world. Besides, I drove, remember? I thought you might need a lift."

Luca grunted and snapped the door shut behind him.

Millie's eyebrow arched, an irreverent sparkle in her Standish hazel eyes. "Well, then. She should have him jumping through her hoops nicely . . . and in very short order, I suspect."

"Keep an eye on her for me, would you?" Chloe smoothed the blanket over her thighs. "I don't want her getting hurt by a Magickal just because she has the misfortune to be my friend and therefore crossed paths with one."

"Of course." Millie waved a graceful hand. "I'll look after all your affairs while you're away. Don't worry about a thing, dear."

"Thank you." Chloe took a deep breath. "All right. Tell me about the alternative arrangements you and Merek have made."

"Yeah, I'd like to hear about this, too." Alex's mouth curved in a small grin. "Millie forgot to mention it to me when I called her."

Millie sniffed. "I did no such thing. If I'd wished to mention it to you, I would have."

His grin stretched into a rare, broad smile, his pale green eyes dancing with amusement. "My mistake."

"Just so." Millie nodded, but her eyes had taken on that sinful twinkle again. It had always amused Chloe to no end to watch the stoic teen wolf and the curmudgeonly old witch play off each other.

Merek's expression remained unreadable when he faced Millie. "Before we do this, Ms. Standish, I have to tell you that my clairvoyance is blank when it comes to your niece. I can offer my skills as a cop, but not my precognition."

That made Millie pause, and she gave the detective a long, penetrating stare. Chloe was impressed that he didn't fidget or squirm. Older, more powerful Magickals than him had broken under Millie's scrutiny before. "Do you think anyone else would be as dedicated to their security as you would?"

"No, ma'am. I would die to keep them safe. *Anything* I can do to protect them, I will, I promise you that."

"I hope that's enough, but I'd rather have you than some team of men who turn on their masters." Millie set her enormous handbag on the end of the bed, pulling out a myriad of strange things. Folded clothes, manila envelopes, a cosmetics bag, a sheaf of paper—Chloe suspected her aunt had put a spell on her purse to make it fit anything she wanted because as enormous as the bag was, it couldn't store all of that. Without help, anyway.

Millie turned to wave Merek forward, only to find he'd already stepped over to loom behind her. He was good at looming, but Millie wasn't any better at letting someone loom over her than Chloe was. She grinned when her aunt gave him an af-

fronted look. He lifted an eyebrow and motioned to the lineup
of items she had on the foot of the bed. The gesture wasn't as
impatient as it would have been if he'd been dealing with
Chloe, but that just proved he was a smart man. No one messed
with Mildred Standish.

Chloe hoped she was just as formidable when she was her
aunt's age.

Moving the pile of clothes to drape across Chloe's feet, Millie smiled. "These are for you, dear."

And that was why she loved Millie so very much. "You're
the best."

"Yes, I know." Her aunt winked at her, but her expression
turned severe just as quickly when she returned her gaze to
Merek. "I collected all the documents you required, Detective
Kingston. I've already spoken to *your* supervisor, and you are
on indefinite paid leave. Make sure my niece and her godson
come through this safely, and you can name your price from
me."

"Thank you, ma'am." He scooped up the envelopes, fishing
out . . . plastic cards? But he examined them closely, squinting
at them, tilting them into the light to see every angle. "These
look good."

"Philip had the contacts; I had the money. Combine those
two and excellent quality can be assured in a relatively short
amount of time."

Alex reached out and deftly plucked the cards from Merek's
fingers, his lupine speed making the movement so fast, Chloe
didn't even see him move. He glanced at them. "Huh."

Then he handed them to Chloe. Identification. Fake identification. Both the cards had her driver's license picture on them,
but neither had her real name. She had to assume there were
cards for Alex and Merek, too. "So we're running."

Merek shrugged and met her gaze. "Like you said, Luca was

going to swoop in and take you where I couldn't be sure you were safe."

"Because the FBI trumps the police. So you called someone who trumped everyone." She gestured the cards in Millie's direction.

"Yeah."

"Good thinking."

His breath whooshed out. "Yeah?"

"You could have warned me." She sniffed, and watched a small grin twitch across his face. His gaze slid from her to Millie and back again; a flash of realization crossed his expression, and then he shrugged, his smile widening.

Chloe winced as something occurred to her. "If we're on the run, there's no way I can take my memory potion. It takes very precise conditions to keep it viable, has insanely complicated ingredients, and a very short shelf life."

"So, you'll know everything Smith wants in a week or two." Merek's grin disappeared, then he sighed. "But that's data Alex already has readily available in his head, so we won't be much worse off than we would have been; we just won't have your potion's unexpected advantage anymore. I don't intend to let anyone close enough to you to find out you can spill secrets."

"I like that plan," Chloe said with a little too much fervor.

Millie watched the byplay, tilting her head as she considered them. She nodded abruptly, but Chloe had no idea what conclusions her aunt had come to. "Philip and I will take Alex back to his house to gather whatever clothing he wants, and Merek will do the same for you, Chloe. I assume you'll want to take your familiar with you, but if not, I will happily house her for you."

Merek glanced at Chloe. "That might be—"

"No. My familiar comes with me. She's been with me since my mom died, and I'm not abandoning her." Chloe refused to think about the awful days after her mother's death or about how Ophelia had come to be her animal companion. She'd done her best to put those events behind her and dredging them up would help no one.

Hands on his hips, Merek stared down at her. "Chloe, it's important that you and Alex change your usual patterns, leave as many of your habits behind as possible. That means no computers for Alex. No gadgets. No modifying the very simple cell phone I give you *for emergencies only* to do anything it shouldn't. No hacking anything. Hell, it means no e-mail. Nothing." He gestured to the trendy clothes on the bed. "You, city girl, get no more makeup, no expensive clothing. No going to Magickal clubs. No more big city life for you."

The look of horror on Alex's face was probably reflected on Chloe's. No city. No lights. No people. It was her worst nightmare summed up in a handful of sentences.

"He's right, dear." Millie's expression held so much understanding and sympathy when she met Chloe's gaze that she had to look away or she knew she'd start tearing up. Only Millie knew why Chloe craved city life and lights, and Chloe wasn't about to explain how pathetic she was to a big bad warlock cop.

"Let me make this clear." Merek looked back and forth between Alex and Chloe. "If you want to live through this, you'll do what I'm telling you. You are one-third of a puzzle they already have two-thirds of. This isn't good news for you."

They had Damien's part of the puzzle, either willingly or by force. She shuddered to think of the ways one might force a vampire as powerful as Damien to bow to one's whims. Torture would only be the jumping off point for negotiations. Another shuddered rippled through her. She didn't want to think about torture techniques. It brought to mind her own recent experiences. Gods help her if she had to survive more of that. If it got worse, she wasn't sure she could. As ugly as surviving what had happened with her mom had been, the night before had still shown Chloe she was even more of a survivor than she'd ever imagined. But she'd also discovered exactly where her breaking point was, and they'd come dangerously close to the point of no return. She didn't want to get that close ever again.

Chloe sniffled, coughed into her fist. "Fine. I'm still not leaving my familiar. She wouldn't stay anyway."

"That is the truth. That cat should have been named Houdini." Her aunt dug deeper into her purse and handed a smaller satchel to Merek. Definitely a bespelled purse. Chloe managed a grin, then felt her mouth sag open when Merek unzipped the satchel. Money. Lots and lots of money. The satchel might even be bespelled for extra space, too. Millie patted Merek's arm. "That's all the cash I had available in my house. There won't be any bank withdrawals for anyone with computer skills to trace. You said smaller bills were better, less noticeable, so that's what you have there. If you need more, I'll make sure you get it."

He took her hand, shook it. "Perfect, Ms. Standish."

"Call me Millie or Aunt Millie." She offered him an arch look. "Only people who make me angry or who I don't like have to call me Ms. Standish."

"Yes, ma'am."

She crooked a finger, and the IDs Chloe held zoomed into her hand. She tucked them and everything else into the satchel. Then she picked up the sheaf of paperwork and leafed through it. "I've rented or bought thirty-seven cabins, small houses, and condos up and down the West Coast and into Idaho, Nevada, and Arizona. Plus, I had several similar properties I owned before. They are all available for your use, or not, as you see fit. My private jet will be leaving Seattle in three hours and stopping at or near every one of these properties. Get off wherever you want, but there will be witnesses who will swear people matching your descriptions got off at every stop. This Smith person will be able to track you down eventually, but this should buy you some time."

The slightly awed look didn't sit well on Merek's features. "That's more than I'd hoped for. Very clever, too."

"Thank you, Aunt Millie." Chloe scooted to the edge of the bed, ready to stand and get on board this runaway train. "For everything. For all of this. It's—"

"That's what family—and, in this case, family money—is for." The older witch glided forward to sweep her into a hug, and it was just like the first time, when she'd come to claim her orphaned niece.

Chloe held on tight, letting herself cling for just a moment before she pulled back. "I love you."

"I love you, too." Millie pushed her hair away from her face, the gesture tender and maternal.

"I'm not sure when I'll see you again, but I'll miss you like crazy." Her throat closing and her heart contracting, Chloe refused to think that the answer to that might be *never.*

5

"I'll be out in just a minute."

Merek just grunted and leaned back against the foot of the hospital bed. Everyone else had gone to take care of business, and Chloe had needed to get ready to leave. Merek had been married before, had had several long-term girlfriends in his life; he knew what "just a minute" translated to in woman-speak. He figured he had a half an hour wait on his hands, at least.

He shook his head, snorted a laugh.

He was insane. That was the official diagnosis. He was completely and utterly insane. Selina had agreed with that assessment when he'd called her that morning to let her know he was going on extended and indefinite leave. She'd also laughed her smoky laugh that this was all over a woman who nullified his precognition. Growling a few choice curse words at her had only made his partner laugh harder.

Hanging up on her would have been satisfying, but the truth was . . . she was right.

Forty-eight hours ago, he'd never have imagined anything

could convince him to put his career aside. Just two days ago, he was a cynical workaholic cop who survived on caffeine and had no real life to speak of. He hadn't wanted one. He'd put all that aside when his wife died. His work had been the only thing that got him through every day, so much so that a lot of days he hadn't even bothered to go home.

Then again, he'd made sure the apartment had been emptied of anything that reminded him of the past. When he'd moved to Seattle from Chicago, he'd gotten rid of every memento of his wife and family. Sold what he could and stored what he couldn't, and then his place had been devoid of anything that would . . . encourage him to stay.

He worked. That was all he did, all he cared about. His whole life was a driving need to keep as many people from going through what he'd been through as possible. It helped with the guilt, the sense of failure. Not a lot, but it helped. Nothing else did, so he went with what worked for him.

And that meant his job. He enjoyed the challenge, liked pitting his mind, body, and abilities against people who were trying to get away with shit. The adrenaline rush beat just about everything but full penetration sex.

Sex and work just circled him right back around to Chloe. The only woman he'd ever lost control with to have sex at work. The only woman he'd ever been willing to give up work for. Brutal honesty had gotten him through the days and months after his best friend's death, his parents' accident, then his wife's murder, and he had to ask himself if he was simply giving up one obsession to replace it with another.

He couldn't imagine getting the craving for Chloe out of his blood, hadn't been able to get her out of his head for two months, hadn't been able to stop himself from going after her the day before. For once, he was grateful to have lost control. It might even be the first time he'd been grateful for such a thing. But if he hadn't, he might have lost her permanently.

No. Just no. That was not an option he was willing to consider. Not now, not ever. Chloe dead.

Not on his watch. And for better or worse, he'd made certain she was his responsibility. Temporarily. Someone like her, someone blank to his clairvoyance, could never be allowed to stay in his life as anything more than a temporary duty. But while he had her, he would give up anything to defend her.

For a man who'd gone from having nothing but his work to hold his attention, he'd had some serious priority shifts in the last day. He now had an irresistible witch to protect, along with her familiar and her teenage werewolf godson. Without any aid from any other law enforcement agency or official. He—they— were on their own.

This was going to go great.

His bags were packed and loaded in his car. He'd done so without hesitation, the same way he'd looked up Chloe's next of kin in her file and found Mildred Standish's personal number. He'd called and laid out the bare facts to the woman, hoping she had the same grit as her niece. From what he'd heard—and who *hadn't* heard of Millie Standish?—he'd had a feeling Chloe was a chip off the old block. Seeing the women in the same room had only confirmed it for him. Without even trying, the women were a force of nature, sweeping in and changing everything in their path. Loyal, tough, smart, protective, and feisty as hell. It was a little scary that he could see exactly what Chloe would be like in a hundred years. It was even scarier that he liked the thought.

He didn't want to think about what that meant.

"All righty, then." The door to the bathroom swung open, and Chloe stepped out, looking fresh and clean and so damn gorgeous he wanted to drag her to the floor, strip her naked, and take her hard until they were both panting. She grinned at him, smoothing a hand down the sleeve of her sweater. "What?"

"Nothing." He checked his watch. Under ten minutes. And she'd even done her makeup. He was impressed. "You ready?"

"As I'll ever be. So, no. But since I don't have a choice, let's get this show on the road." She dumped the used hospital gown on the bed. "Is all of my medical paperwork taken care of?"

"Yeah, you've been discharged. Millie handled it."

Dimples flashed in Chloe's cheeks. "Handy to have around, isn't she?"

"You said it." He shrugged and couldn't help the smile that sprang to his lips. "That old witch is scary as hell, but as long as she likes me, I figure that's just fine."

"Yep." Chloe scooped up her purse and led the way out of her room. "That's the standard reaction to Mildred Standish. Until she decides she doesn't like you. Then the correct reaction is to duck, cover, and run in a zigzag pattern as you try to escape the lightning bolts she sends shooting after you to fry your ass."

He chuckled, put a hand on the small of her back to steer her toward the parking garage and his car. "There's a nice visual."

"Family gatherings are entertaining." She gave a delicate shrug, lowering her voice as they left the Magickal ward of the hospital. "Mostly there's just Millie and me, but when the extended Standish clan descends, it's an Event. Capital *E*, Event. Especially if Aunt Millie and her sister Amaranth dig out their stash of genuine Prohibition bootleg whiskey and start telling war stories." She shot a glance over her shoulder at him, her eyes sparkling. "Then they have to prove who can cast the best spells, and it turns into a proper witches' duel, because we do it *right* in our family, but a witches' duel when you're soused ends up with . . . um . . . *special* results. Funny, but special."

He snorted, but enjoyed the feel of her skin under his fingertips as he held her arm to help her into his car. The passenger side this time. "Cops get called in for *special* things like that going wrong."

Fastening her seatbelt as he slid behind the wheel, she gave another shrug. "It's on private property—a lot of it—and they do have seconds in their duels, so we can keep things from getting out of hand."

"You've been a second?" He couldn't help a grin. The dynamic duo facing down a happy, drunken pair of witches had to be a sight to see. It was stupid, irresponsible, and foolish to engage in that kind of reckless use of magic, but he could picture the hilarity of the situation too clearly not to have to fight back a chuckle.

"For Millie, of course." Chloe waved a dismissive hand through the air, the gesture reminiscent of her aunt. "Amaranth would never lower herself to asking the *halfling,* even though I'm more powerful than a lot of other witches and warlocks in the family. Luckily, being a second just means we know how to douse flames and reverse transformation spells that make old women grow chin hairs and nose warts."

Something in her voice made him cast a sharp glance at her face. "You're a halfling?"

"Mom was a Normal. Grandfather Standish disowned my dad for marrying her." She turned her head away from him to stare out the window as if she'd never before seen the streets that led to her house. "Of course, by the time my parents passed away, the old bastard was long dead, so no one could protest when Millie took me in and reinstated my father's—and, therefore, my—inheritance."

There was more to the story than that, he was sure, but he was also sure she wasn't going to say more about it. He didn't like her keeping things from him. He didn't like that she tried to hold herself apart, stand alone, even though his brain said it was probably the best thing for all concerned. They didn't have to get too deep with each other, even if they were sharing space for the next while. His instincts told his brain that this woman was *his,* and any distance between them was intolerable.

Temporarily. She was a case, a job, and anything more than that was temporary. She was important to him, because she created a void in his visions, because she was just her, but that didn't mean she'd always be important. Just long enough for him to know she wasn't in danger anymore. He hated that he had to keep reminding himself of the simple truth with this assignment.

How the hell had he gotten into this situation?

A pensive frown creased Merek's forehead as he sat on her bed and watched her pack for their little trip. AKA the relocation of her entire life. Better than being dead or tortured some more, so Chloe didn't complain. She just stuffed her life into the two suitcases Merek said she was allowed to take. If she used enlarging spells to fit a few extras in, that was her business. As he'd dictated, she left anything but sensible clothes behind. She put her foot down at no makeup, though.

He leaned back on his hands and crossed his ankles. "Why do you do what you do? You're drugging yourself for your job, so you have to know how dangerous this werewolf project is. It's controversial, at best."

"Yeah, that *is* the best I've heard it called. I don't care much about how controversial it is. Magickal politics are Millie's specialty, not mine." She shrugged and looked away, trying not to notice how delicious his muscular form looked sprawled across her mattress. She cleared her throat and focused on his question, not his lickable body. "I'm doing it for a friend who passed away."

"Alex's mother, you said. A werewolf."

"Yeah." She swallowed past the lump that still formed in her throat all these years later. Losing a loved one never really stopped hurting. "Jaya Nemov. She was best friends with Tess and me in med school. Tess never knew about her or how she really died, of course."

"The full moon Change." Merek sat up, and the bedsprings squeaked under his weight. His gray eyes were serious and sympathetic all at once, making the lump in her throat expand. "I'm sorry you lost her."

"Me, too. She was one of the best people I've ever met." A sad smile curved her lips. "I guess that old Normal saying is right—the good die young."

"Huh." His eyebrow arched, and he pinched the crease in his slacks. "I'm going to live forever."

"Me, too. Cantankerous witch that I am."

He chuckled, and the rich, sensual sound made her want to jump him. She already liked him too much. He was strong and brave and sexy and protective, and he'd volunteered to put his life on hold just to help her and Alex. What kind of man *did* something like that? A good one. She liked him. She wanted him. And she wasn't sure acting on that attraction again was good for either of them in the long run.

So, she jerked around and sorted through her shoes to collect the most comfortable ones she owned. Tossing them at her suitcase, she looked everywhere except at Merek as she searched her room for more things she couldn't live without.

The mattress creaked again as Merek rose to his feet. Having him in her space was unnerving. As many times as she'd relived her night with him in her dreams, she'd never pictured him here. She'd just remembered how it was in his room, in his bed; she hadn't added on to the fantasy. Now she didn't have to fantasize. He was here, and there wasn't a damn thing she could do about it. She had no idea if he'd decide she was still too injured, or if that would just be an excuse to say he thought their doing anything again was a colossal mistake. She wasn't even sure she disagreed with that logic. He *was* her bodyguard now, which changed their relationship, such as it was.

The mere thought of a relationship sent a chill down her spine. It was so much easier when it was just sex. A one-night stand. She refused to let herself think about the fact that none of her other handful of lovers had ever stuck in her head the way he had. Her sex clenched and dampened at the memories parading in erotic detail through her mind, that first night and then the sheer excitement of his taking her against his desk.

Awareness rippled over her skin as he prowled around her room, big and armed and sexy and dangerous on every possible level. His intent gaze sliced into her, and she tried to stomp down on her reaction to him.

"Tell me about her."

"Who, Jaya?" She swayed a bit on her feet, but forced herself to stuff her toiletries into a travel case.

"Yes, Jaya." His eyebrows drew together as if in confusion. Then again, he had no idea where her thoughts had wandered. She rolled her eyes at herself.

"She was . . . awesome." She dropped onto her bed and organized everything into her two suitcases. It might all fit. With some magical help. If she kept talking, maybe Merek wouldn't notice a few spells buzzing through the air. "Jaya was one of those people who grabs onto life and *lives* every single second of it like it's her last. She pulled everyone else into this whirlwind of fun and energy. She was intense. You couldn't help but have a good time when she was around." Those bittersweet memories crashed into her all at once. She swallowed and dropped her face into her hands, pressing her fingertips to her eyelids. "It wasn't until years later that I figured out she lived every moment like it was her last because she knew it might be."

His hard hand closed over her shoulder, more comfort than she'd thought possible in that simple gesture. "She was sick? I thought wolves couldn't—"

"Not sick, exactly." Running her fingers through her hair, she fought the urge to pull him down to the mattress with her. "Her family had a history of dying during the Change. It was like her own personal Sword of Damocles hanging over her head. She pointed that intensity at finding a treatment for the Change, something to make it easier to survive, more controllable. I sometimes wonder if she *knew* that her time was limited, if she somehow sensed that she wouldn't live to see Alex grow up, but she wanted to make sure that she left behind a future brighter than the one she'd faced. I wonder if it was all to save him, rather than to save herself."

He squeezed her shoulder, then slid his hand up and down her back. "She sounds like a hell of a woman."

"She was. She was my best friend and she was just . . . beautiful inside and out. Alex has his father's green eyes, but the bronze skin and dark hair are all Jaya. His face is even a male version of hers." She grinned, finally able to meet his gaze as all the good times streamed through her mind. "Alex was just like her."

"Alex?" The doubt was plain in Merek's voice. "The kid is intense, yeah, but not—"

"Fun? No. Not anymore, anyway. He was there when she died. All I know is that Ivan and Jaya fought that day. A big, rip-roaring shouting match and total relationship meltdown. It was a full moon that night." She seesawed her hand through the air. "Alex and Ivan completed the shift and Jaya . . . didn't. Change can be so unpredictable, and wolf magic fluctuates *so* much at full moon. More than most Magickals would guess, and far more than I realized before I started my research. Though some werewolves maintain control better than others, *anything* that throws a wolf off-balance can be the difference between controlling the full moon shift and not. Jaya's getting into a fight . . ."

"What did they fight about?"

"I don't know. That's all I've ever been able to drag out of Alex. He and his father never talk about her. Absolutely never." Her voice broke on that last sentence, and she cleared her throat. "It's a shame, really, because she was so wonderful. Her life should be celebrated. She should be *remembered.*"

Merek sat down beside her, his hand still warm and solid on her back. "*You* remember her."

"Yeah. I do." She gave a small smile and sighed. "I hope Alex gets to the point that he can ask about her someday. It'd be criminal if the only thing he ever associates with her is fighting and a horrible death."

He pulled her close, tucking her against his chest. "If anyone can help him get there, it's you."

"Thanks." She half laughed, half sighed. He had more faith in her than she did, but she let herself lean against him and absorb some of this strength. Just for a moment, she'd allow herself the weakness. The desire to touch him and taste him was eclipsed only by the need to let him comfort and care for her. The feeling was powerful enough to scare her, so she did the only thing she could do—she ripped herself free of his arms and hurried to her closet to grab a Seattle Seahawks baseball cap she hadn't worn in years.

He reached for her again when she tossed the hat into her suitcase, but she flinched away. Her hormones were rioting, and she didn't trust herself to get near him. Not again. His expression flattened, and he stood to glare down at her. "What's going on, Chloe?"

What was going on was that she wanted him so badly her hands shook like an addict looking for a fix. She fisted her fingers at her sides. They were going to have to play nice for the next few weeks or months or however long it took Luca to wrap up this case with Smith—and she refused to think that he might never catch the guy—so she might as well lay her chips on the table. Alex didn't need a tense environment to live in, and his comfort and safety were more important to her than anything else. She met Merek's gaze squarely. "Look, we're going to be stuck together for a while, so you should know your bodyguard job duties don't include being a gigolo. I appreciate your doing this for Alex and me, and I'm not going to jump you again like I did at the safe house. Your virtue, or whatever's left of it, is safe with me. Not a single seduction spell will I cast."

"Well, that's a shame." He moved around behind her, his breath ruffling the hair at her temple.

She shuddered, snapped her suitcases closed, and lifted them off the mattress. Merek reached around her, took the bags, and dropped them on the floor. Then his hands were on her, turning her to pull her to him, trapping her between his body and the bed.

"I thought I made this clear last night, but if not, allow me to reiterate." His hands slipped up to cup her face, his eyes a stormy gray. "I want you. I have wanted you from the second I laid eyes on you. I fucked you at *work,* for gods' sake. The *only* reason I didn't fuck you at the safe house when you pressed this sweet, soft little body against me was that you'd been *tortured,* and we were in an exposed position. Even then, it was a damn close call. Because I want you, and I have wanted you since the moment I met you. And every single moment since, I've still wanted you."

"Me, too." She swallowed, her pulse pounding in her ears as the simple, stark truth spilled from her lips. "I—I dream about us, about that first night. All the time."

He groaned, his fingertips caressing her face, sliding along her cheekbones and down to her chin to force her to meet his gaze. "We have about a half an hour before Alex, Millie, and her chauffeur / bodyguard / gigolo get here." She huffed out a laugh, and he stepped even closer, his fingers cupping the back of her neck. "That's not as much time as I'd like, but I'm willing if you are. I'm willing to continue this thing between us for as long as we're together on this case."

The half smile that tilted his lips melted any protest she

might have made. She sighed. As if there would have been any protest anyway. The temptation to touch him whenever she could had been irresistible from the first.

"I'm willing," she breathed. If he was, she was. She swayed toward him to close the negligible distance between them. Her breasts flattened against the hard wall of muscle that was his chest.

He leaned down and brushed his lips over hers, a soft caress after the rough claiming in his office. She pressed closer, tempted beyond reason, beyond caution, beyond logic. His lips molded hers, sipping small kisses until she moaned and deepened the contact herself, sweeping her tongue into his mouth. He tasted the same, like warm honey and hot man.

His hands settled on her hips, pulling her tight to his groin to fit her against his thick cock. She arched closer, trying to get his erection right where she needed it. Frustration twisted inside her at the barriers of their clothing. She wanted his hard dick pushing into her. Right now. Her flesh burned, her core melting until she was wetter than she'd ever been in her life. His tongue twined with hers in a sinuous dance, their kisses growing wilder, rougher, but it wasn't enough.

Balling her fingers in his shirt, she tried to communicate her urgency. He sucked her lower lip between his teeth and bit her gently. It did nothing to assuage her. Her nipples hardened to tight peaks, and she wanted his mouth on them, wanted him touching her bare skin. She broke her lips away from his and let her head fall back. Her fingers still fisted in his shirt, and she wanted it gone. "*Naked.*"

The word was more a ragged expression of utter need than a conscious spell, but the golden sparks of her magic answered anyway. Their clothes fell away, dropping to the floor at their feet.

"How the hell did you—" He choked on a startled laugh,

but groaned when she rubbed her breasts against the crisp hair on his chest.

Her heart pounded in her ears, her blood rushing so fast she felt faint. "Touch me, Merek."

"I am. I will." His lips moved down her throat until he could bite down on the sensitive tendon that connected shoulder and neck.

A strangled cry broke from her, need fisting her insides. She captured his hand and slipped it down her torso. He followed her lead, his palm sliding obediently over her skin until he dipped between her legs. "No, I mean *touch me.*"

"*Gods,*" he breathed. He pulled back to meet her gaze, his eyes heavy-lidded and molten silver with lust. The heel of his hand rubbed her clit, making her nerves jump at his touch. Both of their fingers pierced her core, stretched her. His voice became guttural. "You're wet for me."

"Yes," she whispered. Her body arched into their hands, and she guided their movements within her drenched pussy, hot magic from both of them ratcheting up her pleasure. She was going to come; she could feel the clench and release of muscles deep within, building and building until she quivered on the edge of orgasm.

She snapped her fingers around his wrist and jerked his hand away. His eyes widened in surprise when she shoved him onto the bed on his back. After the pain and chaos of last night, she needed to be in control, needed to take, to ravish, to make him groan her name in that deep voice of his.

He seemed to understand because a slow, sexy smile curved his lips, and he licked her cream from his fingers before he tucked his hands behind his head. "I'm all yours, sweetheart. Enjoy."

"I'm going to." She let a fingertip drift down the centerline of his chest. "I hope you will, too."

"Oh, I guarantee it." The heavy muscles in his arms, pecs, and abs flexed as he settled back against the pillows.

Gods, he was gorgeous. She wanted her hands on him, her body rubbing against those hard angles, her sex filled by his long cock. Grinning, she leaned forward to lick his flat brown nipple. It tightened against her lips, and he hissed out a breath.

Hot power rushed through her that she could make this man react to her so strongly, that he was willing to let her use him for both their pleasure. It was headier than any magic she'd ever known. A shiver rippled along her nerves, and her pussy clenched in a helpless spasm. She grazed his nipple with the edge of her teeth and he jerked beneath her, groaning. The sound vibrated through his chest and against her lips.

Her hands moved over his skin, her fingers toying with his other nipple until it was a hard little nub like the one she teased with her mouth. Her other hand slipped down his stomach, her nails scraping a light circle around his navel that had him cursing between clenched teeth.

She hummed in pleasure at his lack of control. Not enough, though. She wanted more. Stroking over his muscular thighs, she touched him everywhere but where she knew he wanted. His hands came down to fist in the sheets, but he made no move to stop her, to take control away from her.

Glancing up at him, she saw that his eyes were pinched closed, a flush of lust running under his tanned flesh, his skin stretched tight across his sharp cheekbones. His teeth were bared in a grimace of what could have been pain if it weren't for the harsh sound of need that ripped from his throat.

She followed the path of her fingers, kissed her way down his chest, sliding her tongue along the hard ridges of his abs, swirling around his belly button. He sucked in a sharp breath, and she nipped at the taut flesh beneath his navel. His body went rigid, a shudder rippling through his muscles.

Beads of pre-cum slipped down his hard shaft. The ragged

sound of his panting echoed in the room. She smiled against his skin, and finally put him out of his misery. A delicate lick at the head of his cock made him strangle on a choke, and the salty flavor of him burst over her tongue.

Her fingers curled around the base of his dick, stroking the soft flesh and the hardness within. She sucked him into her mouth, relaxing her throat to take as much of him as she could. Working him with her hand and her mouth, she had him gritting out swear words, his big body arching into her. It turned her on even more, made her breathing almost as rough as his. The scent of him, of her, of sweat and sex, intoxicated her. She didn't know how much longer she could last—her own wetness slipped down the insides of her thighs, her pussy fisting on emptiness she wanted filled.

"Chloe," he groaned, and the grin that tugged at her lips was smug.

She let him slip from her mouth, then blew a cool stream of air on his moist skin. "Yes. That's my name."

"Chloe!" His body jerked upward, and she heard the sheets rip in his hands.

"Say it again."

"Sweetheart, at this point I'll beg if you want. Fuck me. I want to be inside you right now." His voice strangled when she licked him from base to crown, pulling him between her lips, scraping him lightly with her teeth. "*Chloe!*"

She could almost hear his self-control snap. His hard hands bit into her hips as he jerked her into place over him. His cock pressed for urgent entrance, and she pushed down as he shoved upward. They cried out as he was seated exactly where they both wanted him to be. He filled her so well, his thick cock stretching her channel until she couldn't hold back a low sob.

Tingles raced over her skin, and she knew she wouldn't last long. A few thrusts, and she'd go flying over the edge. She almost whimpered at the mere thought. Sweat beaded at her temples to slip down her skin. She rocked herself on him, taking his cock deep with each roll of her hips. She couldn't stop, couldn't slow down, couldn't savor it. Now. She craved it, the release only he could give her. *Now.* Bracing her hands on his chest gained the leverage she needed to move faster, to take him deeper.

"Chloe," he breathed her name like a prayer, his fingers clenching on her waist as he worked her on his cock.

Their skin slapped together with each movement, the crack of sound filling her bedroom. Gods, it was erotic. She couldn't even draw enough breath to tell him. Her skin felt too hot and so tight she thought she might explode out of it. Contractions built deep within her, her inner muscles clenching around his dick in one long spasm.

He rotated his pelvis under her, and she splintered into orgasm. Throwing her head back, she screamed. Her nails scored his chest, and a wave of magic she couldn't contain rolled from her, only to have Merek return it like a riptide that sucked her under. It was fire and ice and grew more powerful every time they touched. That should have scared her, would have, but she was too far gone to care about anything but the sensations whipping through her body. Her pussy fisted tight again and again, squeezing around his pounding cock.

"Merek," she gasped. "Merek!"

A growl rumbled from him as his body bowed between her thighs. The hot pulse of his come filled her, and he shuddered beneath her. His hard hands held her down, the wide base of his cock stretching her. Orgasm still sent hard tremors through her, making a soft cry spill from her throat. A fierce smile bared his teeth as she clenched on him helplessly. "Just like that, sweetheart. Give me everything."

She shouldn't. She couldn't. She had no choice. Her reaction to him always caught her by surprise, and the way she lost control around him only attracted her to him more. She liked that, wanted it. With the high stakes involved in her work, the only time she really allowed herself to let loose the fetters on her self-control was in bed. And there she craved it. But leaning on any one person for her needs, her pleasure, was a bad thing. Gods, what a mess she was.

Folding in on him, she found herself caught securely against his broad chest. Her muscles felt limp, wrung out, spent. She relaxed for the first time in what seemed like forever. Closing her eyes, she buried her nose in his throat. He smelled so good. Like heat and man and honey, just like he tasted. She smiled at the contrast, but it fit him. His palms stroked in lazy circles on her back while their breathing evened out, their heart rates slowed, and the sweat dried on their skin. She yawned and nuzzled closer, the first tendrils of sleep tugging at her.

She jolted when he lifted her off of him and jackknifed in bed. "Damn it!"

"What?" She rubbed her eyes, trying to focus through the grogginess.

He groaned and rolled off the bed and to his feet in one smooth motion. "Your aunt is going to be here in exactly one—"

The doorbell rang.

"That telling the future thing is kind of freaky sometimes." She stretched against the mattress, arching her back to work out the kinks. He immediately closed his hands over her breasts, bending forward to kiss each one in turn. He sucked her nipples hard, biting at the tight crests. She squealed and laughed, shivering as renewed desire throbbed through her body. "Okay, okay! Freaky, but useful."

"Sadly, yes." His eyes narrowed, and he tilted his head, the callused tips of his fingers still stroking her nipples. "Millie's about to use her key on the door."

"Shit." Chloe scrambled to her feet, pushing his hands away from her breasts, but that didn't cover the creak of her front door swinging open. Scooping her clothes off the floor, she used a spell to shake out the wrinkles. "Hurry up and get dressed!"

His lips twitched as he watched her, but he obligingly reached for his garments. "What, you don't have a spell to put the clothes back on?"

She snorted on a laugh. "I didn't do it on purpose, so, no, I don't have a counterspell handy. You'll just have to do it the Normal way."

"That's okay." His voice was muffled when he pulled his shirt over his head, then his tousled blond head popped into view again. "I'd rather have you take your clothes off for me than put them on."

She laughed outright at that. "Shut up, Kingston!"

"Chloe?" Millie called from outside the bedroom door.

"I'll bring out your bags." Merek sat on the bed to lace his boots, jerking his chin to point Chloe out of the room. "You go head them off before they come in here and see the wreckage."

Her gaze darted around. Gods, the bed was a disaster. Not one of her four pillows was in sight, and the fitted sheet was ripped and balled in the middle of the mattress. The air reeked of sex, so much so that she had a feeling Alex would be able to smell it from out there. Hell, a *stupid* Normal would have been able to figure out what had been going on in here.

Jerking her clothes back on, she used a bit of magic to tidy herself, and prayed no one could sense she'd been freshly fucked. She wasn't ashamed of what she'd done, but that didn't mean she felt the need to advertise.

She stepped out of the bedroom and snapped the door shut behind her. Philip's eyes narrowed; he slid his hands into his pockets, and let his gaze wander around the room as he looked anywhere but at Chloe. Millie's smile was smugly satisfied. She nodded in approval, but thankfully said nothing.

Alex's eyebrows arched, and he didn't bother to hide a grin. "Well, then. I'm going to go make some coffee."

He suited actions to words and strode into the kitchen.

Chloe sighed and went to scoop Ophelia into her cat carrier. She was not happy and distinctly uncooperative. Chloe glared down at her familiar. "Look, you either get in the carrier, which I know you have enough magic to unlatch any time you want, or I can leave you here as werewolf terrorist kibble. What's it going to be?"

Ophelia gave her a slitted-eyed stare, an offended sniff, and turned with her tail waving in the air. She circled the carrier before she stepped in with the kind of queenly air reserved for Marie Antoinette going to the guillotine. Chloe rolled her eyes, snapped the door shut, and engaged the latch. She had no idea how long the cat would deign to remain in there, but she was there for the moment, and that was all Chloe was going to worry about.

Merek walked out of her bedroom and set her suitcases beside Ophelia's carrier. A thought occurred to Chloe, and she turned toward the kitchen. "Alex, you might want to pause on the coffee making. We can pick some up at the airport. They have Starbucks there."

"I broke out the travel mugs." He poked his head out of the kitchen. "This French press you have makes better stuff than Starbucks. Since we're flying in Aunt Millie's private plane, she said we could take it with us. It'll be done before you load Ophelia and your suitcases in the car."

"I'll take care of that." Philip reached for the familiar's carrier while Merek retained possession of Chloe's bags. The two men sized each other up for a moment before Philip grunted. "You take good care of Millie's girl, you hear? I'm not just talking about her safety."

"Philip!" Chloe and Millie echoed, shock in their tone.

Of all the people Chloe would ever have imagined worrying about a man hurting her feelings, Millie's brick house of a boy toy hadn't come anywhere near the top of the list. He hadn't even been *on* the list.

Millie recovered first. "Yes, well. Philip has the right of it, but I think Detective Kingston is smart enough to understand that or I wouldn't be sending Chloe and Alex with him."

"Yes, ma'am. Sir." Merek dipped a nod in Philip's direction, and both of the men headed for the door.

Chloe shook her head, but had no idea what to say at that point. She just sighed, walked over to Millie, and let herself be pulled into a warm hug. The older witch kissed her forehead. "Your detective will check in with me once a week on a secure line, so I'll know you're safe, even if I don't know where you are. Philip arranged everything, including some discreet channels to keep us apprised of Agent Cavalli's investigation." Millie's arms tightened painfully. "If you don't check in, I'll know you're . . ." She let go, brushed her hands off. "You'll be fine. Merek is the best. I checked into him. Of course."

"Of course." Her aunt wouldn't send her with anyone who wasn't the best. Gods, Chloe was going to miss her. Even more than her work, which fed a craving few could understand, she was going to miss the people in her life. Millie. Tess. Even the normally taciturn Philip.

But *people* were the most important thing. Millie had taught that lesson well. The science Chloe developed was always geared toward helping people, improving their lives. Millie's work in the political arena achieved the same ends, just with a different means.

It was ironic that she and Alex had to give up their entire lives, all their people except each other, in order to stay alive, but that was the way the cookie crumbled. It sucked; it wasn't fair, but life wasn't. It was just life, and she wanted to live a lot longer before she saw the end of it. She'd fight to her last breath to make sure Alex got the chance to do the same.

"All right, kiddo. Let's get this show on the road."

6

Four days later they were on the craggy coast of northern California. Chloe flicked her fingers and turned on a lamp before she even entered the living room. Wandering across the room, she lifted the edge of the curtains to peek out the window of their oceanfront condo. She'd have liked to go out onto the balcony and let the sea breeze ruffle her hair, but if Merek found out, he'd freak over the exposed position. He didn't mess around about security, so she propped her shoulder against the wall and contented herself with staring out the closed, locked, and spell-warded window. The moon hovered in the sky, heavy, bright, and almost full.

She wanted to tell herself that this was just a vacation she was on, an extended road trip, but worry gnawed at her. It wasn't just the extra security measures. Alex had become more and more distant as the full moon approached, the silent intensity that burned in his eyes growing more feral with each day that passed. He'd have to Change soon, compelled by the lunar cycles. Worse, she saw a creeping fear haunt his pale gaze, echoes of horror from watching his mother die of Change. It was always like this before full moon, but she'd never spent so much time in close proximity with the boy. They'd never lived together as they were now.

It was awful.

Her determination to find a potion to control the lycanthropic disease redoubled. If Alex was this terrified every month, then she didn't want to know what others went through. She just knew she needed to stop it.

Frustration heaped on top of her worry. If she were home, if none of this had happened, then she might have already finished her experiments. They might already have a prototype for the potion to inhibit full moon Change.

"Damn it." She rubbed a tired hand over her eyes.

Big hands closed over her shoulders, rubbing the tension from her muscles. She sighed as her body went limp. Merek's voice was a low rumble in her ear. "You should have been in bed hours ago."

"I did go to bed hours ago," she groused. She'd gone to bed exactly when Merek and Alex had. And then stared at the ceiling with gritty eyes. "I couldn't sleep."

"Clearly." He pulled her back against his warm chest, wrapping his arms around her waist. "Keeping yourself up at night isn't going to help anyone, sweetheart. You need to rest."

"I know." She sighed, quenched the desire to tell him she hated nights too much to sleep sometimes, and rolled her head on his shoulder to look up at him. He bent forward to brush a light kiss across her temple.

A shiver went through her, the lust that was never far from the surface bubbling up. They'd done their best to be discreet for Alex's sake, but the calm, worldly eyes of her godson missed very little. She didn't try to lie to herself—Alex was no innocent child, whether he was of legal age or not. Outside of that, she wanted no details, and thankfully he'd never felt the need to share. She'd caught the looks he gave her and Merek, but he hadn't felt the need to broach that topic with her either, for which she was even more grateful.

The bottom line was, if she might die, she was going to squeeze every last ounce of living out of the time she had left. That meant she'd turn herself over to the passion that erupted between Merek and her. It was madness, it was stupid, and she didn't care. She didn't want to deny herself or him. She wasn't even sure she *could.* Something about this man had reached down deep inside her from the very first, and pretending she didn't want him was even more stupid than indulging herself.

Though they went to bed separately every night, not one had passed that they hadn't ended up together. Irresistible temptation. "Kiss me."

"I'll do a hell of a lot more than kiss you, sweetheart." Merek stroked his fingers down her torso until he could dip below the edge of her T-shirt.

He let his lips play over hers, a sweet savoring. Fire licked at her belly, spreading liquid heat throughout her body. Her concerns from just moments before drifted away as the endless desire she had for this man enveloped her in a slow fever. His tongue slipped between her lips, deepening the kiss. The taste of honey filled her mouth. She now knew it was because he used it instead of sugar in his coffee. The daily habits, the little details of him, were becoming familiar. All the things he liked best. She bit his lip, sucking it into her mouth, just the way she knew would make him groan. She grinned when the sound vibrated up from his chest.

The hard ridge of his cock burned through the thin material of her pajama pants. Excitement spiraled deep inside her, and her sex slickened. The feel of him, the delightful flavor, the musky masculine scent of him, made her want anything and everything he had to offer. One of his hands slid up her midriff to cup her breast. She broke her mouth away from his and arched herself into his touch.

"Please," she breathed.

"Shh." His talented fingers caressed her nipples, drawing them into tight peaks. He plucked at them, twisting them just enough to make her squirm. Her pussy pulsed in scorching waves, the lips wet with juices. Just that quickly she was ready to beg for him. Gods, the man did it for her.

Her breath sped to shallow panting, a whimper breaking from her throat as the lightest sizzle of magic met her nipple. Now. Gods, now. She wriggled against him, but he tightened his arms around her to hold her in place. He skimmed one hand down her stomach until he dipped beneath the waistband of her pajama bottoms. She wore no underwear, so there was nothing between his fingers and her needy sex.

"Spread for me." His words rumbled like thunder in her ear, and she was more than ready for him.

Easing her legs apart, she tilted her pelvis up in offering. "Touch me."

He did.

First, a light brush over her soaking pussy, a barely there stroke that made her anticipation spike and her breath strangle in her throat. She closed her eyes and swallowed hard. "*Please*, Merek."

"Soon, sweetheart. I promise. Soon." His mouth opened against her throat, and he bit down. At the same time, his fingers opened the lips of her pussy, dipping into her thick cream. His other hand still fondled her breasts, kept her nipples in beaded crests. She could feel how wet she was, and every movement of his hands only made it worse. Goose bumps rippled down her skin as his thumb grazed her throbbing clit.

Every muscle in her body locked at that single touch. A deep shudder passed through her, and she twisted in his embrace. She felt him smile against her neck, then he licked a hot path up to her ear and sucked her lobe between his teeth. A delicate sizzle from the tip of his tongue hummed along her over-stimulated nerves. Tipping her head to the side to give him greater access, she moaned.

His finger stroked her again, drawing circles from her soaking channel to the hard nub of her clit. Her hips undulated with his movements, trying to deepen the contact. He chuckled, and the sound vibrated against her back. Frustration ate at her. She wanted, she *needed.* "Now, now, *now.*"

Digging her nails into his forearm, she tried to force his fingers into her sex. Shock ripped through her when he didn't resist. Two big fingers plunged deep into her pussy, scissoring to stretch her sensitized flesh.

It was more than she could bear.

Her mouth opened in a silent scream, and she came apart. Her sex fisted around his fingers, milking them in endless waves. Lava-like heat spread through every inch of her body, and she threw her head back against his shoulder. The heel of his hand ground against her clit, and his fingers thrust inside her pussy until she crashed headlong into another orgasm. Stars exploded behind her eyes when he sent a spell sparking and dancing from her clit to her channel. Her knees buckled, and he caught her close, still stroking into her sex.

A door down the hall opened, and then the bathroom light flipped on before that door closed. Alex.

She jolted, but it only drove Merek's fingers deeper between her slick folds. She had to bite her lip hard enough to draw blood, to keep from crying out at the delicious sensation. He slipped his hand out of her pants, but not without a final flick of his fingers and sizzle of magic that left her arching and gasping.

"Oh, gods." Her fingers dug into his forearm. "We need a bedroom with a locking door *now.*"

"Yes." He stepped away, reaching to flip off the lamp on their way out.

Her heart thumped hard just thinking about how dark the room would be. "No, leave it on."

"Why? We're going to a bedroom with a locking door *now,*" he drawled, and turned out the light.

The terror was all-consuming, locking her muscles into unresponsive tightness. She couldn't move, couldn't make her body react at all. Cold sweat slicked her skin as the blackness seemed to press down on her, smothering her like a wet blanket. Panic shrieked through her until she began to shiver. The contrast with the fiery lust punched shock through her.

"Chloe?" Merek's hand groped for her in the darkness, and she clung to the contact like a lifeline. "What's wrong?"

"I don't . . . I don't like the dark." The words jerked out past stiff lips.

"Let me get the light, then." His voice had gentled to quiet soothing.

"No, don't leave me!" She hated the shrillness of her tone, but she couldn't let go, couldn't be alone in the blackness. Not again. Not like—

She shuddered away from the thought and threw herself into his arms, needing to recapture the passion of moments before. Her mouth was hungry, consuming, when it met his. He hesitated for a brief moment before he gave her what she wanted. His tongue plunged between her lips as he scooped her up in his arms.

What was going on?

The fear in her voice had made Merek's heart trip, but he ignored that and met her kisses with equal ferocity as he swiftly carried her into the closest bedroom—his. He kicked the door shut just as Alex emerged from the bathroom. The werewolf could make of that whatever he wanted—he knew what they did at night.

Merek strode across the room and sat Chloe on the side of

the bed. He flicked on the bedside lamp, which captured her in a circle of warm light.

Now he could see her expression, the wariness in her eyes that contrasted with the flush of desire in her cheeks. "All right, you want to tell me—"

"Don't just stand there. Come here and finish what you started." She slipped out of her clothes and arched on the mattress, going on the sexual offensive to cover whatever she didn't want to discuss. She stroked her clit for him, teasing more cream from her body. He forced himself to ignore the way his dick throbbed at the erotic sight.

Cajoling entered his tone. "There's nothing you can't tell me, sweetheart. I can help you. You can trust me."

"I'm already trusting you with my life. More important, I'm trusting you with my godson's life." She sat up on the bed. "There's nothing I can do to make being afraid of the dark go away, and talking about it won't help. Therapists with way more training than you have taken a crack at it and failed." She looked away, dropping her sexy pose. "I realize I should have told you about my fear from the beginning, because it makes me more difficult to protect and makes your job harder. I apologize for keeping that from you. It's just not something I even consider discussing with people, so I didn't think about saying anything to you."

"But you won't tell me where the fear came from?"

"No." Her eyes closed tight, her arms crossing defensively over her breasts. "That part isn't relevant to anyone but me."

He sighed at how stiff her words were. More secrets she was keeping from him, but he couldn't force her to tell him everything, and somehow he knew pushing would make her less likely to talk in the future. "Someday you'll trust me with it, Chloe."

Her laugh was a painful thing to hear. "It wouldn't solve anything."

"Maybe not, but I'd still like to know." Gods, but didn't he know how that could be? A wound so deep nothing would ever fix it. A problem so huge nothing could overcome it. He understood that kind of pain, and what it took to live with it.

He settled himself on the bed beside her, stroking his fingertips over her jaw until she looked at him again. "What do you need, sweetheart?"

"You." A little smile tilted up one side of her mouth. "I don't want to think about this at all. It's bad enough without dwelling on it, you know? I just want to pretend the last ten minutes didn't happen, and to get back to where we were before."

"The last ten minutes did happen, and I'm glad they did. This was something I needed to know." He leaned forward and brushed a kiss over her mouth.

"I wish it wasn't." Her hands pressed to his chest, stroking over his T-shirt. She lifted her lips to his, tentative, as if she feared he'd push her away. The thought made him ache inside.

"Come here." His voice was gruffer than he intended, but he pulled her into his arms, and she came willingly. Her arms wrapped around his neck, her mouth slanting under his as she kissed him harder, her tongue probing for entrance. His cock surged with need as her taste exploded over his taste buds.

Her hands tugged at the bottom of his shirt, and he yanked it over his head. Then her bare breasts rubbed against his flesh, and he groaned. She explored him with her fingers, teased his nipples, stroked his stomach. When she reached for his dick, he broke, shuddered, jerked to his feet to shove his sweats down his legs.

The heat in her eyes as she took in his body made him burn.

Gods, it had never been so hot for him. Her touch, her scent, the eagerness with which she responded to him. His hunger for her went far beyond the physical, but the physical was so fucking good. His cock was so hard, it ached, and he needed inside her so badly he was shaking. He couldn't wait another minute.

Crawling onto the bed beside her, he pressed her thighs flat to the mattress and mounted her. "Chloe, I need you."

"Have me." She held her arms out to him. Her hands slid up his biceps to his shoulders, her legs wrapping around his waist. She chuckled low in her belly, and it rubbed her against his dick. He gritted his teeth to keep from coming then and there.

"Now," he groaned. And then he was inside her, no gentleness, just lust and sharp craving driving him to orgasm. His self-discipline went up in smoke as it usually did with her.

His hips bucked, and he slammed his cock into her hot, sleek sheath. She was tight, wet, and the feel of her inner muscles gripping his cock each time he thrust inside her made him lose what was left of his sanity.

"Kiss me." She licked her lips, and her face was rosy with passion. Passion that was just for him. He liked that. He liked that far more than he should. Her eyes were heavy-lidded, a tiny, knowing smile kicking up the corner of her mouth as she deliberately fisted her pussy around his cock.

"*Fuck*, Chloe." His breath whistled out between clenched teeth. "Do that again, and this will be over right now."

Her grin turned evil, so he did what she'd asked. He kissed her. If he didn't distract the woman, she'd let that inventive mind of hers cause all kinds of trouble. He chuckled as he plunged his tongue between her lips to the same rhythm he set between her legs. A helpless moan was her only response.

Tilting his head, he sipped at her lips before twining his tongue with hers again. The taste of her was almost narcotic. Fire twisted in his gut, heat and need wrenching through him as he picked up his pace. Their skin smacked together, the impact loud in the small bedroom. She gasped against his mouth when he rubbed over her clit. He was going to come soon, and he was going to take her with him. He wanted to feel that hot milking of her pussy on his cock.

Sweat sealed their bodies when they pressed together, made them slippery when they moved apart. She walked her feet up the backs of his thighs, pushing down to keep him close. He sucked her bottom lip between his teeth and scraped the swollen flesh while he pulled back and broke the kiss. "*Gods*, Chloe. This is fucking incredible."

"Oh, yeah." She slipped her palms down his back to grab his ass and pull him deeper into her. A laugh bubbled out of her, and she arched her hips up to meet his, clenching her inner muscles tight around him when he withdrew to thrust back in. "Faster, Merek. *Harder.* I love it."

How was he ever going to give her up?

It was the last coherent thought he had before the world dissolved around him, and he exploded into orgasm. Desperately, he reached between them and flicked his finger over her clit, pouring hot waves of magic into the touch. Her entire body arched, stiffened, and she convulsed around his cock. He jetted into her slick pussy, and heard her sob his name. He groaned, the sound half pleasure and half pain. It went on and on, but was over too soon, his come pumping deep inside her as her sheath fisted on him. More. He wanted more. Always with her, he wanted *more.* He wanted to stay inside her forever.

Her hands slipped up and down his sweat-dampened back before falling limply to the pillow beside her head. "*Mmm.* That was just what I needed. I bet I'll sleep *really* well now."

He chuckled, letting his forehead rest between her breasts. "So, I'm a sleeping pill now. You're welcome. I think."

Turning his head, he nuzzled and kissed the inner curve of one plump breast. His hand petted her hip, the silkiness of her skin irresistible. He couldn't get enough of touching her. A part of him suspected he might never get enough, and the thought worried him far less than it should. He'd been in far deeper than he should have been since the very beginning, and he didn't even want to wonder why. There was no end in sight, so he could only control the here and now. And at that moment all he wanted was to sleep with his woman in his arms.

Using the last bit of strength he had left, he shifted to the side so he wasn't crushing her, but could stay inside her. Yes. Perfect.

Automatically, he reached out to turn off the light, and felt her tense beside him. It was only then that he realized they'd never once slept with all the lights out. Normally, they just crashed into slumber after sex, but what he had thought was a mere oversight had been deliberate on her part. He should know by now not to assume anything with Chloe. Unlike with other people, he couldn't predict her reactions or the reasons behind them. He hesitated briefly, then switched the lamp to its lowest setting. "Is that all right?"

"Yes, that's fine."

When he didn't push her for more answers about what could make an adult woman so scared of the dark, the tension leeched out of her muscles. She swallowed, and he could almost feel her groping for something else to talk about. "I was thinking... before you came into the living room..."

"You know, you think too much, Doctor." He kissed her to take any sting out of the words.

Humming against his lips, she broke away after a long moment. "No, I mean... The full moon's in a couple of days. We need to get Alex somewhere safe."

Somewhere safe for him to shift. Somewhere it would be unlikely that anyone would look for him at full moon, when werewolves were forced to change shape. The process was grotesque, and Merek couldn't imagine it was anything less than torturous. He'd watched wolves shift before when they were trying to evade capture. The sound of every bone in the body breaking in rapid succession was one he'd never forget. A shudder racked him. He swallowed to rid his mouth of the faint taint of bile. These were not the kind of thoughts he wanted to be having after a mattress session with Chloe. He sighed and stroked his fingers down her hip again, but his mind refused to shut down.

Full moon was going to be a problem, Chloe was right about that. Depending on how long this job lasted, he would have to deal with this every month.

Shifting was what wolves *did*, and he wasn't sure what exactly it was about full moon shifts that made them more dangerous, but a lot of wolves died that way. Maybe it was that they were compelled and so weren't totally in control of the Change. Maybe it was the added stress on top of an already dangerous situation. It didn't really matter, other than how it affected Alex.

Merek sighed, burying his nose into the soft hair at Chloe's temple. "There's a couple of places up in eastern Oregon, remote campgrounds, that would be good."

Nodding, she turned her head for a full kiss. "Places where no one can tell the difference between the werewolves howling and the real wolves?"

"Yeah, and run by Magickals who wouldn't think anything of a little howling at that time of the month." He obliged her, letting his lips play over hers.

"Okay." She pulled away, then came back for another round. "How long will it take us to get there?"

"We can be there before nightfall if we hit the road first thing in the morning."

"Okay, sounds good." The lines of worry eased from her face. She yawned and snuggled into him, her eyes blinking slowly. "I'll be good to go as soon as I get coffee."

"Can you sleep *now*?"

"Yes, thank you, Detective." She pinched his side, but he felt the silent laugh that shook her chest. "If I'm lucky, Alex will be up first and have coffee ready. He's a good kid like that."

Yeah, he was a good kid like that. The wolf had treated Merek with courteous caution from the beginning, and nothing had changed. If Alex had a problem with Merek and Chloe's relationship, he hadn't said anything. Then again, the teen didn't say much anyway. He just watched and waited for Merek to fuck something up—his distrust of adult males was plain to see, and from what little Chloe had said about Ivan Nemov, the kid had a right to his misgivings. There was nothing Merek could do about that, so he just went about his business with Chloe and keeping them all safe and treated the kid with the same tolerance and cool civility that he received. Whether or not that was the best approach to take, he had no idea, but he did know he wasn't about to give up the pleasure of being with Chloe.

He smiled when she cuddled closer, sighing in soft contentment. Smoothing her inky hair back, he let himself relax, let his thoughts drift where they would. They'd made it out of Seattle without incident, and the few days since had been spent in placid normalcy, but his shoulder blades still twitched. They weren't out of danger. Even as he understood that, he cursed his inability to know what danger was coming. He'd never had to fly blind during a case before—even a case that was off the record. It was disconcerting as hell, and he didn't like it, but there was no putting the brakes on this runaway train. He'd chosen to contact Millie, and Chloe had willingly gone along with their plans without a single complaint.

She trusted him whether she wanted to admit it or not. She *would* trust him enough to tell him about her fear of the night someday.

Why that was so vital to him, he didn't know, but it was. He wanted her trust as much as he wanted the woman herself. She'd gotten under his skin that first night, and every moment that had passed since he'd seen her again had only sharpened the addiction.

It also sharpened the urgency of keeping her safe. Her and Alex. Despite the constant cold shoulder, he liked the kid, thought he'd handled the upheavals to his life with a maturity people three times his age couldn't manage.

Merek had a feeling if anything happened to either of them, he'd never forgive himself. A huge, gaping hole would be ripped into his heart, and he doubted he'd ever really recover. They'd become that important to him, that quickly.

He swallowed, and Chloe gave a sleepy murmur, burrowing deeper into his chest. Her lips brushed his skin when she spoke. "Sleep now, remember?"

"Yeah. Sleep now." He pulled in a breath, smelled the sweetness of her skin, and felt something loosen inside him, a constriction that had been there for so many years, he didn't recall his life without it.

Letting out the breath on a shaky sigh, he squeezed his eyes closed. He expected to stay awake, working things over, his mind obsessed with the problems presented to it, but it didn't happen. Drowsiness swept over him, dragging him under. It wasn't like him to ever unwind, but when had he acted like himself since Hurricane Chloe had swept back into his life? A smile touched his mouth, and he went to sleep with it still on his face.

7

The sun was just beginning to set when they made it to the lakeside campground. The elf who ran the place was delighted to rent them the last site he had. Chloe had handled most of that transaction because Merek had given the elf the oddest look imaginable. She had a feeling her warlock had seen something ugly in the elf's future, and Chloe was very sure she did not want to know what it was.

She sighed and shoved her hair out of her face. When Merek said they were headed for the ass end of nowhere, the man wasn't kidding. They were sleeping in an honest to goodness *tepee*. She was clearly in an alternate reality. The real her was back in Seattle sipping a latte with Tess, lamenting a recent run-in at work with That Jackass Damien. The real her was *not* trying to wrestle her familiar into said tepee, while Merek and Alex did very little to smother their guffaws as they did something manly with red meat over open flames.

"Come *on*, Ophelia." The cat hissed and took a swipe at her with claws bared. Chloe managed to get out of the way. This time. She had several long scratches down both forearms. "The other option is sleeping alone in an SUV. I can't let you run around in the wilderness. There are bears and real wolves and things. This isn't Seattle, baby. We are not in Kansas anymore."

With a graceful sideways leap, Ophelia made a dive for the tepee's exit. A quick spell blasted from Chloe's fingers in a beam that she hoped looked like a flashlight to any Normal who might be camping along this lake. The familiar shot backward and whipped around to snarl at Chloe, her fur standing on end.

"I know this isn't any fun, baby," she crooned, holding out a placating hand and praying she didn't get it torn to shreds. If anyone understood her familiar's hatred of the isolated wilderness, it was Chloe. She wanted civilization back as much as her cat did. "Next time, we'll have a real house with a real kitchen, and we'll stay in a real town with a real grocery store to buy you gourmet kitty food. I promise."

Ophelia growled, her tail thrashing, but her fur settled into a smooth layer again.

"A real litter box, too. I'll even make Merek clean it for you while you watch." The cat had taken an instant liking to Merek, which Chloe could neither explain nor justify, but she was too grateful to care. She didn't want to think about how difficult this trip would be if Ophelia had disliked anyone in their party.

"Gee, thanks. Throw me under the bus." Merek's deep voice preceded him into the tepee as he crawled through the opening. He held an unopened can of cat food in one hand. Sitting cross-legged on one of the single-sized futon mattresses ringing the inside of the tepee, he cracked the lid on the can and held it enticingly toward Ophelia. "Come here, sugar. Don't let roughing it upset you. It's only temporary."

The familiar sniffed, her tail still snapping in irritated little jerks. After a few tense moments, she relented, gliding over to Merek and climbing onto his lap where she allowed him to hold the can for her to eat out of. He rolled his eyes, but gamely kneaded his big hand down the Siamese's narrow back until she closed her eyes in ecstasy and purred.

Chloe's heart squeezed at how good he'd been with her familiar. And her. And her godson. He'd been amazing about everything. She never would have suspected someone who liked to be in control as much as he did could be so . . . tolerant. Kind. Sweet.

She also stared at her familiar in blatant jealousy. Who would have thought that would ever happen? But she'd love to climb in Merek's lap and have him slide his hands all over her. If this business with being on the run was ever over, she was locking herself up with the man for a week straight until she burned him out of her system. This level of intensity and craving just couldn't go on this way. She'd go crazy.

Licking her lips, she looked up to find Merek's heated gaze moving over her face. A wicked knowing reflected in his eyes. "I want you, too."

Her breath froze in her lungs, her heart slamming against her ribcage. Need fisted deep inside her, tightening some muscles, loosening others, and she was damp and ready for sex in seconds. Sucking in a lungful of air, she forced herself to look away from him. "There's no walls in this thing, no doors we can close. Alex—"

"I know." He sighed, lifted a sleeping Ophelia off his legs, and set her on the mattress beside him. "That doesn't mean I don't want you. It doesn't mean I won't be lying in my sleeping bag, thinking about you, and wishing I had you under me."

She closed her eyes and willed that mental image not to form. No such luck. She could too easily imagine herself stripped and spread beneath him while his cock filled her until she screamed because it felt so fucking good. A shiver ripped through her, and her nipples tightened to the point of pain. She grabbed a jacket from her suitcase and jerked it on to cover her breasts.

Merek chuckled as he watched her, but she refused to look at him or she knew she'd jump him. Then they'd see who was under whom. Luckily for her self-restraint, Alex called from outside the tepee. "Hey, you two. Dinner's done. Hurry up before the bugs get it."

She winced. "Fighting off Godzilla-sized insects for my food. Ah, the glamorous life."

A snort was Merek's only response before he crawled out of the opening, stood, then turned to help her to her feet as she crab-walked through. She looked out across the gorgeous lake, at the sheer red rock cliffs that dropped straight to the water's edge on the far side of the lake. She drew in a deep breath of cold, clean air. The last rays of the sun shimmered across the cliffs and made the waves glitter. "Well, it's pretty, even if we have to fight for our food."

He grinned, looped an arm around her neck, and reeled her in to pop a kiss on her forehead. Gods, it felt good to have a man touch her, not just for sex, but with the little affectionate gestures, the private glances and smiles that spoke of secrets only they knew. It was something she'd never let anyone close enough to enjoy before—even the years with Damien had never been more than a good professional relationship with hot sex on the side. This thing with Merek scared her, but it felt too good to stop. The sex was one thing, but this was something entirely different. Something vastly more intimate. Caring.

Terrifying.

Her heart rate kicked up a notch, and a twist of anxiety tightened her insides. She swallowed, and managed a weak smile for Alex. They all took seats around the picnic table, and Merek and Chloe pointedly did not mention the fact that Alex's hamburger was rare to the point of raw. The moon flickered in the darkening sky, and a silent Alex stared at it, his eyes gleaming with untamed wildness as a shudder went through him.

"We'll be staying here for a few days, until full moon passes, then I think we'll head further inland." Merek, being Merek, didn't skirt around the issue that was on everyone's mind. "We'll find some place similar to this next month. If there's anything more than this you need, let us know, and we'll make sure you get it."

"Thanks. I will." Alex's chin dipped in a nod, polite, but not trusting. He unbent enough to meet Merek's gaze. "This should be fine, though. Just...a place to run that's isolated enough that I won't get into too much trouble."

"Yeah. Not a lot of Normals around here. I asked." The warlock shrugged, crunching on a potato chip.

"That's helpful, actually. If we can stay somewhere away from Normals next time, too, that would be best." A faint smile touched the werewolf's lips. "I can't stop the Change, but I *can* keep from rampaging and biting anyone. It's not easy, but I can do it. Fewer Normals to tempt me is...better."

Merek gave an easy nod, totally accepting of the wolf's nature, which made Alex relax in his seat. "I'll make sure we have appropriate accommodations for you." A grin crinkled the corners of his gray eyes. "Though you may have to explain the situation to Ophelia."

Alex barked out a laugh. His gaze slid to Chloe. "Did she scratch you up too badly?"

She held up her arms to show the long scratches. "Not too badly considering how pissed she was, but she did get me a couple of times."

Merek frowned, grabbed her wrists, and bent his head to inspect the damage. He glanced at the lantern burning on the edge of the table, and it glowed brighter. Far brighter than a lantern could actually glow. The flames dancing in the fire pit roared higher, casting their light across the table and Chloe's arms. Alex made a small, impressed noise in the back of his throat, but he, too, leaned forward to get a good look at the scratches.

Warmth spread from Merek's callused fingertips in waves as he stroked over the scraped flesh. His touch was barely there, the delicate brush of a butterfly's wings, but the heat of his skin, the power of his magic, burrowed deep inside her. Goose bumps spread up her arms and down her body until she shivered. She closed her eyes and swallowed, trying to keep the incessant longing at bay.

"Am I hurting you?" His voice was low, but the anxious edge to the words made her eyes fly open.

"No, you're not hurting me," she whispered. In fact, the ache in her arms had faded to nothing. When she glanced down the scratches were gone, healed by his spell.

That was sweet. Alex's voice echoed in her mind, and he leaned further over the table to get a better look. He narrowed his gaze, and she could almost feel the sweep of his lupine senses moving over her, checking her injuries. *Gone. I didn't know anyone who wasn't a Magickal doctor could heal like that.*

"I can't do anything fancy, but cops have to have first aid training." Merek's gaze sharpened on Alex's face. "Your fangs are showing."

He winced, pushing to his feet. "I'm going to go Change in the tepee. It . . . makes it easier to stay in control at full moon if you make a regular habit of shifting a couple of days before."

Putting action into words, he strode away, and a few moments later, Chloe tensed at the distinct and horrifying sound of every bone in the human body snapping and reforming into a new shape. Her stomach heaved a bit, and she clamped a hand over her mouth. Merek rubbed a hand up and down her arm. "I hate that noise, too."

"You never really get used to it, do you?" She pitched her voice low, hoping Alex was too involved in his shift to eavesdrop.

Merek shrugged, again with that quiet acceptance. "If you're a wolf, I imagine you do. Or if you spend enough time around wolves, but I haven't, so no."

Alex, now in full wolf form, shot from the tepee, shaking from head to tail. He froze when he came into the moonlight, his gaze lifting to the heavy orb. His chest expanded in a deep breath, and then he threw his head back, and let loose a long, keening howl. It was answered from several different directions. Chloe's eyebrows arched. Real wolves or other werewolves? She couldn't tell, but she'd bet a werewolf could.

Alex loped over, his long body lithe, his fur as dark as his human hair, but shaded with lighter brown and tawny. Chloe reached out to scratch behind his ears. He closed his pale eyes and leaned trustingly into her touch. She stroked the rough silk of his coat and bent forward to drop a kiss on his muzzle.

"Did you freak out Ophelia?"

His tongue lolled out in a wolfish grin. *No, she's asleep. The fur would have flown otherwise.*

"Your fur, not hers, I bet." Chloe looked down her nose at him. "My familiar is feisty."

He snorted, then froze, every muscle in the wolf's body going on alert as he stared at a copse of trees beyond their campsite. Chloe and Merek turned in unison to follow his line of sight.

A slim young wolf slipped from the underbrush, staring at Alex, eyes gleaming in the moonlight. He glanced back at them, instinct warring with caution as his body shuddered. *I know it isn't smart, but I sense no deception from her. She's just another werewolf here for full moon.*

Merek closed his eyes and swore softly. "Be careful. Don't run too far."

I'll be back in a few hours. With that final thought, Alex spun on his haunches and launched himself into the trees. The bushes rustled slightly as he passed, but soon there was nothing to indicate the wolves had ever been there.

Chloe bit her lower lip, the darkness closing in around her as her godson disappeared. Too many worries warred for dominance inside her, and she swallowed.

"He'll be all right." Merek reached out to catch her hand.

"I know. I'd know if he wasn't." She tapped a finger to her temple. "The voices in my head would tell me so."

His eyebrows arched. "That is an entirely disturbing mental image."

"Says the man who can see the end of days in his head. You can just leave my little voices alone, thank you very much."

He snorted. "Fair enough."

She shivered, pulled her hand away from his, and wrapped her arms around herself. Instinct, more than anything, drove her to her feet. Anxiety sliced through as the darkness deepened. She tried to reassure herself that there were other people close by. She could even see the faint flicker of distant campfires, but it wasn't the reassuring bustle of a vibrant city.

Distraction, that was what she needed, but reaching for Merek would only make him ask questions. His gray eyes already saw more than she'd like. After last night, he definitely understood something was wrong with her. He'd sense her desperation was for something far deeper than sex.

Pathetic. Clingy. Needy.

The last thing she wanted from any lover was pity, especially not from Merek. She winced and stepped further away from him and closer to the light of the fire, drawn like a moth to a flame. Her jaw tightened as she clenched her teeth. She'd done so much to conquer her fears, had come so far, but it took everything she had to move past the fire and toward the blackness of the rippling lake. Every step away from the brightness of the flames sounded like a death knell, though her feet hardly made a sound on the soft shore.

She toed off her shoes and left them behind to let the chilly water lap around her feet. Making a quick decision, she stripped out of her clothes and tossed them toward her shoes. Then she waded into the lake until she could dive below the surface. It felt like a fist closed around her chest, it was so cold, but some defiant triumph burst within her. She was out here—she wasn't huddled in terror beside the fire.

Then the complete darkness of it punched through her minor victory, and she clawed her way to the surface, spinning in the water until she could see the dancing flames again, beckoning to her.

"Chloe!" Merek stood on the shore outlined by the fire's light, his arms crossed, his feet braced apart. "What are you doing?"

Shoving her hair out of her eyes, she arched her eyebrows. "Uh ... skinny-dipping?"

Relief she hated herself for feeling exploded inside her, obliterating what was left of her triumph. Merek was here, and he would never let anything bad happen to her. She rolled her eyes in self-disgust at her weakness.

"The lake has to be freezing."

She treaded water. "So come warm me up."

Shaking his head, he beckoned to her. "Come out of there, and I will."

"Chicken." Feeling outrageously brave, she skimmed a hand across the top of the lake, sending water spraying in his direction.

He snorted, but jerked his T-shirt over his head and dropped it to the ground where she'd tossed her things. The rest of his clothes joined the pile. The flickering light cast shadows on his bare skin as he moved. Gods, he was a beautiful man.

His muscled legs flexed and stretched with every movement, and he was built like some great predatory cat. Huge and golden as a lion, his coloring only showcased by the amber firelight. Broad shoulders and heavy pecs tapered to a hard slab of a stomach and narrow flanks. Her gaze caught there and went no further. His cock stood in a hard arc, and her entire body clenched with want.

Every single sense she had focused on him, and even the uneasiness in the pit of her belly at the deepening night faded before the sensations he generated within her. It was unnerving that anything could hold that fear at bay, but then he towed her through the water and into his arms and nothing else mattered.

A wave of warmth enveloped her, as shocking as the cold had been when she'd entered the lake, and she gasped. "You used a heating spell on the water. That's cheating."

"Hell, yes. It's fucking cold in here." He hauled her closer until she was plastered against him, his erection prodding her belly. "I don't make a habit of icing down my cock right before I put it in a woman."

A shriek of laughter ripped from her. She buried her face in his neck, giggles bubbling out of her for several moments before she could speak. "Oh, wow. That's so romantic."

"It's more romantic than a case of the wilts, I promise." He shifted his stance, and it was then she realized he was standing, tall enough to touch the bottom of the lake.

"That's still cheating." She nipped at his throat, sucking his flesh while she held it between her teeth.

"Yeah, well. I'm a warlock, honey, not Superman." He thrust himself against her, long and hard and so hot it made her want to whimper. "I work with what I've got."

"You have more than enough. Share."

He snickered, but his broad palms cupped her bottom, lifting her into his hard length. The play of all those muscles against her skin, the rush of water around them, pressing them together, was incredibly erotic.

She twined her arms around his neck and her legs around his waist. Just opening herself for him made her heart trip and then pound in her chest. Her nipples rasped against the soft hair on his chest, and she rubbed her breasts against him to increase the stimulation. Her breath sped to shallow pants, and she could feel his breath brushing over her lips. She had to taste him, needed that honey flavor filling her mouth.

Flicking out her tongue, she ran it along his bottom lip, pressing for entrance. He groaned, letting her take his mouth, tangling his tongue with hers, while his hands moved over her back and buttocks. His fingers dipped between the globes of her ass, parting the cheeks so that water swirled in to caress her heated flesh.

Excitement blasted through her when his fingertips followed the water, teasing her anus until she shuddered and pushed back against his probing touch. She wanted. Oh, gods, she wanted. She ripped her mouth from his, throwing her head back to gasp for air. His finger slid deeper inside her, stroking her rear passage.

"Merek," she pleaded. She didn't even know for what. Her hips rocked against him, blindly seeking more of him. All of him.

"I'm going to fuck you here," he whispered, sucking kisses down her neck. "Not tonight, but soon."

Then he bit her throat, and her body flashed over into orgasm. She sobbed, arching as spasms rocked through her. Her pussy fisted on nothingness as his finger worked her anus, thrusting deep and fast. The water around them began to steam and hiss as her magic exploded into boiling heat. "Please, Merek."

"That didn't please you?" He licked the spot he'd bitten, his voice teasing and warm. His cool breath against her damp flesh made her shiver, her nipples tighten even further.

"You know it did." She closed her eyes and pulled her bottom lip between her teeth. His flavor was still there, lingering on her swollen mouth. Her sex clenched, her needs not quite satisfied. "I want you inside me."

His finger moved within her ass, stretching her even further. "I am inside you."

"You're going to make me say it, aren't you?" She pinched his shoulder when he hummed an agreement. "Fine. I want your cock in my pussy." She grinned and writhed against him in a way that made him groan, but also made wicked heat flood her system. Teasing him meant teasing herself. Her voice dropped to a low purr. "I want you inside me. Both ways. I want you to make me come for you, make me squeeze your cock so tight you can't even think. I want you to make it so good for me, I forget my own name."

"*Fuck*, Chloe." He lifted her so she could take his cock inside her, but she could feel how his body shook in reaction to what she'd said. It was heady, knowing she could make this big, powerful warlock shudder with want. For her and only her.

Sliding her hands into his hair, she pulled his head back so she could kiss him again. He arched his hips, pressing slowly into her pussy, and she moaned at how good it felt. Inch by inch, his thickness stretched her walls to their limit. Sweat slipped down her flesh until it reached the waterline; the cool night air combined with the heated lake made her shudder at the contrast. Even the magic warming the water around them was nothing compared to the white-hot need they generated between them.

He rocked into her, and she sighed into his mouth, twining her tongue with his. The kiss went wild in moments, and they bit and sucked at each other's mouths in their urgency. Their breaths were mere gulps of air as their lips clung, fed from each other.

Her legs tightened around his hips, giving her leverage to lift and lower herself on his cock. His finger pushed deeper into her ass, rubbing his thrusting cock through the thin layer of flesh separating them. The sensation was incredible . . . and then he used magic. The spell was wicked, dark with passion. It sizzled along her nerves, sparking from his penetrating fingertip. Her breath seized as it hit her, dragged her into a place where there was nothing but this moment with him, his hands, his mouth, his cock.

Power fizzed through her, their energies blending, merging until they were one, locked together in a search for surcease. The water swirled around them and between them, sealed them together, growing hotter and hotter as it caressed their skin. She could *feel* his desire, how every plunge into her made his control of his magic slip a little. She fed her own needs back to him, the way tingles raced down her flesh, the way she couldn't hold back the pleasure spells. Fire and ecstasy, fueled by their bodies and their magic, whipped the lake into a whirlpool around them. It surged as they did, caught in the storm with them.

The muscles in her legs strained as she clung to him, rode him as fast as she could. He growled deep in his throat and plunged into her, his cock, his finger, taking all of her. She screamed into his mouth, her back bowing as she came. Her nerves convulsed, her sex pulsing around him as pleasure rocketed through her. His pleasure, her pleasure. It became one, dark and hot and greedy, consuming them. His come flooded her pussy, and she flexed around his cock, milking him until they both cried out. She tried to pull her mouth from his, tried to sob, but his free hand wrapped in her hair, holding her to him, plunging his tongue between her lips. Arching helplessly, she fisted around his thrusting cock again and again, moaning against his mouth, her sex so sensitized she came each time he entered her.

She collapsed in his arms, boneless. If he hadn't tightened his hold on her, she'd have gone under. He gathered her close, kissed her forehead, and carried her up to the shore. Sagging to his knees as they cleared the water, he groaned, the sound of a man barely conscious.

"Can you think?" she gasped.

"Nope." He chuckled. "Do you remember your name?"

"Nuh-uh." She sighed, shivering as a stiff breeze chilled her. Pushing out of his embrace, she went to their discarded clothing to get something to cover herself. Twitching her fingers, she warmed the air, sent it in a swift flow to encase Merek as well.

"Nice," he said.

Joining her at their tangled pile of clothes, he bent and scooped up two items, reaching over to hand her one of them.

She blinked down at what he'd given her, then shot him a grin. "*Two* towels? You knew you were coming in before you even—"

"Yeah, so?" He rubbed the terry cloth over himself swiftly, then reached for his shorts.

Following his lead, she scrubbed the water from her skin, then wrapped the towel around her wet hair. "Why'd you tell me to get out, then?"

"Because it's freezing in there, and it wasn't until I hit the water that I thought to use a heating spell. Before that I was hoping I wouldn't have to come in after you, but this is *you* we're talking about."

She grinned, shook the sand from her clothes, stuffed herself into them and her shoes, and hurried for the fire. The apprehension she'd never quite rid herself of came back with sudden force without the distraction of sex. She tossed another log on the fire, using magic to speed the burn, and soon golden light poured over their campsite.

"Where's the big lantern?" She plopped down on a tree stump on one side of the blaze while Merek sat opposite her on a giant log.

"I took it into the tepee so I could get the towels."

"Ah." After that, a companionable silence stretched between them, punctuated only by the pop and crackle of the sputtering flames.

He sighed, lifted his gaze to the sky, and smiled. "They're beautiful, aren't they?"

Squinting upward, she didn't see anything out of the ordinary. "The stars?"

"Yeah, you don't see them this clearly in the city. Too much light."

She craved all that light with a suddenness that made her shake. An ocean of streetlamps and taillights and glowing windows. People. Thousands of people around her, and lots of lights. Electricity and all the other conveniences right down the block. Restaurants that delivered. Cell phones and e-mail and all kinds of ways to get in touch with people.

"I'll take the city any day, thanks." She tried to keep her voice teasing, but knew he saw too much, as usual.

When she met his gaze, his expression had sobered. "Will you tell me about it?"

Because the question was gentle rather than accusing, she found she couldn't pretend to misunderstand him. She closed her eyes and tugged the towel away from her hair. "What do you want to know, exactly?"

"Everything."

She flinched a little. Everything. No one really wanted everything. She had way too much baggage to ever dump it all on any one person. A soft breeze stirred, and it chilled her damp hair. She'd been wet that day, too. And cold. So damn cold.

"I know something bad happened, sweetheart."

Of course. Why else would a grown woman be scared enough of the dark, she still needed a night-light? Hot tears of shame pricked her eyes, and she blinked them back. She'd come to terms with her fears and what she could and couldn't deal with years ago. This trip stomped on all her shiny red buttons, but that didn't change anything.

A sigh eased passed her lips. "I was seven years old. . . . No, wait. You're going to need some family history. You know I'm half-Normal, and that my grandfather disowned my dad for marrying my mom, but you don't know that they had to run away to escape from Grandfather Standish's vengeance. He tried to ruin Dad's career so he'd come begging for family handouts. Dad was a doctor, you know."

"Like you." His voice was low; obviously he wasn't intending to rush her. She had a feeling he'd sit there and listen for as long as she wanted to talk. It was as sweet as it was scary.

She shook her head. "No, he was a practicing physician. A country doctor. He and Mom escaped to Montana, out in the middle of nowhere, like fifteen miles from the nearest town." Magickals either lost themselves in the anonymity of a sprawling metropolis, where anything odd a stranger did would be written off and dismissed, or they lived in the boonies, where they didn't interact with people often enough for them to notice anything odd. "The people in town thought he was just into homeopathic medicine with his herbal remedies, but he could make them better, and they didn't ask questions besides that." A faint smile curved her lips. "He used to let me help grind the herbs and mix them."

"Potions."

"Yeah, I inherited the knack from him." Her smile widened, then faded just as quickly. "He passed away when I was five. He got hit by a drunk driver going around a blind curve at over a hundred miles an hour. Magic can't always save you, you know?"

"Yeah. My parents died in a car crash, too. They were gone before anything could save them."

She nodded. "They said Dad died instantly. I hope so."

He swore softly, leaning toward her, but not leaving his seat, as though he understood she'd never get through this story without breaking down if he held her in his arms and comforted her. "I'm sorry, Chloe."

"I ... *felt* it when he passed away. That was the first time my precognition presented itself." Her voice went almost clinical, a doctor diagnosing. She swallowed, feeling like anything but a level-headed scientist. "My little voices warning of bad things coming."

"Sweetheart ..."

She shook her head, staring into the fire as she started the worst of it. Her hands balled into knots to hide the way they started to tremble. "They didn't warn me the day my mom died. Or, if they did, I don't remember it. Maybe I didn't pay attention. I didn't know anything about magic, then. Not really. By the time I was seven, my dad was already sort of ... fuzzy ... in my head. The stories Mom told about him sounded like fairy tales from the books she read to me at night." She held her hands out toward the flames, wishing the warmth could seep inside her, but she felt the ice freezing her very soul. "I think maybe Mom thought I was Normal like her because I hadn't done anything like my dad could do."

"You didn't tell her about the voices when your dad died?"

"No. I didn't know what they were, what they meant. Not until years later." Not until Millie had told her. By then it was too late. Far too late for any of them.

"How did she die?"

Such a simple question, and such a complicated answer. "There was a storm. A massive storm. It knocked out our electricity and phone lines, washed out the roads, made mud slide down the mountains, and left us totally stranded." She pulled in a slow, deep breath. "So, when Mom slipped and cut herself while she was chopping some kindling, there was no way to get help." Her laugh was dry, painful. "If I'd known then what I know now, if *Dad* had still been alive, my mom wouldn't be dead. But there was just so much blood, and it happened so fast, she was gone before I really understood what was going on."

And she'd been alone with a dead body that used to belong to her mother. She didn't tell Merek how she'd huddled in the corner of their living room, too scared of the blank, staring eyes of that corpse to move. How she'd vomited at the smell. How she'd sobbed until there were no more tears left, but she was trapped for two more days until the storm passed.

Even when it was over, no one came for them. No one knew they needed help. No one cared.

"I went for help, but the storm had washed away trees and rocks, so the landmarks were all wrong. I got lost. When night came, it was pitch black because there were still too many clouds to see the stars. It was so dark, and I was so alone." Over and over again, she'd gotten lost in the gloom of that alien landscape. For as long as she lived, she'd never forget the utter sense of aloneness, of isolation. Her stomach turned, but she forced back the nausea. "Ophelia found me there."

"Ophelia was in the woods?" The question, quiet as it was, startled her back into reality. For a few moments she'd been so lost in the telling, she'd forgotten he was there.

She cleared her throat. "Yeah. She doesn't like the wilderness any more than I do. I don't know how or why a Siamese purebred familiar got all the way out there. All I know is there was a bear, and I got between it and its cub by accident. It was going to tear me apart." She snorted, shook her head, and smiled. "Then there was this mangy, half-starved cat attacking the hell out of that bear's face while I ran."

"Suicidal cat." But his tone was almost admiring.

"Yeah, well. I named her that for a reason. She caught up with me after she was done with the bear, and she's been with me ever since." Chloe rubbed her nose, remembering the freezing cold at night, the meager warmth of Ophelia's skinny body as they curled together in the blackness. The hunger and terror.

Those details she kept to herself. There was only so much she could strip bare for anyone. No one really wanted everything. She picked up a twig and spun it between her fingers. "It took me another two days to make it to town and another week for them to track down my next of kin."

Both she and her familiar had been malnourished and dehydrated when they'd staggered into the sheriff's department. Chloe had almost thought it was a delusion, finally reaching light and warmth and *people.* People with food and water.

"Millie came and claimed you."

"She did."

"And you've been in Seattle ever since."

"No, I went away to college and med school. I didn't come back until I did my residency." She'd had to get away or she'd known she'd never be able to. For years, she'd had nightmares, terrified of being alone in the darkness. She'd clung to Millie like the lifeline to sanity she'd been for a broken young girl. It would have been too easy to let her aunt shelter her, coddle her, protect her from life, but she'd never have been a whole person. The thought of *needing* anyone as much as she'd needed Millie then still had the power to terrify her.

She'd had to prove to herself she could be alone, that she could cope with the night, even if it meant sleeping with a lamp turned on or getting up to stare at the millions of twinkling lights of the city around her to remind herself she was *not* lost in the woods anymore.

She'd made her own way, such as it was.

Merek stood up and walked around to her side of the dwindling campfire. "You've always been in big cities since then though? Until now?"

A smile twisted her lips. "Yeah, I'm a wimp like that. City

girl all the way with my cute clothes and nightclubs, like you said. Los Angeles and New York for school. I did a year of foreign exchange in London." She shrugged, looked away. "Lots of people and lots of light, even at night."

His hand appeared in her line of vision, his fingers offered in invitation. "Come on."

"I think I just want to sit here for a while." She felt... drained. Emptied out after telling him all that she had. As if she had nothing left.

He just reached down and scooped her up to carry her to bed. She stiffened for a moment, wrapped her arms around his neck for balance, but then went limp against him. He felt so good, so warm when she was frozen inside. She wanted to tell herself it was the dip in the icy lake, but she hadn't the energy left to lie to herself. For once, she didn't want to be brave. She wanted to let him hold her and make her feel safe in this nightmare she was reliving, but she couldn't.

With Alex sharing their "room" tonight, she was sleeping alone. Best get back to sucking it up like a big girl and dealing with the darkness. She'd done it for years, and the last thing a man like Merek needed was a clingy woman. The last thing she wanted was to *be* that kind of woman.

She'd stand on her own two feet, no matter how much it scared her.

Gods, seven years old. Merek shook his head. She'd been just a baby. Emotion he didn't want to feel, let alone put a name to, banded so tight around his chest he couldn't breathe. He swallowed hard; he didn't ever want to put her down, wanted to make sure she never went through anything like that again.

And yet she was already going through it again. Voluntarily. For Alex. So he could be safe for his full moon Change.

Merek closed his eyes for a moment, feeling that band tighten. He'd seen a lot of shit in his life, had been through more than his fair share, but it made his hands shake to think of anything else happening to her, even with his intimate knowledge of just how many things could go wrong for people.

All he could do tonight was make damn sure that she didn't have to be alone in the dark. Hell, if that was the worst of the fears she'd come out of all of that with—he shook his head again. He'd thought it was the worry and maybe nightmares from being tortured that kept her awake at night, but now he wasn't so sure. Maybe it was all of those things, but he'd never met a stronger person in his life. She humbled him.

"I don't need to be carried, Merek. I can stand." She wriggled to try to get down when they got inside the tepee.

He tightened his arms and kissed her forehead, savoring the feel of her against him, vital and alive. It so easily could have been different. He could so easily have missed out on the chance of ever knowing her. The thought hit him like a blow. "I can't stay with you tonight, but you don't have to go to sleep alone. We have some time before Alex gets back from his nocturnal activities."

A breathy laugh escaped her. "Nocturnal activities, huh? Is that what they call it these days?"

"That's right." He let her feet slide to the floor, but kept her snug against him, so she was still on her tiptoes with her fingers linked behind his neck.

She glanced at her sleeping bag and then back up at him. "So you're just planning to lie there and hold me until I fall asleep?"

"Yep." He dropped his forehead to hers and dragged in her feminine scent, grateful beyond words that she was here with him, that she was the person she was. Unstoppable force of nature, and he wouldn't have it any other way, even when she made him crazy.

"I won't want you just to hold me if we're that close and in a horizontal position."

He closed his eyes and ran his hands up and down her back, a laugh straggling out of him as his body had a predictable reaction to her words. "Whatever you need, sweetheart."

"Nocturnal activities, I think." And then she pulled him down for a kiss.

It was like setting a match to a powder keg. All the emotions roiling around inside him suddenly had a focus, somewhere to go. The relief was so sharp it almost drove him to his knees.

He wanted to go slow, wanted to be gentle, to show her how he'd come to cherish her. Hell, he wanted to be in control enough to do any of those things. Instead, he jerked at her shirt, wrenching it over her head. He didn't even bother to remove her bra before he latched onto her nipple. He sucked her through the lace, used the fabric to stimulate her to a thrusting little nub. His fingers offered the same rough treatment to her other nipple, and she squealed when he bit her lightly.

"Merek!" Her fingers splayed over his chest, moved down his T-shirt to his pants, and she fumbled with his fly. Her hand on his cock was enough to make him wild, lust eating away at his restraint. He divested them both of their clothing in short order and dragged her down to her sleeping bag.

He jerked her thighs wide, and thrust himself deep inside her. She hissed between her teeth, not quite wet enough for his entry to be easy. He shuddered and buried his face in the crook of her neck, a low groan ripping from his throat. "I'm sorry. I couldn't wait."

She stroked her hands down his back, turning her head to kiss his ear. "Then you'd better make it up to me."

A chuckle slipped out, and he lifted his head to look down at her. "Would two or three orgasms before I get to come be penance enough?"

She sniffed. "Three."

"I'll see what I can do."

"Good." Humor glinted in her eyes, the shifting kaleido-scope of greens and browns, blues and golds, all the clearer from this close.

He licked his fingertips, lifting his torso to be able to reach between them. Stroking his damp fingers over her clit made her gasp and writhe, which forced his cock even deeper inside her. They both groaned, but he continued toying with her while her flesh grew wetter, her muscles flexing around his shaft. She squirmed beneath him, the gold flecks in her eyes glowing with magic.

"Do you want me to use spells, or should we do this the old-fashioned way?" He let his fingertips circle her clit with slow, deliberate promise, so she'd know exactly what she was in for.

She lifted her hips into his caress. "Is that really a question?"

Chuckling, he let a spell vibrate down his arm and out through his hand. Her eyes went wide, and she screamed, arch-ing as she came for him, her pussy fisting around him. A wave of her magic hit him, skated over his skin, and lodged in his belly, a slow fire that made his cock jerk. He had to grit his teeth and run through police procedure in his mind to keep from coming with her.

"That's one," he said when he could speak again. Sliding out of her made him groan, but he knew he wouldn't last if he stayed inside her for her next orgasm.

Kissing his way down her torso, he let his tongue flick out to taste each plush nipple in turn. They tightened for him, dark-ening to a deep raspberry. He sucked one hard, and his fingers plucked and twisted the other. Sending a light shock from the tip of his tongue made her jolt and squeal. Her thighs closed around one of his, and she rubbed herself against him.

He grinned, kissed his way upward to lick her throat, and sent a swift tingle to her from every inch of skin that touched her. She shivered, gooseflesh breaking out. Working her with his thigh, he rocked against her pelvis until she gasped his name in his ear, nipped at his shoulder, and sucked on his earlobe. "Please, Merek. I'm going to come again. Please."

He rode her clit with his leg, flexing the muscles until they burned with the strain. Her nails raked down his back, sending wicked pleasure into his flesh, a spell that made him choke with need. She arched under him, the magic they used cycling, reverberating, expanding their ecstasy until a hoarse cry burst from his throat. Her wetness increased, the scent intoxicating as it dampened the hair on his thigh. Gods, he wanted inside her, wanted that wet heat hugging his cock. He groaned against her neck, biting down on the tendon.

"Merek!" Her fingers dug deep into his shoulders, and he felt her pussy spasm against his leg. She gave a little sob as she bucked in his arms. He held her in place, sliding down to kiss the soft curve of her belly, nip at her navel, until he reached the part of her he wanted most. She whimpered, "Oh, gods. I don't think I can . . ."

"Nuh-uh. Two more for you, and one for me. No backing out now, Standish." How many times would he need to make her come before she was exhausted enough to sleep through a dark night in the wilderness? He was about to find out. Flicking his tongue against her swollen clit, he heard her broken moan.

"Please," she whispered, but her fingers slid into his hair, holding him close to her slick sex. Gooseflesh broke over his scalp from a fresh pleasure spell. His hips arched in reflex, rubbing his cock against her sleeping bag.

It felt too good, and he fought to keep from moving his body in the same rhythm he worked hers. Turning his head, he bit the inside of her thigh. Hard. She choked, her fingers clenched painfully in his hair, and her back bowed. "Yes, Merek!"

Forcing her thighs flat to the sleeping bag, he opened her for his feasting. The sweetness of her cream flowed into his mouth, and he buried his tongue in her soaking pussy, thrusting until he felt her excitement crest. Her low cries, her pleading moans, kissed his ears. He formed his lips around her clit, sucking it hard. Sinking his fingers into her hot sex, he stroked her until she could take three fingers easily. Her channel clamped down on him, and he bit her clit, holding it between his teeth as he flicked his tongue rapidly across the little nub.

"Merek . . . Oh, gods. Oh, *gods!*"

The feel of her squeezing around his fingers, the scent of her musky passion, the sobbing cries, snapped his control. He bolted upward, settling on top of her, and shoving her thighs even wider with his. He thrust deep, the last of her contractions wringing his cock. Kissing her lips, he let her taste her own wetness while he began moving within her. He couldn't hold back, couldn't stop.

Inside the tepee, he didn't have to worry about a Normal seeing the lightning bolts of his favored pleasure spells like he had in the lake. Here, he could make her writhe and scream for him. He licked a slow path up the side of her throat, sending a jolt here and there with the very tip of his tongue. She sucked in a breath, but arched her neck for him. Her nails raked down his back, her own spells making the pleasure-pain burn beneath his skin and spread.

The pace he set was hard, pounding, punishing. She wrapped her legs around his waist, lifting herself into his thrusts.

"Sweetheart, you feel so fucking good." And so fucking tight. Her passage was so narrow and swollen, she squeezed him in an iron grip.

Grinding his hips downward, he sent a bolt of magic sizzling into her hard little clit, down the length of his cock and into her creamy pussy, stimulating them both until they groaned and shuddered at the intensity.

She squirmed beneath him with a gasp, her lush breasts rubbing against his chest. "Merek! Gods, yes. I love it when you— *Merek!*"

His name on her lips was enough to send him over the edge. He forced his eyes to remain open, to watch her come with him. He loved the look on her face as those sharp hazel eyes glazed with fulfillment. Fulfillment he'd given her. It was the most potent aphrodisiac he'd ever known. His back hunched, his hips bucked, and he slammed his dick hilt-deep into her sleek pussy. He jetted his come into her, letting go of the unraveling edges of what remained of his discipline. "Chloe!"

Long, long moments later reality began to return by degrees. He lay sprawled on top of her, breathing in the female scent of her. He had to be crushing her, so he hauled himself up onto his elbows to keep from smothering her.

Gods, he'd been wild, out of control, savaging her. He winced as his gaze snagged on a lurid bite mark forming just below her collarbone. It wouldn't be visible with a shirt on, but he'd know it was there, know he'd marked her. What the hell was wrong with him that he liked that idea? He wasn't one of the fanged races, but it didn't stop the primitive, possessive pleasure that coursed through him at seeing *his* bite on *his* woman.

She could heal the mark in the morning, and she'd probably hex his ass if she knew what he was thinking. But she hadn't said so much as a word since they'd climaxed. Concern punched through him. He swallowed a hard lump of dread, and forced his gaze away from the bruise.

"Are you all right? Did I hurt you?"

But she was already asleep, her hair fanned out on the pillow, her cheeks ruddy, and her breasts rising and falling in the slow cadence of deep slumber. He let out the breath he hadn't realized he'd been holding, and couldn't help the smile of satisfaction that curled his lips. Sliding out of her made him grit his teeth and sweat break out on his forehead. Gods, but he wanted her. Still. Again. Always.

Rifling through her suitcase produced a nightshirt, which he managed to work over her head without waking her. If he lingered when tugging the shirt down over her breasts, smooth belly, and supple thighs, no one would ever know except him. She was so beautiful.

He forced himself to move away from her to go and dig through their camping supplies until he came up with a small, battery-powered lantern. Flipping it onto its lowest setting, he deposited it beside her. The batteries were new, so they should last all night long. Then he went and gathered up Ophelia. She mewed in annoyance, but he petted her until she relaxed. Laying her in the sleeping bag with Chloe, he covered them both up. He might not be able to hold her, but he wouldn't make her spend the night alone.

Bending forward, he kissed her forehead gently, so as not to awaken her. "Sleep all night, and have only sweet dreams."

It was a benediction, a prayer, a wish, and if he was lucky, a spell that would make it so. Her inner demons could unravel his magic, but he hoped they slept tonight, too.

8

"I want everything we don't absolutely need in the morning loaded in the car tonight before Alex heads out." Merek growled the command as he picked up Chloe's biggest suitcase and his own duffel bag.

Alex and Chloe stared at him for a long moment, but then Alex shrugged and went to get his stuff. Chloe plucked a few things from her smaller suitcase and then closed the lid. "I'll keep out the clothes I'm wearing tomorrow. We can just load up the rest."

"Okay, I'll do the same," Alex said as he shuffled clothes around, zipped up his backpack, and slung it over his shoulder. Then he followed Merek to the car and helped him stow all their gear.

When they were done, the only things left out were the sleeping bags and pillows, two lanterns, and a few personal items.

Still, Merek's shoulders twitched. It was an itch he couldn't scratch, and it had started just as they were cleaning up after dinner. The feeling had only intensified as the sun sunk toward the horizon. He had no idea what was coming, but he knew something was. He didn't even know *when* it was coming. Tonight, tomorrow, next week.

He. Didn't. Know.

Fuck.

Pinching the bridge of his nose, he suppressed the frustration that roared within him. There was nothing he could do about this now. His precognition was unreliable in this situation. He could only be as prepared as he could be. It was ironic that he normally had to have a stranglehold on his sight, and now that he'd give anything to call it up, it had abandoned him to the same blind fate that most people dealt with all the time.

"Hey." Chloe's softness pressed to his back, her arms wrapping around his waist from behind. "You want to tell me about it?"

He sighed and let his hand drop away from his face. The lake stretched before him, as smooth and unruffled on the surface as he usually was. The thought didn't reassure him at all. "There's nothing to tell. I don't know anything. I can't *see.*"

"You're doing the best you can." She pressed her forehead between his shoulder blades, her fingers moving in soothing circles on his stomach.

He caught her hand in his, flattening it to his belly. Much more of her stroking and his body would respond with embarrassing enthusiasm. "It might not be enough."

"I know that." She slipped around until she leaned against his front. Tipping her head back, she met his gaze. "Alex knows that. There aren't any guarantees."

"If anything happened—" He choked off the sentence, unable to finish it, but he forced the words to grate out. "I can't watch you die, Chloe. I can't."

"You won't have to." She propped her chin against his chest, cuddling closer. "I know you'll get us through this. We're going to be fine."

He snorted to cover the depth of his reaction to her trust in him. He'd wanted it, and now he had it. "Did the voices tell you that?"

She pinched his butt. "No, my precognition isn't really strong enough for that. I just know that I trust you, and I have faith that we'll come out of this okay. I have to believe that."

"Why?"

A sigh flattened his T-shirt against his chest before she dropped her arms and stepped away from him. "Because you and Alex don't. So, that's my job."

He caught her hand, keeping her close. She gave him a soft smile when he lifted her fingers to his lips and kissed them. "Thank you."

She shook her head. "Thank *you*. For everything."

For coming along on this case with her and Alex? For last night? The words hovered on the tip of his tongue. He wanted to know if her gratitude was specific to *her*, to *them*, or just for his being a cop. Why he was making that distinction now, when he normally thought of himself as a cop first and foremost, was beyond him.

He was saved from making a bumbling ass of himself by Alex. "The moon's going to rise in about ten minutes. You guys need anything from me before I shift? I like to Change before the moon goes up. I don't know if that makes my chances any better because I can already feel how it pulls at my bones, but..."

The kid trailed to a babbling close, his fingers clenching and unclenching, his eyes red-rimmed, his body twitching with all the signs of a junkie just off a bender.

Merek nodded. "Do what you have to do. We'll be here when you get back. I want to head out at first light, so you can crash in the car on the drive."

"Sounds good." Alex nodded with the speed and elasticity of one of those wobbly-headed dolls. "I'll be back as soon as the moon starts to set."

"Take care of yourself." Chloe stepped forward, lifted up on tiptoe, and popped a kiss on his cheek. "Try not to get in any trouble."

He flashed a quick grin, which bared his long, curved fangs. "I never do."

"I know." She stepped back while he paced in a restless circle. "You're an awesome kid. Young man. Whatever."

"Thanks." That wild smile shone again, then a shudder rippled through him as the last rays of the sun began to fade from the horizon. "Gotta go."

Spinning, he all but flowed into the tepee, his body so primed to Change it'd probably taken all his control to stay in human form as long as he had.

Merek tensed as he heard the kid shifting, and held his breath, waiting to see if Alex made it over or if they lost him right there. Chloe reached back for his hand blindly. He took her hand, hauled her to his side, and felt her flinch at each sound of a bone breaking. Sweat popped out on his forehead, trickling down his temple and sticking his shirt to his back. His gut churned as the silence stretched on for long, long moments and there was no sign of Alex.

Somehow, this hadn't occurred to him as a possibility, that they might lose the contained young wolf just because he was a wolf. Merek's jaw clenched. He should have seen it coming. The boy's mother had died the same way, Chloe had told him so. He let go of her hand, met her haunted gaze for a fleeting moment, and then strode toward the tepee. "I'll check on him."

Check and see if he'd made it through, but the eerie silence was damning. Every footfall rang too loudly in his ears. He didn't want to go in, didn't want to see, didn't want to *know*. His heart pounded in slow, painful thuds. Sucking in a deep breath, he braced himself as he reached the tepee's opening.

I'm here. Alex's telepathic voice sounded in Merek's mind, and relief hit him with the subtle force of a freight train. The wolf stepped outside, but ugly memories lurked in the pale eyes as they met Merek's. *It's always . . . harder at first at full moon. And then it's way too easy.*

"I understand." He laid a hand on the wolf's back, one of the few times he'd deliberately touched the wary boy. The muscles twitched beneath his hand.

Do you? The question was sharp edged, brittle.

"I have my own powers that are a bitch to control. They don't threaten my life, but I can relate to some of what you go through." Leaving his hand where it was, he sent a wave of soothing calm to the vibrating young wolf. Full moon fever wasn't easy for a wolf to fight, and with his pack in Seattle, Alex wouldn't have had to work as hard, would have had older wolves to help and guide him. He'd have had the protection and freedom of running on pack land.

The muzzle dipped in a nod. *Maybe you do get it.*

He kept up the stream of discipline and control that flowed from his hand to the wolf, knew from the way Alex quivered that he felt the magic, but didn't try to escape it. Good. Anything Merek could do to help, he would, and he wanted the werewolf to know it. "Chloe and I can never understand exactly what you go through, but we're here if and when you need us. Believe that, if nothing else."

The wolf's eyes closed, and he finally leaped sideways and shook. *I believe you, but I have to go. Now. The need to run is ripping me up inside.*

"Go. We'll be here."

Alex shot forward, passed Chloe, and slid to a stop at the lake's shore to fling back his head and bay at the moon.

The lonesome sound ended in a howl of agony when the lupine body jerked sideways as though struck by an invisible sledgehammer. The report of a rifle came a split second later, followed by the reverberating gut-punch of Merek's warding spell being breached, and then time assumed the elastic quality of battle.

Merek launched himself forward, knocking Chloe to the ground in the same motion as he pulled his weapon from his concealed holster and fired into the stand of trees north of their campsite, just beyond the stretch of his warding spells.

"Fuck," he snarled. How many of Smith's men were there? He stretched his senses, found four distinct energies lurking beyond the line of trees. Not good.

"Alex!" Chloe screamed; terror and rage rang clear in her voice. Well, at least she wasn't going hysterical on him. Then again, it was Chloe.

She tried to crawl out from under him, and he shoved her back to the ground. Bullets slapped into the dirt around them, made it spray in their faces. "Stay down, damn it!"

"Alex was shot, damn it," she retorted, flinching as he returned fire on the terrorists.

"I'd like for him to be the only one, so stay where you are." He felt the bullets exploding through his shields, then the hot slicing blade of the Magickals combining their abilities to rupture the warding spell entirely. They were powerful; he could feel the strength that only came with age.

Sweat filmed his skin, made his clothes cling to his flesh. He ignored it, shoved the discomfort away. That didn't matter now. Only Chloe and Alex mattered. He could see the kid convulsing on the beach, his lupine body jerking spasmodically in the flickering firelight. Fear coated Merek's tongue, but then he locked any emotion away until there was nothing left but the heightened senses and intensified magic of battle fever.

The overwhelming silence pounded against his ears. Gunfire had ceased, but he knew they were moving, separating. He waited, every muscle tense, and he leaned more heavily on Chloe, silently telling her to be still. Alex's harsh groans made her quiver, but exposing themselves on the beach would be suicide. Merek prayed harder than he ever had in his life to any deity who would listen that the kid hung on until Merek could get to him.

A twig snapped, far too close for Merek's comfort. He threw out his free hand, and a ball of flames exploded outward. It hit a man, highlighting him and the deadly rifle he carried. This was the one who'd shot Alex. Cold rage coalesced inside Merek, and he blasted another stream of fire into the Magickal. The scent of cooking meat made his stomach jolt, but the flaming corpse hit the ground before the guttural scream finished echoing against the surrounding mountains.

Something moved between Merek and the fire, a shadow almost too fast to be anything but another flicker of dancing firelight. It was an enemy, he could feel the magic, taste it in his mouth. Vampire. Half-shifted, so it had enormous bat wings stretching from its back. Meaning they didn't give a shit that a Normal might catch a glimpse. Anyone that careless was especially dangerous. Even most Magickal criminals obeyed the laws against Normal interactions because if you fucked that law in a big enough way, it carried an automatic death sentence.

They needed to get out of here. Now.

The vampire swished through the air above them, dropping something large on the far side of the fire. Another terrorist? He couldn't tell. The bloodsucker came back, sweeping forward to hover right over them, and Merek knew they were caught. He flipped over, weapon extended, aiming for the wings. A few shots hit, the explosive ammunition designed for Magickals lighting up the night. Blood rained down on him in hot torrents, drenching his clothes. Shock showed in the red eyes that gleamed like embers in a pale face. The vampire screeched, its broken wing contorting so he dropped to flop like a great wounded bird on the ground.

Snapping a fresh clip into his gun, Merek rolled into a

crouch. He wrapped an arm around Chloe's waist and hauled her up next to him. He scuttled to the far side of the tepee, dragging her in his wake. The cover was pretty fucking feeble, but vampires could see in the dark, and he couldn't. He kept his senses open as wide as possible, trying to pinpoint the other terrorists.

Fishing in his pocket, he jerked out his keys. He shoved them into Chloe's hand and leaned close to breathe in her ear. "Get to the car, and I'll get Alex."

He could hear her swallow, feel her turn her head away from the fire and toward the pitch blackness that swallowed up the SUV. Tension screamed through her, and he waited for her to master her terror, knowing that she would. "I—I don't . . ." She shuddered. "Okay."

"That's my girl." He squeezed her hand, curling her fingers over the keys. "If we're not there in five minutes, I want you to get out of here. Contact Luca and Millie."

"No." She jerked her head around to stare up at him, her pupils huge. "I won't do that."

His fingers clenched over hers. "Chloe—"

"I won't leave you alone in the dark." Another shudder went through her, but she dropped his hand and moved away. Toward the SUV, as he'd told her. "I can't. Don't even ask it."

He knew that was the best he would get, so he didn't say anything else. Not allowing himself a last look at her, he forced himself to focus on getting to Alex. He could only hope the kid was as stubborn a survivor as Merek had always taken him for. Tonight, it would mean the difference between living or dying.

Merek could feel his power flowing hot and wild through his body, and he tried to rein it in, bury it until he needed to use it. Find the balance between awareness of other Magickals, and hiding his own presence from *their* awareness. Too bad he sucked at invisibility spells.

He slid from behind the tepee, ghosting into the few trees

near their campsite to try to avoid casting shadows for them to see. The underbrush to his left moved, the noise created by something far too big to be an animal. His heartbeat slowed to a dull thud in his chest, and he lifted his weapon as he slid forward to look.

Whatever was moving through the bushes wasn't trying to be quiet. He could hear the breath whistling out of a pair of lungs. The scent of blood came to him, but the energy was that of neither of the Magickals he'd dealt with so far. It seemed familiar somehow, but he didn't know why.

Then he knew. His pistol was trained on the elf who'd rented the campsite to them the day before. And the man was dying, slow and bloody, just as Merek had seen in his vision the moment he'd looked at the elf. Shit. He sighed softly and knelt beside the pathetic specimen crawling forward on his belly. A single glance, even in the semidarkness, told Merek the other man wasn't going to make it.

"I'm sorry," the man choked. He met Merek's gaze, reaching out to fist his fingers in the leg of Merek's pants. "Reward . . . for people matching your description. I called last night. Sorry. Didn't know."

His grip went slack as he began coughing up dark liquid. Merek shook off his hand and stood, knowing there was nothing he could do for the elf now. Part of him was glad he didn't have to. The man had turned them over for money, and Merek had little pity for the fate that had befallen him.

"He broke so easily." The dispassionate, almost regretful, voice sounded from his left, but whoever was there already had him. "But his blood was sweet. We brought him along as a snack for later. Pity."

Merek turned only his head to see what he was dealing with. Vampire, from the fangs and the blood-tasting comment—different from the one he'd shot from the sky. A wolf would have had to shift at full moon, so only one fanged race was in human form tonight. One look at his face, and a fresh explosion of adrenaline raced through Merek's veins. He knew this man, whose red hair gleamed like a copper penny. "Gregor."

"Good to see you again, Kingston." His tone was pleasant, bland enough to be discussing the weather. Then again, murder was everyday business for the vampire, so this might be just that boring for him. This was no recruit for Smith's cause, but a mercenary who whored his deadly skills out to the highest bidder.

Merek shrugged, easing one hand off the butt of his weapon to try to angle his fingers in the bloodsucker's direction. "I wish I could say the same, but my day is never good when I run into you."

Gregor laughed easily. "I'm flattered, Detective, I really am. Now, are you going to try to use that hand to cast or are you going to be reasonable?"

As usual, the vampire carried no weapons. He didn't need them. Merek didn't want to think about what he'd do to Chloe or Alex if he got his hands on them.

That wouldn't happen. Merek wouldn't let it. Playing in his favor was the fact that Gregor couldn't know Merek's best weapon—his precognition—was toast in this situation. He'd take any advantage he could get, even one based on a false assumption.

He let a knife-thin smile curve his lips. "When have I ever been reasonable?"

The vampire grinned, anticipation flashing in his gaze. His eyes burned red around the edges. "I was hoping you'd say that."

Instead of moving his hands as Gregor expected, Merek slammed his toe into the ribs of the dying elf at his feet. The shriek that ripped through the air made the vampire flinch, but before Merek could launch a spell at him, Gregor had used his superhuman speed to disappear. The underbrush didn't even rustle with his passing.

A wolf's howl roared from the lakeshore, the sound of a cornered, angry animal.

Alex.

Pivoting on his heel, Merek bolted out of the trees and toward the beach. His pistol was up and ready, but he kept one hand free for casting. The vampire with the broken wing hunched over Alex, the tip of one wing dragging in the sand behind him. His talons were bared, arching with deadly purpose toward the young wolf's throat.

He couldn't get a shot off. The vampire was too close to Alex. Flicking his fingers, he fired a percussive boom into the air. The vampire slammed his hands over his sensitive ears, crying out hoarsely. Alex writhed on the ground, one half-Changed arm covering his head to block the noise. Gregor's enraged bellow sounded in the distance behind Merek.

Not even pausing in his movements, Merek launched himself forward to catch the vampire around the waist and roll him away from the wolf. Fleshy wings tangled around them, and Merek tore at the skin trying to get loose. The vampire screeched, slashing his talons down Merek's bicep, and Merek lost his weapon as his arm spasmed.

Pain.

It exploded into his body, reverberated through his skull until he thought it would split. Black spots spun in front of his eyes, and the need to vomit cut through the adrenaline pumping through his system.

The vampire hissed, and only the thought of those talons biting into him again cleared his head enough to react. He swung blindly, slamming his fist into the vampire's mouth. The fangs ripped through his knuckles.

Hard bones from the top of one massive wing clipped him in the jaw. He swayed, caught the top of the wing near the shoulder and blasted through the flesh, bone, and cartilage with a fireball. When the vampire shrieked and bucked under him, Merek was ready, rolling toward the severed wing to escape being entangled again.

Staggering to his feet, he opened his hand. "Gun," he ordered, and the universe obeyed. His weapon whooshed through the air and smacked into his palm.

The amount of magic he was using began to drag at him, his energy sapping. And they weren't out of the woods yet. His body shook from the strain, but he moved toward Alex, dropping to his knees beside the boy. Alex had regressed to a half-shift, the monstrous form worthy of any Hollywood depiction of werewolves, twice the height and breadth of any human. Three times as heavy, too.

Alex's hand was pressed tightly over the bullet hole in his side, but blood still flowed between his fingers. Merek grabbed Alex's free arm, hoisted him up, and hauled both of them to their feet. "Keep pressure on that wound."

Will do. The voice was a bare whisper in his mind. Still, it meant the boy was conscious and aware of his surroundings. That helped. Marginally.

I'm bleeding pretty badly. You're slashed up. The vampires can track the scent of our blood.

"They can?" Merek didn't bother swearing. Gregor was still out there, and that thought alone sent ice flowing through his veins.

Luca said so. It's how he tracked me down the day my dad disappeared and Smith's men were hunting me.

Shit. He wished that was a skill Luca possessed personally and not a purview of the entire vampire race, but he couldn't take the chance of assuming these vampires couldn't track them the same way. This sounded like just the kind of thing the Vampire Conclave would want kept secret from other Magickal races.

Alex staggered with every step, his legs giving out from under him as his bones broke and reformed over and over again, transitioning between the half-shift and human forms and back again. Spittle-laced gurgles of agony spilled from the boy's mouth.

He tensed against Merek, trying to pull away, but not strong enough to do so. *Get Chloe out of here!*

"Not leaving you," Merek grunted.

Shaking his head, Alex again tried unsuccessfully to escape Merek's hold. *She can't die because . . . of me. Not . . . another one.*

He didn't know what that meant, and at the moment, he didn't give a flying rat's ass.

"Sorry, son. Not happening. I won't do it." He paused to fire at the sound of movement behind them. A vampiric hiss answered him. "She wouldn't leave without you, anyway."

Fuck! The wolfish face snapped its jaw, fangs dripping as he bared them. Then the facial bones broke, the muzzle retracting, and Alex's human face surfaced. He choked on a breath, sagging against Merek's side.

"Concentrate on getting to the car."

"I'm with you," he rasped. Pushing forward one unsteady step at a time, he took as much of his weight off of Merek as possible while keeping hold of him for balance. The boy's jaw clenched on a groan of pain, his face set in grim lines, but he kept moving.

Merek's respect for the kid doubled, but he focused on keeping them moving. Blood dripped steadily down his arm, the wound weakening the muscles and making them burn with a ferocity that made him want to howl. The adrenaline rush wasn't enough to overcome the pain of it, but he gritted his teeth and rocked Alex and himself forward.

He hitched the boy higher, trying not to lose his grip. A low snarl of warning vibrated from the boy's chest. Merek was already swinging his weapon around, squeezing the trigger when Gregor and a woman who moved with the competence of a trained operative came within range.

His bullets hit, but though the vampire staggered, he kept coming. The woman dove for the ground, rolling away while she fired off shots with both her weapon and her magic. Both missed, but the percussive force of her spell sent Merek and Alex staggering backward. The smile on Gregor's face as he advanced had that same anticipation he'd worn before; this time the eyes flashed full red. Merek squeezed the trigger again.

The distinctive click of an empty weapon sounded from his pistol. He dropped it, lifting his hand to send a blast into the bloodsucker that he knew wouldn't have enough effect. Merek moved in front of Alex, spreading his fingers and feeling his exhausted power gather more slowly than the vampire could move.

The whine of a car accelerating cut through Merek's mind, and then the SUV plowed into Gregor and sent him flying. Brakes squealed as Chloe pulled up beside them. The doors whipped open, and her eyes were wide and wild. Her knuckles were white on the steering wheel, and Ophelia hunched on the dashboard, hissing.

Merek stuffed Alex in the backseat, then shoved Chloe over in the front seat, slammed both doors shut with what was left of his own magic, and hit the accelerator. "Everyone stay down!"

His words were all but lost as the rear window shattered from a flying bullet.

"Chloe, will you keep your head down?"

"No! I'm going to help Alex." She flipped down the console between the front seats and squirmed through the narrow opening, maneuvering onto her knees on the floorboard behind the passenger seat.

"Ophelia, get off the damn dashboard," Merek barked. Chloe heard a small thump and assumed her familiar had obeyed.

She flinched as another spray of bullets hit the car. The dull slap of metal hitting metal made her insides freeze with terror. Gods, don't let them hit anything important. She rocked sideways, slamming her chin into the door as Merek swerved hard. The tires squealed, spinning for purchase before they raced down a bumpy road.

Alex lay sprawled across the backseat, one hand pressed to his side while the other held tight to the back of the bench seat. The werewolf, at least, was strong enough to hold himself in place as the SUV swung around tight turns and switchbacks in the road. His eyes were pinched closed, a muscle ticked in his clenched jaw, and his normally tanned face was ashen.

There was blood everywhere.

All over the floor, Alex's naked body, pooling on the leather seat. Seeping into her jeans. Chloe felt the color leech out of her face. This was why she'd gone into pharmaceutical research rather than into practicing medicine. The stench of blood, the blank eyes of hurt, dying people. It reminded her too much of her mother.

A shudder ripped through her, but she shook herself, forced those memories into the deepest, darkest corner of her soul and locked them in tight. Alex needed her now. Her fears from that day *would not* be allowed to take someone else from her.

"Let me see, Alex." She tugged his hand away from his side to get a better look at what she was dealing with.

"It's silver," he gasped, his body twitching and writhing. "Gods, it burns. It's like my insides are on fire. Help me, Chloe. Please, help me." The pleading in those green eyes gripped her insides tight. Memories of him rushed at her: a gap-toothed little boy, a stringy adolescent, and as he was now, almost full-grown, but just as beloved.

Silver. Oh, gods. The bullet hadn't hit a vital organ or he'd be dead already, but the wound didn't look good. The flesh around the entry was charred and beginning to fester. The speed of werewolf healing meant the allergic reaction to silver also intensified. She tried to keep her voice reassuring as she spoke to her godson. "I'll help you, honey. Just hang in there."

"You're going to have to take the bullet out before it dissolves into his bloodstream," Merek boomed from the front seat, meeting her gaze briefly in the rearview mirror.

"I know," she shouted back over the wind. "I'm getting the first aid kit." And a lantern for some light. She pressed Alex's hand back over the wound, and he choked on a groan.

Merek seemed to have found them a straight road to speed down, but trying to remove a silver bullet from a werewolf was tricky even under ideal conditions. These were not ideal conditions.

Shit. Shit. Shit.

Shoving herself up on shaky legs that weren't helped at all by the moving vehicle, she tried to ease over Alex and into the back of the packed SUV. The various crates and bags were a tumbled mess littered with shattered glass. She tried to remember which ones held which items. After a few minutes of frantic searching, she came up with the small lantern Merek had given her to sleep with.

Where was the fucking first aid kit? Chloe wanted to snarl, but knew it wouldn't help. Wind rushed through the broken window, the cold air chilling her to the bone. Her fingers felt stiff with it as she fumbled through another crate of camping equipment, but she ignored the slight discomfort. It was nothing compared to what Alex was going through.

There. Relief washed through her as she spotted the large

white box with a red cross on it. Wrapping her hand around the handle, she yanked it out from under the ice chest. Maneuvering back over the seat with her treasures was a complete bitch. Her leg slipped out from under her when she was halfway, and she crashed on to Alex's legs.

He jackknifed upright, his eyes wild and fangs bared in a grimace of pain. *Fuck!*

His voice roared so loudly in her mind she wanted to whimper and slap her hands over her ears, but knew that wouldn't do a damn thing. "Lie back down, Alex."

The feral gleam in his eyes didn't fade, but he obeyed jerkily. Flipping the lantern on high, she wedged it between his chest and the seat. It cast a bright light over the area she had to work with. Not great, but much better than trying to pull out a bullet in the dark.

Running over everything she remembered from med school about werewolves and silver as well as bullet extractions, she straddled her godson's thighs and tried to keep her balance as Merek wheeled the SUV up what had to be a highway on-ramp. It didn't matter. Their safety was his job, helping Alex was hers.

She cracked open the first aid kit and rifled through the contents. Antiseptic, bandages of all sizes, a few vials of herbal infusions. The most useful thing in there for pulling the bullet out was a pair of tweezers that she knew wouldn't be useful at all.

Okay. She could do this with magic. She'd never tried it herself, but she knew it could be done. Her heart gave a sickening lurch. If she messed it up, missed even a single sliver of silver and it got into his bloodstream, he'd be dead by morning. No pressure. She wiped her sweaty palms on her shirt and noticed Alex's pain-filled eyes latched on her every movement. She didn't even bother with a reassuring smile.

Gods, please. She closed her eyes for a moment and sent up a silent, fervent prayer.

Sucking in a deep breath almost made her gag on the sickly sweet scent of blood. She gritted her teeth and placed her hand over his wound, seeking the metal with her magic. She'd never even watched anyone do this before, even in her rotation in the ER. She didn't know a spell to do what she wanted to do, but she focused as hard as she could, working every single fragment of the silver back up through the hole it had left behind while Alex's claws shredded the rental SUV's upholstery.

His skin smoked and sizzled as each silver piece oozed out. Blood so dark it was black flowed in a thick, sluggish stream from the wound. His muscles spasmed and sweat poured down his face, mixing with tears as he sobbed in agony.

Moonlight shown in the window, slicing across Alex's face. His eyes went wolfish, fangs extending as he gurgled on a growl. She swallowed at the sight. "How are you even in human form right now?"

"Silver," he choked out. "Leave . . . some of it in, so I can . . . stay human. Rampaging right now would be . . . a bad idea."

"No. It could kill you." She recalled vividly the bronze searing into her wrists, and that was an *external* application of the metal witches were allergic to.

"Better than me trying to rip you and Merek apart so I can go bite and Change some Normals." Another sob heaved from his chest, and he turned his face away from her. "So they can live through this every month."

She scanned the wound with her magic, closing her eyes to focus better. "All the silver is gone already."

Shit. The word was no more than a weary whisper in her head.

"I wouldn't have done it anyway." Drawing on all the magic she had within her, she began to heal the putrid flesh the bullet had left behind. Bringing new, healthy tissue to the surface, sealing the wound. When it was done, she placed a bandage over the area and let the animal magic flowing through the boy's veins do the rest of the healing for her. Now that there was no contact with silver, he should be better within a few hours. Sooner, if he hadn't lost so much blood. She hoped. The moon might still be full and in the sky when he was healed, which was a worry. "We'll deal with it if you somehow manage to get up the energy to rampage, but I couldn't risk your life by leaving silver inside you."

He sagged against the seat, every muscle going limp. Tear tracks made clean furrows in the grime on his face. Pain still dug grooves beside his eyes and mouth, but the flesh no longer pulled taut across his cheekbones. He flinched and slammed his eyes closed when a moonbeam hit him in the face.

She smoothed his hair away from his forehead. "You won't have to be like this forever, Alex. I *will* find a way to stop this."

His pale eyes cracked open and met hers, his expression too serious and adult. "If these assholes don't get there first. They'd have wolves on their knees trying to get some of the drug. Any of us would do anything to not have to fight full moon fever. *I* would give anything."

"I know." Leaning to the side, she dug into the rear of the SUV until she came up with a mylar space blanket. "Luca won't let Smith win. We just have to stay alive long enough for me to finish my research."

Alex snorted. "I'm good with that."

She tucked the blanket around him to help him conserve as much body heat as possible. She hoped the allergic reaction to silver didn't mean they'd be facing an infection. If it came to that, she was making Merek take them to a hospital with a Magickal ward. He'd do it, too. Merek always took care of them, even if it meant bullets and dark spells were flying.

She swung her leg off Alex so she could stand on the floor, but had to bend so she didn't hit her head on the roof. She hung on to the back of Merek's seat when they bounced over a pothole. "We'll make it through this, Alex."

"Okay." There wasn't a single ounce of conviction in the wolf's voice, and he was clearly humoring her.

She sighed. He didn't believe her, but what could she say to convince him? She didn't know that everything would be all right. Squirming along the seat so she could sit with Alex's head in her lap, she tried to ignore the drying blood all over her clothes.

"It might be better if you sat in the front seat. Away from me." He closed his eyes, but the claws of one hand still sank deep into the backseat every time the moonlight touched him. His fangs clenched tight, his jaw flexing.

It wasn't that he was worried about turning her into a were-wolf. None of the Magickal races could combine, and she was already a witch. Even if an elf married a wolf, they could have a wolf child or an elf child, or some of each, but a hybrid was a Magickal impossibility. If Alex's rampage made him bite Chloe, it could kill her the way any traumatic injury could, but she wouldn't turn wolf.

She stroked her hand down his sweat-soaked hair. "You would never hurt me, Alex. No matter how bad it got. Not even the full moon could change that."

His green eyes fixed on her face, as if he was trying to absorb some of her certainty, and her heart broke at the expression on his face. He let go of the front seat, reaching up for her hand. She grabbed his hand, squeezed it tight, and ignored the sharp talons that tipped each finger. His throat moved as he swallowed. "I love you, Chloe."

"I love you, too, kiddo." She let go of his hand, set it on his chest, and tucked the blanket tighter around him. "Try to sleep."

"Thanks. For everything." His voice slurred, and his thick lashes made dark crescents on his cheeks. "You too, Merek."

She had no idea how he heard, but it almost sounded like

Merek was speaking softly in their ears. "No problem. That's my job."

Leaning back in her seat, she suddenly realized she was exhausted. Sweat and other people's blood made her clothes sticky, and her muscles began shaking with reaction. She rubbed her hands up and down her arms to stop from shivering. Her heavy use of unfamiliar magic had drained what was left of her energy.

Even the cold didn't seem to be slapping her awake. She met Merek's gaze in the rearview mirror, her heart turning over at the concern in his gaze. She offered a tired smile. "We need to get Alex cleaned up."

"We all need to clean up." His deep voice was as steady and sure as always, still a comforting murmur in her ear. What spell he was using to do that, she didn't know, but she liked it. She let her chin drop to her chest and her eyelids droop. "Don't worry, sweetheart. I'll handle it. Get some rest."

As if that was all the permission she needed, she fell headlong into oblivion.

9

Chloe blinked blurry eyes, unsure exactly what was wrong, but knowing something had changed. It took her a moment to realize the car had stopped moving. A rush of air and squeak of hinges announced the opening of the door across from her. Ophelia stirred from where she'd curled herself around Alex's head, half her body draped across his neck and shoulder and the other half on Chloe's leg.

She turned her head to watch Merek wrap the space blanket tightly around Alex before he hoisted the teen up and over his shoulder. Alex did little more than groan, but the confirmation that he was still breathing was oddly reassuring. The weight of his head lifting from her leg made her limb tingle, and she flexed her toes to get her circulation going.

Picking up her familiar, she opened the other door and slid down to let her feet touch the cracked cement of a parking lot behind a cheap-looking motel. Except for a few feeble lights, the lot was shadowed and dark. Probably best considering the shape the SUV was in. Still, standing around in the gloom made chills run through her. She tried not to look at the bullet holes gouged into the side of the SUV, tried not to think about how endless the night seemed with only a few overhead lights to guide her way.

The muscles in her legs protested when she hobbled around the end of the car, one of her calves cramping so hard she hissed out a breath. Merek glanced at her sharply. "You okay?"

"Fine," she lied. "Where are we?"

"A few hours over the border into Idaho."

Hugging Ophelia tighter, she tried not to limp. "Which room are we in?"

"Numbers seven and eight. They have an adjoining door." He dangled two sets of keys from his index finger. She snagged them and led the way to the nearest room, unlocking the heavy door and pushing her way in with one shoulder.

Feeling along the wall by the door for the light switch, she relaxed a little when the room flooded with brightness. She held the door open for Merek and watched him bypass the two double beds to deposit Alex in the bathroom. The pipes rattled in the wall as he turned on the water. Out of habit that Merek had drilled into her, she shut and bolted the door and then closed the curtains as tight as possible so no one could see in.

Then she went around and turned on every single lamp in the room and opened the adjoining door to do the same in the second room. This one had only a king-sized bed. "I'll stay in there with Alex, and you can have the big bed in here. Then your legs won't hang off the end."

"Thanks," he said as he appeared in the doorway. "I'm going to bring in what I can salvage from the car. Why don't you—"

"Get Alex hosed down so when you come back you can carry him to bed?" She slid past him to do just that.

"Yeah." He'd never sounded so weary, and her heart clenched. He was as covered in gore as she was, and she stared at the gruesome sight he made for three full seconds before she shook herself and kept moving. He glanced down at himself.

"Don't worry. The clerk won't remember me or anything about us."

"Those memory spells sure do come in handy sometimes, don't they?" She had to force herself away from the desire to cling to Merek and make sure he was all right. To hover over him, grab him, and hold on tight. If something happened to Alex or Merek and she was left alone . . . Her belly jolted at the punch of pain and panic that thought caused. No. She could not—*would* not—lose either of them. She refused to even consider the possibility, despite what had happened tonight.

As if he understood her need to hold him, Merek caught her around the waist and pulled her close. She shouldn't let herself lean on him, should pull back instead of letting him draw her in. It would only make it worse if she cared too much, but he ignored the filth coating both them and pressed her to his side. She caved in to her need and rested her head on his shoulder. Reaching up, she cupped his jaw in her palm, stroking her thumb over the rough stubble there.

He tilted her head back and kissed her. The heat that always bloomed between them filled her body, and it was the first time she'd felt warm in what seemed like forever. She suckled his bottom lip, and he groaned, burying his hand in her hair. He nipped at her lips before sweeping his tongue into her mouth.

Her body liquefied at the deeper intimacy, her sex clenching, nipples tightening, skin sensitizing until the rasp of his beard against her face was pure eroticism. His fingers cradled her head, his big body a welcoming fire that tempted her. It was so sweet, tears stung her eyes, and she felt that weakness try to overtake her, the need to desperately hold on, and forced herself to stumble back, away from the solid warmth he provided.

"I'm going to check on Alex before the tub overflows," she gasped and fled.

Skittering into the bathroom, she snatched up a thin washcloth from the pile on the vanity, and knelt beside the bathtub

Alex was sprawled in. His long legs were bent awkwardly, and the water had already turned bright pink from the blood on his skin. Gingerly, she peeled the soaked bandage away from his side and tossed it in the garbage can. She wet down the cloth and wiped away as many of the rusty blotches from his skin as possible. Then she drained the tub and refilled it before she grabbed another washrag.

She noted his skin tone looked better, not as deathly pale. His breathing was deep and even in true sleep, and the area around the wound looked pink and healthy, not enflamed or hot to the touch. Good. He was healing nicely. If things continued along this course, he would be back to normal by morning, without even a scar to remind him of the shooting. A physical scar, anyway. The kid had far too many internal scars, and she feared this would add one more. She sighed and scooped water up to rinse the shampoo provided by the motel out of his hair.

"Everything's in the room, and I fed the cat." Merek came in and set the first aid kit on the counter as she pulled the plug on the drain again. "Just in case he needs another bandage."

"Thanks. I don't think he does, actually. Toss me a few towels and help me dry him off." A sheet of thin white terry cloth draped over her shoulder a second later, and then Merek wedged himself in next to her to lift Alex up and towel him down. When he was relatively dry, Merek picked the teen up as gently as he would a newborn and carried him into the room to tuck into bed.

The front of her shirt was soaked, and pink droplets hit the carpet in a steady stream. She winced. "Man, I wouldn't want to be the maids who get to clean this room in the morning."

Merek left her standing beside the bed, picked up his duffel bag, and went into his room to change clothes. When he came back he nodded to her smallest suitcase. "This is the only one that survived. Go into the bathroom, strip down, and hand me your clothes. I'm going to take the towels and our bloody laundry with me when I torch the SUV."

"T-torch the SUV?" she echoed blankly. She knew what he was saying should make sense to her, but it didn't.

Merek reached out and caught her chin in his hand. "Sweetheart, Alex told me Luca said vampires can track the scent of our blood. We were leaking a hell of a lot of it, so depending on how sensitive they are, they might find the SUV pretty easily."

"It's soaked with Alex's blood."

"Yeah. We're ditching the car. I'm going to take it outside of town, burn it, dump it in the river we passed, and hope that throws them off a bit. I'll do what I can to mask my scent on the way back." He returned to his room for a moment and came back with a revolver. "I'm leaving this with you. Anyone but me tries to come into either room, and I want you to use it. Understood?"

A jerky nod was the best she could do as she accepted the heavy weapon. "I ran over a man today. If that's not proof I'm capable of hurting people before they hurt me, I don't know what is."

"Good girl, and thank you for saving my ass, too." He ran a hand down her hair, which had been a windblown, tangled mess *before* he'd kissed her.

She gestured to the sleeping Alex. "You saved ours first."

"That's what I'm here for." He flashed a brief grin. "Go take a quick shower. Then I want your clothes and all the dirty towels."

Picking up her suitcase, she shuffled into the bathroom, and obediently scrubbed herself clean in the fastest shower of all time. She'd have liked to linger and pamper herself under the hot stream of water, but instead winced as the soap insinuated itself into all the little scrapes and bruises on her skin. Drying off used the last of the thin towels, and she was in a pair of yoga pants and a shirt under a minute later.

"Be careful," she whispered and handed Merek everything from the bathroom, including the bloody bandage she'd fished out of the garbage.

"I will." And then he was gone.

Not letting herself peek out the curtain as he drove away, she set the revolver on the nightstand and pulled up the one chair in the room next to Alex's bed. He looked better, but he was bound to now that he wasn't covered in his own blood. She didn't know how long she sat there in tense silence, watching over Alex, feeling grit burn her eyes, listening for any noise outside. An eternity.

She jolted when the doorknob rattled, snatched up the gun, and held it at the ready. Relief made her wilt back into her chair when Merek's voice came through. "It's me."

He was even filthier than he had been, dirt and sweat making streaks down his face. His gray eyes stood out in pale contrast. Exhausted strain made brackets around his mouth. "I'm going to clean up, get a few hours sleep. We'll take a cab to the small airport here, which opens at seven in the morning. We're going to be on the first flight out. I don't care where it's headed."

"Okay." She stared at Merek for a long moment, drinking in the sight of him. Some of the tension inside her eased at having him back with her. She knew that was dangerous, but they'd gone so far over the line tonight, she didn't know if they'd ever get back to safe emotional ground.

His stride wavered a little as he walked into his room. Frowning, she hurried after him, shut the adjoining door so their conversation wouldn't disturb the sleeping wolf, and followed Merek into his bathroom. He was gingerly tugging his shirt away from his arm, and it was then that she realized he was injured.

A long gouge ran up the length of one bicep and came to a ragged stop just above his elbow. It was ugly, swollen, caked with clotted blood. A trickle of red ran down his arm. "It broke open again on the way back."

"Oh, gods," she choked. "How bad are you hurt? Why didn't you *tell* me you were hurt?" This, after everything with Alex, was too much for her. It piled on top of her until she felt moisture welling up in her eyes. The pain, the gut-wrenching terror, the exhaustion.

"Sweetheart—"

"Gods." A tear slipped down her cheek, something deep inside her crumpling under the force of her fear. "How the hell did *this* happen? This can't be real. I'm just a *scientist*. I don't . . . I don't hurt people, I don't . . . Alex was *shot*, for gods' sake. I had to pull a bullet out of my godson's gut."

"*Look at me*," Merek ordered, cupping her face in his hands. "Take a deep breath."

She sucked in a breath, and her chest hitched on a sob, but she locked her gaze on his dirt and blood-streaked face. The dried crimson stains did little to calm her, but she swallowed and forced herself to get a stranglehold on her control. Blinking away the tears still clinging to her lashes, she let the air ease out of her lungs. "Okay. Okay, I'm calm."

"Good." He stroked his fingers down her cheek, and she leaned into the comforting touch. "I know this is nuts, honey, and nothing I can say will make it less so."

"I know." She sighed. "It just . . . hit me all of a sudden."

"That happens." His smile was crooked. He dropped his hands and yanked his T-shirt over his head. Even the blood crusted on his skin didn't stop her mouth from watering at the sight of all that naked flesh. He unsnapped his fly, the hiss of his zipper loud in the small bathroom, and then he was deliciously nude. "Once our flight takes off from here, we'll take a bunch of connections and bounce around different cities before we get off. I don't know how or if they can track us from one plane to the next, but I doubt it."

She thought about what she knew of vampiric hypersenses and tried hard not to stare at Merek's sculpted ass. "It doesn't seem feasible, no."

To give herself something else to do, she leaned to the side and plucked up one of the threadbare hand towels provided by the motel, hosed it down in the sink, and started dabbing at his arm.

"Good. We're not risking it though. We'll keep moving." He flinched, but angled himself to the side to give her a better look so she could clean him up.

Pressing her palm over the wound, she closed her eyes and pulled up the dredges of her magic to disinfect and heal the ugly gash. She felt the flesh close under her fingers, but the effort sucked away the few reserves of strength she had. When she opened her eyes, she saw the skin was still swollen and pink, but it was as healed as she could get it. Wolves and vampires had magical healing abilities that left no scars, but unlike Alex, Merek would be physically marked by this night forever.

The muscles flexed as he tested his arm. "Nice. Much better than I could do. Thanks, Doc."

"Anytime." She tossed the towel down and laid a hand on his chest, just to feel the vital warmth of him. He was here; he was alive. They were all okay. This time. Her fingers moved in circles on his skin, stroking unconsciously as she absorbed the reality of him.

Slanting her a sinful look that was her only warning, he looped his good arm around her waist and swung her into the bathtub. "Keep me company while I shower. Strip."

"Are you sure you're up for that? I mean, your arm still has to be sore, and you must be bone tired because I know *I* am." Her mouth snapped shut when he just took her hand and wrapped it around his hardening erection. She grinned a little. "I guess you're up for it."

"I guess so. Not enough energy left for any pleasure spells, so we're doing this the Normal way." He shook his head, his smile rueful. "I'm half-dead, and I still want you." And then he dropped his mouth to hers and all but inhaled her. The desperation in his touch reached down deep inside her, and her own chaotic emotions imploded.

She shoved her tongue into his mouth, drowning in the taste of him. He tugged at the hem of her shirt, pulling it up. The time it took to break the kiss and get her top over her head annoyed her. Her arms twined around his neck while he lobbed her shirt at the vanity, and she stood on tiptoe to press herself against his long, hard body. His teeth grazed her neck, and her pussy fisted, dampened, pulsed with want.

The pipes squealed in the wall, and Merek twisted so he blocked the initial blast of icy water. When had he turned on the faucet? Did it matter? She held on to him as he maneuvered them around until her back pressed to the wall, the tile cool on her flesh, and she gasped. Beads of water soaked through her clothes, trailed down her legs in a sensual caress.

Big hands cupped her hips, fingers hooking in the waistband of her pants to work them and her panties down. She kicked them away, impatient for the full length of his naked body against hers. The pleasure of it made her arch. Closer, deeper, yes.

The hair on his chest stimulated her nipples; the heat of his skin set her on fire. She stroked her fingers over him, needing to touch as much of him as she could reach, to assure herself that he was safe and whole. He bent her backward over his arm and closed his lips over her nipple, flicking the taut crest with his tongue, sucking it deep into his mouth.

A mew erupted from her mouth, and her nails dug into his chest as she tried to communicate her craving. He merely switched to her other nipple and offered it the same erotic treatment. Her body undulated against his, but it only served to make her burn hotter.

The water trickling down her flesh made her shiver. His lips sipped at her skin, her collarbone, her throat, her jaw, her nose, her eyelids. His hands moved over her body much the same way hers slid across his rougher flesh ... a reassurance, a reverent worship.

"Chloe," his voice was a breathless whisper, and the look in his eyes was so hot and tender, it made her heart stop.

And then utter panic hit.

No. She could feel it, the last of her defenses beginning to crack and crumble. A sob caught in her throat. She couldn't do it. She couldn't *need* him. Not like that. Not permanently. She refused. She would never, ever need anyone like that again. Not so much that losing them would shatter her.

Jerking back, she tried to rip herself from his embrace. Her hormones screamed a protest, but her mind knew better. Stumbling back, she tangled in her wet clothes and slipped on the slick tub. She would have fallen if Merek hadn't grabbed her, spun her so her front was plastered against the tile wall.

He pinned her there, his heavy weight keeping her upright. "Too late to run now, sweetheart."

She hated that he might be right. Gods help her, but he felt good, amazing, perfect. His hand drew back and smacked against the fleshy part of her upper thigh, and she jolted, all her tight, twisting emotions snapping. His hard body made hers melt, made her thoughts dissolve and swirl down the drain with the water. There was only Merek, only this moment. The future didn't matter; the past was nothing. The present was everything. The present was—"Merek."

"Chloe." He kissed the nape of her neck, nipped at it.

Her heart hammered in her chest, blood pumping through her hot and fast. Flattening her palms to the shower wall, she sighed at the mix of incredible sensations. The thick steam in the air, the hot water, his slick skin sliding against hers. His hard muscles pressed to her back, and she arched her ass to rub herself against the heavy arc of his cock.

It was too much, and not enough. She wanted more, and knew she couldn't have it, couldn't even ask for it. How could she defend herself against *herself*? Those unruly, incendiary emotions she didn't want wrenched at her insides.

Wrapping his arms around her, he filled his hands with her breasts. She moaned when he tweaked her nipples. He circled them with the callused tips of his fingers until they were so stiff she thought she'd scream. When he pinched them hard and rolled them between his fingers, she had to bite her lip to keep from doing just that. So good. It was so perfect. He knew just how to touch her, just how to play her to make her give him anything and everything he wanted. Moisture burned her eyes while lust and craving clawed at her like wild things.

One of his hands moved to follow the slide of water droplets down her belly until he toyed with the soaking curls between her thighs. She let her head fall back against his shoulder, closing her eyes to savor the streaking ecstasy. If tears mingled with the water on her face, she hoped he didn't notice.

Those wicked fingers dipped in to stroke her clit, and her hands slithered down the slick wall until she could latch onto his forearm, pressing him deeper into her sex.

"More," she pleaded. "Please, more."

Two big fingers pushed into her pussy, and her muscles squeezed around him. His groan vibrated against her back. "So hot and tight for me, sweetheart. So creamy I can't wait to get inside you."

"Don't wait." Her head rolled on his broad shoulder, and she squirmed when his cock slipped between the globes of her ass.

He hummed in his throat and began pumping his long digits into her, adding another and another until she was stretched to the limit. Her wetness increased each time he filled her, the slide so exquisite she thought she'd die. She gasped for air, the thick steam making it that much harder to breathe.

"Inside me." Another tear glided down her cheek. "Now. Please, now."

"Soon." He kissed the side of her throat, suckled the sensitive spot that connected her neck and shoulder.

It excited her more that she knew he'd fuck her when he was damn good and ready, no matter how she begged or teased. It was why she liked pushing his control, even as she utterly relied on that same quality.

The shower pounded down on them, the hot water nothing compared to the heat they generated. It sealed them together, made their skin slip and slide in an erotic dance that sent her pulse tripping. His hips bucked until the head of his cock nudged his plunging fingers, just barely stroked the lips of her pussy. Her nails dug into his arms, desperation beating through her.

He froze behind her, all movement jerking to a stop, and his breath erupted in a painful hiss. "Arm."

"Oh. Gods." Her fingers relaxed, and she jerked her hand away, regret washing through her. She turned her head to kiss his shoulder, her hands petting his skin in apology. "I'm so sorry."

A rusty chuckle answered her. "Yes. Kiss me, lick me, touch me. Show me how sorry you are."

Reaching around to grab the outsides of his muscular thighs, she grinned a little. "I'd be happy to kiss, lick, touch . . . or suck any part of you. Because I'm really, really sorry, of course."

"Of course." He bit the side of her neck just hard enough to make her jolt. Her insides clenched, and she whimpered when he withdrew his fingers from her greedy sex. "Later, I'm going to let you suck me hard, but right now I need inside your sweet little pussy so bad I'm dying."

His fingers pulled her slick lips wide, held her open so his cock could spear into her pussy. One of her hands reached back to sink into his wet hair, and she twisted her torso enough that she could draw him down for a kiss. A shudder racked her body as his fingers toyed with her clit, tugged at her plumped pussy lips to emphasize just how wide he stretched her. He was big and hot and hard, and she screamed into his mouth when he pinched her clit.

It was perfect. Her throat closed on the need to cry, and she tightened her fingers in his hair as she ravaged his mouth, wanting him as close as he could be. Closer, after the terror of this evening, she needed all of him. He buried himself deep inside her, and it didn't feel like enough to satisfy her craving for him. Nothing ever could, and she sobbed against his lips.

He released her mouth. "Shh. Shh. It's all right, sweetheart. We're all right. I'm here. You're not alone."

Something so huge and beautiful it scared her to even acknowledge it expanded in her chest until she couldn't breathe, could only hold on to him and hope it would never end, that it would always be this good, this sweet, this intense. Those weak, damnable tears continued to escape, and she couldn't stop shuddering as the jumbled emotions collided with the inexorable, rising tide of ecstasy.

"Merek," she gasped, clamping her inner muscles on his cock.

He groaned; his hips rammed deep, slapping against her ass, driving her into the slippery tiles. "Chloe. My Chloe."

Fiery tingles broke down her limbs, and she felt orgasm building deep inside her. Moans spilled from her throat every time he entered her. He rubbed her clit in time with his thrusts, hard and fast, the movements designed to shove her past her endurance.

He changed the angle of his penetration, and it was so right it sent her spinning. The breath froze in her lungs as her muscles gathered into one enormous pulse of pleasure. Her channel locked tight on his cock, and his hoarse groan and deep shudder told her she'd dragged him over the edge with her. Her fingers bunched in the wetness of his hair, holding him close as her pussy throbbed around him in waves so powerful she sobbed again. His hot come flooded her, and he rolled his hips, thrusting still deeper into her slick sex. She sagged against him, shutting her eyes as the physical and emotional storm swept through her, changed everything in its path, and left her drifting in its wake.

He stood there with her until the water turned chilly, his big hands stroking over her skin, cupping her breasts, her hips, the curve of her belly. Somehow he knew she needed the closeness as much as she'd needed the sexual release he could give her. Maybe he needed it too, because he didn't stop touching her even after his cock softened and slid from her body. He planted light kisses everywhere he could reach. He crooned to her, a soft wordless rumble of soothing comfort and assurance.

She stirred when the water turned off, felt like she was floating as he lifted her into his arms. "How long do we have until we have to catch our flight?"

Setting her on the counter, he ignored her gasp as the cold tile touched her bare backside. The sharp contrast with her hot, over-sensitized flesh made her shudder. He grabbed a towel and dried her, his touch gentle. "A couple of hours, maybe."

"Okay." She took the terry cloth from him and worked on her hair. "How did they find us today? Was it the blood tracking?"

He pulled another towel from the stack and swiped at the moisture on his skin. "No, they put out a reward for us in the Magickal community, and the elf who ran the campgrounds turned us in."

"Asshole." Her jaw clenched so tight the muscles twitched,

her teeth grinding together as she fought the desire to hunt the bastard down and hurt him. Bad.

Merek looked away, shrugged. "He's dead. They killed him."

That gave her pause, and she managed to wrench open her locked jaw to growl, "I wouldn't have wished him dead, but considering the danger he put us in and what happened to Alex, I can't say I'm sorry."

"I kicked him when he was down." He wiped the towel over his face and then scrubbed at his hair.

She blinked at him. "Seriously?"

"I needed a distraction." His tone was defensive, but the look on his face was completely unrepentant.

Again, she just blinked. "I'm not sure if I should laugh or be horrified."

He wrapped the towel around his waist. "A little of both probably isn't out of line."

"All righty, then." A grin broke across her face as she hopped off the counter to pick up her discarded shirt. Then she remembered that her yoga pants hadn't fared so well. "Um . . . you're going to need to go get me some clothes from my room. I can dry these magically, but not that fast. Not after all I've burned through tonight."

"Okay." He dropped a kiss on her mouth, came back for another quick taste, and then pulled away with a rueful smile and a shake of his head. "Be back in a minute."

"Thanks."

The last thing Merek wanted was to go rooting around in Chloe's bespelled bottomless suitcase looking for clothes. He'd rather keep her naked, wrapped in his arms, while he got the only few hours of sleep he was likely to get for some time. His eyes burned with fatigue, and he shut his mind off from the fact that she'd tried to pull away from him in the shower.

Why it pissed him off so badly that she would want to put

any distance between them, he didn't want to contemplate. He was too fucking tired to contemplate anything right now. He just wanted a bed and Chloe to share it with him. Shucking his towel and leaving it wherever it happened to fall, he jerked on a pair of sweats and a shirt from his duffle.

"Damn it, Ophelia, I don't want to hurt you. Get out of the way."

A deep snarl that he wasn't sure was from Alex or the cat sounded clearly through the door joining the two rooms. Merek eased it open to see a fully dressed and alert Alex facing down a pissed off cat who stood, back arched and hair on end, directly in front of the exit.

Bloody scratches were already healing themselves on Alex's hands and arms, so he'd been tangling with the familiar for at least a few minutes, if not longer.

"Going somewhere?" Merek kept his voice mild, his arms crossed over his chest.

The teen inhaled sharply, surprise flaring in his pale eyes as he whipped around. Then his jaw flexed, and he pulled his backpack over his shoulders. "Yes."

Merek shook his head. "You can't do that."

"What the hell do you care?" Frustrated rage flashed across the teen's normally impassive face. "This way you can keep Chloe safe. I'm a liability."

Merek pushed away from the doorjamb and crossed to plant himself directly in front of the wolf. "We all have things about us that make us liabilities. We learn to work with our limitations."

Shaking his head hard, Alex sent a fulminating glare toward Ophelia. "I won't be responsible for another—"

"It wasn't your fault your mother died, any more than it would be your fault if Smith's men killed Chloe." No, that was a responsibility that would fall squarely on Merek's shoulders if he failed to keep her safe.

"If you guys had spent a few more minutes in the shower, I'd have been history." A huff of breath that sounded close to a sob emerged. "Damn cat."

He closed his hand tightly over Alex's shoulder. "You can't do that to Chloe. She would never forgive herself. Ever." Merek knew enough about her now to know how true that was. "She'd tear off and go searching for you herself, and Smith's men would catch up to her in under a day."

Alex shut his eyes, but not before a sheen of moisture showed. "I can't stay."

"Can you honestly do that to her? Just walk away and never look back?" For a moment, the young man's future wavered before Merek's eyes, superimposing over the boy before him. A tall man, smiling down at a woman holding a wolf cub in her arms. Then another flash of the same man, sitting alone in a darkened room, bitterness poisoning his expression. Different possibilities? Different events in the same time line? The images disintegrated before Merek could tell.

Those green eyes locked on his face. "Can *you*? Isn't that what you're going to do if Luca ever closes the case and we get out of this?"

"I'm not the kind of guy who's into hit it and quit it with his women. That's not my style. I don't play those kinds of games." But that wasn't the whole story. He'd gone into each of his relationships since his wife's death knowing when it would end and how. His heart had never been involved, and though he'd cared for the women, he'd known there would be no deeper demand on his time or emotions than he'd already foreseen.

With Chloe, everything was different.

Merek sighed and dropped his hand from the kid's shoulder. What the hell did you say to a kid who'd been dragged away from his life, had a bullet dug out of him, didn't trust men for shit because his dad was an asshole, and said asshole dad had disappeared without a backward glance? Merek had no fucking clue. He didn't even think there *was* a right thing to say. "Look, I know your dad bailed on you in every possible way after your mom died, but—"

Alex cut him off with a snort.

"*But* if I was really looking to dick someone around or to score an easy lay, this isn't how I'd do it."

"Yeah, I guess not." Alex shoved a hand through his dark hair and looked away.

Merek sighed and waited for those green eyes to meet his again, too damn exhausted to care if he put his foot in this one. "I get why you don't want to trust me, but I'm not your father. I'm in this until the end. I'm not going to bail on you when the brown stuff splatters. I haven't yet, and I won't."

"It's not just *you* or my dad or anyone else, it's . . . shit." The wolf sniffed and scrubbed at his bloodshot eyes, grief and guilt ripping through the façade of indifference. "I was completely useless back there. I couldn't help either of you, even if I hadn't been shot. Not against a full-grown vampire or Fae or . . . hell, not even against another wolf." His hands lifted, flexed until the muscles in his forearms stood out. "Some of it is instinct, you know? Just being a wolf. But I *know* computers, electronics. Aside from the instincts, I don't know shit about guns or spells or fighting."

"I can teach you to defend yourself. Even against spells, even though you can't cast them like I can." He gestured to the door. "If *you* don't bail on *us,* that is. I can help you hone those wolf instincts even more."

Wariness and old pain flashed in the boy's eyes, but it wrestled with the desire to believe. "Why would you do that?"

Nothing but sheer honesty was going to keep this from turning into a total clusterfuck that Chloe would never forgive him for, so Merek laid it out there. "Because I can. Because I'll take any edge I can with protecting your godmother. Because I like you, and you need to know how to save yourself when the time comes. And, yeah, you might have been someone who was just along for the ride because I wanted to keep an eye on Chloe and she wasn't going anywhere without you, but you're a good person. There aren't a lot of those in the world."

"Don't I know it." Alex rubbed his side where the bullet had struck, his ancient, weary eyes meeting Merek's. They searched his face for a long time, looking for gods knew what, but Merek met his gaze without flinching.

Finally, his face guarded by his usual inscrutable mask, Alex nodded. "I'll stay."

10
─────────

Merek kept them hopping from one plane to another for three days straight, bouncing from one coast to the other, sleeping in airport hotels, only to drag them out of bed to do it all over again. The pace he set for them was grueling, but he had to make sure Gregor wasn't behind them. Or any of Smith's other operatives. Merek wanted to be as sure as he could that they could drop off the map again, so he pushed them all to the breaking point. Neither Chloe nor Alex said a word of complaint, but their expressions took on a perpetual look of bleak exhaustion. When Merek glanced in the mirror, he saw the haggard strain on his own face.

Even Ophelia went where she was told, which was a first. They'd had to abandon the cat carrier the day they left Seattle because she just wasn't having it. He'd even put some hexes on the thing to try to keep her temporarily contained, but Millie was right—the cat was a little Houdini. The spells he'd used had worked at locking down hardened Magickal criminals, but not Chloe's familiar.

Traveling with an animal on an airplane would have been a

dead giveaway, but the cat had sniffed at him and gone transparent as soon as he'd voiced the thought. Not even a ripple in the air around her showed where she passed. The damn familiar was better at invisibility spells than he was. He couldn't even sense her with his magic, nor could Alex sniff her out. How she got through or around airport security and stayed clear of the thousands of feet ready to step on her, he never knew. He didn't want to know how she managed without a litter box.

He kept a sharp eye on Alex to make sure the boy didn't try to give them the slip during their travels, but he spent most of their flights unconscious. Part of his exhaustion might be the lingering effects of the silver penetrating his system. Merek suspected Ophelia literally sat on the kid to make sure he stayed where she wanted him, but couldn't be certain.

Chloe staggered a little as they left the airport in Phoenix and the wave of desert heat slapped them in the faces. Both Merek and Alex reached out hands to steady her, and she managed a ghost of a smile for them. "Where to next?"

"Not far. An apartment building across town." He steered her toward the shuttle to the rental car lot, Alex falling into step behind them.

"You mean, we're staying here for longer than a layover? We can sleep in a bed for eight whole hours?" The look she gave him was so hopeful he had to grin. That her hazel eyes were bloodshot and bleary made him want to pull her into his arms, but he nudged her along and kept an eye out for anything or anyone out of place.

They made it to the rental office and drove to the apartment without incident. Chloe made him stop at a pizza parlor for takeout on the way, and he could hear Alex's stomach growling from the backseat.

Merek made them wait while he checked the place out, searched the furnished apartment for anything off, swept it with his magic to see if there were lingering vibrations from another Magickal. Nothing. When he loosed the reins on his precognition, the past of the building swept to him with stunning clarity. He saw them breaking ground on the site before it went up, and time swept forward until long after they'd left the place. The space of days they would be there was a gaping maw in his visions, but the time directly after showed no evidence of violence. No blood spatter, no bullet holes riddling the walls. Nothing.

He motioned Alex and Chloe forward, watched them trundle in, dump the pizza off in the kitchen, and separate into bedrooms to drop their stuff. Chloe paused to turn on every lamp and hit every light switch along the way. He'd seen them do the same thing many times before, and the normalcy of it felt good. He was swinging the door shut when Ophelia's yowl made him pause. He didn't bother looking around for her, just waited for her skinny body to begin stropping his ankles while she dropped her invisibility spell. Snapping the door shut, he secured the lock and set warding spells on the apartment. Then he stooped down to pick the familiar up and carry her into the kitchen to wait for Alex and Chloe.

They'd be under five minutes unloading everything, and he knew Chloe was currently managing to hog every inch of counter space in the bathroom. A smile twitched across his lips before it faded, and his gut twisted as something besides the need to outpace Gregor seeped into his consciousness. He was starting to like them too much, know them too well. The problem with forced proximity was it also forced intimacy. He hadn't let anyone this close for this long since . . . since his family. Since his wife. He sighed and rubbed a hand over the back of his neck. Fuck.

No, the problem wasn't that he was stuck with them now that he'd agreed to keep them safe. The problem was he *liked* it. He liked *them,* liked knowing their routines. He liked being around Alex, who hated not having his gadgets, but had managed to find books on nanotechnology in airport stores.

Merek sensed a basic similarity between himself and the kid. They were both too watchful, too serious, too alone. And that was where Chloe came in, a mouthy, acerbic counterbalance to them both. Despite all her own baggage, she managed to remain optimistic that obstacles could be overcome. She was smart, brave, and when the chips were down, she fought. She survived. He admired that in anyone, let alone someone with a traumatized childhood. He just liked her.

Under other circumstances, he might have been able to convince himself it was just her body, just the chemistry they generated between the sheets, but the stolen moments they snatched for sex were buried under the time they spent just being together. He liked watching her tease Alex into laughing, liked flopping down in front of a television in whatever random hotel they happened to be in to watch some cheesy program, only to spend most of the time cracking up because not one of them could keep their sarcastic comments to themselves.

They were in danger; they were on the run. . . . At this point, they could all be wanted fugitives, and he wouldn't know. Nothing about it should have been comfortable. He was ready to fall over from exhaustion and strain, but he couldn't think of anywhere in the world he'd rather be than right here, or any other people he'd rather be with.

"This pizza is going to be cold before we eat it if you two don't get a move on." He shook his head to clear his wayward thoughts, and jumped when Ophelia dug her claws into his leg. He detached her from his flesh with a grunt, and petted her until she sighed and purred.

"Coming!" Chloe called, and the way her voice echoed told him he was right and she was spreading her things out in the bathroom. His lips tugged in a reluctant grin.

Alex dragged in from his room, propping himself against the counter across from Merek. Cocking his head, he listened for something Merek couldn't hear. His eyes squinted into an almost-smile. "We could just eat without her."

At that second, Chloe appeared in her doorway. "Thanks a lot, brat."

Alex just snorted a little laugh, grabbed the stack of paper plates from the pizza place, and divvied them up. Ophelia gave an imperious mew, and Alex obediently went to retrieve a can of food from Chloe's suitcase. No doubt about it, the cat had them well trained.

A giggle drew Merek's attention to Chloe, who was shaking her head at her familiar. Her gaze met his, and they both grinned, then chuckled, then laughed until they were holding their sides. Alex came back, popped the top off the can, and set it in front of the cat. "What'd I miss?"

Chloe waved a hand helplessly in the air, and Merek had to grab it to keep her upright. "N-Nothing. It's not even really that funny."

A fresh spate of laughter rolled out of him, and he grabbed a napkin to wipe his eyes. "No, it's just tension relief, and the fact that the cat has us at her beck and call."

The strangest look entered Alex's eyes as his gaze went from the familiar, back to the bedroom door, and then down to stare at his hand as if it belonged to someone else. "Man, if the pack could see me now, a wolf playing fetch for a cat."

And that just set them all off again.

"Oh, gods." Chloe leaned weakly against Merek's side, and he let himself enjoy the feel of her. "Okay, really. We need to eat and get some sleep. We are way too giddy."

"Even cold pizza and lukewarm lettuce sounds good to me right now." Alex flipped open the first of four cardboard boxes, and handed Chloe the plastic container with the salad she'd in-sisted they get.

She forked a portion of greens onto everyone's plate while the wolf served up gooey slices of combination pizza. Merek's stomach rumbled like he hadn't eaten in a month, but this was the first meal they'd had without tension humming through their muscles in days. They didn't even bother sitting at the table, they just fell on their food like ravenous animals, and not even Chloe bothered to try to spark up a conversation.

When they'd cleaned their plates, and both Merek and Alex had gone back for thirds, the kid sighed with deep satisfaction.

"Exactly," Merek said.

Chloe snorted and heaved herself away from his side. "All right, let's tidy up and hit the sack."

Any other day, that would have been the most exciting thing she could say to him, but the exhaustion weighed down on his very bones now that his hunger had been satiated. Pushing to his feet, he grabbed the empty pizza and salad containers, while Chloe stuck the leftover slices in the fridge and Alex gathered the dirty plates and Ophelia's empty can of cat food. Then he went rummaging through the cabinets with Chloe to try to find a garbage bag. The apartment was furnished, but besides that, supplies were limited.

A deep sigh echoed from the cabinet Chloe had her head in. "Looks like cold pizza for breakfast, and then we need a grocery store."

Alex hummed an agreement. "Yeah, less fast food would be nice for a while. I'm getting sick of it."

Eyebrows arching, Merek blinked at the wolf for a moment. "That's got to be the first time in history a teenage boy has said that. You're a mutant, kid."

"Gee, thanks." Alex actually grinned at him.

Ignoring them both, Chloe continued rifling through the contents of the kitchen until she found what she was looking for. "Thank the gods there's coffee here. Instant coffee, so it'll taste like tar mixed with drain cleaner, but it'll be caffeinated, so I don't care."

"What a trooper." Alex gave her a one-armed hug, and she ruffled his hair, making Merek smile. Nice kid. He hoped the boy grew up to be a better man than his father. Narrowing his eyes, he focused on Alex. And saw nothing. He bit back a curse, his muscles going rigid. It wasn't the static-fuzzed picture he usually saw when he looked at the wolf, but a huge blankness.

What the hell did that mean?

Only that the kid would be important to him. He sighed. The kid was already important to him. So was Chloe.

As always, frustration clawed at him that his gift denied him the ability to protect those who mattered the most to him. The future was his to shape and command unless it really counted. Powerful and powerless at the same time. He fucking hated it. It was his job, his *duty*, to protect people using every weapon at his disposal. Bitterly ironic that what usually made him so valuable in just these situations was completely beyond his recall or control. He shoved a hand through his hair and turned away, moving to double-check the doors and windows as well as his magical shields.

Plastic rustled while Alex and Chloe stuffed the garbage in a bag, and then there was a long pause during which he could sense Alex speaking telepathically to Chloe. Then his voice filled Merek's mind. *I'm headed for bed. Need anything before I go?*

"No, thanks. Sleep well."

A chuckle rippled through his thoughts. *No worries on that one.*

Merek glanced back at Chloe, seeing only the woman and nothing of her future or past. He didn't even have to try to harness his abilities with her. His muscles wound tighter as he faced her. "You should go, too."

"Not just yet." She leaned back against the counter, folded her arms, and met his eyes with her sharp hazel ones. "Why do you do that?"

"What?"

"Every now and then you stare at me, tense up, and get this awful *look* in your eyes." Her eyebrows lifted. "Are you seeing something bad in my future? If so, I'd like to know. I can take it."

"No. I still can't see your future." His hands flexed at his sides. "I just realized I can't see Alex's either."

She nodded, but her gaze didn't waver. "Could you ever?"

"Yeah, although . . . it was fuzzy. Like a television screen on the blink. Sometimes the picture was clear; sometimes there was nothing but static." He forked his fingers through his hair, hating the truth. There was a lot of shit he could handle, but this was one thing he'd never be able to accept. "It's like that with my partner Selina, too, but not with Alex anymore."

"So now you can't see him either." She shifted, settling more comfortably against the countertop.

"No," he growled. "Not at all. It's just blank."

"Why?" He could almost see the scientist's wheels spinning, running experimental scenarios in her head. The woman had to test everything. Him, his control, herself, her abilities, the world around her. "You're this amazing clairvoyant, even Luca sounded in awe of your skills, so why are some people blank and some not? What makes your sight go on the fritz like that?"

"It's complicated." He swallowed and let his chin drop to his chest. "The last person I couldn't see anything with was my wife. Before her, my best friend growing up. Before him, my parents."

"So, people who are important to you in some way." Her eyes narrowed, her head tilting as she considered. "Or people who *become* important."

"Yeah. The one and only vision I ever had of my wife was the first time I touched her. I shook her hand to introduce myself and got this flash of our wedding, where it would be, how she would look, how I would feel. Just this one single moment that burned into my brain." One he'd done everything in his power to make come true. Good thing she'd been a scattered artist with no desire to ever *plan* anything, because most women he'd ever heard of would have balked at his controlling every aspect of their wedding. He'd just known he had to have that moment, that vision, that feeling.

Now, it felt like a different person had been married to her, loved her. He wasn't that man anymore, young and with just enough cocky idealism left to think he could save the world. He suppressed a snort. He didn't even want to be that man anymore. Turning away from Chloe, he stared blindly at an ugly watercolor print hanging on the wall.

"Something bad happened to her, didn't it?" Her voice was soft, undemanding. He didn't have to answer her if he didn't want to. He sensed she wouldn't press the issue. So, why would he tell her anything? He hadn't spoken to anyone about this since ... ever. Maybe it was the exhaustion that made him answer, maybe it was some heretofore unrevealed need to connect, maybe it was just Chloe and what she did to him.

"Yeah. Something bad." Him. *He* had happened to his wife. If he'd walked away that first day, if he'd never shaken her hand, she might be alive and well today. The thought was a punch to the stomach, even to this day. "It's worse than that."

"Worse than something bad happening?"

"I can't—I can't even remember her face anymore." Guilt dragged vicious claws down his flesh. She'd died because she was his wife, and a decade later he couldn't even recall what she had looked like. Ten years was nothing in a Magickal's five centuries-long life. If they survived to a natural death. His wife hadn't gotten that chance.

"What?" Chloe's arms looped around his waist, and her body warmed his back as she rested her cheek between his shoulder blades.

He swallowed. "My wife. I can't remember her face. If I focus on most people, I can see every detail of their lives, from the day they were born to the day they'll die. All the possibilities. I can see them as clearly as if I were standing there with them." He closed his eyes. "It's not like that with the people who'll have the biggest impact on my life. And her face has faded from my mind until I have to concentrate to remember it. Even then, it's blurry, like one of those grainy old photographs."

Her lips brushed over his back. "I'm sorry."

Just that. He could feel her sympathy radiating from her, seeping into his skin, but she didn't coddle or fuss, didn't demand to know more, didn't ask questions. She just held him the way he'd never let anyone hold him since his family died. Not for comfort or solace or need. He kept the world at arm's length, and he liked it that way.

He'd had sex since his wife's death; he'd even had a relationship or two, but he'd always ended things before it got too deep. He'd always been able to foresee that it wouldn't go too deep. A humorless smile curved his lips that the one woman who appealed to him most was the only one who tried to run when things got intense. Not that she could push him away even if she wanted to in their current situation, but she didn't demand more than he was willing to give.

The problem was she didn't have to demand it, did she? He'd already given up his entire life for her, given everything for her. Cold clutched at his belly, twisting inside him, but he couldn't deny the thought. He was always honest with himself about who he was and what he wanted. He made no excuses to himself or anyone else about what he was. Most of the time, he was a cynical bastard, the product of his life and circumstances.

But with Chloe, he dared to hope . . . for far too many things, most of which he didn't even want to acknowledge.

"What was her name?" Chloe linked her fingers together on his chest, dragging his attention back to a story he didn't want to tell.

"Laura." He sighed. Everything tangled up inside him. The past, the present, the future. Things that he saw so clearly for other people, but not with himself.

Her fingers moved in reassuring circles on his chest. "That's a nice name."

"She was a nice girl." True, and not even close to the whole picture of who she'd been.

"Can you tell me what happened to her?"

He didn't want to. Gods, but he didn't. Not when the ugliness of it was etched into his mind, the memories that he couldn't forget. But since Chloe had had the guts to tell him her worst nightmare, he couldn't deny her the same. "She died."

Chloe just waited, her arms secure around his waist. It was easier not looking her in the eyes, not having to see the expression on her face when he told her the truth. "We lived in Chicago—I grew up there. I was a new detective assigned to their MTF Violent Crimes Unit. It was one of my first cases." One he hadn't had the experience to handle, though he hadn't realized it at the time. He cleared his throat, pushed out the words that would revolt the average person. "A real bitch, too. A serial killer was targeting Magickal women, sexually assaulting them with wands, and then stabbing them to death with knives from their own kitchens."

"Wands?" She stirred against his back, her arms tightening.

He could hear the surprise in her voice. Only little kids first learning magic used wands as a focusing tool. An adult Magickal would never need one, and wouldn't want to be that indiscreet anyway. "Yeah. Wands."

"That's sick."

"Yeah." But he'd seen worse since then, much worse. At the time, it had horrified him, added another callus to his already scarred soul. "We arrested a guy who met the profile, had no alibis, and knew way too much about the crime scenes to be uninvolved."

"And the wands?" Her fingers balled in his T-shirt, but she didn't recoil. He had a feeling the stubborn witch was going to stand there for as long as he wanted to keep talking, no matter how bad it got.

A brief smile touched his lips, and he covered her small, warm hands with his. "He was on a kind of antidepressant that caused impotence. All the pieces fit. We thought we had our guy."

"You didn't." The words came out a whisper, and a tiny shiver went through her.

"No." He snorted. In retrospect, he should have seen it, should have understood the case would get personal when he couldn't get a clear precog read on anything. "Instead, we just pissed the real killer off by giving credit to someone else."

She didn't ask how this related to his wife, but he could feel her going rigid behind him, knew she'd already guessed what had happened to Laura. Bile burned the back of his throat, threatening to choke him. Cold spread through him, freezing around his heart. Gods, he didn't know if he could say it. Didn't know if he could force out the words he'd never said to anyone. So he told her about his wife, instead of what had ended her life. That much, at least, he could manage.

"Laura, she was a Fae artist, you know? She had that stereotypical flakiness. Hell, she owned it, played it up. Frustrated the hell out of me, sometimes, but that was just her." A sigh eased out of him. They'd been so young, so damn sure of themselves. "She forgot to set the warding spells on the house. Wasn't the first time." And he'd given her hell about it every time, but Laura was Laura was Laura. She'd apologized, promised to remember, and then a week or two would go by and he'd come home to an unprotected house.

He was silent so long, lost in his own thoughts, that he jerked when Chloe spoke. "Who did it if it wasn't the guy you arrested?"

"His twin sister. That was how he'd known about the crime scenes. She told him."

"A woman did that? To other women?" Her palms flattened against his stomach, and he could feel the deep breath she dragged into her lungs. He heard the trained medical professional in her voice next. "That's a fairly rare psychopathic trait to find in women."

He nodded even though he doubted she could see it. "They were both abused as kids by their father. Seriously abused. Sexually. With wands, among other things."

"Oh, gods." Horrified woman washed the doctor away, and she wedged herself even closer to his back.

"I came home and...found Laura like that." His belly heaved as the memories he'd have given anything to burn from his mind assaulted him in vivid, gruesome succession. The wand had still been inside her, a knife from a set her parents had given them for a wedding present protruding from her chest, her eyes blank, and her face waxen. He'd slipped in the ocean of blood around her, fallen in it before he'd reached her side. His mind had known she was gone, but he'd still radioed for an ambulance, praying someone could undo what had been done, that somehow the awful metallic stench of blood would be gone and she'd be there, smiling at him and telling him she'd burned dinner so it was Chinese takeout again. "We'd only been married five months, and it was over. I lost her."

"And you blamed yourself." The soft sob was almost his undoing, and he jerked away, every muscle in his body shaking. She came around him anyway, took his face in her hands. Like him, she wouldn't let him run away. She blinked back tears and searched his face. "You still do. Blame yourself. Your clairvoyance. For not seeing what was coming, for not saving her."

He choked on a breath, but met her eyes and told the truth. "Yes."

"It wasn't your fault." Her fingers stroked over his jaw, and he wanted to lean closer, wanted to rip himself away from the tenderness that was so absent from his life.

Words, the ugly, vicious truth, wrenched from his gut. "She died because of my case, because she was my wife, because *I couldn't see to save her.*"

"You can't save everyone, Merck." A wealth of sympathy, of understanding, filled her eyes. The knowledge of a woman who *could* have saved her mother if she'd possessed the skills she did now. "When it's time for someone to go, it's time."

"No. No, that's not always true." He couldn't allow himself so easy an excuse. Hadn't he wanted to? Hadn't he tried? But he'd been through this in his mind so many times, and then had forced himself to bury it deep inside and move on before he drove himself mad. "There are a lot of possibilities for when people's lives are over. That's what I see most of the time when I look into the future. The past is solid; the present is always in flux while people are making decisions, but the future is all possibilities. Roads people can take, choices people can make. If I had known what was coming, if I had made different choices, maybe it would have been a later possibility for their deaths."

Her inky brows lifted. "*Their* deaths?"

A harsh chortle crackled from his chest. "All those people I couldn't see? My parents, my best friend, my wife? They're dead. A murder, a car accident, a mugging gone wrong. *All* of them died. Horribly, unnecessarily."

And he'd never let anyone that close ever again. Until now, until he'd had no choice. Until the alternative had been worse than letting someone in.

"You're never going to know that for sure. You can't torture yourself for being human. You're not a god, no matter how powerful your abilities are." She slid her arms around him and pressed her nose to his chest, squeezed him tight. "You're not Superman, remember?"

He laughed, hot moisture stinging the backs of his eyes. He rubbed his hand over them until he knew he wouldn't embarrass the hell out of himself. "Yeah. I know."

Sliding out of his arms, she took his hand and tugged him into the bedroom. He followed without protest, too drained to deal with anything else. Some of the weight on his chest had shifted, the ice cracking, just from telling her the truth. He pulled in a deep breath, stood placid while she undressed them both and urged him into bed.

She settled against him, hooked her leg over his thigh, and sighed. "You know, you had that same look on your face the night I met you."

He grunted, pulled her closer. "What look?"

"That stony-faced, the-world-fucking-sucks-ass look." She kissed his chest. "The one you got when you watched Alex and me tonight. Same expression."

The night he'd met her came back with perfect clarity. When he thought about it, he usually focused on how it ended, not how it began. He blinked the grit from his eyes. "That about sums up that day, yeah."

"Why?" She leaned up a little, propped her chin on his chest to meet his gaze.

Trailing his fingers over her silky hip, he let himself be distracted for just a moment, let himself savor the feel of her. Then he dragged in a breath, smelled her sweetness. "You know how I said Selina's fate fuzzes in and out for me? Sometimes I see it and sometimes I don't?"

More understanding and empathy than he could ever deserve shone in her eyes, though she looked as tired as he felt. "What did you see about her? How bad was it?"

"I saw her death." His shoulder jerked in a shrug. Seeing death was just a part of his reality, as a clairvoyant and as a cop. It was tougher with people he knew, but there wasn't anything he could do about it. "It's going to be bloody and ugly and just as gruesome as—"

Laura's. He didn't say it out loud, but Chloe knew what he meant. It was a relief that someone knew; just the telling, the sharing had helped ease some of the oppressive weight of failure and guilt inside him.

He cleared his throat. "It'll happen soon, within the next year." He'd seen it that day, and had gone to a bar to rinse the bitterness of it away. Instead, Chloe had walked in before he'd finished his first beer.

"Did you tell her?" The bottom of her foot brushed up and down his calf.

Shaking his head, he gave a rueful smile. If Chloe knew more about his partner, she'd know the elf was always three steps ahead of everyone, even without extraordinary precognitive abilities. "I didn't need to. She knows."

"She does?" Chloe blinked.

"Some Magickals can sense it when the end is near." He brushed her hair away from her face, rubbing a shiny, blue-black lock between his fingers before tucking it behind her ear. "Selina is old, almost at the end of her natural life anyway."

Her chin dug into his chest when she shook her head. "The death you're talking about isn't the natural end of life."

"No." He let his breath ease out slowly. "No, it's not."

She drew patterns on his chest with the tip of her finger, and even as exhausted as he was, he felt his body stir. He almost groaned. There was no way he was doing anything about it right now. Later, definitely. She smiled at him as if she knew what he was thinking. "So, you're there and I walk in and you can't see my fate and you like your women like that?"

He snorted and arched his eyebrows in disbelief. "After my

wife? You think I wouldn't run like my ass was on fire from a woman whose future I couldn't see?"

Her nose wrinkled. "Yeah, good point."

Pulling her up until she was draped across his chest, he kissed her soft mouth. "You were irresistible. The last thing I wanted was to look at someone and see the end of them, know exactly how numbered their days were. Even if they were going to live as long as Selina, I didn't want to see it." He shifted her until she straddled his hips, slipping his erection into her hot sheath, wanting that connection. Her sigh was all pleasure, and she shut her eyes and relaxed bonelessly against him. His palms cupped her hips, and his tension unwound as well. "With you, sweetheart? I couldn't see anything. Not so much as a flash like I had with Laura. Nothing. I didn't even have to hold back my precognition. It got the night off for some R & R. So did I."

Her smile was smug, but her eyes remained closed. "Glad I could help take your mind off things."

Listening to her breathing even out, he knew the exact moment she slipped over into sleep. He could feel blissful unconsciousness coming to claim him as well, and he fought it off just long enough to check the magical shields on the apartment.

Chloe made a little sound in her sleep, and burrowed into him. He held her tight, needing her near more than he'd ever needed anything in his life. Shutting his eyes, he sighed. Even his last thought wasn't enough to keep exhaustion from dragging him under.

Losing her now just might kill him.

Hot moisture coated Merek's cock when his eyes flared open the next morning. Chloe's tongue worked along the underside of his dick as she sucked him hard. A harsh groan broke the silence in the room, and he laced his fingers in her silky hair, holding her in place. He barely remembered to throw a spell up to muffle the sounds in their room before he cried out. He felt the head of his dick hit the back of her throat.

"Gods. Yes. Chloe. Please. I . . ." The words were broken, barely coherent fragments of thought, his control spinning away as he arched off the mattress, needing to fuck that talented mouth.

She chuckled, and the vibrations against his shaft damn near made him come. His fingers clenched in her hair, and he gritted his teeth to hold off orgasm as long as possible. This was too good to end so soon.

He shuddered as she licked and tasted him, swirling her hot, wet tongue around the head of his cock. A hoarse sound of pleasure wrenched up from his chest. His body bowed in a tight arc, his hips jerking upward without any direction from his mind.

Gods, if she used any kind of magic on him—

The thought had no more than drifted to the front of his consciousness when he felt a slow sizzle slide down his flesh as she sucked him deep. He jackknifed on the mattress, caught her shoulders and had her on her back before she could do more than moan a protest.

"I was having fun."

"So was I," he growled. "A little too much fun."

He forced her thighs wide with his, and filled her with one quick jab. She gasped, arching underneath him. Her legs wound around his hips, and her hands rose to clutch at his shoulders. "Hurry, Merek."

Restraint had slipped through his fingers, and he didn't need any urging. He couldn't have slowed down if he'd had a gun pressed to his temple. He needed her, craved her. Now. Right now.

After the gut-wrenching emotions of the night before, the mindless ecstasy she offered him now was more than he could resist. She wanted it, he wanted it, and he wanted it with her. Only with her.

Her slim thighs wrapped tight around his waist. "Yes! Yes, yes, *yes*. Just like that. So good... right there. Oh, please. Merek!"

"Ah, gods." It was too much, listening to her litany of pleasure. His hips bucked, driving his cock into her sweet heat with brutal force. She was right there with him, dragging her nails down his back, sobbing for him to move faster, harder, deeper. And he gave her what they both needed. The feel of her sleek sheath gripping his cock was so damn good.

The bedsprings squeaked beneath them, and the headboard thudded against the wall. Slapping skin, harsh cries, low moans, gasping sobs. A carnal symphony of lust.

All of it turned him on even more. Everything about her did.

Seduction spells flowed back and forth between them, shoving them higher. His heart pounded in his ears, drowning out every other sound. There was only her, only this. Her mouth opened in a silent scream when he sent a pulse of his own lust dancing over her flesh. Golden light burnished her skin, made her a fiery goddess in his arms as an unholy gleam lit her eyes. She spread her fingers wide on his chest, and white-hot lightning arced from her to him, sizzling his nerves until he was on the edge of orgasm.

"Fuck, *yes*. Baby, that's just—" He didn't bother trying to gather enough wits to finish the sentence. Instead, he thrust deep, ground his hips against her clit. He knew now exactly which angle would make her—

"Merek!" Her hands seized his biceps in a frantic grip as she twisted beneath him. "Faster. Please. Yes. Merek. Please. Fuck me harder."

He couldn't stop a smug smile. There was no ecstasy as potent as a woman begging for more. When she gave him the same smug smile and deliberately fisted her pussy on his dick, he knew he wouldn't last much longer. He didn't even want to. "Now. Right now."

"Yes!" She arched underneath him, and heated spells from her gripped his cock each time he plunged into her slick channel. Desperation made his movements harsh, frantic. So close. He reached between them and thumbed her clit, tweaking it with a spell that made her gasp and explode in his arms.

Her pleasure hit him in a wave that dragged him under, and he let it, welcomed it.

When he came, the rush was more intense than anything he'd ever known. It burned him from the inside out, ripping at his very soul. For once, he didn't fight, didn't resist, didn't try to hold on to any kind of control. His body jerked, come jetting from him as her pussy contracted around his cock. She sobbed his name, and he worked her as long as possible, shoving his dick deep, wringing them both out.

"Chloe," he groaned. He sank down on her with the vague wish that he could stay inside her forever, that the pleasure he found with her would never end. He shuddered, buried his face in crook of her neck, and licked the salty sweetness of her flesh.

She sighed and shivered, trailing her fingertips in long, slow sweeps over his back. "Good morning, by the way."

Laughter burst out of his throat, and he wrapped his arms around her, rolling until she sprawled on top of him. The swift movement had her squealing and clutching at him, but the giggle that burst from her when she braced herself over him and flipped her hair out of her face so he could see the sparkle in her eyes made a tenderness he'd rarely experienced in his life squeeze his chest.

"Chloe, I—"

He'd never know what he might have said, because she swooped down and caught his mouth with her lush lips. It was slow and soft, her unique flavor on his tongue, her scent in his nose, her silken skin rubbing over his body. They were both breathing hard when she lifted her head, and she shot him a wicked grin. "Gods, I love the taste of you."

"Ah, sweetheart. You're good for me." He sat up and cradled her close, kissing her forehead.

Some of the light dimmed in her eyes, and her smile slipped a bit. She glanced away. "Yeah, I'm so good for you I'm going to get you shot one of these days."

"Hey, now." Frowning, he crooked a finger under her chin and forced her to look at him. "Where did that come from? What happened to you being the hopeful one?"

Shaking her head, she pressed her lips together. "I don't know. I'm just...worried." A faint smile creased her cheeks. "I'm always worried. About you and Alex...and me, of course."

He sighed, brushing her hair out of her eyes and away from her face. He wished he could spare her this, but he knew he couldn't, so he gave her honesty instead. "I'm not going to tell you not to worry, Chloe. I'll do my best to make sure that's all you have to deal with, but you already know my best may not be good enough."

The words burned as they came out, and he wished like hell he didn't have to say them, but he wouldn't lie to her, not ever. Not even to spare himself. Especially not then. He dropped his forehead to hers and pushed away the self-loathing he felt for having failed to protect them. Like he'd failed others before them. He'd done everything he could.

"No, I—" She shook her head, kissed him. "I *trust* you to help us. You have to know that. I trust you the way I could never trust anyone else, and it scares me even to tell you that, but it's true." Her fingers flexed against his shoulders, and she shrugged helplessly. "I just...I don't know what you get out of this. You could die—"

A laugh huffed out. "Honey, that's just the job. That's what I do."

"Yeah, I know you deal with it every day, but why leave your job for *this*?" She waved her hand around to encompass the room, the apartment, their whole situation. "Are Alex and I just the job? Is it because you couldn't see my future? I mean . . . I've wondered this from the beginning, but was too scared to ask in case you regained your sanity. After what happened in Oregon, I can't *not* ask. It's not just a vague *maybe*. It's a very real possibility. You could end up dead because of us. Why would you do that?"

He stroked his fingers up and down her spine, working his answer over in his mind. Some of it was obvious; some of it he didn't know the answers to himself. He hadn't when he started; he still didn't. He doubted that would satisfy his curious little scientist. Smiling, he kissed the tip of her nose. "Some of it is the job, I'll admit. I don't like to see innocent people get caught in the crossfire, and I do what I can to stop it. Also, I'd love to do anything I could to help nail Smith's ass to the wall. If chasing you trips him up and makes him do something stupid or draws him out in the open for Cavalli to catch, then that's fine by me."

"I never pictured myself as terrorist bait." She winced and shifted to try to get off his lap. "I'm glad you can—"

"I'm not done yet." He held her in place, tightening his arms around her. "It's not just the job. It's not just because I can't see your future. That's more likely to make me turn around and walk away." That wasn't strictly true, because before he'd met her, the number of people he couldn't see the future for could be counted on one hand, with fingers left over. He just couldn't imagine approaching such a person without all the caution reserved for live explosives. "I care about you and Alex. Not just because of the job, but because of *you*. Both of you. And admitting that scares the hell out of *me*. The inability to see with you means you'll be important to me, but it doesn't let me know how or why. Or for how long." He shrugged. "I made my own choices, and I'm here willingly. I would die for you."

"I know. I saw you risk your life to go get Alex." She closed her eyes. "I don't *want* you to die for me. Us." Her dark lashes swept up, and her gaze met his. She cupped his face between her palms. "I care about you, too. You can say it was your choice, but I would feel responsible forever if anything happened to you."

Catching her hand in his, he turned his head and kissed the center of her palm. "I know *exactly* what you mean, sweetheart."

She sighed. "I'm getting that memo. It just . . . sucks, you know?"

"No arguments here." He dropped a quick kiss on her full lips, then went back for another, slower, longer kiss. His cock stirred, and he groaned before he forced himself to pull away. He hated to worry her more, but he had to let her in on his agenda for the day. "I'm going to need to leave Alex and you alone for a few hours while I take care of something."

A frown drew her eyebrows together and her kiss-swollen mouth downward. She crossed her arms over her bare breasts. "Oh? What do you need to take care of?"

He couldn't resist it—he brushed his lips over the cleavage she presented. "I need to see someone about resupplying my ammunition cache. I can only carry so much with me at one time, and I blew through some in Oregon."

She shivered at the reminder, but didn't shy away from the discussion. "There has to be a sporting goods place that has what you need around here. Arizona's a red state, right? They have to have guns here."

His lips twitched. "It's not that simple, Doc."

"How come?"

"Think about it. Would a regular, Normal bullet work on, say, a werewolf?"

"No." She blinked. "Oh." Blinked again. "Well, shit."

He did grin, then. "There are limited places to buy the kind of ammo I need, and we need this to be off the record. We're trying to fly under the radar, remember?"

"Yeah. I recall," she retorted drily. He watched her brows draw together as she thought about it for a second. "You can't possibly have a separate kind of bullet for each Magickal species. You'd never know what kind of person you'd be shooting at next. What if you were ready for werewolves with silver bullets and got attacked by elves? Silver wouldn't be nearly as effective."

"Head of the class, Dr. Standish." His cock reacted as she idly stroked his skin while thinking. Since he didn't have time to indulge himself again before he had to get going, he forced himself to lift her off his lap.

"So . . . what do you use?" She settled against the headboard, tucking the sheet around her. "There's no known chemical, herb, metal, or alloy that effects *every* Magickal species."

Grabbing his duffle off the floor, he tossed it on the bed and pulled out clothes, his extra revolver, and his last clip of bullets for his regular weapon. He'd had to drop his other spare in Oregon, but two guns meant he could leave one with Chloe and still remain armed himself. It was enough. "We use bullets that are explosive, armor-piercing rounds that have fragments of *every* metal, alloy, chemical, etcetera, known to ward off Magickal species."

"Bronze for witches, silver for werewolves, iron for Fae and elves, and . . . what for vampires?" She waved a hand through the air. "They're only allergic to daylight—oh, you're using a sunbeam spell as part of the explosion in the explosive round."

"Yep." Ejecting a bullet from the magazine, he handed it to her. For most people, it wouldn't look any different from a regular bullet, but if Chloe tested the material inside with her magic, she'd sense something entirely different. "There's not enough to damage a Magickal like a pure round made from the one thing they're allergic to would, but it'll slow any Magickal down, regardless of species, and emptying a clip into someone will do the job."

Her eyes narrowed as she focused on the bullet, turning it this way and that in her hand. She glanced up at him for a brief moment. "I'm not going to ask if you know that from personal experience."

"Good, don't ask." He snagged the round from her hand, slid it back into the clip, and set the clip on the nightstand next to his weapon. He handed Chloe the revolver.

"Crap. You do know." She checked the safety on the gun as he had shown her, ignoring the incredulous brow he arched in her direction. "The bullet I pulled from Alex was pure silver."

"Yeah, that shot was just for him." He'd thought of this too, had come to only one conclusion. "I'm guessing they wanted to incapacitate him so he was easier to manage while they took care of us." It also meant they hadn't really cared if they killed the boy, as long as they delivered to Smith one of the two people who had the information he wanted.

She swallowed, balled her fingers in the sheet, and gave him a smile edged in desperation. "Right. So. You have to have very specialized ammunition. What are you going to do?"

He shrugged and gathered his pile of clothes. "An old friend of Selina's in the area will probably give me whatever he has lying around."

"So, no one they could connect you to." She laid the revolver beside her on the bed, drew her knees up, and rested her chin on them. "But stopping in Phoenix wasn't just a random choice."

"No, it wasn't." He bent to brush a kiss over her cheek, then turned for the bathroom. "But believe me, no one would connect me to this person."

Laughter tinged her voice. "That good, huh?"

"We met. Once." He glanced back. "It wasn't pleasant."

She took a breath, her face sobering. "How do you know he'll help you?"

"I don't." He was pretty sure. Mostly. The vision he had of events before him was hazy, but that he could see *anything* told him Alex and Chloe weren't directly involved with what he was going to do. In any case, if he was wrong, he didn't want them with him. "If everything goes according to plan, I'll pick up groceries on the way back. If I'm not back by nightfall—"

"You'll be back." Her face set in stubborn lines.

"Chloe." He made the word a warning, an admonishment.

She averted her face, refusing to look at him. "I know what to do, Merek. I will if I have to, but I won't have to. You'll be back."

Arguing with her wouldn't help, so he left it at that and got down to business. Chloe had a grocery list ready for him when he got out of the shower, and a solemn nod from Alex was all he got from the wolf before he was out the door with a slice of cold pizza in his hand.

Time to see the most obnoxious Normal the gods had ever cursed the earth with.

II

An hour later, Merek was circling the car around a block on the outskirts of Phoenix. The route he'd taken here had been as circuitous as he could make it, and he took his time checking out the address he was looking for.

The place was modest and unassuming. A tidy little house on a tidy little street. Nothing special or different about it except the very abnormal Normal man who lived inside.

Theodore Holmes.

The last living vampire hunter.

Or, the last one Merek had ever heard of, and only then because Selina had told him. Assuming the old bastard *was* still among the living, but he thought Selina would have mentioned his dying, if for no other reason than the man had hated Merek's guts on sight and it amused the hell out of her. That he got on Merek's last nerve amused her even more.

He parked the car several blocks away and walked back to the house. Stepping onto the porch, he kept his hands loose at his sides and in plain sight. If Holmes still lived here, he already knew Merek was there, and probably had a weapon or five trained on him.

Something wavered on the edge of his senses, an irritating scrape over his nerves. "I know you're there, Holmes."

"What the hell do you want?" The voice emerged from an intercom next to the door. It was gruff with age, but didn't betray a creak of weakness.

"Your help." Merek huffed out a laugh, glancing up into a video camera mounted to the porch roof. If anyone had told him a month ago he'd be here, he'd have told them to get their precognition retested.

Holmes's door swung open, his sharp blue eyes sweeping over Merek and the street behind him. As Merek had suspected, there was a compact pistol leveled on his chest. "Did Grayson send you?"

"What do you think?" Merek didn't so much as twitch, taking a long moment to look Holmes over as thoroughly as he'd been inspected. It was none of Holmes's concern that adrenaline hummed in Merek's veins, his heart leaping at seeing the business end of a weapon, a dozen defensive spells swirling into his mind, ready to disarm and dismantle the threat.

"I think you've stirred up a hornet's nest." Holmes lowered the weapon slightly. "There's nothing I can do to bail you out of that much trouble."

"Let's make this conversation more private." Merek nodded his head toward the shadowy interior of the house. He wasn't saying any more than he already had out in the open.

The old man grunted. "Fine."

Stepping back, Holmes allowed Merek to pass in front of him and shut the door behind them, reengaging whatever security systems were in place. That little pistol remained trained on Merek while they walked through the house to a small kitchen.

He sat at a scarred wooden table, scanning the room for the exits should he need to make a quick escape.

Everything in the place was functional, if shabby around the edges. A feminine touch showed in some of the decorations, and Merek wondered if Holmes had ever been married. Then he banished the thought. He didn't want to know about the man's personal life, and Holmes would probably shoot him just for wondering.

Merek's clairvoyance leaped at the hint of a question, and his time with Alex and Chloe had loosened his grip on his power, so a vision exploded through his mind. He saw a woman... years ago, when the furnishing had been new. A wife. Pretty, with a wry smile. Not a hunter, but she handed a rifle to Holmes and kissed him good-bye, so not ignorant of his profession. Sweat gathered along Merek's hairline, his hands fisting on the tabletop. His vision dragged him into the near future, two options stabbing themselves into his thoughts. A wiry teenage girl dancing around this kitchen before hugging the old man tight. She had Holmes's sharp blue eyes and the wife's wry grin. Something about her face was familiar, as if Merek had seen it before, but he couldn't put his finger on where. Merek shook his head, and the vision crashed into the second option. Selina's dead face blew past his eyes, the same scene he'd seen the day he'd met Chloe, but now the view expanded and he saw Holmes's broken body beside his partner's, a neat bullet hole between the old man's eyes.

"What do you want?" The question was just as rude and unwelcoming as the first time it was asked, and it jolted Merek back to the present.

Sucking in a deep breath, he got his usual tight-fisted grip on his precognition, and forced his hands to relax on the tabletop. "The first thing I need is Magickal ammo."

"What makes you think I'd have any?" Holmes's shoulder

jerked in a shrug as he laid the pistol down, still pointed squarely at Merek. "Illegal for unauthorized Normals to have that stuff—that's how you get a sweeper team to go through your house, remove your contraband, and mess with your memories."

One eyebrow arched at that utter bullshit. As if that kind of threat had ever intimidated a vampire hunter. "I need some Magickal ammo for a Glock and a .38 Special."

"Yeah, yeah, I heard you twice the first time." Holmes's chair scraped back when he stood. "It's down in the basement."

"I'll wait here while you get it." He'd also wait for the sweat to dry and his muscles to stop trembling in reaction to his intense vision.

The other man thumped across the room to the cellar door. "Watch him, Boleyn."

A German shepherd came into view from down a short hallway, its nails clicking against the linoleum floor. With its odd bicolored eyes—one blue and one brown—the dog looked suspiciously like a slimmer, female version of Selina's familiar. The thing snapped its jaws once before sitting down to stare at Merek as if he looked better than the canine's next meal. Just as Selina's familiar liked to do. Merek would bet Millie Standish's fortune this was a familiar from the same litter. He'd never heard of a familiar attaching itself to a Normal. Then again, this Normal wasn't very normal. He shrugged. Now wasn't the time to be curious about a retired vampire hunter. He had bigger worries, and he didn't want to invite any more clairvoyant episodes.

He didn't hear the Normal return, but he sensed that same irritating presence approach so he turned his head to watch Holmes come up the basement steps carrying a couple of boxes of ammunition. He dropped them on the table. "Now, you wanna tell me why you can't just get your own at work?"

A casual shrug and a mild tone from Merek would likely annoy the Normal, but he didn't really care. "I've taken an extended vacation."

Holmes grunted and resumed his seat. "Most vacations don't end up with two people dead—one of them roasted alive."

"He shot a teenage boy." A blood-soaked memory that would haunt Merek for the rest of his days. He had far too many of them.

The old man's eyes honed in on him, pinning Merek in place. "Vampire?"

Now it was his turn to grunt. "Werewolf."

"Mangy animals," Holmes grumbled, then shrugged. "But they don't like vampires any more than I do."

Merek didn't even want to get into an argument with the man about his hatred for vampires. Hate was an irrational thing, and he wanted to get out of here without a bullet hole in his own hide. A small smile tilted up the corner of his lips. "I torched one vampire's wings off, and a lady friend of mine ran another down with an SUV."

"Good woman." A rare smile crossed the man's face, wrinkles deepening around his eyes.

"One of the best." Merek ran a hand through his hair. "She's the reason I'm on vacation. And the werewolf boy."

"Vacation." The Normal gave a derisive snort.

"I know you keep your ear to the ground in the Magickal community. How bad is it?" Merek leveled a serious gaze on the vampire hunter. He wanted the perspective of someone besides Millie and her bodyguard. Holmes's take would be about as different as possible, and the human wouldn't spare Merek any ugly details.

"They want you for questioning about the killings of those people in Oregon. That old Standish witch is keeping things quiet in the Council, stopping an all-out manhunt, but some strange rumblings are going on in the werewolf packs. Don't know if it's related or not, but things look to come to a head soon." Holmes rolled his shoulders. "As for you . . . Most say you've gone rogue, and the Witch Coven is covering it up since you're one of theirs."

"What do you think?" Merek tapped his fingers against the table, chewing over what Holmes had said.

"Selina'd be after you herself if you'd gone rogue." He made an impatient gesture with an age-spotted hand. "Sounds a little too much like someone's looking for you and wants as many eyes doing the looking as possible. They had a reward out for information about your whereabouts, and now you're wanted for questioning. The Magickal you torched wasn't some innocent bystander. Got a record as long as my dick."

There was a mental image Merek would have to take bleach to. He reached out and pulled the boxes of bullets toward him, opening them to check the rounds and test them for viability. They were good. "There were a couple of other operatives there. One was Gregor—"

"Shit." Holmes sat back in his chair with a low whistle, the first real sign of surprise crossing his face. "You are in some trouble, boy."

Merek choked on a short laugh. "I'm aware."

A long moment of silence passed while both men contemplated the new information they had. Holmes's gaze met Merek's. "You better bury yourself deep. Stay away from the Magickal world. Go totally Normal."

"We're going to." It was the same conclusion Merek had reached. One he wouldn't be letting Millie know about when he checked in with her next. No more using her properties, just the cash she'd given them. Nothing related to Magickals in any way.

"Trailing around that werewolf boy is gonna trip you up once a month." The old man's face went blank. "They know to look for him, know he's a weakness. That'll be a problem."

Meaning he should cut his losses and ditch Alex. Merek's hand tightened around the boxes until the metal casings ground together. He eased his grip and unclenched his jaw. "Maybe, but he's my problem, and no one's going to touch him."

"You said he was shot."

He managed a growl. "My lady friend is a doctor. Kid pulled through just fine."

"Lucky."

"Very." He stood abruptly, more than ready to leave, and offered his hand to the other man. "Thanks for your help."

Holmes hesitated a beat before grasping his hand and shaking it. His grip was strong enough to belie his age. "Wasn't for you."

"I know. I'll thank Selina when I'm back from my vacation." Merek dropped the old man's hand, scooped up the supplies he'd come for, and moved to slip out the backdoor. "I'd appreciate if you let me surprise her about my visit."

"I'm not saying a damn thing, boy. Get the hell out of my house." Holmes used a keypad to disengage his security system and jerked open the door. "For your sake, I hope we don't meet again."

"From your lips to the gods' ears." Merek stepped out and didn't look back. "I had a vision of your future, Holmes. You have a choice coming up. Stay with a young girl or go to your death with Selina."

"I'm retired." Holmes's tone was hoarse.

Merek shrugged, still unwilling to turn around and see the look people got when he mentioned an unpleasant future. "Maybe an old case you were involved in with her cropped up. A dead end of some kind caught a new break."

Even as the words came from his mouth, he knew they were true.

Holmes sucked in an audible breath. "Who was the girl?"

Then he strangled on a tight laugh. "Never mind. There's only one person it could be. My granddaughter, Riley."

"That sounds right." Merek glanced back and sighed at the white-lipped expression on the old man's face. "The girl means more to you than any case, so do yourself a favor. Choose the living. Let the past die."

Hadn't he done the same when he'd gone with Chloe and Alex instead of letting his own history keep him in the familiarity of work and the comfort of old bitterness? Then again, he had no idea if this would end well for any of them, so what was he doing giving advice to anyone?

Chloe sat on the couch with a mug of steaming hot, corrosive, and foul coffee cupped between her palms. The revolver lay loaded on the coffee table in front of her. Twilight had grown longer and longer, and Merek was still out. She tried not to worry. Too much. She still had some time.

Luckily—or perhaps, unluckily—she had plenty to occupy her mind. Merek had admitted he *cared*. It still warmed her deep inside, but he'd also confessed how caring scared him. Merek was never going to be a man who admitted to any weakness easily. And his revelations about his wife explained so much about the man she'd come to know. Why he felt the need to control every detail, why he was so overprotective, why he was a diehard cynic.

Unfortunately, her years in med school, internships, and residencies meant she could picture the crime scenes he'd described all too clearly. Her heart ached for the young man who'd had to go through that with someone he loved. Who had to live with the weight of responsibility riding his shoulders. Gods, what a nightmare.

She imagined any man, especially a cop, would have felt some guilt over what happened, but Merek's clairvoyance made his guilt that much more oppressive. She didn't know how he'd lived through it and made it out sane. He was possibly the strongest person she'd ever known. And one of the kindest, most considerate, and most compassionate.

The man confused her. He was a study in contradictions, all of which she found fascinating. He made her feel what she didn't want to, which scared the crap out of her, and he also made her feel safer than she had in her entire life. Even with terrorists chasing them down, ready to torture her or Alex for the information locked in their heads.

No. Just no.

A sigh slid out, and she grimaced when she sipped her awful excuse for coffee. The instant stuff was just offensive to her sensibilities. No self-respecting Seattleite should ever have to touch this crap. She took another swig, and felt the caffeine start to kick in even as the acidic liquid burned her belly.

She tensed when she heard the doorknob, but relaxed when the voices in her head gave a reassuring whisper and she felt the easing of the shield spells around the apartment. Merek. Anyone else would have to breach the spell; only he and she and Alex could pass through it without incredible magical energy expended or harm coming to them.

Setting her coffee on the table, she resisted the urge to throw herself at him when he came in the door and make sure he was uninjured. He knew how to take care of himself. She had no doubts about that. So instead of wringing her hands like an idiotic weakling, she picked up the gun as he walked in and she carried it with her as she went to the kitchen to make him a cup of the nasty tar. He was as addicted as she and Alex were, so any coffee was better than no coffee. She hoped he'd remembered to get some real stuff at the store.

He dropped the bazillion grocery sacks he had looped around his arms on the floor and counter, then accepted the coffee cup she handed him and took a deep swig. She motioned to the revolver she'd placed on the counter. "Mission accomplished?"

"Yep, we're fully loaded. Ammo's in there somewhere, but I had to take the long way to get there and back. Sorry it took so long, but I couldn't risk being followed." He frowned down at the mug in his hand. "This has honey in it."

"Yeah, so?" She lifted an eyebrow, digging into the bags and separating out things that required refrigeration.

"You haven't unloaded the bag with the honey in it." Rifling through the sea of plastic, he came up with a bear-shaped container full of golden liquid.

She shrugged and went back to her sorting. "We ate at Kentucky Fried Chicken when we flew through Lexington, remember? I snagged you a handful of those little honey packets they give out for their biscuits."

"Ah. Thanks for looking out for me." He blinked at her, looked down at the coffee, then sipped it again. Something unreadable moved across his expression, but he said nothing more.

The bag holding the milk had another plastic bottle in it. She pulled it out and stared at it uncomprehendingly for a moment. Massage oil and lubricant in one.

"For later." Merek's low rumble made heat pool in her belly. He bent forward to nip at the lower curve of her ass, and she jolted in shock. Her nipples tightened, her sex dampening as all the erotic possibilities raced through her mind of what he might have planned for her. Then he snagged the small bottle from her hand and stuffed it in his pocket just before Alex came out of his room with a technical manual dangling from his fingers.

A hot blush washed up her cheeks, and she gave them a weak smile.

Alex and Merek greeted each other with manly slaps on the back, and Merek sent her a look that promised all manner of wicked things when the wolf turned away to drop his book and start helping.

"Hey, check this out." Alex rummaged around in a bulging shopping bag.

"What?" She peered around his shoulder to watch him unload one night-light after another until over a dozen were lined up along the counter.

Most of them were plain old night-lights, but a few of them were truly hideous. One was shaped like a deer carved into a fake log, another looked like a plastic moose's head, and another was made out of what might have once been a pinecone. The last was a deformed seashell. With glitter. She picked that one up with the very tips of her thumb and forefinger and held it out as if it were something smelly. "What is *this*, exactly?"

Merek arched his brows and shrugged, but a grin broke through. "Hey, I cleaned out the store. The other options were scented, and I figured if we mixed six of those with a werewolf nose in the house, he might vomit on us as payback."

"Thanks. Really. I mean that." Alex's voice was fervent as he yanked the wrapping off of each light. "Thank you."

Chloe snorted, but had to turn away to hide the tears welling in her eyes. She stuffed the refrigerated items into the fridge and freezer, blinking until the moisture was gone. Alex knew she liked lights on at night, and Merek knew exactly why she was terrified of the dark, and neither of them thought she was a wimp.

And Merek . . . He was controlled, but not controlling. He didn't try to control *them*. He accepted them just as they were, and controlled all the details around them to make sure they had everything they needed. Alex's werewolf need to Change at full moon was just another detail. Merek wasn't annoyed by it, didn't act pissed off by the inconvenience. He just handled it.

Now that he knew she was afraid of the dark and why, he didn't try to talk her out of it, try to reason with her or tell her to grow up and get over it; he just went out and bought her an entire store's worth of night-lights.

That was the moment, right there, that she fell all the way in love with him. She'd been fighting it, avoiding it, and ignoring it for days now, but that did it. She loved him. Completely, utterly loved him.

She just had no idea what she could do about it. After what he'd told her about his wife, she couldn't imagine that he'd ever want to deal with loving anyone ever again. Not when it meant he also had to deal with the fact that he couldn't see her future and any bad things coming down the pipeline. That was assuming he even felt some of this wrenching, terrifying, wonderful emotion that was threatening to consume her soul.

The worst part was, she wasn't even sure she could blame him for not wanting any part of this. No one understood better than she did that some wounds just never healed, some fears could never be overcome. And if you couldn't fix it, you just had to live with it any way you could. Merek wasn't asking her to change, so how could she try to force him to live with his worst nightmare permanently?

She couldn't.

The rest of the evening passed in a daze. She barely noticed when Alex pushed all the furniture in the living room against one wall, Merek set up a force field so they didn't break anything or make noise that would disturb the neighbors, and the two practiced close quarters combat. The television show they watched after made both males howl with laughter, but she stared into space petting a purring Ophelia.

Her thoughts ricocheted around in her mind until she wanted to scream. She couldn't even talk to anyone about it, especially not Merek. If she were home, she'd have Millie and Tess to ask for advice, but as it stood, she was totally alone in a sea of maleness that either wouldn't want to know or wouldn't get what she was going through. Gods, this sucked. It hurt. It hurt to love someone and have to keep it locked inside. It hurt to have to protect someone from the most amazing thing she'd ever experienced.

The TV program ended so she kissed Alex good night and wandered into the bathroom to brush her teeth before bed. When she bent forward to spit out the toothpaste, she saw Merek reflected in the mirror behind her, and she damn near choked on her toothbrush.

Waiting for her to finish with her coughing fit, he propped his broad shoulder on the doorjamb, Ophelia draped across one brawny forearm, purring while he stroked her. "Something's on your mind, sweetheart."

Too many somethings. A flush sped up her cheeks, and she rinsed her toothbrush off, set it aside, and splashed cool water on her face. Unaccustomed nerves jangled inside her. Crossing such a huge threshold in her heart, and having to do it alone, suddenly froze her with terror. How did she act around him now? How did she keep him from noticing? He was the most observant man she'd ever known. He never missed anything about her, not a hitch in her breathing, a sigh, a change of mood. He watched, he listened, and he cared.

And she loved him for it.

"Is this about yesterday?" His gaze shuttered, his expression going blank.

It took a moment for the question to process, and she yanked her mind from her own issues and focused on him. She turned to face him. "No, this isn't about yesterday, or anything you said."

"You sure?" His gaze moved over her, but no emotion showed there. "You know you can talk to me if something is wrong." A tiny smile hovered at the corners of his mouth. "I can take it."

A repeat of her own words that had kicked off the discussion of his precognition and his wife. She let a laugh huff out and pushed away from the vanity. Taking Ophelia from his arms, she set the familiar on the ground. "Go play in the living room, sugar."

The cat darted away, and Chloe stepped into Merek's embrace. Her heart turned over when his strong arms immediately closed around her, and she buried her nose against his warm chest, inhaling the scent of him and sweat and the lingering smell of laundry soap on his shirt.

"I know you can handle anything." But then he might feel obligated if she dumped her feelings all over him. The only thing worse than being in love alone was being the object of pity from the person you loved. Her belly lurched at the thought. No. No, she wouldn't do that to him, wouldn't cling or revert to her old childhood neediness. He deserved better than that, and so did she. She sighed, pressed her hands to his chest, and gazed up at him. "This isn't something you need to handle. I can figure it out on my own, but I appreciate the offer to listen more than you know."

He didn't look happy with that, just as he'd been displeased any other time she'd withheld information from him, but he gave a reluctant nod. "Just remember, you don't have to go through anything alone right now, Chloe. I'm here to make sure you're all right. I can't do that effectively if you don't tell me when something is wrong."

How she kept the tears from welling up in her eyes, she'd never know, but instead she managed a smile for him. "When something is *wrong*, I'll let you know. I have some stuff to figure out, but nothing is wrong. I promise."

Things were far too right, and that's where she hit her current snag. His hands stroked up and down her back, and his gaze searched her face. A spurt of alarm darted through her. He would know if he looked too deep. Of course he would. He was Merek.

Time for a distraction.

Rising up on tiptoe, she brushed her lips over his chin, his jaw. "Kiss me, Merek. Take my mind off of things."

"I can't believe I'm saying this." He leaned down and feathered a kiss over her mouth. "But I'd rather you tell me what you need your mind taken off of."

She smiled against his lips, running her tongue along the curve of the bottom one. "My mind is always on you. And bad men. And you. And you when you're being a bad man."

His arms tightened around her, pulling her flush against all of those hard angles. He kissed her hard once, twice. "I'm always good."

"Prove it." She arched her back, rubbed herself against the steely length of his erection, and felt the insidious heat begin to leech the strength out of her muscles. Her body molded itself to his, her nipples beaded to chafe against the soft satin of her bra.

Shifting her around until the doorjamb pressed into her back, he pinned her there while he swooped in for a thorough kiss that had her up on her tiptoes again to get closer. His tongue swept into her mouth, and his honeyed flavor made her moan. The man was addicting, and she never wanted to get enough. She wanted him forever. Their tongues mated, twined, dancing until their breathing was ragged. She cupped his jaw in her palms, wanting to show him with actions how much she craved him, needed him, *loved* him. Everything she couldn't say out loud, she put into that kiss.

Renewed magic shivered beneath her skin, waiting to be tapped. She let it loose, let the heat and longing she felt pour from her to him. Her need was returned to her in a throbbing echo of his magic, the hot male thrum of it seeping into her very bones. Her sex went slick with juices, her nipples so tight they ached for the feel of his hands on them.

Jerking away, he stared down at her, his pupils so huge that only a thin rim of silver remained. His lips were as red and swollen as hers felt. His chest heaved with each bellowing breath. "Bed. Now."

"Yes."

He swept her off her feet, carried her to the king-sized mattress, and dumped her on it. With a flick of his fingers, the bedroom door swished closed and locked. Oh. She'd forgotten all about that when she'd told Ophelia to leave. Oops.

Holding his hand out, fingers splayed, he intoned, "Naked."

She arched in startled reflex as her clothes fell away and left her bare to his gaze. He was just as nude, and she let herself look at him. Golden muscles rippled in the lamplight, hard cock dripping pre-cum, gray eyes flashing silver with barely leashed power.

His eyes closed for just a moment, and a wave of magic swept out from him, tingled as it passed over her skin. She felt a boost in the strength of the shields around the apartment. A smile tilted her lips. Safety first. Always in command of the details. She understood his obsession better now, and for all of their sakes, she was grateful for it, if not for the events that made him so conscientious. Still, she wouldn't change the man for anything. She loved him just as he was.

When he looked at her again, she held out her arms and let her grin widen. "Come here."

"Not just yet." He shook his head, taking a moment to trail his gaze over her body. The air-conditioned breeze in the room made her nipples bead tighter, and she felt the heat of his gaze touch her skin.

She let her legs fall open against the mattress. His nostrils flared as he dragged in the scent of her wetness. He licked his lips, his gaze locked on her pussy. She knew her folds would be swollen and slick with cream. A little smile curled the corners of her lips, and she cupped her breasts, circling the areolas and teasing herself while she teased the man watching her. The rapacious look on his face, the way lust tightened his features, told her exactly what kind of effect her actions had.

When she let one hand drift down her torso until she could dip her fingers into her wet sex and rub her hardened clit, Merek's resistance snapped. His hand shot out with that startling speed of his, wrapping around her wrist to pull her fingers up to his mouth. Leaning forward, he sucked the juices from her fingertips. Then he set her palm back on her breast. "You do that, I'll handle this."

And then his mouth was on her, his hot tongue licking at her damp flesh. Her body arched off the bed, and his hands controlled the motion. He held her legs flat to the bed, shoving them open with his broad shoulders. Slipping her fingers into his hair, she tugged him nearer, excitement a twisting thing inside her. The feel of his lips closing over her clit, suckling her, made her scream as orgasm broke through her in a rush so overpowering, she couldn't contain the explosion.

Pulses continued to hit her in rippling waves as he teased her with his tongue. She lay limp on the bed, dazed and unsure how he'd made her come so fast without using any kind of seduction spell. Then she gave a breathless chuckle, her heart still thumping in her chest. Her chemistry with Merek was the most powerful turn-on she'd ever come in contact with. Spontaneous combustion. Contentment spread through her limbs, and she sighed when he rolled off her.

"Hold on to the headboard." The rumble of his voice was deep and rich. Commanding. Sexy.

She reached her hands up, grasped the bottom of the headboard, and used the leverage to lift her body toward him. Something hot and burning with magic wrapped around her wrists, locking her in place.

Her breath caught, and she froze. Tugging on the spell bindings, she found she couldn't escape. The last time she'd been tied down had been . . . A horrible flash of a Fae woman's face flooded her mind, dark magic seeping into her skin, bronze burning her flesh. She shuddered, jerking spasmodically at the golden chords that glowed around her wrists.

Heart pounding, her gaze flew to Merek where he sat beside her, but not close enough to touch her. His expression was quiet, knowing. He waited to see what she would do, how she would take this utterly vulnerable position.

She swallowed, feeling more stripped bare than she ever had in her life. "I'm not sure . . ."

"Just say 'safe,' and the spell unravels." His hand closed around her thigh, and she realized her legs weren't bound.

"I can get loose any time I want?" She licked her lips, and his gaze followed the motion, the gray sparking with silver as he watched her.

He nodded. "Any time you want, sweetheart. Trust me."

"I do." More than that, she loved him. If this was the only way she could tell him, then so be it. She relaxed against the bindings and offered him a smile. "I want you."

A grin broke over his angular face, and he shook his head. "You are the most amazing woman I have ever met."

"Come show me how much you appreciate my amazing-ness." She let her gaze lock on his thick cock, and licked her lips again with slow relish.

He bent forward to scoop his pants off the floor, slid his hand into the front pocket, and pulled out the little bottle he'd tucked in there earlier. "I'm going to show you exactly how much I appreciate every single inch of you."

Her breathing shallowed out to nothing, and she swallowed. Oh, gods. The thought of him fucking her ass made her palms dampen and her heart hammer. A blush suffused her face, burning with scorching heat. "Yes."

"I told you. Amazing." He gave a flashing grin, tossed the bottle onto the mattress beside her, grabbed her ankles, and yanked her down the bed. The spell rope stretched, so her wrists were still bound, pulled straight over her head.

The distinct creaking *pop* of the bottle opening made her shiver in anticipation. He brushed his lips over hers, a brief kiss before he drizzled the cool oil over her hot skin. Her moan was a helpless sound and made his lips curl in a satisfied smile.

Then his big hands stroked her.

He took his time, worked the oil deep into her flesh, using hot little pleasure spells to make her gasp in shock or sigh in delight. He started at her feet, pressed his thumbs into her arches until her toes curled. Her ankles and calves were massaged, her knees kissed, her thighs opened so he could blow a breath on the puffy, wet folds of her pussy. A spell lit her sex; fire and ice had her shuddering with lust that made her heart rate rocket.

But he didn't touch her there, just left her aching, needing. Needing him. Always him. "Merek."

"Shh. Just relax, sweetheart." His voice was as seductive as any magic ever dreamed up, sliding over her sensitive nerves like warm velvet. A little rough, a little soft, totally rich and decadent.

More oil slicked her thighs, the curve of her belly, the softness of her breasts. He swirled his blunt nails over her nipples, coaxing them to tight points. His strong fingers worked her shoulders and arms before he rolled her over and kneed her thighs apart.

"Close your eyes." He bent forward to kiss the nape of her neck, between her shoulder blades, the small of her back, each globe of her buttocks.

A purr was the only answer she could give as she obeyed him. For once, she wasn't afraid of the darkness. Merek was there, and everything in her focused on him.

Time drifted as she let herself float on a cloud of sensuality. There was nothing in the world except the magic of his hands and what they did to her body. Her muscles were pliant, warm and soft, all tension melting away as she turned herself over to him and anything he wanted to do to her. She knew he'd make it good for her.

He kneaded her neck and shoulders and back, and her pulse picked up speed as he cupped her ass in his big palms. Slipping a hand under her belly, he lifted her hips and slid a pillow underneath her. She sucked in a deep breath when he knelt in the vee of her thighs, spreading her wider. Cooler oil trickled between her buttocks as he parted the cheeks, the liquid quickly heating when it touched her skin. Her breath seized at the sharp difference between her overheating flesh and the chilly oil. His slick fingers trailed down, teased the rim of her anus.

Desire punched through her, and her body flexed as she arched herself higher for him. "Take me there, Merek."

"Here?" One finger probed at the tight ring of muscle, pressing just the tip into her ass.

"Yes," she gasped. She moaned and lifted herself into his hand as he began to stretch her anus for penetration, her arms jerking against the bindings. Her racing heart thudded against her ribcage, heat flowing through her veins.

His finger worked deeper, massaging until he could slip in a second digit. He thrust slowly, the oil making the slide exquisite.

"Merek, please," she breathed. She twisted in her bonds. Even though she had no desire to escape, she couldn't stop moving.

"Pleasing you is part of my plan." He brushed a kiss over her shoulder, nipped at the flesh.

A choked laugh ended in a gasp as he added a third finger to her ass. "I like this plan."

His low chuckle made her grin into the pillow. "I had a feeling you would."

Those diabolical fingers pumped slowly in and out of her ass, widening her passage until she thought she'd die. Her hips undulated, her ultrasensitive nipples chafing on the smooth sheets. She whimpered and closed her eyes, turning herself over to the sensations she couldn't control, didn't want to control. She wanted to feel, wanted to experience every moment of Merek's touch.

She bit her pillow when his cock replaced his fingers, the head nudging into her anus. It stung, he was so big, but she breathed through the pleasure-pain. He gripped her waist, his heavy thighs forcing her legs even wider for him as he surged deeper into her ass. He froze when she cried out, bucking against the glowing bonds around her wrists.

"Are you all right?" His grasp tightened when she didn't answer. "Chloe?"

"Give me a second." She forced her body to loosen up, muscle by muscle, accepting the thick penetration of his cock. He shifted a little, and a ripple of pleasure went through her. Just that small movement, and more juices flooded her pussy. "Okay. I'm ready."

Torment roughened his tone. "I don't want to hurt you. We can stop now, if—"

"No." She rolled her hips experimentally, using the spell ropes to gain some leverage. A gasp ripped from her as the slippery oil made the first few inches of his cock slide in and out of her ass, each stroke easier as she relaxed.

Goose bumps broke out across her skin as he began to rock with her, tiny plunges that made ecstasy streak through her. His palms skimmed up her back, down again, gentling her. His voice was a deep growl that urged her onward.

"Faster," she breathed, writhing in the bespelled cage of her bonds.

He obeyed her, his thrusts picking up speed and force until his muscled stomach spanked against her backside. Her sex fisted each time he entered her ass, and need sliced through her like a werewolf's claws. She moaned, bowing her back until the bonds snapped tight. He kissed the nape of her neck, his breath whispering against her hot, damp skin. "You feel so good, Chloe. Amazing."

I love you. The words were there, hovering on the tip of her tongue, but she bit them back. "More. Please, more."

He rotated his pelvis against her, and she cried out at the pleasure that flooded her. He gave her more, just not as much as she needed. She tightened her muscles around his cock, and he groaned, the helpless sound vibrating against her back. "Yes, Chloe. More. Give me more."

The ropes glowed brighter as their passion built, blinding her until she had to close her eyes to escape the light, but that only focused her more on the physical: the glide of their oil-slicked and sweat-dampened skin; the rough hair at his groin that stimulated her; the groans between each gasping breath; the flex and release of muscles as they moved together.

It was pure magic, no pleasure spells required.

He slid his hand between her body and the pillow he'd placed under her hips, forcing her to arch her ass higher into his thrusts. She sobbed and then screamed when his hand dipped between her thighs and rubbed over her wet folds. Every deep thrust rubbed her clit against his stroking fingers. "Merek! I need . . . I can't . . . *please!*"

She knew she made no sense, but somehow he knew what she was begging for. His hips bucked faster, driving his cock even deeper than he'd ever been before. His fingers pressed down directly on her clit, and she exploded into an orgasm that left her shrieking, sobbing, and heaving under him.

A rough groan from him told her she'd dragged him along with her, and soon he filled her ass with hot fluids. Great shudders racked his body, and he wrapped his arms around her to hold her close.

"Gods," he gasped. "That was . . . amazing."

"Amazing." She echoed the word at the same time, a bubble of sweet laughter slipping from her. "Yeah. It really was."

Moments later, her arms went slack as he released her from the spell binding. She collapsed against the bed, cooing in delight when his long fingers worked any remaining tension from her muscles. He tugged up the covers and settled beside her, tucking her into his warm body.

Her hands fisted in the covers when he flipped off the lamp on the bedside table. Then she grinned. One of his truly hideous night-lights shone from a wall socket. The seashell light. From the glow in the room, she'd guess he'd plugged one into every available socket. She sighed and leaned back into him, relaxing.

"Not too dark?" He kissed her temple.

She shook her head. "Nope."

He'd noticed. Of course he had. This was Merek. Her smile widened.

No wonder she loved him.

12

Something was wrong.

Every hair on the back of Merek's neck rose, his instincts shivering to life. In the three weeks since they'd left Arizona, he hadn't had a hint of suspicion that anything was amiss, but he stood looking at the woman behind the ticket counter at the Portland airport, and he knew. The way her eyes widened slightly when she entered his information into the computer, the way her bored expression flattened to emptiness.

They'd been blown.

"You know what? I need to make a call before I check in." He gave the lady a grin he hoped looked genuine, swept his falsified passport out of her hand, and stepped back to let the next impatient traveler buy him a few seconds before she called security. From the corner of his eye, he noted when she picked up a phone.

Alex and Chloe were occupying a few of the uncomfortable chairs grouped near the ticketing area. They hadn't checked in yet. Merek insisted they switch things around when they flew. Sometimes they paired off; sometimes they all traveled separately. Same plane, but they didn't sit together, didn't acknowledge each other. Nothing would link them.

This time, Merek had been alone, the others together. He thanked the gods he'd gotten in line first. Digging through his duffle for a cell phone he didn't need, he pretended to lose his grip and scatter the contents on the floor near their chairs.

Alex hopped up to help him gather his belongings. Merek offered a thankful smile and kept his tone cheerful. "Our IDs have been flagged, and security is on the way. I'll handle them." He nodded an easy farewell to Alex and Chloe, as if he'd never met them before and never expected to see them again. He could only pray he did see them again. Soon. But he had to get them out of here now. "I want you to very casually walk away from me, get in a cab, and leave the airport. I'll meet you in exactly two hours in the mystery section at Powell's." The bookstore was enormous, the size of a full city block, and had gobbled up the surrounding stores into a sprawling maze of interconnected buildings. It was packed with people and a warren of bookshelves easy to get lost in. The perfect place to disappear, if necessary. "If I'm not there on time, you know what to do."

Chloe gave him a dismissive wave before she set her purse in her lap and rooted around in it. She came up with a tube of gloss, slicked it on her lips, and dropped it back into the abyss of her bag.

"Come on, honey. Let's go." She gave Alex an impatient glance as she stood, looped her purse over her shoulder, then picked up her suitcase and walked away.

"I hate Oregon." Alex shrugged into his backpack and followed her. Neither of them looked back, and they hopped into a cab. A relieved breath eased out of Merek's lungs when they pulled away from the curb and sped away.

They were safe. For now.

The relief was short-lived. A uniformed guard slid into view.

He wasn't Normal. Elf, maybe. Senses Merek had honed as a cop made that conclusion register before he'd even given the question his full attention.

A shimmer formed before his eyes, visions of how this could play out. Now that Alex and Chloe were out of the picture, he could see again. Possibilities, chances, probabilities. Some were uglier than others. He discarded those, making a snap decision, which made still more potentials dance before him, overlaying the reality of the bustling airport. Reflex kept the two pictures sharp, allowed him to react to what was true and interpret what was possible.

Adrenaline ripped through his system as his heart picked up speed, but he controlled the need to run, to fight, to hunt those who hunted him. Pulling in a deep breath, he let it ease out. Before it had completely left his lungs, he'd shifted his duffle to his left shoulder, leaving his right hand free if he needed to grab the weapon tucked into the small of his back, concealed by his jacket.

Ducking into a men's room, he used a pocketknife to jimmy the door to a janitor's closet and shut it behind him. No spells, nothing for another Magickal to detect.

The restroom door opened, and the elf stepped in. Merek froze, unsure how developed the elf's senses were. He might be able to detect a life-form in here, but Merek's visions showed that wasn't likely.

Another possibility sliced into his mind, crystal clear and certain. A second security guard would walk in behind the first, helping with the search for Merek. The second man was the greater danger, and more likely to find what he was looking for. The two of them together could take Merek. If that happened, he was on an unstoppable collision course with Smith. As much as he'd like a piece of that bastard, it would leave no one to protect Chloe and Alex.

Fuck.

Slapping open the door, he grabbed the passing elf from behind. The swift squeak of the bathroom door behind him told Merek the second man had entered. Struggling with the elf, Merek felt a nightstick slam into the back of his skull. There was heavy magic to power the blow. Dark spots exploded before his eyes, and he felt himself falling. The breath blasted from his lungs when he made impact with the tile floor, and he choked when the elf landed on top of him. Sucking in air, he swung out, a quick snap of fist meeting jaw and the first security guard slumped against Merek's chest. He blinked hard, trying to clear the cartwheeling stars, and heard the baton whistling toward his head again. He jolted, heaved out from under the unconscious elf, who took the blow instead.

The world spun in sickening circles before him, a kaleidoscope of colors. He lifted a hand, shot out a spell, and it collided midair with one launched by the second guard. The burst of light made his stomach lurch, and he let himself collapse flat to the tile, narrowly missing being hit by another spell. He flicked his fingers, took the guard out at the knees. He'd meant to go higher, hit the chest, but his aim wasn't quite straight.

A scream from the guard as he collapsed to the floor beside his companion rang in Merek's ears, jabbing into his brain. He jackknifed in reaction, but the movement made him sicker. He saw the guard with both hands locked around his leg, writhing in agony. Merek wheezed, sent a final spell, and left the second guard drooling beside the first.

Rolling to his hands and knees, Merek grabbed for one of the porcelain sinks to drag himself slowly to his feet. Then he bent forward and vomited his guts up.

Even with his skull ringing, the future still played out before his eyes. Only now the overlapping layers of vision made him gag on whatever was left in his stomach. The paths he needed to take to make it back to the welcoming blankness of his people rooted in his thoughts. He rinsed his mouth, wiped the sweat from his forehead, staggered to the janitor's closet to pick up his duffle, and escaped.

The red and white marquee sign that read POWELL'S BOOKS—USED & NEW BOOKS was the most welcome thing Merek had ever seen. The drizzling rain felt like a hammer blow every time a drop landed on his skin, and he wanted to get out of it. His gaze swept the street one last time before he crossed toward the mammoth bookstore.

His movements were slower than he liked, his step careful. He was on autopilot. Just make sure no one followed him. Just get to Alex and Chloe. Just be certain they were safe.

The lights inside the store blinded him when he walked in, and he shuddered, fighting a wave of nausea. He paused for a long moment, trying to remember where he was going. Mystery. The mystery section at Powell's. Where he'd told them to meet him.

Reading the signs to get to the right area hurt his eyes, the words blurring and streaking, a halo of light forming around every person he passed.

And there they were. Two dark heads of hair bent together, one so deep a brown it was almost black, one a shining blue-black like a raven's wing. Chloe. She looked up at him, pushing that raven hair from her face. Her relieved smile made his heart skip a beat, but then her grin faded when she got a good look at him.

"Merek, what happened?"

"Took..." Somehow his tongue didn't want to shape the words correctly, but he forced himself to speak distinctly. "Took a knock to the head from an airport security guard."

Alex's hand closed around his shoulder, and Merek startled because he hadn't seen the wolf move. The quick motion was like an anvil slamming into him, and his view tilted sideways.

"I've got you, Merek." It was Alex's voice, but he sounded

like he'd spoken from a great distance. Hadn't the boy just been next to him? Merek thought so, but he wasn't quite sure. He blinked a few times, but couldn't see clearly, couldn't think clearly.

He blinked again, and things had changed. What, he wasn't sure, but he felt a shift in space and time. A soft rocking motion told him he was in a moving vehicle. It was disorienting, and he didn't like that, but when he pulled in a breath, he smelled his lover's sweet scent. "Chloe."

"Yes, Merek. I'm here." Her hand stroked his forehead, and it felt good. *He* felt good, energized, but that wasn't right either.

"I got hit by a police baton." He frowned up at the gray fabric that covered the ceiling of the car. He was in a tilted back passenger seat. Chloe perched in the backseat behind him. Turning his head, he saw Alex behind the wheel.

Alex's green eyes left the road for a moment, and they reflected a deep concern. "Yeah, you had a pretty nasty concussion. Chloe put you under a healing spell, so you'd sleep until you were completely better."

"I didn't want to try to do any kind of quick healing on you. The brain can be so delicate to work with, and I just don't have the skills to rush it." Her fingers brushed through Merek's hair, and he felt her testing him with her magic. "This was the best I could do."

He reached up and caught her hand. "You did good, sweetheart. I feel fine. Great, in fact."

Groping under his seat, he felt for the lever so he could sit up. The sun was setting, its light breaking through the overcast clouds. There were trees and a few houses along the road, but nothing else to indicate their location. A prickle of unease ran down his spine. "Where are we?"

This vehicle wasn't a rental, of that Merek was certain. Someone's graduation tassel hung from the rearview mirror, and his shoes stuck to the soda on the floorboards. Whoever owned this car was a total slob. The long silence made him glance around. Chloe was wedged into the middle of a nonexistent backseat. Ophelia sat beside her, using the back of Alex's seat as a scratching post.

He looked to Alex again. "Do I want to know where the car came from?"

"Stole it," he replied, more cheerful than Merek had ever heard him. "I reprogrammed the onboard computer and scrambled some records so the owner will have a bitch of a time proving the car even belonged to him in order to report it stolen. We switched out the plates of six cars in a mall parking lot of similar makes and models, then drove over to a parking garage at Portland State University and did the same."

Smart. It would take them a while to sort that mess out. Merek wasn't going to say it out loud. "You want to tell me what all this is for? Where are we, and where exactly are we going in this stolen vehicle?"

He could feel the tension ratchet up in the small car, saw Alex glance in the rearview mirror to meet Chloe's eyes. The teen swallowed. "Yeah. There's a story for that."

"So." Chloe took a deep breath. "Here's what we figured. We can't use the IDs or credit cards Millie gave us, and if those are blown, then any of the properties she owns are out as well. We haven't been using them, but not using them has seriously depleted our cash fund. And now we *can't* use them because we don't know which are covered by Smith's men and which aren't."

Alex took up the thread of the explanation as he slowed the vehicle to make a turn onto a narrow two-lane road. "We need somewhere safe, somewhere I can Change, somewhere away from Magickals, somewhere not related to anyone we know."

"And..." Back to Chloe, and Merek was already sure he wasn't going to like where this was going any more than he liked riding in a stolen car. These two were too damn smart. "We *are* running low on cash, but contacting Millie for more would be a bad plan, since they probably know she helped us with the IDs."

He scrubbed a hand down his face. "Cut to the chase. Where have we gone?"

"You're going to be pissed." The glance Alex gave him was worried, and that in itself worried Merek.

"We stopped and picked up groceries after we . . . after we got off the ferry from . . . Seattle," Chloe whispered the last word, as though that would somehow dampen the effect.

He jerked around in his seat to stare at her. "No."

"Yes." The stubbornly mutinous look was so familiar he wanted to shake her. He usually found it endearing, but he was usually in control of the situation. "It's already done anyway. We're here."

He snarled. "You know how far werewolf senses can stretch!"

Rearing back against the seat, she held up a placating hand. "Well, we just passed *through* Seattle. We didn't stop. We're on Bainbridge Island."

As if that would reassure him. "You have to be kidding me."

"Tess's aunt and uncle have a house here." Her fingers linked together in her lap, and she began reciting calm, scientific facts as though reading a checklist. "They're on sabbatical in Rome, and I know the security code to their place. They have no connection to me; I've only been here once with Tess, when the system was installed, and I never even met them. More important, no Magickal is going to expect another Magickal to be there."

He clenched his jaw, looking for a way around her facts. "I don't like it."

"Do you have a better idea for where Alex can Change?" Her hands lifted and fell back to her lap in a helpless gesture.

"We have no ID to rent a car or house or campsite and not enough cash to convince anyone to look the other way."

Of course he didn't have a better plan. Damn it. "This is a bad idea."

"We're already here. If anyone was going to sense us, it's a done deal. We can take a ferry back, if you want, but we might as well stay until the full moon is over. It's just for a few days, and it'll buy us the time we need to figure out what to do next. We know it's not ideal, but we don't have that kind of option on the table, do we?" Alex spoke for the first time in several minutes.

"No, we don't." Chloe reached over and patted the boy on the shoulder. "I think this is the best plan we can get in the limited time we have until full moon."

Fuck. Fuck, fuck, *fuck.* Merek rounded on the kid. "Can you control yourself surrounded by that many Normals?"

"Yes." His Adam's apple bobbed as he swallowed, but the obstinate set of his jaw said he was serious.

"You're sure?"

"Yes. I can." He nodded for emphasis, taking his eyes off the road for a split second to glance back at Chloe, the person who'd believed in him first, who had trusted him and reassured him when he'd had a silver bullet punched through his gut. Then he met Merek's gaze, his green eyes clear and certain. "I won't hurt anyone. I can control it."

"Shit." Merek slumped, his face dropping into his hand for a moment. He rubbed his fingers against his eyes.

"It's going to be okay." Chloe patted his shoulder, and it pissed him off more that he liked her touch, craved it.

"This is a bad—"

"Do you have a better one?" Her fingers tightened on his shoulder, a reassuring squeeze, an apology. He shrugged out of her grip.

"I would have said so if I did." He sighed and dropped his hand.

"I know."

The last place he wanted them to be was Seattle, but the damnable truth was he didn't have a better idea of where to go to keep Alex safe for the full moon. Chloe was right about all of it, and their future was as foggy to Merek as it always had been. This could be the perfect plan, or it could be utter disaster. All he could do now was mitigate any damage.

He jerked the cell phone out of his pocket and flipped it open. He placed a secure call to Millie, got her voice mail and left her a message, then he tried Luca. Same thing. He tried to rein in a growl. "Cavalli, this is Kingston. We're on Bainbridge Island for the full moon. Don't send anyone over to check on us because I don't want undue attention. I'll call again if anything goes down, so be prepared to send in the cavalry."

Closing the phone, he watched a barn-like two-story house come into view. Another wave of icy, impotent fury ripped through him. He just hoped this wasn't the mistake that got them killed. Or captured. With Smith's track record, Merek wasn't sure which one would be the better option. Probably death.

"Fuck."

"Fuck."

Chloe slapped her hand against the shingled siding of the Jones's house and glared at the keypad as if she could will it to do what she wanted.

"What?" Alex's quiet voice sounded behind her.

"The security code isn't working." She blew out a frustrated breath, shrugging her shoulders to work out the tension. Hours of sitting cramped in the miniscule backseat while she hovered over a pale, unconscious Merek had done nothing to make this easier. She'd never forget the way her heart had literally stopped when her strong warlock had keeled over. The fact that he was obviously annoyed with the situation didn't help either. She didn't even want to consider his reaction when he found out she couldn't get in the house as she'd claimed she could.

The wolf nudged her out of the way to scrutinize the panel. "Are you sure it's the right one?"

"It's Tess's date of birth." She lifted her hands and let them drop. "So, yes, I'm sure."

He rocked back on his heels, sliding his hands in his pockets. His dark brows drew together as he thought, then he gave a definitive nod. "I can get around this."

"What are we getting around?" Merek rumbled from the far side of the porch. He mounted the steps, a few grocery bags gripped in his hands. Alex had stayed in the car with the sleeping Merek while Chloe had stocked up with enough supplies to hole up until after full moon.

If they could get into the house. Chloe's muscles tightened even further as dread curdled in her belly. She hated this, hated not being on the same side as Merek. Neither of them was backing down, because they both thought they were right. She pulled in a deep breath. "They've changed the security code, but Alex says he can get around it."

The teen glanced back at Merek. "I'm going to have to break the no gadget modification rule."

He snorted. "You already broke that when you hijacked the car."

A flashing grin answered that, and Chloe rolled her eyes. She actually thought her godson might be having the time of his life with this little day trip. Sicko. "Even if you can disable the security system, that won't get it to unlock the door like Tess made it do. And there will be *no magic* used here. Nothing to make it obvious Magickals are in residence. No spells."

The kid cocked his head, considered the problem, offered: "I can use a little wolf strength on it. One quick push, and we'll be in."

Merek gave a growl worthy of a werewolf, his gaze flinty as it slid over her. Oh, yeah. He was not happy about this little snafu. She couldn't even blame him. She should have considered that Tess would have her uncle change the code. Probably on a regular basis. Merek slid his wallet out of his back pocket and flipped it open, pulling out a few metal tools. "We can do this with no magic of any kind."

Interest flickered in Alex's eyes, and he arched an eyebrow. "You know how to pick locks? Sweet."

"Security system first." Merek jerked his chin toward the keypad, and Alex's enthusiasm slid away until he wore his most solemn expression.

"Right." The wolf fished his cell phone out of his pocket, then dug some tools out of his backpack. Unfastening the face of the panel, he pulled it out to reveal the maze of wires inside. He hooked his cell phone into the wires, and the screen lit with information Chloe had never seen on a phone before. He got to work, his face set in lines of fierce concentration.

A few minutes later, the panel beeped, went black, and then flashed back to life. Alex set the keypad back in place and typed in a series of numbers. "Okay, I wiped everything and reset the code to 9-8-7-6-5-4-3-2-1-0. Lame, but easy to remember."

Chloe finished his thought for him. "But having to wipe everything also means the keystrokes to unlock the door aren't in the program anymore."

"Yep, and that would take equipment I don't have with me." He shrugged. "What's a little breaking and entering after grand theft auto?" Pulling her out of the way, he motioned Merek forward. "Your turn."

The reminder of all the laws they were bending just made her warlock scowl more ferociously, and she sighed. He had the door opened in under forty-five seconds, which Alex clocked on his wristwatch. Chloe went in to the guest bedroom on the ground floor and put away her belongings. It stung more than she could have imagined when Merek followed Alex up the stairs to claim rooms on the second floor.

Ophelia padded into Chloe's room and made herself at home on the bed. Chloe took a moment to pet her, and then went to close all the curtains on the bottom floor, knowing Merek would do the same upstairs. She watched the sunlight fading on the cloudy horizon as she shut the last set of blinds.

Turning on every light she passed on the way to the kitchen, she went searching for pots and pans to cook dinner. After a minute or two, she heard the males tromp downstairs and out the door to finish unloading the car. Neither of them was speaking, which didn't bode well for the evening. She wondered how long Merek could hold on to a grudge. Not long, she hoped, but she didn't know him well enough to be certain.

They spent the next hour mostly silent, and Alex turned in early, without getting his usual self-defense lesson from Merek. The boy just escaped to his bedroom upstairs for a loud television show. She had an idea that he was hoping to drown out any arguments they might have. That he assumed they'd default to screaming made her heart ache and told her things about Jaya's home life that she wished she didn't know.

Merek left her in the kitchen to do the dishes and stalked into the living room. She heard him rustling around, but couldn't figure out what he was doing. She went to peek at him, couldn't see anything, but could still hear him moving. Frowning, she stepped into the room and saw him kneeling near a wall, a pile of night-lights next to him on the floor while he fitted one into a socket.

Her lips shook when she opened her mouth, and she had to press them together for a moment before she thought she could talk without tearing up. Even pissed off and not speaking to her, he was still taking care of her, plugging in night-lights to save her from the dark.

"I love you," she blurted. The words just fell out, shocking the shit out of her. Until they were out there, she hadn't known she was going to say them.

His muscles went rigid, his head turning slowly to stare at her in utter, dumbfounded shock. "You can't." His eyes went stormy, turbulent with too many emotions for her to decipher. The words that came from his mouth sounded rough and desperate. "We've been together under some extreme circumstances—"

"Save the police psychobabble for someone else, Detective. I'm the one with the medical degree, remember? I know what love is, and I love you." She spat the words at him, but the fury burned itself out as quickly as it flared. She felt as if she'd been kicked in the stomach. Again, she needed someone more than they'd ever need her, like she'd needed Millie as a child. But she wouldn't cling or make demands. She refused to be that person ever again. Not even for him. "You don't have to feel the same, but don't try to tell me what *I* feel."

"I won't." He rose to his feet, the stunned look still glazing his eyes. His mouth opened, closed, but he just stood there staring at her until she couldn't take it anymore.

"Good night, Merek. Sleep well. I'll see you in the morning." Turning on her heel, she marched into her room and shut the door behind her.

She collapsed on the bed and dropped her face into her trembling hands. It hurt. Gods, how it hurt. Tears burned her eyes, but she refused to cry. She had expected this. Even then, it felt like her heart was shredding into tiny pieces, and she was bleeding to death from internal wounds. It was one thing to *think* she was in love alone, it was another to *know* it.

Yet, it was something of a relief. She had said it. It was out there. She didn't have to hide it or worry that he'd figure it out and feel guilty or obligated. Obviously, he hadn't felt obligated.

He'd tried to talk her out of it. A laugh that was almost a sob bubbled out, and she clamped her hand over her mouth to stop it. Shoving her head between her knees, she sucked in slow, deep breaths until the need to cry—or vomit—passed.

When she felt like she had a modicum of control back, she sighed and sat up. Pushing herself to her feet made her muscles ache, and she swayed a little. She clenched her jaw and willed her body to do what she wanted. There was nothing to do except put one foot in front of the other and get on with it. Survive. That was her specialty, wasn't it? A painful smile flicked over her face. She shook herself and went to shower and get ready for bed. She hadn't slept alone in almost a month, and she didn't relish the thought of doing so tonight. It wasn't just the sex. She wanted Merek near, wanted his arms around her in the night, the security of his embrace.

That wasn't going to happen.

Scrabbling for something—*anything*—else to think about, her mind turned to the issue of the upcoming full moon and Alex's forced Change. It felt like so much longer than a single month since she'd had to dig a silver bullet out of her godson's body. Her belly tightened at the thought. She never wanted to live through another night like that for the rest of her life. An ironic grin twisted her lips. There were several nights in her life she'd rather not think about again.

She stuffed those thoughts away and made herself come up with a new topic, like when this whole situation was over and they could go back to their lives. Alex could be his computer genius self, headed for college soon. Merek could go back to the police department. She could resume her research on lycanthropy. The potion she'd made for herself had worn off weeks ago, so she now remembered her work, but there was nothing she could do about it cut off from her lab the way she was.

Even if they had the breakthrough she knew they were on the verge of, it would still take years of testing and refining to perfect the treatment. They'd tried everything they could think of to block or regulate hormone release, inhibit magic. Synthetic chemicals, plant extracts, herbs. Everything. Some were more useful than others, but nothing had quite gotten there. The mix they had now was close. Very, very close.

She sighed in familiar frustration, scrubbing shampoo into her hair as if she could stimulate her brain into thinking up the answer. But nothing new came to her as she rinsed off, or as she hopped out of the shower, or as she finished preparing for bed. A disgusted growl rumbled in her chest. She'd gone over and over this so many times. The only thing she'd ever seen keep a werewolf in human form on full moon was when Alex was shot with a silver bullet.

"Silver." She jerked as if she'd been shot herself. Holy shit. That was *it*. Yes! If they used the current formula they had and added trace amounts of silver, it just might work. She could keep Alex from having to Change. She could save him, just as Jaya had always dreamed. She could increase the life expectancy of an entire Magickal race. Elation bubbled up inside her, and she danced out of the bathroom, twirling in a wobbly pirouette. "Silver, silver, sil*ver*."

"What about silver?"

"Gah!" She jolted, reeling back until she bounced off the doorjamb. Clapping her hand against her chest, she tried to slow her rocketing heartbeat as she stared at Merek lounging across her bed. "Gods, you scared me."

"Sorry." Though he didn't sound remorseful. "What about silver?"

A huge smile bloomed across her face, and at that moment she didn't care that she was on his shit list or that he didn't want her like she wanted him. *Years* of her work had just clicked into place. This used to be what she lived for—she stomped down on the thought that she'd have to learn to live for it again. "I think that's it. What'll refine the formula we were working on. If we add trace amounts of silver, it would stop the Change."

His eyes narrowed in thought. "It took more than trace amounts to stop Alex's Change last month. It almost killed him in the process."

"Yes, but we aren't going to shoot anyone, and we won't have the complications of trauma and blood loss. Plus, trace amounts combined with the other chemicals we're using just *might* do the trick. I have to run tests. Lots of tests." She slammed her hands on her hips. "I want my lab back, damn it."

He jerked upright, his fingers fisting at his sides. "Too bad. If you think for even a second you're taking a field trip over to Seattle, you're out of your mind."

She huffed out a breath, and her elation dimmed. "Please. I'm not an idiot, despite what you may think."

"I never said you were an idiot." He sighed, his hands unknotting.

"We did our best in a bad situation, Merek. I know you're not comfortable being this close to Seattle, and neither am I, but you were unavailable for consultation at the time." The ghastly pale expression on his face from that morning flashed through her mind. "I'm sorry if you don't like this, but we couldn't stay where we were, and I made an executive decision."

"I know. I know you did your best, and I appreciate your hauling my unconscious ass along for the ride." He shook his head. "I'm not happy with this situation, but that means I'm worried *for* you, not angry *at* you."

"Thank you for making that distinction. And you're welcome. You would have done the same." But he still hadn't addressed how she'd spilled out her love all over him and he'd looked at her like she'd sprouted horns and a forked tail.

He met her gaze, and she knew his thinking had followed the same path as hers. "Are you angry at me?"

"No." Not angry, hurt. She swallowed and looked away, unable to hold his gaze. "I'm not mad."

"Do you want me to leave?"

The question sent a pang through her, and self-preservation warred with need. "No."

"Good." His breath eased out. "There are some ... things we don't agree on, but I don't want to fight."

Things. Like whether she could or should love him. Like whether they should have come to this island. Yeah. There were some *things* they didn't see eye to eye on. It was unlikely they'd come to an accord on either issue.

"I don't want to fight either." She offered him a wavering smile. "I just solved years worth of research. I think. We should celebrate."

"Celebrate." A naughty smiled flashed, the only warning she had before his hand shot out, snapped around her wrist in an iron grip, and jerked her facedown across his lap.

A squeak erupted from her, and her breath rushed out of her lungs as she hit the hard muscles of his thighs. Her hands bunched in the bedspread, her nose a bare inch from the soft fabric. "Merek!"

"What?" His voice was a silken purr. He stroked his fingers up the back of her calf, making her shiver. Excitement whipped through her, and her nipples went rock hard in moments. "This isn't the kind of celebration you had in mind?"

Her short laugh was incredulous. "You want to give me a celebratory spanking?"

Cool air rushed over her thighs as he drew her nightgown up and tossed it over her head. Her breath heaved in little pants, anticipation twisting within her as he cupped her buttocks in his palm. "Can you think of a better way to commemorate the occasion?"

She couldn't.

His fingers hooked in the waistband of her panties and began working them down her legs. "Let's get rid of these."

A slow whimper trickled from her lips, and she arched her hips to help him ease the lace off of her. Shrugging, she let her nightgown fall forward off her arms and onto the floor, leaving her naked. Her tongue twisted into knots, and she could do little more than moan when his callused fingers caressed the bare globes of her backside.

"You have the sweetest little ass," he growled.

"Oh, gods, Merek. I don't know if—"

A sharp swat cut her off. "Too late to run, remember sweetheart?" He stroked her stinging flesh. She closed her eyes and tightened her grip on the bedspread. Far too late to run. From herself, from him, from how she felt about him. She shuddered, and he smacked her backside harder.

"Merek, I—"

"Tell me you don't want this, and I'll stop." He cupped both throbbing cheeks, then dipped between them to find the hot, slippery center of her. Her pussy flexed around his fingers when he penetrated her.

She panted, lifting her hips into the rough stroking of his fingers. Her mind whirled, and she scrambled to keep hold of her wits.

"Chloe—"

"Don't stop!" She grabbed the leg of his jeans when he moved as if to set her aside. Everything in her rebelled at his withdrawing now. She didn't think she could handle being left alone. Her feelings were too raw and tumbled, from agony to elation to lust and back to agony. "Don't stop. We're celebrating."

"Yes, we are."

She smiled against the bedspread when she felt his fingers slide over her backside again. His cock was an iron bar against her hip, so she knew that no matter how jumbled his own emotions were, he did want her. It was enough. It had to be. Even if it hurt that she *knew* he might not be capable of giving her more. She understood why he might not want her to love him. His lost family would make him just as wary of love, of needing anyone, as she had always been. But it was too late to save herself. It had been from the very beginning, whether she'd admitted it or not. So, she'd take what she could get for as long as she could get it. She pressed herself into his stroking hand, raising her ass to fit against his palm.

His hand lifted away from her skin, came back down in a light pat that made her whimper in frustration. That wasn't what she wanted. She needed the intensity that would burn away everything else. The love, the anguish. All of it. She undulated on his lap, sighing when he slapped her left cheek, then her right. Hard. Harder.

Desire slammed into her, no slow building tide, but a crashing wave that dragged her under and drowned her. Wetness coated the lips of her pussy, and her inner walls contracted. Quicker, sharper swats, randomly spread over her ass, her upper thighs. Her flesh swelled, stung, burned. She cried out when he stopped, moaned when he thrust his hand between her legs. He flicked her clit, and she jolted, let out a broken groan. Filling her sex with three thick fingers, he worked her slowly, but it wasn't enough. She bowed her back, pushing them both faster.

"None of that, sweetheart," he scolded. And he took his hand away from her needy pussy and brought it down hard on her ass. The crack of flesh on flesh aroused her. Only with Merek would she want this; only with Merek could she surrender everything.

Each sharp spank reverberated through her entire body, made her sex clench, made her wetter. She was so close. He wasn't even inside her, and she was going to come for him.

When he paused again to tease her clit and fuck her pussy with his fingers, she shattered. Fiery heat and icy tingles sluiced over her flesh as her sex spasmed again and again. He smacked her ass, building her need until she crested once more, bucked helplessly against his hand.

Her heart pounded, made the blood roar in her ears. She turned her head to look up at him and meet his beautiful eyes. His face was tight with lust, red staining his high cheekbones. His chest heaved with each breath as he stared down at her.

"Make love with me, Merek." A low sob ripped from her when he cupped her aching backside. "Let's forget everything. Just for the night. Please, Merek. I want you." A tear slipped free when she heard his defeated groan.

Ignoring the voices in her head that whispered this might, in fact, be her last night with him, she turned herself over to his pleasure. Whatever tomorrow brought, she intended to enjoy these final hours with him.

For the first time in her life, she wished the night would never end.

Forget? Merek wanted to forget everything, just as she'd said. Forget he'd failed to defend himself well enough and *they'd* had to drag *him* to safety. Forget that he'd woken to find they were a stone's throw away from danger. Forget he couldn't keep her forever. Forget that she *loved* him.

He clamped down on that thought so fast, it made his own head spin. No. Not again. Never again. He knew that road only led to a dead end. *Her* dead end. He couldn't live with that. *Never* again. This was temporary. He'd always known that, and her love changed nothing. In fact, it only made it more necessary to walk away from her. Soon. An instinct that wasn't clairvoyance told him it would all be over soon. How and why and exactly when was beyond his abilities.

More than ever before, he hated his own weakness and how it kept him from protecting her.

He closed his eyes when her fingers brushed his leg, wrenching him back to the present, to the grinding needs of his body. His cock throbbed, so stiff with his lust, he shook. She lay nude, draped across his lap, her pale skin flushed from his spanking, cream slicking her thighs from where she'd come for him.

"Merek," she whispered, and he broke.

Hauling her upright, he pulled her astride his thighs. He shoved his hand into her hair, held her still for his kiss. This time, this once, he had to have all of her, had to give her everything. No holding back, no pretending this dance wouldn't end. She melted against him, thrusting her tongue into his mouth. He groaned and locked his arms around her, so she was plastered against him. Gods, the feel of her was unbearable it was so perfect.

Her fingers slid under his shirt, pulling it over his head, and he shuddered, loving her hands on him. Her touch fulfilled needs he wasn't even willing to admit he had. He just wanted her, wanted more. He slid one hand down to cup the soft, smooth curve of her ass and pull her tighter to him. She moaned and twisted in his arms, rubbing her nipples over his chest, her movement driving him crazy.

He used his grip on the silken strands of her hair to pull her head back so he could bite his way down her slim throat. The taste of her, the feminine smell of her, sank hooks of need inside him. She arched her body into him, her legs wrapping around his hips as she tried to ride his dick through his pants. He forced her back into a deeper bend so he could suck her little nipples into his mouth one at a time. He drew hard on the tight crests, batting them with his tongue, shoving them against the roof of his mouth.

A choked cry spilled from her throat, and the musky scent of her arousal intensified. Her hands scrabbled for purchase on his back, and he could feel the heat and magic gather inside her. "No spells, sweetheart. Not here. Not tonight. No spells."

"Merek, I need you." Her voice was whisper-soft, but he heard it anyway. "No spells. Just you."

She didn't say she loved him again, and he told himself it was for the best, that he didn't want to hear the words. Even as he recognized the lie, he forced himself to set her away from him, and caught her elbow when she staggered, her eyes glazed and her expression dazed with lust. It made his cock ache to be buried inside her.

"Yes. Now." He stripped out of his boxers, pants and boots, left them in a tangled heap on the floor. He reached for her, and she met him halfway, pressing herself against his chest and rising on tiptoe to kiss him.

Having her in his embrace made some white-hot emotion expand in his chest until he couldn't breathe. He crushed that, wrestling it into the deepest, darkest corner of his soul where he wouldn't have to acknowledge it. Instead, he focused on the physical, on Chloe, on his woman in his arms. A groan rumbled in his chest. He slid his hands down her back, palmed the hot globes of her ass, and smiled against her mouth when she whimpered and wriggled.

The satin skin of her belly rubbed over his cock, and he choked. He backed her up until she hit the bed, smoothly rolling them onto the mattress. She hissed when her buttocks slid against the sheets, and some dark, possessive part of himself liked that she could feel his mark on her, that she'd be wearing it for a while since she wasn't allowed to use a healing spell on herself. Every time she moved, sat, lay in bed, she'd be reminded of him. Oh, yes. He liked that a lot.

Shifting them onto their sides, he pulled her close, looped her thigh over his. "Is this all right? Not too painful?"

"Good. Perfect. Yes." She wound her fingers through his

hair, tugging him close for a kiss. Her tongue twined with his, and he cherished the moment with her. A moment that was slipping through his fingers. He couldn't remember the last time anything had felt so right. Before Chloe . . . years. Maybe never.

He held her tighter, every inch of her welded to his front. Yes. He wanted that. The head of his cock brushed her wet core, and she jolted forward, tilting her hips in offering. He wanted to wait, to draw this time out as long as possible, but he couldn't. He needed her too much. A quick thrust, and he was hilted inside her, squeezed tight by her heated channel.

Closing his eyes, he had to grit his teeth to keep from coming then and there. Only Chloe could shred his control like this, and the emotional knot within him twisted at the knowledge that far too soon there would be nothing and no one that could do this to him. Just as he'd always preferred it. He blew out a harsh breath, ran his hands over every part of her he could reach, as if he could burn the feel of her into his mind, as if the memory could sustain him.

Somehow, she understood, touched him everywhere, kissed him deeper, gave him exactly what he needed. Everything. They rocked together slowly, savored each other. Sweat sealed their bodies, and their breathing grew ragged between kisses, as her breasts slid against his chest, and his pelvis rubbed over her clitoris. The fire that built within him wanted to rage out of control, but he couldn't let this end. Not now. Not yet.

Not yet.

Her sex began to clench around his cock every time he entered her, and he held on to his restraint by the tips of his fingers. The little cries and moans that spilled from her lips told him just how close she was to coming for him. She writhed against him like a cat in heat. Orgasm fisted in his belly, shudders racking his body. His groan was as helpless and hopeless as he felt. Too soon. Too soon to let go. Too soon to lose her.

"Merek," she sobbed, ripping her mouth from his. She arched hard, the muscles in her thighs tensing as she impaled herself on his cock, took him deep, deeper than before.

The way her pussy milked him made his thoughts scatter, made orgasm inevitable. He pounded inside her, let her drag him into the abyss. Come spurted from him, filled her tight channel, and still he held himself deep, unwilling to lose this connection with her.

They shivered together, arms wrapped around each other, aftershocks quaking through both of them. She buried her face in his chest, and he could feel the wetness of her tears. His emotions gave another vicious wrench, but he ignored them, refused to accept them. Later. Later, he would deal with his own feelings.

Now was for Chloe.

He cradled her close, stroking back her damp hair. "Shh. Don't cry, sweetheart. Shh. Don't cry."

She kissed him fiercely in response, demanding without words that he make her forget. Everything. Her tongue thrust into his mouth, and his cock went rock hard, thrusting into her pussy.

And he held her tight, pushed away reality, made love with her again and again and again. Just for the night. Just as she'd asked.

It was all he had to give her.

13

"Chloe!"

Windows exploded in the living room, and the choked cough of silenced gunfire reported just before the shrill squeal of a woman in pain.

"Chloe!"

She bolted upright, her name coming at her from too many directions. Merek's bellow beside her as he flipped her off the bed and onto the floor, covering her with his heavy body. Alex's mental shout from upstairs she didn't have the ability to answer. The cry from the living room had been in a woman's voice. "Tess?"

More gunfire, more shattering glass and breaking wood. "Are you here, Chloe?"

"Merek, that's Tess." She wheezed out a breath while he crushed her into the carpet. The glint of light off the dull black metal of his pistol made her swallow. It was too much like the last time, when Alex was shot. She pressed her forehead to the floor, regret lancing through her. "I'm sorry, Merek. You were right. We should never have come here."

He grunted, stuffing the revolver into her hand. Then he jerked on his shirt, grabbed his pants, and rolled to shove himself into them. "There was no way to have known for sure, sweetheart. Stay here, stay down. I'm going to see what kind of mess we're in."

"Broken glass. Put on your boots." He did, and she clutched the revolver closer, scooting to put her back into a corner behind the bed and away from the windows. "Alex. Make sure Alex—"

"I will." He nodded a quick approval when he saw where she'd moved.

Resisting the urge to shove him to the floor and protect *him*, she returned his nod. "Be careful."

"I will," he repeated. Then he disappeared, leading with his pistol out into the hallway.

Gods, she was naked. All she had was a revolver. She shoved down on a hysterical giggle, sucked in a breath, and dredged up the magic inside her. Too late to pretend there were no Magickals here, right? She fought down another laugh.

"Clothes," she ordered in a low voice. She closed her eyes tight, heard a rush of air, felt a hint of heat from the spell, and when she looked down again, she was dressed. Shoes to shirt, fully dressed. That was a first, but she didn't have time to wonder about it.

Her heart hammered in her chest, and she tried to slow it, tried to control her breathing so she could hear anything that was going on outside the bedroom. Who was here besides Tess? How many of them were there? Where was Alex? Where was Merek? She didn't know, could only sense people moving around her, perceive the faintest creaks of floorboards as they ghosted along. A huge thump sounded against the wall, and her night-light flickered wildly beside her, but its glow was soon dimmed by the streaks of dawn filtering through the heavy curtains.

Clamping her mouth closed to keep in a scream, she shifted her grip on the revolver, held it ready in case anything tried to get inside her room. The thumping continued, muffled shouts and grunts, the impact of flesh on flesh as two large people struck each other. But who? Merek? Other men? She didn't know. Merek would know. Alex would be able to sense it, but this wasn't her area of expertise. So she sat, trying not to tremble, and waited for whatever came next.

A lupine howl echoed above her. Alex!

She shot to her feet, her gaze pinned on the ceiling, and she strained with all her might to hear anything, *anything* that might tell her he was all right. The door to her room exploded inward, screeching on twisted hinges to embed itself in the wall.

A huge, half-shifted wolf barreled in, a gun in each hand. His feral gaze locked on her, but her revolver was already pointed at him. He wasn't Merek or Alex or Tess. That was all she needed to know.

Her heart stopped, her hands trembled, but she pulled the trigger again and again until the gun clicked. Empty.

Merek watched the werewolf stumble back, a blank look of shock on his face as he dropped one gun and clutched at the bleeding holes in his chest. Not a shred of sympathy passed through Merek as he wrenched the man's other gun from his hand and used it to put six bullets in his skull. He fell. Dead. Even a wolf's healing magic wouldn't bring him back from that.

Tucking the pistol away as a spare, he grabbed the fallen weapon and tossed it to Chloe. She caught it, letting the spent revolver clatter to the floor. Her face was pale, but her step was steady as she walked to his side. She looked up at him, her eyes huge, her lips shaking, yet her voice was calm. "Is Alex okay? I heard him yell."

"He's fine. Cavalli went to help him out." Merek ejected the clip in his pistol and shoved in a fresh one, pulled back the slide, and chambered the first round. He kept his senses open, ready to detect an approaching attack.

Chloe fell in behind him when he moved down the hall to the front of the house. She spoke in a soft whisper, "Luca's here?"

The breathy tone was almost lost in a roar of gunfire overhead. A hissing shriek of an injured vampire made his ears ring. If Cavalli failed and Alex got injured in any way, Merek would personally end the bloodsucking son of a bitch.

"He followed Tess, who got a report of a code change from the security company as well as the code someone tried to input before making the change. She figured it might be you, so she came to check it out instead of just calling the cops." He swung her into the kitchen and down to the floor behind the island. A bruised, battered, and sopping wet Tess was already crouched there, a neat little compact pistol in her hands. He nodded to her. "By the time our vampiric friend pried that information out of her, he realized that Smith's men were following them and that he couldn't call to warn us because I didn't fucking leave him my number on the message."

A muscle in Tess's cheek twitched. "Maybe I would have been a little more forthcoming if your vampiric friend had ever told me the truth about anything. At all." She swallowed, shook her head. "Vampire."

"Yeah, and I'm a witch." Chloe shrugged, her face still too pale for Merek's liking. "So is Aunt Millie. Merek is a warlock, and Alex is—"

"A werewolf," Tess interrupted, stuffing a lock of her dripping red hair behind her ear. "Luca the liar filled me in on those little details after his fangs popped out when my boat was capsized by some kind of . . . of *force field.*"

"Spell. Not force field." Chloe swallowed and met Merek's gaze. "How long do you think we have until the Normal police get here? Or the cavalry you told Luca to have standing by?"

"The spell hit while he was calling in. I'm pretty sure his phone's at the bottom of the Puget Sound." Tess didn't look at either of them. "The cavalry's not coming."

"I put a silencing spell on the place after the windows shattered." He didn't need to tell Chloe the Magickal Council would expect them to die before they revealed themselves to Normals. Their lives were not worth every Magickal person's. It was the ugly reality of living with magic. "If we're lucky, no Normals are coming."

"Luck. Right. We've done so well with that lately." Chloe's chest lifted in slow, deep breaths, and he wished like hell they were in a place where he could comfort her, but they weren't and he couldn't, so he turned away and did his job.

The women fell silent when he lifted his hand. Something . . . swept along his senses. A person. Magickal. Hiding under an invisibility spell. He drew in a lungful of air, let half of it out. The brush of a footstep sounded to his left. He swung around the edge of the island. Fired two shots toward what he hoped was the chest.

Flames exploded outward, and he ducked back behind the island, throwing up a shielding spell to protect them, but the effort cost him. Fuck. This Magickal was old, powerful. Fire engulfed them, red and orange light flowing around his shield like liquid. Sweat sluiced down his skin as the heat hit him. Chloe yanked Tess closer to him, threw her own magic around them.

The heat lessened, and he swiveled around, taking a blind shot through the shield. He felt the reverberation as it pierced, but a short scream ended the flood of flames. Chloe collapsed against his side, panting. "Okay?"

"Fine. You? Tess?"

"Good," Tess choked.

"Me, too." Chloe patted his arm and chest as if looking for injuries. He used his free hand to catch hers, squeeze in brief reassurance, and then set her aside.

He forced his muscles to cooperate, to not shake from the outpouring of magic. Pushing himself up into a crouch, he kept the shield as strong as he could, and took a quick look at what they were facing. A woman lay sprawled on her back, her mouth gaping open and closed like a landed fish, a clear shot through her throat. Hovering over her was a vampire.

Not Cavalli.

Merek squeezed off another shot and tucked himself back behind the island as the vampire returned fire. He jolted and Chloe screamed in pain as the bullet ricocheted off their shield and exploded into the refrigerator. Shoving Chloe back against the cabinet door, he clamped a hand across her mouth, and looked up. He wasn't surprised to see the vampire perched on top of the island, fangs bared in a horrific smile.

They both fired. And hit.

The vampire barely jerked as blood bloomed from his chest, and Merek groaned as white-hot agony sliced into his thigh. Chloe dropped her gun to dive for his leg and the crimson that spurted upward. Femoral artery. His mind registered the severity of the wound, even as his instincts kept him moving. The vampire leaped to the counter across from them, laughed as Tess's Normal bullets hit him and did even less damage than Merek's one shot. He followed the bloodsucker with his weapon, but his body felt weak, his muscles unresponsive.

His aim wavered, the vampire's didn't, and he knew he'd failed.

A shadow that moved with unnatural speed sailed over the island and crashed into the vampire. Cavalli. They slammed through the wall and into the living room. Furious hissing and blows too swift to sound real echoed through the cloud of white plaster.

Chloe's healing spell wrapped around his leg, sealed the entry and exit wounds from the bullet, and began to weave the muscle and sinew back together. It fucking hurt. A lot. It felt like hot pokers jabbed into his leg, and stars burst before his eyes. He gritted his teeth and bore it, gurgled on a groan, sweat stinging his eyes.

"Merek! A little help, please." Alex's call was so mild, Merek knew the kid was up to his neck in a fight he couldn't handle. A short howl ended in a whoosh of escaped breath. Someone had gut-punched the kid.

Scrambling to his feet, he grabbed the counter to keep his leg from collapsing under him. Pain stabbed from his thigh straight to his skull. The healing wasn't done, but it was good enough that he wasn't going to bleed out. "You two stay here. Chloe, pick up your gun."

She fumbled in the pool of his blood to retrieve the pistol. Her hands shook, her lips colorless, her mouth pinched. The look in her eyes was haunted as she wiped the blood off her hands and onto her pants. "Be careful. Help Alex."

Not bothering to waste time with a response, he turned away from her and stumbled out of the kitchen, almost tripping over the body of the woman he'd killed. He had to get to Alex.

Chloe watched him walk away, and it took everything in her not to scream for him to come back. She'd never wanted to hold on to anyone so tightly in her entire life. This need made her childhood clinging to Millie seem like nothing. It was terrifying and unstoppable. Only the fact that Alex needed help kept her mouth shut.

Tess shifted beside her. "What can we do? My bullets aren't doing shit against these guys."

"No, you need special ammunition designed for Magickals." An idea began to percolate. Rocking herself onto her hands and knees, Chloe crawled forward until she could reach the cleaning supplies under the sink. She glanced back at Tess. "Normal stuff is especially ineffective against vampires and werewolves. Because of their healing abilities."

"I see."

A sick feeling crawled through Chloe at the expressionless mask her friend wore, but what could she say? Tess wasn't an idiot. The conclusions she was obviously coming to were pretty damn accurate. "I'm sorry I lied to you, Tess. I'm sorry we all lied to you."

"Did you have a choice?"

Pulling out every cleaning solution she could get her hands on, she lined them up on the floor to see what she had to work with. "No, but that doesn't make it suck less."

"That's for damn sure." Tess's voice went hoarse, and her eyes closed for a moment. When she opened them, she was back in control, the mask firmly in place. "What can we do?"

"I can make some explosives." Chloe didn't mention that the Council would probably order Tess's memory altered so she wouldn't know about magic after this was over. She also didn't tell her friend that she didn't have enough magic left to generate a flame spell like Merek and she had blocked. A few nasty potions were the best she could do. She rifled through the cabinets under the island until she came up with a few plastic containers.

"This has the ammo you'll need." Handing her gun over to her friend, Chloe set to work on the incendiaries.

"Okay." Tess's face was milk white, which made her mottled bruises stand out in ugly contrast, but her tone was serene. "So, we're burning my uncle's house down?"

Chloe focused on the chemicals she was mixing, letting magic slip from her as she worked, tweaking the compounds to do exactly what she wanted. "No, the people will burn, the building will be fine."

Both women studiously ignored the shouts, grunts, and gunfire from other parts of the house. Tess swallowed audibly. "How is that possible? A magic spell?"

"A magic potion, actually." A flicker of skepticism crossed

the Normal's face, and Chloe managed a grin. "Trust me, this is what I do."

Tess flinched a little and looked away, checking her weapon. "Trust. Right."

The smile slid off Chloe's face, and she sealed a few of the containers. This was the worst possible way Tess could have found out, and Chloe didn't have a clue what to say to her best friend. So much had happened since they'd last seen each other, so many changes for both of them. Luca and Merek, for starters. She wanted to *talk* to Tess, connect like they used to do with just a glance, but this was neither the time nor the place. It would have to wait—*if* they ever got the chance. *If* the Council didn't have Tess's memories wiped. *If* they survived this at all.

A shadow moved to their left, someone slipping through the shafts of sunshine coming from the hole Luca had made in the wall between the kitchen and the living room.

Beware. danger. Beware! Chloe's clairaudience kicked off right on cue, letting her know for sure it wasn't someone on their side of this fight.

"Heads up," Chloe whispered when that ominous shadow flickered again. She hoisted one of her concoctions.

"I saw it." The redhead flipped her damp hair back over her shoulder with a nonchalant shrug. "Ready when you are."

They didn't have long to wait. Agony burst in Chloe's skull, and she wailed. Pain screamed along every nerve ending in her body, and though she knew it wasn't real, she would have sworn fire ants swarmed over her flesh, biting and burning. Tess writhed on the blood-smeared linoleum beside her, caught in the same evil telepathic spell.

Spasms racked Chloe's muscles, and her hand clenched and unclenched around the plastic canister. A man moved into the light, his hands outstretched as he focused more of the spell on Tess. She lifted in a hard arc off the floor, an inhuman sound ripping from her throat. Chloe forced her fingers to move through the pain, pointed the container at the man, and used the tiny spurt of magic she could muster to pop the lid off.

The potion exploded forth, spraying the man from head to toe in a quick shower. He blinked down at her for a moment, his spell slacking off until both women collapsed to the floor. Chloe could tell the moment her potion took effect. His eyes widened, and then he gave a guttural shout, slapping at his clothes, dancing in a frenzied circle as his skin began to melt like wax.

She didn't stop to watch the carnage. Crawling through the drying pool of Merek's blood, she grabbed Tess and shook her hard. The Normal woman gasped at the touch, bolting upright with a cry. "Tess, honey, it's okay. We—"

The sharp report of a gun cut her off as Tess swung the pistol around and dropped the melting man with one shot. Hot crimson splattered them as he hit the floor, still twitching and groaning. Tess swayed where she sat, sweat making clean trails down her face. "That was *not* an exploding magic potion."

"No, that one was more corrosive than combustible." Chloe gathered up her other containers, ignoring the way her hands trembled and the shocks of pain that continued to fire through her nerves.

They both flinched when something heavy crashed into the wall beside Luca's makeshift doorway. Tess pointed the gun at the opening and Chloe hefted another canister, ready to launch it at anything that came through.

Instead, they saw Luca roll by, wrestling with a vampire and a half-shifted werewolf. The scene was appallingly clear, each man bleeding from multiple wounds, clothes slashed to shreds from jagged claws, Luca cursing in fluent Italian as he grappled for the upper hand against his two opponents.

The house grew brighter by the minute as morning light managed to filter around the shades that Merek and Chloe had drawn to keep out prying eyes. At the moment it was also keeping out the sun that would burn Luca and the other vampires in the house. Much as she'd like to torch the hell out of the terrorists, she couldn't do that to Luca.

The bad guys didn't have those kinds of scruples.

The vampire terrorist hissed and ducked away from the sunbeams, but he opened the front door while the enormous wolf launched a struggling Luca outside.

Slashes of fire carved burns on his face. Every exposed inch of skin boiled and sizzled, and an animalistic shriek of sheer agony assaulted Chloe's ears as he writhed in the sunlight.

Tess bolted forward, a horrified cry on her lips. Chloe managed to hit the vampire with her flame potion before he touched her friend, and he hit the floor, rolling to try to put out the fire. As if Chloe would have made it that easy for him. Tess emptied the rest of her bullets into the werewolf, two shots to the heart and three to the head. He fell, his body contorting as his bones snapped and retracted back to human form. Chloe stayed where she was, ready to use her potions on anything that moved.

Throwing herself on top of Luca, Tess did her best to shield him from the light, and somehow managed to pull, push, and heave him back into the house. Chloe slammed the door closed behind them. The stench of scorched, blackened flesh made her stomach turn.

Tess's eyes were wide, blank with utter shock as she watched her lover's fangs protrude from his gums. "Luca? *Luca!*"

He choked, his eyes little more than slits in his swollen, distorted face. "*Mia diletta.*"

A tear slid down her cheek. "I'm here. Tell me what to do. Tell me what you need."

"Leave me." He closed his eyes and turned his face away, but not before Chloe saw his hungry gaze lock on her friend's throat.

"What?" A short sob racked the Normal woman, disbelief coloring her words. "No, Luca. You're hurt. You need help."

Chloe put her hand on her friend's shoulder, her heart breaking as she saw the ugly truth. One of these two was going to die, and there was nothing she could do to stop it. "He needs to feed, Tess. He'd need a lot of blood to heal from this, and if you stay close, he'll attack you and drain you. He won't mean to, but he won't be able to help it. Come away, honey. You need to leave him."

A brilliant explosion that sounded like fireworks brought her head around, and she saw Merek and Alex locked in a deadly showdown with four other Magickals. Gods, there were just so many of them. They took out two and three more seemed to be ready to take their place. An exhausted sob caught in her throat when Merek's bloodshot gray eyes met hers.

Chloe looked as drained as he felt. Every muscle and tendon in Merek's body ached. His very bones ached. He'd burned through more magic in the last hour than he'd known he possessed. He was spent. Shoving that thought away, he made himself keep moving and blocked a punch by a beefy elf. He rolled his shoulder, brought his knuckles up in a quick jab to the big man's kidneys, adding as much magic as he could to the blow. It wasn't much, but it made the other man grunt and stagger backward into a werewolf terrorist, giving Merek precious seconds to breathe.

He saw when things went south the moment before they did. Alex was holding his own against a warlock who was as drained as the rest of them. It was the female vampire who fucked things. Time stretched into slow motion as he watched her slam a fresh magazine into a Beretta and swing it around to point at Alex. Merek didn't hesitate, didn't think, just launched himself forward and prayed he made it in time. One step, two, and he was airborne, catching the wolf around waist and sending the boy crashing to the carpet.

Merek's body jerked as searing heat and power slammed into his back, his side, his chest, spinning him around like a puppet with broken strings. Another strike to his chest, and one to his injured leg that drove him into the floor.

Some part of his mind knew they were bullets, that he'd been shot. More than once. But a haze swam through his consciousness, and he couldn't seem to piece everything together. They were still in danger. He should do something, but what that was drifted just beyond his grasp.

There was screaming, and golden flames danced in front of him, driving away the enemies. That was good. Alex stood over him, fangs bared, a roar of anguish and rage rending the air. Merek blinked in confusion as the world revolved around him. Someone was rolling him onto his back.

"No! Please, no." Chloe swirled before his eyes, her precious face tear-streaked. Her hands were frantic as they ripped open his shirt, but he knew she didn't have enough magic left to stop all the bleeding. He could feel blood pumping out of him with every beat of his heart. "Don't leave me, Merek. I need you. I love you! Please don't leave me alone. *Please!*"

He wanted to reach for her, wanted to touch her so badly, but he couldn't make his arms move. Couldn't speak, couldn't warn her to run before they came for her, could only stare up into her hazel eyes. Her broken pleading trailed off into ragged weeping as she used all of her energy to try to pull bullets from his body. A body he felt disconnected from. There was no pain, no panic . . . nothing.

It was funny. All this time, he'd worried about failing her, about failing Alex, about not being able to protect them because he couldn't see their future. About someone else he cared for dying on him. Now, he was going to fucking die on them, and who would protect them then?

Blackness edged into his vision, and he coughed, his mouth flooding with his own blood.

It tasted bitter.

14

_____

Chloe woke to darkness.

It took everything she had not to scream as blind terror exploded through her. Her blood froze in her veins; her heart stopped and then jackhammered against her breastbone. The blackness closed in around her, suffocating her. She lay on her side, and her hands were bound behind her, bronze blistering her flesh. Her fingers trembled, and she fisted them tight, trying to fight down the need to gag.

She didn't know where she was, just that she was bronze-bound and alone in the vast, gloomy nothing.

It was the sum of all her fears. Her stomach heaved at the thought, and she swallowed bitter bile that coated her tongue. Sweat slid down her face to burn her eyes. Tremors ran through her muscles, and she panted, her face pressed to the hard, cold floor.

Something landed on her back, and she bucked, biting back a terrified shriek. Whatever was on her rolled away, but she knew it wasn't gone. She could hear it breathing. She went rigid, waiting for the next nightmare to materialize. Sandpaper rasped against her left cheek, and she flinched away from the harsh sensation.

"Prrp." Ophelia laid a paw against her cheek, then rubbed herself down Chloe's torso. How her familiar had gotten here, Chloe would never be able to guess. The cat crawled over her and settled against her back, vibrating with a purr. A few seconds later, the bronze shackles clanked to the metal floor.

Chloe choked, freed, but reminded far too much of being stranded with her familiar in the forest as a child. Only this was worse, because now she knew the danger she was in, knew there were people out there counting on her to help them and not just herself. She couldn't give in to her fears; as much as she wanted to curl up and sob as she once had, she didn't have time for any weakness.

Alex and Tess needed her.

She got a vice grip on her control, pulling her injured wrists into her chest. Forcing her mind to focus on healing spells helped drag her back from the abyss. She clenched her jaw to stop her teeth from chattering. Wherever she was, there were vampires and werewolves out there, and they could hear if she made too much noise.

Swallowing hard, she forced back the darts of panic that shot through her. Memories exploded through her mind. Merek shot, bleeding out faster than she could extract the bullets and seal the wounds. A screaming and struggling Tess hauled away from Luca by a werewolf. Alex roaring, so much grief on his face it hurt to recall it. He'd left her with Merek, shooting forward to attack those who'd hurt a man they both loved. The teen's body had frozen after no more than two steps, his muscles flexing in uncoordinated jolts as if he were struggling against himself. His eyelids fluttered, and he shook his head hard, prying them open. A vampire stood across the room, her gaze locked on Alex's face—hypnotizing him into unconsciousness.

Chloe had stopped healing Merek long enough to heave one of her fire canisters at the bloodsucker, but the other woman had stepped smoothly out of its path. She didn't even lose eye contact with Alex. Merek choked, blood gushing from his mouth and nose. Energy she didn't know she had poured into him for the spells, and she'd felt her own grip on reality, on life, begin to fade. Jerking, she'd tried to refocus on Alex, searched for him . . . and was caught by the vampire's gaze herself.

That was the last thing she remembered, before now.

Patting her hands along the hollow metal floor, she tried to feel for anything that would orient her. A van? The space felt small enough for that. She fended off a wave of dizziness as the darkness assaulted her once more. A tiny part of her couldn't believe this had happened again. Trapped in the black, scorched by bronze, those she loved most lost to her, perhaps forever. She snorted, tears stinging her eyes, hysteria rising.

No. She was no longer a scared child. She refused to let her fears rule her, refused to let them freeze her up. She didn't know where she was, but she knew it was nowhere she wanted to be. She didn't know where Alex and Tess were, but she doubted it was any safer. Luca and Merek were—

Agony poured through her like acid, and she pushed that away as well. Not now. If she survived this, there would be plenty of time for grief. Years. Decades. Centuries.

She shuddered, but made herself complete her train of thought. As far as she knew, both men were dead. No one was coming to save them. No one was going to protect them. No one was going to get them out of this. That was her job now.

Cracking open her senses, she tried to stretch out her magic and see if there was anyone else within reach. Nothing stirred outside the van, but there was a flurry of activity in the distance. Her ears buzzed with the life forces of many different kinds of Magickals. Mostly wolves, which only made her belly cramp tighter. She'd never felt so many wolves in one place at one time. This was not good.

Her hand came into contact with the side of the van, and she got to her knees to try to feel around for the door. Quietly. Was the van parked on the street? In a garage? Could she scream for help? If she did, would anyone but the wolves hear her? She didn't know so she couldn't risk it.

The hinges for the rear door bumped under her questing fingers, and a spurt of triumph went through her. She slid over on her knees to find the middle. If she could use her magic to unlock and ease the door open . . .

But the doors creaked open, and a shaft of light pierced the gloom. A pale streak told her Ophelia had bolted, disappearing to the gods knew where. Chloe turned her face into the brightness, relief so huge it made her shake coursing through her body. She sent a fireball through the narrow opening, and heard an angry shout on the other side. One door whipped open, and a gun pointed at her face. Shit.

"Are you going to behave, or am I going to have to put you back into the cuffs?"

Blinking away the light, she focused on the man with a familiar, quiet voice. She couldn't keep her mouth from falling open, then it snapped shut on a snarl as welcome rage rolled over her. Her fists clenched to keep from torching the treacherous asshole. "Peyton."

"You remember me." He grasped her upper arm and pulled her from the van. Every muscle screamed a protest at the quick movement.

"Hard to forget a man who helped torture you." She jerked away from him, but he held on with disgustingly little effort. His jacket lay in a smoking heap on the cement floor, and she smirked.

"Let's get moving. Your friends are waiting for you." He

propelled her across a large loading dock. "We'd have moved you at the same time, but it took quite a few men to handle young Nemov. Someone trained the boy well."

"Detective Kingston." As much as she'd like to fry his nerves with a spell, she managed to stop herself from following through with the thought. He was taking her to Alex and Tess, and acting rashly wouldn't help any of them. She would need all the magic she could marshal to get them out of this. She refused to consider any other option. They *would* get out of this. She satisfied her ire by spitting out, "They killed him and Agent Cavalli, you know. I hope you're happy, traitor."

Some emotion flickered in his eyes, but was soon gone, and his face became a smooth mask. "No, I didn't know. This way, please, Dr. Standish."

Since she didn't have a real choice, she let him lead her through a secured door and down a long, brightly lit hallway. It looked like they were in an office building, which was so ordinary it was disconcerting. They passed armed men and women who nodded to Peyton and looked her over like so much prey. She clenched her jaw, lifted her chin, and refused to cower.

They sped up endless floors in an elevator, but there was no dial or buttons to say exactly how many. Peyton pushed her out to turn into a few interior hallways, and she lost track of where they'd gone as they wound deeper into the building. The wolf swished a keycard in front of several security panels to get them through a series of doors. She could smell the familiar scent of a laboratory, and her insides twisted tighter. If they tortured her again, she had no defenses left against telling them everything about the formula.

Stepping into a room that was, indeed, equipped as a lab, she wasn't surprised to see Ivan Nemov standing there with a handful of other Magickals. He looked like hell warmed over, and Chloe couldn't summon a single scrap of sympathy. He'd sold out her research to terrorists, gotten Damien and his pregnant fiancée murdered, and abandoned his only child. She offered him a baleful stare, and he winced and glanced away.

Toward Alex.

She couldn't prevent the cry that burst out, and Peyton hauled her closer when she tried to break for Alex. He was in a *cage*. And he wasn't the only one. An unconscious Tess lolled against the bars in the cage next to him. So many cages. Dozens of wolves were locked into silver dog kennels, some in human form, some in animal form, but there wasn't enough room to stand up, let alone half-shift. Shredded newspaper on the floors of the cages was the only thing between them and the silver. She winced when a wolf rolled over and yelped in pain as it brushed the bars.

Her mouth worked for a moment before she could form a coherent sentence through the horror. "What the hell is this?"

"Dr. Nemov's grand experiment." A slender man pushed away from the large lab table in the middle of the room. "It's nice to finally meet you, Dr. Standish. I've heard so many good things about your work."

"Leonard Smith." She didn't need his nod of confirmation to know. What startled her was the complete lack of evil in his eyes. A man who'd orchestrated all this should have a face twisted and deformed with malice, but he just looked like a middle manager appropriate to the office building they stood in. She swallowed, pushed away the inane thoughts, and refocused on what was important. "How are so many werewolves missing and no one reported anything?"

She knew before the words were past her lips. These weren't registered wolves. These were Normals they'd turned into werewolves. Smith's words rang in her mind again: *Dr. Nemov's grand experiment.* Her gaze swung to Ivan. "How could you?"

"For Jaya. For Alex," he rasped, his Russian accent thickening. Eyes as green as Alex's met hers. They burned with an intensity that bordered on fanatical. "Our work wasn't going fast enough. There are too many regulations on our experiments. We were so close to a breakthrough, and it would have still meant years of verification testing. *Years.* We've already lost so many years. Every month means more of us don't make the Change; more of us die. I already lost my wife. I won't lose my son."

The utter blankness on Alex's face when she looked at him told her Ivan had already lost his son, whether he was alive or not. Her soul ached for the boy, but she made herself address Smith. "I won't help you with this. It's illegal and immoral. Dr. Nemov seems to have forgotten his oaths to medical ethics."

"I agree with you," Smith responded with a benign smile. "Ivan's work is a regrettable means to an end for me, one I don't relish, but necessity wins out."

"What end could possibly be worth *this?*" She waved a hand at the people caged like mindless animals. At her godson and her best friend.

"Freedom," he said simply. "The pack leaders are ineffective. How long did they fail to get this kind of research funded? Instead of granting werewolves a modicum of independence, they sold us out to the vampires, who will be more than happy to control treatment, to make slavering dogs of our entire race." He arched an eyebrow and spread his hands. "Deny they despise us, Dr. Standish."

She licked her lips, swallowed, scrambled for some logic when her mind spewed repulsion. "Vampires despise everyone, but they had the means to pay for the experiments."

An impatient gesture from Smith stopped anything else she might say. "Werewolves have stood apart too long, hiding behind the walls of pack lands and the hive-minded obedience of pack law. It's time to take our own destiny in hand."

For the most part, she agreed with him. Right up until he got

to the part about killing people and letting Ivan Change innocent Normals into wolfish lab rats. The terrorist's face and
voice were calm, his manner implacable. There would be no
reasoning with this man. He was a hero in his own mind, a sav-
ior.

Smith gave her a smile that was almost regretful. "I'm afraid
Dr. Nemov has run into a wall with his work. He needs you to
finish the formula." He paused, waited for her to speak, and
arched an eyebrow when she didn't. "I understand your reti-
cence, truly I do. However, I must have an *effective* treatment,
so you'll understand if I feel the need to build some safeguards
into your timeline."

"Safeguards?" Ivan's blond brows lifted. Apparently, he
wasn't in on all of Smith's plans. Chloe braced herself, not
knowing how bad it could get, but knowing it was going to be
ugly.

Smith ignored the other wolf and glanced at his watch. "You
have roughly ten hours until the sun sets, and the full moon
rises. When that happens, we'll take whatever you've come up
with and administer it to your young pup, there." He nodded
to Alex's cage; the boy's expression remained bland. "Just to
make certain he can both control the Change *and* the rampage,
we'll put your friend in the cage with him."

Chloe's lungs seized, her heart skipping several beats. No.
Gods, no. If the mixture wasn't perfect, it could be lethal. It
most likely would be, and she'd have killed her godson, a boy
she loved as much as she could any child of her own. If it *didn't*
kill him immediately, but left him unable to resist the rampage,
her best friend would be bitten . . . or worse. Every ounce of
blood rushed out of Chloe's face so fast, tingles pricked at her
cheeks. Peyton actually had to hug her close to keep her legs
from collapsing under her. Her belly revolted at his touch, and
she locked her knees to pull away from him.

A shocked breath whistled out of Ivan's throat.

"*What?* Smith, I came to you with this. I gave you everything! You can't think to use my son. We have plenty of other wolves for that!" He gesticulated wildly, sweeping a hand toward the many kennels. His eyes flashed with feral light, and he turned on Smith with bared fangs. Smith drew a weapon from his coat, pointing it at Ivan's head; the scientist froze, nostrils flaring at the scent of danger.

"Yes, plenty of wolves, but none who would make Dr. Standish give me what I want when I want it. You don't seem to realize that neither my funds nor my patience are limitless." He sighed, shook his head. "I believe we've exhausted your usefulness, Doctor."

And then he pulled the trigger. Once. Twice. Three times.

Ivan crumpled to the floor, and Chloe stared blankly at the broken body, the blood spreading out from under him. Shock made her limbs go numb, and she braced her hand on the table to keep from toppling. Smith tucked his gun away and motioned to the other two people in the room, a man and a woman, to take care of the mess.

She recognized them both. The Fae woman who'd helped Peyton torture her, and the vampire she'd hit with the SUV. His shock of brilliant red hair gave him away. He offered her a befanged grin as he walked past carrying one end of Ivan's body. "No hard feelings about running me over. It's a dirty business."

"Gregor," Smith's tone was reproving. The two people walked through a doorway into what had to be a morgue. There were a lot of bodies. Ivan's failed experiments? Normals who hadn't made the Change to wolf? People who'd gotten in Smith's way? Probably all of the above.

Smith waved a hand at Gregor when they came back into the room to mop up the blood. "Unfortunately, operating outside the law means dealing with some unsavory characters—"

The vampire smiled affably and made no comment.

"—but Gregor is the best at what he does. He'll be keeping an eye on you today. Another safeguard."

"Fine, but I need Alex. He's an expert in computers, and he's worked in my lab before. Let him help me." Because she didn't think she could stand looking at him trapped in that kennel while she formulated her potions. It was bad enough with Tess unconscious, but Alex would be watching her, knowing what would happen if she fucked up. Downward rushes of cold dread made her insides shake as it continued to hit her just how much was at stake. She met Smith's gaze and shrugged with a nonchalance she didn't feel. "You killed the only other person who might have been useful."

"Since his life is on the line . . . it only seems fair. Be aware this room has been specifically designed by Normals and warded by Magickals to prevent unauthorized entry and exit. With the *guests* we have staying here, it's proved necessary." He motioned for the Fae woman to open Alex's cage. The boy didn't hesitate, bolting forward. A shield snapped around the Fae, and Alex ricocheted off of it. Smith smiled indulgently, and it sent a chill down Chloe's spine. "Come, Peyton. Let's leave them to it. Gregor, Sasha, watch them."

The two werewolves glided out, Peyton glancing back to send her a long look she couldn't read. Gregor gave Chloe a smile that told her he would enjoy himself immensely if she tried anything stupid. Alex glared at him, moving to her side. She reached for his hand, her grasp tightening in reassurance. The Fae woman, Sasha, positioned herself by the door and stood at the ready with a deadly little pistol in her hand.

"Okay, let's do this." Chloe ignored both terrorists, took a deep breath, and got to work. There weren't many hours between now and sundown to get it right, and she could *not* mess this up.

Lives depended on it.

* * *

Pain echoed through Merek's torso, a pounding drum that should have ... hurt more. It was the lack of agony that brought him to full consciousness. He let his eyes crack open, careful not to move. The iron stench of blood filled his nose, but he lay on something soft. Where was he? More important, where were Chloe and Alex?

"Ah, you're awake, my friend. Good. I'd hoped those healing spells I used on you would work, but casting isn't an expertise of my kind. I'm afraid my methods are rudimentary at best, so you'll wear those scars for the rest of your life." Luca's voice sounded from his left, so Merek turned his head before he fully opened his eyes. "You're lucky Dr. Standish managed to remove all the bullets before she was taken, and before the bronze got into your system, or there would have been little I could do in the state I was in. You don't want to know how I managed the transfusion you needed."

Luca rose from the chair he was lounging in. "They cut the phone lines, and our cells were victims of the battle, so we've been isolated from any outside contact all day."

Merek had never seen a vampire so pale, cheeks sunken in, eyes ringed with dark circles. He rolled his tongue around in the parched desert of his mouth to generate some moisture. "You need to feed."

A faint grin curved the other man's lips, the tip of one fang flashing in the lamplight. "Yes, well. I've had enough to keep me going, but I'm not about to suck your blood, now, am I? After all the effort I went to, to get more into you."

Blankets had been nailed over the windows, so there was no telling what time of day it was. No way of knowing how long it had been since Alex and Chloe were taken. Utter failure stabbed into Merek. He'd failed the people he cared for most. Again. Failed to protect them, failed to keep himself from getting shot, failed to stop them from being taken by terrorists.

Cold sweat broke out on his forehead. Everything he'd promised them and Millie and himself, he'd failed at, and now his people—his *family*—were in the hands of Leonard Smith. Merek didn't even know if they were still alive, and the thought alone made bile burn the back of his throat. He swallowed hard, shoved away the yawning sense of desolation, and got a hold of his emotions. If there was a chance, no matter how slim, that they could be saved, Merek and Luca had to act now. Lying around feeling sorry for himself would help no one.

"What about Smith's people?" Merek sat up slowly on the living room sofa, waiting to see if the world would spin. It stayed steady, though every muscle in his chest and back protested the movement. The bullet wounds had healed to tender scar tissue. Not pleasant, but manageable. "Any of those bastards still breathing?"

"Funny you should ask." Luca nudged a man sprawled across the floor, wet with blood and his own urine. Elf, by the points of his ears. He groaned, twitching away from Luca's boot. The vampire crouched beside him, his fangs bared in what only a fool would call a smile. "You have blood and information. I need both."

"Fuck you, Cavalli," the elf spat. When he turned his head, Merek could see that the flesh on half his face had been melted. The victim of some kind of flame spell? Had Chloe done it? He knew he hadn't. The clawing need to get to Chloe, to know where she was, tore through him, but he gave the scene before him an impassive stare. He wouldn't fail again by giving this terrorist even the slightest advantage.

"Ah, good." Luca's purr could rival Ophelia's at her best. Talons extended from his fingertips, and he used one to bring the elf's head around to face him. "You know who I am. I'm not going to bother making threats because if you were someone who cowed to them you wouldn't be working for Smith.

The only thing I will say before I drain you dry is that you've taken my woman, and I cannot abide that. I want her back."

"Smith is probably going to toy with your bitch a bit before he kills her." The elf winced when Luca's deadly talon slid along his scorched flesh. "Too bad I'll miss it. And don't even think you can mesmerize me, bloodsucker. I'm stronger than that."

"I'm sure you are. For the moment." The vampire sank his fingers into the melted clumps of the elf's hair, pulling back the man's head to expose his neck. "The more blood I take, the weaker you become, and the easier it is to mesmerize you. I wish I could say I'd try to make it painless for you, but we both know I won't."

"Fuck y—" The elf's voice whistled to a high-pitched scream as Luca drove his fangs deep into the other man's throat.

Long moments passed while the elf gurgled and struggled helplessly in the vampire's grasp. His hands scrabbled and clawed at the carpet, his squeals growing fainter and fainter.

"Much more, and there'll be nothing left to mesmerize, Cavalli." Merek kept his voice nonchalant as he looked around at the carnage strewn through the house. Or at least, the parts of the house he could see. Congealed blood sprayed across every wall and added to the reek of death. Broken bodies littered the floors, and it was obvious many of them had seen Luca's fangs before they went. Merek flexed his arm and saw the distinct twin puncture marks on the inside of his elbow. Luca was right—he didn't want to know how the transfusion had happened. He just wanted Chloe and Alex back, safe. He didn't give a damn how many people Luca and he had to kill to make that happen. Ruthless desperation burned everything else away. If there was even a possibility of saving his people, he'd do whatever it took.

Luca ripped his fangs away and threw his head back, blood

pouring from his mouth to coat his chin and mat his soul patch. He gasped for breath, shaking his head like a dog until the crimson liquid went flying to add another layer of spatter to the walls. His eyes shone in the way only a predatory animal's could.

He used his hand fisted in the elf's hair to jerk him up until their gazes were level. Luca's voice dropped to a low, chilling hiss. "Tell me what I want to know. Where is Smith? Where has he taken the women and the boy?"

A groan rattled from the elf's chest. He stared blindly into the vampire's eyes, his pupils expanding until they nearly eclipsed the blue irises. His fingers twitched against the floor, some last token of resistance. "Mercer Tower."

Merek leaned forward, his fists balling on his thighs. Impatience thrummed through him, but he shoved it aside. "Mercer Tower downtown?"

But the man was dead, as drained as Luca had promised.

The vampire dropped the lifeless body, swiping a hand down his face. "How's your invisibility spell?"

Merek blinked at the non sequitur, but answered anyway. Whatever the vampire had in mind, he was game. Anything. Anything to save them. Anything not to fail them again. "Not great. Normals can't see through it, but any Magickal worth his salt can sense it, if not look right through it."

"Blocking Normals is good enough for me. It's nightfall, and that will help us as well." Ruddiness flushed Luca's cheeks, and he looked healthier than Merek had ever seen him. The big vampire rose to his full height, flexing his arms into curves the way a bodybuilder would. His eyes burned to red, his fangs and talons exploding to their full, terrifying lengths. Muscles corded in his neck and face, veins bulging as he strained. A sound similar to that of a werewolf's Change rent the air, bones snapping, cloth tearing as massive wings exploded from the vampire's back. They flexed out, black tissue stretched taut between each hinge of bone. "I think I can get us there faster than a boat or calling in a helicopter would."

"Sounds like a plan." Merek shook his head, climbing to his feet. His leg ached like a son of a bitch, but he ignored it. Pain didn't matter. Exhaustion was nothing. Only getting to his family. "Remind me never to piss you off."

Luca flicked dismissive fingers, his talons clicking together. "You're too intelligent for that anyway."

"Thanks for the vote of confidence . . . and the healing."

"I needed your skills." The vampire shrugged as he made the cold-blooded statement, but gave him an intense look, his eyes narrowing. "You realize your superiors at the police department may not be willing to look the other way if they get wind of everything we do tonight."

Shrugging in return, Merek met the other man's stare. What was a job compared to Chloe and Alex? Nothing. It was that simple.

The considering expression didn't change. "For whatever it's worth, I'd look the other way . . . if I were your superior."

"Let's just focus on everyone surviving." Dredging up as much magic as he could, Merek threw a cloaking invisibility spell over them both.

The vampire gave a hum of approval as they disappeared from sight. "Shall we go?"

15

She was out of time.

Smith entered the room, and Chloe just stared at him, so mentally, physically, and emotionally drained, she couldn't even think beyond the dread that had become a living force inside her.

A smile graced his face, and she'd already learned to hate that look on his face. He left the door open behind him, and she got the feeling he did it just to taunt her. Probably to taunt the wolves he had trapped in here as well. They'd begun to writhe and snap as dusk drew closer, salivating at the scent of a Normal in the room. Tess had huddled in her cage since she'd regained consciousness, silent, eyes glassy and vacant. Chloe had wanted to comfort her friend, but she didn't have the time or energy to spare, not for grief or kindness or even human decency.

Alex had worked with her in desperate tandem, telepathically stuffing information he'd pulled off his father's computer into her overloaded mind. The awesome speed with which the boy could process data overwhelmed her, left her staggering, but she'd pushed through because she had no other choice. Combined with her own theories, she'd refined Ivan's version of the formula until she had something that might work. Might. Possibly.

Helpless anger wrenched inside her. It should be tested and retested before it was ever administered to a human subject, but that obviously had no bearing on a terrorist's agenda.

Tremors shook her body as she drew a syringe of the potion from the large beaker she was working with. She set it on the table and stepped back while Smith prowled forward. Revulsion crawled over her skin when his arm brushed hers. His glance told her he knew how he affected her. She gritted her teeth, but said nothing.

"I think the honor of giving the first dose should be yours, don't you, Doctor? You should see the fruits of your labor." Smith's gesture went from the syringe to Alex.

The boy shuddered, his struggle with Change obvious. The moon would rise soon, and she'd seen the self-loathing fill his green eyes every time he'd glanced at Tess's cage, the smell of a Normal as tempting to him as it was to the other wolves.

Smith's smile widened, and it was even more horrifying than it had been before. His fangs bared, but that was the only sign that Change affected him at all. Only a very old wolf could have that level of control. "Let's make this complete. Sasha, let the Normal out. We'll see how young Nemov does."

A dazed Tess clambered out of her kennel, held upright by the Fae woman, who kept a weapon pointed at her, even though she just stood there and rocked in place. The wolves went wild, slamming against the doors to their cages, howling when they hit the silver bars. The din pounded on Chloe's eardrums, and she wanted nothing more than to slap her hands over her ears and pretend this wasn't happening.

Alex stood at soldierly attention, his gaze glued to a blank wall, but his fangs protruded over his bottom lip. His telepathic voice was as calm as ever. *Just do it, Chloe. There's nothing else we can do now except play his game. He'll just kill us outright if we don't.*

He was going to kill them all anyway. They weren't on his side, so they were just a liability that had exhausted its usefulness. It was bitterly ironic that for once Alex was the one with the most hope. Chloe couldn't dredge up a shred of it. Not anymore. Swallowing down a huge lump in her throat, she picked up the syringe and approached her godson. "I'm sorry, Alex."

Those green eyes moved over her face, his internal voice rough with emotion he didn't let show. *Don't be sorry. The last month has been the best of my life, and I know how pathetic that sounds, but it's true. If it has to end this way, I'm glad I had the time. Living with you and Merek. A family. People who stuck it out with me.* He tugged his shirtsleeve up, baring his arm for her. His telepathic tone became matter of fact. *Smith's going to have to shift for full moon, too, as well as any wolf he has working for him. I hacked the security system in this place, and you should have a twenty-minute window right when the moon goes up. Get out if you can. I wish I could have done more to help you.* He didn't blink, didn't flinch when the needle pierced his skin, though the trace amounts of silver in the potion would burn like lava in a wolf's veins. Chloe clenched her jaw and refused to give in to the sobs building in her chest. *Picking you as my godmother was the best thing my parents ever did for me. Don't ever blame yourself for this. I love you.*

"I love you, too," she breathed and dropped the empty syringe to the table. Then she grabbed his hand, and waited for the inevitable with him, this boy who was neither her flesh nor her blood, but was still hers.

His young body began to shake, and his grip tightened as he fell to his knees with a keen of animalistic pain. She went down beside him, steadying him with a hand on his shoulder. Trying to keep the panic out of her voice, she sucked in a breath. "Alex? Alex, tell me what's going on. What do you feel? I can try some healing spells if you talk to me."

Never had she felt the inadequacy of her healing skills as sharply as she did now. Treating his bullet wound was nothing compared to this—a poison she'd administered herself. Her heart hammered in her chest, guilt and nausea roiling in her until she wanted to scream.

"No. No!" A large form came hurtling through the open door, and gunfire rang hollowly in the wide lab. Peyton. Chloe's heart stopped as the man moved with stunning speed.

The Fae, Sasha, stumbled back as a bullet hit her. She screamed when she slammed into the wolf cages, and those who could reach her latched onto her limbs, her clothes, her hair. Spells shot out from her in wild sparks as she made noises worthy of the trapped and terrified animals who grabbed her.

Gregor and Smith dove into action to try to tackle Peyton. Both wolves shifted midair, the crunch of bone barely audible over the clamor from Sasha. Blood sprayed from bullets and teeth, talons and claws. Peyton's gaze met Chloe's for a single instant, and his telepathic command pierced her mind. *Run!*

Alex was already standing, jerking and twitching as if he were having a seizure, but on his feet. That was enough to spur Chloe into action. She leaped for the tottering Tess, drew back her hand, and slapped her friend as hard as she could. "Tess, get it together. Let's *go!*"

The redhead blinked as if waking up from a deep slumber, but Chloe wasn't about to lose this opportunity. She grabbed her friend's arm and hauled her toward the door, shoving Alex along in front of her. He moved, not as fast as a werewolf should be able to, but they were out of the room without being hit by any stray bullets or spells.

They reached a door to an outside hallway, and it wouldn't open. "No. Damn it." Chloe slammed her fist against it, already feeling the pulsating waves of shielding magic that would be difficult to dismantle, even if she knew how to magically disarm a door, which she didn't.

A gurgle came from Alex's mouth, spittle falling from his lips. *My hack . . . should have . . .*

The door clicked, the small, lighted panel beside it flashing from red to green. *"Yes."*

Hope she'd lost so recently came rocketing back, and Chloe prayed to whatever deity was paying attention that they made it out of here, that they could get help. Wrenching open the door, she gathered every scrap of magic she had and pushed against the shield spells around the labs. The spells became a visible blue force field, rippling every time Chloe rammed her power into it. Sweat coursed down her face, stuck her clothes to her skin. A shaky opening began to slice through the shield, and Alex shoved the smaller women through it.

"No, you are coming with us, young man. That. Is. Final." Chloe latched on to his hand, drew on his energy, and used it to widen the opening just enough to yank him over to her side. She lurched forward, almost face-planted into the floor, and made Alex stumble, both of them shaking. They'd have gone down, but Tess latched on to her other wrist, held her up, and steadied the wolf.

"O-okay." Tess's voice was shaky, but her grip was firm as she held on to both of them. "How do we get out of here?"

Swiping the sweat from her brow, Chloe cast a frantic look around. A cacophony of roaring came from the lab behind them, followed by the sound of someone crashing into something solid. Or *through* something solid, like a wall. The thought made ice run through her veins. Whatever they did, getting away from this spot was imperative. There was no telling how long Peyton could or would keep fighting, or how long they had before someone came to investigate the breach in the spell shield. She moved to Alex's other side and grabbed the boy's arm. He still swayed where he stood, shivering and panting through clenched fangs.

"Let's just keep moving." Chloe pushed them forward and Tess nodded, helping her prop the wolf up so they could shuffle into an ungainly trot. They ignored the elevators and followed the signs for the emergency staircase.

Spilling out onto a cement landing, they faced a sign that said they were on the hundredth floor. Tess leaned over the rail to look down. "I have bad news."

"I really don't want any bad news," Chloe wheezed as she hefted more of Alex's weight. The kid was pure muscle and getting heavier by the second. She hoped that was just her perception and that he wasn't starting a half-shift. They'd never be able to carry him then. Panic made her heart trip, but she refused to give in now.

Tess glanced back over her shoulder. "Well, suck it up, princess, because that's what you're getting. We have to go up, maybe use a door for a higher floor. There are people coming up these stairs at a run. Listen."

It was faint, but there was definitely the pounding of footsteps from further down, and moving at much faster speeds than a human could run. Since any sane werewolf was running on pack land or locked in for the full moon, she had to assume that meant vampires. Or, worse, *not* sane werewolves. Neither option was one she wanted to deal with. "All right. Up we go. Let's get out of Smithville."

Heaving Alex up the steps one at a time, her heart broke every time he tripped and stumbled. His breath came out at a pant, sweat pouring down his face. He didn't even pause to wipe it away, just used one hand on the railing to help haul himself up the stairs. Filtering as much of her own healing energy to him as she could spare, she took a moment to be grateful he didn't tell them to leave him, because they didn't have time for that argument. The little genius had to know she wouldn't do it. Neither would Tess, when she wasn't damn near catatonic.

All three of them staggered drunkenly up to the landing one floor above where they had started, only to find there was no going any further. They'd reached the roof. "Oh, fuck."

"Better out there than sardined on a stairway," Tess stated, shoving on the metal bar that opened the door.

A piercing alarm shrieked when it swung wide, and Chloe winced, but worked with Tess to jockey Alex through the opening.

"Can you use your magic woo-woo to booby trap the door?" Tess gave her a hopeful look, swatted the heavy metal door shut, and shrugged. "Because there went any element of surprise we had about where we got off the stairwell."

"They can track us by scent anyway. They're werewolves. And vampires. Both are coming after us, so they'll find us in the next minute or so." Alex sucked in a deep breath of the cool air, untainted by the oppressive fear and human waste of the laboratory. "I can smell them."

He pushed away from their support, managed a few steps on his own before he threw his head back to stare at the full moon peeking out from between the clouds. Chloe used the free moment to press her hands against the door. Booby trap. She'd never tried to booby trap anything in her entire life. Closing her eyes, she concentrated on what she wanted, letting her ugly emotions feed the energy needed for the spell. Pain, agony, fire, corrosion, death for whoever opened the door. She twisted the words into an endless litany in her mind, building a shield around the door, a shield that sparked with red and orange and white-hot flames. Heat radiated from the metal surface in front of her, and she gasped, jolting backward.

"Holy freaking shit," Tess breathed.

No kidding. The door had expanded, warping, melting into its frame. The shield around it shimmered, smelled of molten iron, and whispered of ominous things. Chloe shook out her hands, ridding herself of the dark energy the spell had generated.

A choking sound from Alex brought her around to face him, and a low sob from the boy made her hurry to his side. She cupped his cheeks between her palms. "Alex, honey. You can't freak out on me now. I know it's not good, but the other option was dying in a silver cage. We'll find a way out of this. I know we will."

"No." He shook his head, a single tear streaking down his face, and he swiped it away, embarrassment reflecting in his eyes. "It's full moon, and I'm still *human*." He flung his arms out, extending and retracting his claws. "Look. I can shift, but I don't *have* to. We did it, Chloe. It *worked*."

"Gods." She didn't know what else to say. So many things spun through her mind, wild hope, crazy scientific possibilities, deathly terror because the danger was nowhere near past. She grabbed for something real, something sane. "The side effects aren't good, because you weren't doing so hot."

He snorted. "A few minutes for the healing magic to kick in, but that's nothing if it means wolves don't have to worry about dying. Some tests, some tweaking. But *look* at me. I'm not even having to fight for it, and I'm human."

Something enormous slammed into the door, making them both jolt back to ugly reality. Tess called from where she was prowling around the edge of the building. "Could we hold off on the celebration until we're out of here, please?"

Stumbling back from the door, they all gathered near the railing. Twinkling city lights stretched in a panorama around them, brightly lit high-rises and the Space Needle piercing the sky, with the Puget Sound a dark swath in the distance. Chloe was almost ashamed of the relief that rushed through her at being back in a metropolis, surrounded by millions of lights. "Well, we're downtown. As if that helps from up here."

Wind rushed up, pushing them back from the edge of the building. This time, when whoever was at the door pounded on the metal, he or she got through it. Chloe groaned at the shock that punched through her with breath-stealing force as her shield gave way. Then a great explosion shook the very air around them when the door blew. They ducked, hitting the hard cement surface of the roof. Screams, flames, the putrid stink of burning flesh.

Chloe stared in stunned silence, unable to believe what she had wrought. Bodies on fire danced in grotesque patterns across the roof, some moving so fast they made streaks in the darkness. Slowly, they collapsed. Dead. She knew they were dead.

"Holy shit," Tess gasped.

Even Alex turned to give Chloe an incredulous look. Shaking her head in mute silence, she clenched her quaking fingers. "I don't know how I did that."

A quiver ran through the wolf's body, and his nostrils expanded as he pulled in a deep breath. "Smith's coming. Gregor and Sasha. A female wolf, too. Get ready."

No Peyton. Had he survived the fight? Had he run as soon as he had the opportunity? Chloe still associated the man with the burn of bronze against her skin, so she wasn't ready to trust that he'd helped them for some altruistic reason. For all she knew, he was hoping to overthrow Smith and take over and they'd just provided a handy excuse. She wasn't willing to trust much of anything anymore.

And then there was no more time for thinking.

The wolves are mine. Alex tensed beside her, his muscles twisting and flexing as he grew into a monstrous half-shift. His dark skin went pitch black, his facial bones stretching into a muzzle with massive, dripping fangs. The tall boy grew to a height of almost seven feet, and his ropy young muscles swelled to a rippling sinew so huge he exploded from his baggy T-shirt.

Parts of him shrank in and others thrust forward, making grotesque sucking and crackling sound effects.

It took place in a handful of seconds, but those terrifying moments stayed with a person forever. Tess choked and swayed, her eyes forming perfect circles as she stared at the transformed Alex. A deep roar ripped loose from the teen, answered when two other half-shifted wolves plunged through the smoking doorway. They leaped forward, dropping into crouches to survey their prey.

A noise that was almost a chuckle rippled from Alex before he launched himself toward them. Chloe grabbed for his arm, wanting to hold him back, but he was moving faster than her reflexes could keep up with. She missed, crying out as the three half-animals collided with the crunch of shattering bones.

"Get down!" Red streaked through the night, and Tess dove to knock Chloe off her feet as a spellbomb exploded where she'd been standing.

Tess covered both of their heads with her arms, and Chloe automatically threw up a shield around them. The next bomb exploded like shooting fireworks against her warding spell, and she jerked when the dark magic ruptured her shield. It was a blow to the solar plexus that left her gasping, and before she'd managed to recover, Tess bounded off her, which gave Gregor the opportunity to drag her away from Chloe's protection.

That left Sasha blasting another spell at Chloe, who threw up another shield to block it, but sprawled onto her backside when it struck.

Her heart pounded so loudly in her ears, all she could hear was the rush of blood. Magic hummed beneath her skin, waiting for her to direct it. She wracked her brain for any self-defense spells she knew. Merek's teaching of Alex hadn't included lessons in casting because wolves couldn't cast well. Chloe didn't think she could do any of the physical moves they'd drilled. The only magic she was proficient at was what she used at home and at work. Potion making, practical everyday magic. Merek would know the right spells if he were here, and her heart cinched so hard thinking of him that she gasped with the pain. Tears pricked her eyes. There was another kind of spell she'd used recently, with Merek. Seduction spells. She staggered under the weight of agony that threatened to crush her, and she desperately tried to shove it away, to remain numb.

The Fae woman's face swam before her tear-glazed eyes.

That face had haunted her dreams for weeks. The woman who'd tortured her, ripped her already-fragile sense of safety away in a handful of moments. Rage exploded inside her, and she didn't need the spells. Her magic simply reacted as she wanted it to; the simple magic she used with Merek turned dark and deadly.

Massive bolts of lightning shot from her fingertips, sizzling toward the other woman. Sasha tried to set a magical shield around herself, but the amount of fury behind Chloe's spell meant some of it got through.

A cold smile of satisfaction curled Chloe's lips as she watched utter shock widen the Fae's eyes. Then her body began to writhe as the lightning hit her, arced around her, bit into her flesh. A harsh scream wrenched from her throat. The shield before her wavered, and Chloe used the momentary lapse to her advantage. A part of her was stunned at her own ruthlessness, while the rest of her simply reacted.

Another round of lightning forked from her hands, slamming into the Fae. The anger inside Chloe was nowhere near burning out, and she fed it into the spell. Flashes of memory erupted in her mind. Her own torture by this woman. Barely escaping the last full moon with Alex. Tess's betrayed, hurt expression when she'd found out they'd all lied to her. The stench of Luca's flesh igniting in the morning sun. Blood covering Merek's body, his beloved gray eyes going blank. A raw sob tore from Chloe, but she didn't allow herself to stop.

What remained of Sasha's shield disintegrated in a shower of blue sparks, and Chloe hit the other woman again and again. The shrieks that came from the Fae were barely human, a wild sound of pain. The noise trailed off as she finally passed out, but her body kept jerking spasmodically under the hits of lightning.

Chloe could kill the other woman. She *wanted* to kill her. For Merek, for Alex, for herself, for being part of an organization that had harmed so many she loved. She stood on the edge of a precipice she'd never faced before. Violence, rage . . . murder.

For Merek, she pulled back, shut down the magic. For Alex and Tess, she didn't allow herself to look at what her hate had produced. It would fuel her nightmares for years to come.

She had won the fight, but no sense of victory stole through her as she turned away. She was numb, finally, and she welcomed it. Anything to keep from feeling, from coping with what she had seen and done. She staggered only a step or two before she ran toward the sound of a scream in the night. High-pitched and terrified. Only a woman's voice could make a noise like that. Tess.

The sound cut off so abruptly it sent chills racing over Chloe's flesh. She paused, staring blindly into the cloud-shadowed darkness. Gods, she fucking hated the dark. "Tess!"

Where had the sound come from? She didn't know which way to go now. Shit. The glare from the city lights only made it harder to see.

"*Tess!*"

The scream came again, ending in a gurgling choke. Chloe's heart hammered against her breastbone, and she shot forward, sprinting through the night and praying the roof stayed even underneath her.

The clouds parted, and moonlight gilded the gruesome scene before her. Gregor circled Tess, fangs bared and dripping pink foam. Blood poured from a series of bite marks around Tess's throat, but she was still on her feet, still fighting. The vampire feigned left, darting right in a blur of speed, but Tess had already dived for the ground, both fists swinging in blind arcs.

She connected, hard.

The vampire staggered back maybe an inch, but Tess kicked out with her foot and swept him off his feet.

Damn impressive for a Normal to be holding her own against a full-grown male vamp. Chloe shook herself, and torched the bloodsucker with her lightning. He jolted and spun, hunching forward in a hissing roar that made her heart stop. He came at her, fangs gleaming in the moonlight.

Chloe glanced around, frantic. A weapon. She needed a weapon. Spells alone wouldn't do much to a vampire. Only sunlight would, and it was nighttime. She sliced him with lightning again, concentrating hard on the glow of it. Sunshine. She needed it to be sunshine. Her magic answered her commands eagerly. The crackle of it lifted the hair on the back of her neck. A ball formed between her hands, so brilliant she had to turn her face away and close her eyes.

A hoarse shout from Gregor, and the stink of burnt flesh told her the spell was working. It was too much to maintain for long, but when she blinked her eyes open, there was no one near her. Not Gregor, not Tess.

The hollow crash of metal sounded as the torched vampire ricocheted off the doorframe before streaking through the open door and into the bowels of the building, clearly deciding this wasn't a fight he could win.

Good.

She didn't have a moment for relief as Alex came tumbling by with Smith. The teen wolf's flesh was shredded to ribbons, his face a barely recognizable mass of blood and broken bones.

The slightly smaller female wolf tackled a pursuing Tess.

Lashing backward with her foot, Tess caught the she-wolf in the chest. The wolf grunted, but Tess didn't have time to do more than roll over before the she-wolf was on her again. The Normal used the heel of her hand to snap the she-wolf's muzzle back and up. Both let out an agonized howl as Tess gripped her now broken wrist and the she-wolf tripped back.

Chloe didn't know what to do, who to try to save. Alex punched all ten talons into Smith's sides, and the bigger wolf howled in rage, pummeling the boy with fists that sounded like concrete impacting flesh.

Tess's shriek spun Chloe back toward the other fight. The she-wolf had the Normal on her back, hunching over her body, a taloned hand around her friend's throat. Tess thrashed for air, for life.

"Get *off* her, bitch." Chloe drew back a hand, flung a fireball over the she-wolf's head, searing her back, but not doing much damage. She had to get the wolf away from Tess. She had to.

Gods help her.

The she-wolf writhed in pain, her huge, half-shifted form crushing Tess. Chloe rushed forward, throwing all of her weight behind the push, but her strength was no match for any were-wolf. The she-wolf whipped around and sank her fangs into Tess's thigh, ripping through cloth and flesh.

"*No!*" Bitten. Tess had been bitten by a wolf on full moon, the time of Change. Oh. Gods.

Silver. silver. SILVER. Find Silver. A chorus of whispers sounded off in Chloe's head. Werewolves were allergic to silver.

Tess. Tess had a silver necklace she wore all the time. It glinted in the moonlight. Chloe reached over, jerking it off her friend's neck.

The wolf arched back, jaws gaping, Tess's blood leaking from the side of her mouth, to howl her triumph at the moon. "*Aaaa-oooh.*"

Chloe cupped her friend's necklace in her palm, thrust it into the she-wolf's mouth, and lit up another fireball to force the melting silver to coat the inside of the wolf bitch's throat.

The wolf's jaw locked around Chloe's wrist, and her fangs made screaming agony shoot up Chloe's arm and directly into her brain. She stared into the female wolf's eyes as the silver ripped into her bloodstream, killing her quickly and painfully. Her every breath and every heartbeat sped her demise. Her feral eyes glazed over with death in moments. The crunch and crackle of Change sounded as her body shriveled back into its human form. Chloe wrenched her injured arm out of the wolf's mouth, whispering a few healing spells to stop the bleeding, but Tess needed her energy far more.

Slamming her hand over Tess's femoral artery, Chloe felt the pressure of each heartbeat pulsing blood between her fingers. She closed her mind to doing the same thing for Merek that morning. He was gone, but Tess could still live. Even with Chloe's full weight pressing down on the bite, some blood escaped. She focused her magic on healing the wound. It didn't matter if her friend had been bitten if she didn't survive the initial injury.

Down. get down. DOWN.

The whispering echo of premonition hit Chloe so hard she swayed before she ducked. Just in time. A hulking half-shifted werewolf sailed over her head, skidding into the dark and out of sight. Smith. She heard him scrabble against the rooftop, leaping back for round two. She cast a shield so hard he ricocheted off and kept on flying to hit the railing, but he didn't go over.

I regret that your death was always going to be necessary, but at least you were more useful than Dr. Nemov. The wolf projected the thought as he righted himself and shook all over, like a wet dog. He stalked her slowly, his eyes looking for an opening.

"You're full of shit, Smith. If you really regretted what you did, you would have stopped years ago. My only comfort is knowing that when my aunt finds out about this, she'll make sure you never use *my* formula to get what you want. If anyone has the power to stop you, she does." Chloe's energy levels were in the toilet, and she had very little magic left. This night had taken its toll. She swayed to her feet, tottering, planting her feet to keep from toppling as she watched him circle Tess and her. Easy prey. She lifted her chin and glared at him. "Just get on with it and quit playing with your food, you filthy *animal.*"

Smith bayed at the full moon and charged her. He bounced off her warding spell, and she sliced at him with red flames. Seared fur roiled and stank. Noxious fumes hit her in the face. He roared with pain and rage, letting out an unholy keen. The blood-chilling sound froze her for a second too long. He crashed through her weakened shield, knocking her away from Tess.

They rolled over and over until Chloe slammed hard onto her back, doubling over and gagging as her breath exploded out. His knee made hard contact with her ribs, and a few of them gave way. Hot pain tore through her torso, shooting through her in nauseating waves. He straddled her, pushing his crushing weight down on her waist, and she felt herself blacking out until he snaked out an arm and clawed her from shoulder to breast. His talons slashed through skin and muscle, making her scream, raw and high-pitched.

Thrusting the sound forward with magic, she made the shriek worthy of a banshee. Smith reared back, loosing an agonized howl, slamming his hands over his sensitive ears. She scrabbled back on the hard pavement, breaking nails and skinning palms in her effort to get out from under him.

She skidded into the corner of the rooftop. Trapped, but at the moment the railing was the only thing holding her upright. Blood spilled, heavy and thick, from her chest. She pressed a hand over the wound, but it proved too large to cover. Her breathing hitched in torturously, every inhale and exhale a conscious effort. She had never known real pain before this moment.

The moon went dark behind clouds, and she could barely see him in the remaining gloom. Only the reflection of his eyes showed, which looked demonic and horrifying. The night had never been more terrifying than at this moment. Her heart raced like that of the cornered prey she was. She fought to keep from blacking out, clamping her hand tighter over her shoulder.

Smith's rancid breath blasted into her face as he closed in. She slammed her eyes shut and lit up a flare in his face. He staggered back, blinded by the light as she shot the sparks as high into the air as her waning magic could make them go. Maybe they'd bring help. Maybe Alex and Tess would be saved. She had no faith left for herself. What little energy she had went into sending up the flare.

Smith came back, of course. She knew he would. Werewolves were bigger, stronger, faster, and she had no more tricks up her sleeve. She sagged against the rail, consciousness fading in and out.

She wasn't sure if what she saw was real or pure dream, but it made a weak smile curve her lips.

Ophelia, her suicidal escape artist familiar, came streaking through the dark. She leaped onto Smith and dug in with vicious precision, hooking claws into his eyes and sinking teeth into his left ear.

The massive wolf howled with rage, trying to buck her off. He spun and twisted like a maddened rodeo bull. She hung on, though. He backed into Chloe, tripping and crashing. Something in her knee gave way where he stepped on it. She tried to scream again, but went into a fit of hacking coughs, which increased the pain ripping across her chest. He and Ophelia flailed over the rail.

"*Ophelia*," she wheezed as loud as she could, which just made her cough harder.

"Meow," the familiar returned, and Chloe started. Ophelia had gone over the rail. Chloe knew she had. She'd seen her.

It was a dream. It had to be.

Because an enormous dark angel swooped from the sky and brought her Merek. He cradled her close, kissed her mouth, and she tasted honey. He said her name over and over again, but she couldn't draw in enough air to speak.

The angel transformed into Luca, who sagged to his knees beside Tess. "*Mia diletta?*"

There was no response. Maybe Tess had died, too. If this was death, it hurt enough to steal Chloe's breath away. She couldn't see Alex. She hoped that meant he'd survived.

"No," Luca choked out the word, then he screamed it. "*No!*"

A tear ran unchecked down his cheek, dripping off of his chin. He lifted Tess gently against his chest and rocked her, a deep sob racking his body as he buried his face against her long hair.

Chloe blinked slowly, aware that Merek was talking to her. Or maybe he was talking to Luca. She wasn't sure. She was just glad she could see him. One last time.

The darkness she hated so much closed in and took her away from him.

16

The astringent smells of a hospital assaulted Chloe's nose. It confused her, left her disoriented. Was she back in med school? Her residency? She licked her lips, found them cracked. Her body ached, but she couldn't remember why.

Soft light shone through her eyelids, and when she opened them, she saw an atrocious seashell night-light. With glitter. A smile curved her lips, and a snort of laughter ended on a sob. For a single moment, her heart flew.

Merek!

Then a pair of slim legs crossed at the ankles came into sharp focus. She looked up to find Selina reading a file beside the bed. Chloe frowned, even more confused, and questions tumbled out. "Where am I? How did I get here? What are you doing here?"

"The Magickal ward of Harborview. I imagine Cavalli and Kingston carted your battered carcass here. And Kingston asked me and your aunt Millie to handle things for him, look in on you and the two wolves, take care of your familiar." The elf's eyebrows arched, then she reached out to press a button that lifted Chloe into a sitting position. "Any other questions?"

"Two wolves?" Chloe's dream collided with reality, spinning her deeper into uncertainty. Hazy images formed. Ophelia, the angel, Luca's wretched sobbing, Tess bitten by a wolf, Merek. The odd sensation of wind rushing over her, soaring over the city, wings beating. She shook her head and got to the most pressing point. "They're alive?"

"Alex Nemov and Tess Jones are both alive, yes." Something flickered in the detective's eyes. "For the moment. It's been three days, and Dr. Jones is still in critical condition and under constant watch. Nemov is conscious and responsive, but..." She shrugged one shoulder. "The doctors are doing everything they can."

"Good. That's good." Chloe's voice sounded fuzzy to her own ears. She had to see them. Twists of guilt and sorrow wrenched at her insides. If she hadn't insisted on going to Bainbridge Island, they might not be in this mess. She closed her eyes for a moment and swallowed. "Luca and Merek are both alive?"

A hint of a smile twitched up the sides of Selina's mouth. "Again, for the moment. They're tracking down Smith and what's left of his operation."

"Smith's alive?" Chloe blinked. She'd started thinking her dream wasn't a dream at all. The angel was obviously Luca in a vampiric half-shift, so pieces had started falling into place. "How could even a werewolf survive a hundred-story drop and walk—*run*—away?"

Selina spread her hands in an eloquent gesture. "He's an older werewolf, so I guess he was powerful enough to manage to heal and get out of there before the authorities arrived on the scene. Plus, it was full moon. Who knows what wolves can really do on those nights?"

"What about the other wolves that Smith had?" The awful memory of those poor souls trapped in cages would remain with her for the rest of her life. "What happened to them?"

"All of Smith's men are being hunted down." Selina spoke

slowly, as if she thought Chloe was too out of it to have heard her the first time. But it told her the detective didn't know about those wolves. Were they dead? Alive? Had the FBI or the All-Magickal Council covered it up? She'd have to call Millie and ask.

Chloe nodded, tried to keep her expression vague. "Right. Of course." She pulled in a deep breath, a knot within her unwinding. "And when they're done, Merek will be back to work in Seattle."

Alive, whole, and within reach. She wanted to be in his arms again so badly, to hear the steady beat of his heart under her ear, just to talk to him and make sure he was okay. She didn't know what form their relationship would take when things returned to normal, but if he was alive and things *could* go back to normal, that was more than she could have wished for a few days before. It was enough.

"Actually, no." The detective bent down to tuck her file into a leather satchel. "Since you mention it, Kingston doesn't work for the Seattle PD anymore."

Chloe sat in stunned silence for several seconds before she choked out, "He quit?"

"Cavalli offered him a spot on his team, and he took it." Selina straightened and crossed her legs the other way.

"What about you?" Chloe was still trying to wrap her mind around Merek quitting. He was a cop. His job was his life. It defined him. "You're his partner. He loves working with you."

The detective shoved an impatient hand through her hair, revealing an elfin ear. "I told him if he didn't make this jump he was a damn fool. No one passes up the chance to work with Luca Cavalli. The bloodsucker's been dancing around it for a couple of years now, yanking Kingston in for a case here and there, but it looks like the FBI managed to pry its head out of its collective ass."

"Why would you encourage him to leave?"

Selina stared at her for a long, long time before she answered. "He's the best partner I've ever had, so I'm not thrilled to see him go, but..." A resigned smile twisted her lips. "We both know I'm going to bite it soon, so there's no reason for him to hold himself back for me. Or to stick around and watch."

It was eerie how accepting the woman was, and considering how Alex, Tess, and Chloe had fought so hard to live, it was almost offensive to her. "You're pretty calm about the thought of dying."

The elf sighed, her narrow shoulders dipping in a shrug, the gesture weary. "I'm old, and I'm tired. It's time. Even if I didn't go as soon as I think I'm going to, I'd only have another fifty to sixty years, max, before age got me. After several centuries, I've seen enough to know fifty years won't make much difference one way or another."

"I see." What she said made sense, but Chloe guessed she was just too young to truly understand. Even in her darkest moment, Chloe had never welcomed death. She couldn't imagine assuming that attitude. It just wasn't her, but she had less than a century under her belt, so she was willing to concede the view would be different from where Selina was sitting.

"No, you don't." Selina snorted and rose to her feet, leaning down to snag her satchel. She gestured to a blue duffel bag beside the bed. "Your aunt left you some clothes before she went to visit Alex."

"I want to see him." The words were out of Chloe's mouth before she realized she might not be up to moving around much. She'd been ignoring it as much as possible, but she hurt. All over. Every inch of her throbbed, and it was obvious the IV in her arm was feeding her painkillers, so she didn't want to know what shape she would be in without them. "I want to see Tess, too. Now."

"I'll get a nurse on my way out." Selina looped her bag over her shoulder. "I'll stop by and check on you again tomorrow."

"Thanks." Chloe pushed herself higher against the pillows, ignoring the ache in her knee. "And thanks for coming."

"Not a problem."

It took almost an hour before she was showered, swathed in a fluffy robe, and transferred to a wheelchair. The process was humiliatingly slow and arduous. It didn't help that halfway through, a doctor came in to poke and prod at her injuries. He assured her she'd make a full recovery and that the healing spells were being administered over an extended time period to ensure that she wouldn't scar and that she'd retain full mobility. She'd be *just dandy* in a few days. By the time he was done with his examination, she wanted to snarl at him to get the hell out of her way or she'd wheel her own self down to Alex and Tess's rooms.

When she finally got to see Tess, she found herself sitting alone in a viewing room. Her friend was incoherent and obviously on some serious painkillers of her own. She was strapped to her hospital bed, multiple IVs and sensors attached to her. Her body twitched constantly, and she sweated, moaned, and mumbled under her breath. Incipient Change made her bones break over and over again, though she was not quite shifting forms.

Chloe's breath caught when her friend arched against her restraints, fangs punching through her gums. Tess's eyes went feral, her skin and hair darkened, and she snarled, twisting into a half-shift before slamming back against the mattress and regressing to human form.

The lycanthropic disease was slowly morphing every cell in her body, until she would be a full werewolf. If she survived. What Alex was simply born with, Tess would suffer through for nearly a week before the pain stopped and she regained some control of her faculties. Even then, they wouldn't know if she was successfully Changed until she made it through her first full moon shift. Chloe could picture every step of the Change, the way it affected every molecule. Her research spared her no details.

Turning her head, Tess had a moment of lucidity when she looked at Chloe through the glass separating them. "How could you do this to me? You lied, and now I have to lie. Luca lied! Everyone lied. . . . It was all a lie." She sobbed, her shoulder jerking upward as if some invisible force propelled the joint. "Everything's breaking and breaking."

As if to emphasize the point, every bone in her arm snapped. Chloe clamped a hand over her mouth, closing her eyes against the accusations on Tess's face. There was nothing Chloe could say. It *was* her fault. If she'd walked away from the Normal when she should have, Tess would never have come into contact with Luca or Smith or Smith's she-wolf. If Chloe hadn't lied and kept lying, she wouldn't have turned her best friend's entire life into a lie.

A gentle hand settled on her shoulder, jerking her out of her misery. "It's not your fault. She won't even remember she said any of that to you when she's done Changing."

Peyton. Chloe's muscles squealed in protest when she whipped around to look at the wolf behind her. She gritted her teeth to stop a groan of pain and offered him a cool stare. "So, you're not dead."

"Not this time, no." He gestured to a chair against the wall. "Do you mind if I sit?"

She shrugged. "If you aren't dead, then why aren't you in jail?"

Pulling the chair to her side, he eased into it and sighed. "Because, despite all appearances, I'm not a criminal." He angled a glance at her. "I am—I *was*—undercover."

"You were a double agent." Blatant disbelief colored her voice, but she couldn't help it. "So, torturing me was just part of your cover? Because I have to tell you, you suck at your job if you're supposed to protect innocent people."

A dimple tucked into his cheek, but that was as close as he came to an actual grin. "I had to prove myself to Smith. They don't just let you in to terrorist groups if you know the secret handshake."

"Uh huh." She crossed her arms over her chest, then dropped them when the motion pulled at injured tissue. "If that was an attempt at an apology, you suck at those, too."

"Thank you, Doctor. For the record, that wasn't an apology," he retorted drily. "I had a choice that night. I could either give them you, or I could give them Ivan Nemov's son. I thought you'd prefer the call I made." He arched an eyebrow, but she remained stubbornly silent. "If you don't believe me, and you still think I should be locked up, maybe you should check your precognition and see if it's telling you to run from the big, bad wolf."

She glared at him, but couldn't deny that the voices in her head were silent. No warnings of danger whispered around her. "Fine. It doesn't mean I trust you as far as I can throw you, but you're not completely evil."

"Thank you, Doctor." If possible, his tone went even drier. "My superiors will be so pleased by your professional assessment of my character."

"You know I'm not that kind of doctor. Even if I were, you'd be beyond my help." She rolled her eyes at his sarcasm, but his words caught her anyway. "Your superiors—Luca—knew you were a double agent, right? Did he tell you which of us—"

"No. I mean, yes, of course he knew. It was his idea for me to infiltrate Smith's organization. But, no, I made the decision to sacrifice you instead of Alex." He tugged at the leg of his pants, twitching out a nonexistent wrinkle. "Which I'm sure Kingston will want to discuss with me when he gets back."

"He knows I would want Alex spared, if a choice had to be made."

"It did." Peyton shrugged fatalistically. "Whether he wants to acknowledge that or not is the real question."

"You'll forgive me if I kind of hope he punches you in the face really hard." She gave the wolf a saccharine smile, then decided to change the subject, just to throw him off. He might be able to answer one of her many questions for her. "What happened to the wolves Smith had locked up?"

"The same thing that's going to happen to your friend." He angled his chin toward Tess. "I've spoken to the local pack, explained what happened, and vouched for all of the new wolves. They'll be trained as Magickals and given a place in the pack, if they want to join." He hooked an ankle over his opposite knee. "The All-Magickal Council is paying for the training, and for all their medical bills. Your aunt had a hand in that."

"Of course, she did." Chloe smiled. Millie would have been all over this, just as Chloe had told Smith. Millie had her fingers in every political pie, and anything that involved her niece's case would have garnered special attention. Chloe couldn't wait to see her again. She'd missed the old witch.

Peyton shifted in his seat. "I volunteered to train Dr. Jones myself. She worked as a pathologist for the Normal side of the FBI, so our people are eager to get their hands on her. She'll be useful to us once she's wolf-trained."

"What does Luca think about that?"

His face went carefully blank. If he'd been difficult to read before, now he was impossible. "Cavalli is a vampire. Dr. Jones is a werewolf. Or she will be when she pulls through this."

That he stated it as a fact made Chloe thaw toward him just a little. He had no doubt that Tess would make the Change to wolf successfully. But he was right about Luca and Tess's relationship. Vampires didn't mix their blood with anyone else's, especially not their animalistic cousins. Before, Luca *might* have been allowed to turn her into a vampire, but now . . . Whatever possibility there had been for the two lovers was over.

Chloe ached for all the blows her friend had received, and for all those that were still coming. She hoped Peyton was right and Tess wouldn't remember what she'd said, that she'd let Chloe help her. Selfishly, she hoped she didn't lose her best friend.

She turned on Peyton. "You'd better do a good job training

her. She'd better be welcomed into the wolf packs with open arms."

"I will. She will." Peyton rested his hand on his thigh, his manner and tone as unruffled as ever. "You have my word on that."

Her mouth worked for a moment as she examined his face. She wished she could tell if he was lying, but the man made his living going undercover and convincing evil people he was evil, too. The clear memory of bronze blistering her skin the two other times she'd met him made her voice rough. "Your word doesn't mean much to me, Peyton. You hurt her in *any way*, decide to torture her to save someone else or to save your own ass, and I will hound you to the ends of the earth. I will take you apart piece by piece, slowly, and nail your wolfie hide to the wall. Is that in any way unclear to you?"

The corners of his lips twitched as if he was fighting a smile, but it never formed. "We're clear."

"Good." Her eyes narrowed to slits. "I'm not kidding either. I don't care if you're a law enforcement officer or if it's illegal to threaten you. I *will* do what I'm telling you."

"I believe you. Ma'am." He tipped his chin in a respectful nod.

She sniffed. "Well, at least you're not an idiot."

The twitch was a bit more pronounced this time, and his midnight blue eyes glittered. "Kingston's going to have his hands full with you."

The words were like a punch to the heart. Merek. Gods, she missed him; she wanted him *here*. Her chin lifted. "Whether he does or not is none of your business."

Peyton nodded. "Then I'll only say that I'm glad Dr. Jones has friends in the Magickal community as fiercely protective as you to look out for her. Whether you believe it yet or not, I'll look out for her, too. I would *never* hurt her."

"We'll see." She settled deeper into her wheelchair and watched Tess in the awful throes of Change.

"Yes, we will."

Merek lay on his belly in the middle of the forest, gazing down the sights of a high-powered rifle loaded with pure silver rounds. He ignored the discomfort of the cold mud seeping into his clothes and sliding over his skin to form a sticky crust. None of that mattered. Not the chill, the pouring rain, the filth. With the exception of Gregor, who'd managed to disappear as he always did, they'd hunted the fleeing members of the terrorist cell for more than a week, picking them off one by one until only Smith remained, cornered in a shack in the middle of the wilderness. They had him surrounded, and he'd have scented them all by now, would know he was fucked.

It would be finished soon.

A dozen possible ways it could go down flipped through Merek's mind, too much in flux for him to know which would be the true outcome, but all of them ended in the terrorist's capture or death, and that was all Merek cared about.

That he could see the future of this made relief coil in his gut. Whatever might happen, he knew this no longer tangled with Chloe or Alex's lives. And they *had* lives to look forward to. No thanks to him.

He clenched his jaw, let the self-disgust sluice off his back like so much rainwater. They were free of him now, so it didn't matter if his heart still stopped every time he even thought about how he'd arrived too late to do a damn thing for them besides get them to a hospital before they bled out. It didn't matter if he wanted to vomit when he recalled them covered in gore. It didn't matter if he had to concentrate even now to make his hands stop shaking at the thought of how close they'd come to dying. Minutes had counted. *Seconds* had counted.

The report from Peyton of what had happened had been grim, but Merek had read every word so many times he'd memorized it. The handful of times he'd called to check on Alex, neither of them had mentioned that he'd watched his father get gunned down before his eyes. The boy had been through enough without that, but he would come through it just fine. Chloe would make sure of it.

Gods, *Chloe*. Merek didn't even let himself consider how she was doing. He shut his mind to all thought of her. The pain was too crippling to deal with. Nothing would ever make it right again.

Movement in his sights snapped his focus back to the task at hand. Smith erupted from the shack, a howling monster with bloodied fangs. A flurry of staccato conversation in his earpiece let Merek know they had men down inside the house, and none of the other agents outside could get a clear shot. He could. His body hummed with tension, and he drew in a calming breath of clean, evergreen-scented air. Then he let half of it out, his hands going rock steady.

For Alex, for Chloe, for himself, for all the rage, the pain, the anguish this man had caused so many other people, he squeezed the trigger.

The rifle recoiled against his shoulder, and almost simultaneously, a bloom of crimson spurted from Smith's torso. The wolf jerked, his look of mild surprise clear through the powerful scope. Then he collapsed, folding in on himself in the rain-washed mud, a hand pressed to the wound in his chest.

Right through the heart.

"Good. I'll see you when you get back to Seattle."

"Right." Merek pinched the bridge of his nose, hunched over on the rickety desk chair in his motel room. He'd called Alex the moment he'd returned, hadn't even bothered to wash the grime off first. The kid would want to know it was over.

A short pause fuzzed through the line. "Chloe's about to walk in; I can smell her. You want to talk to her?"

"No. No, you can tell her." Need exploded through him, so fierce it scared the shit out of him. "I have to go."

He slammed the receiver down before he gave in to temptation. Burying his face in his hands, he sucked in a breath. It was better this way. Better for her, better for him. He'd promised the kid he wouldn't bail on him, but they wouldn't be living together, and the distance would keep Merek sane.

But Chloe. He couldn't see her and not want her, want her and not touch her, touch her and not claim her as his. Always. Forever. *His.*

To do so would trap them in the same nightmare. He couldn't do that to either of them.

Gods, he missed her though. Even with the grueling hours Luca had had the entire team putting in, Merek couldn't stop missing Chloe. The few moments he had alone, his body burned for her; he woke up hard for her. The craving never ended.

He shoved to his feet, stripped on the way to the bathroom, and stepped into the tub. A shower and eight full hours of sleep before he headed back to the city would help him come to grips with the fact that he'd never have her again, that life as he knew it was over. No more Seattle PD. No more people sharing his living space. No more family. No more Chloe.

Chloe. Wide hazel eyes, a brilliant mind, a sharp tongue, a soft body. He missed her. Everything about her. How he'd survive without her, he didn't know, but he knew he'd never forgive himself if she died on his watch. So he had to let her go, for both of their sakes. It was over, and if he didn't like it, if he kept waking up wanting her, it was just the price he had to pay.

He leaned his forehead against the shower wall and closed his eyes as the water ran down his body, rinsing away the shampoo. Even with his decision clear in his mind, he couldn't stop the vivid memories of the last time he'd shared a shower with Chloe, the feel of her slick sheath tight around his cock. Her face flashed through his thoughts, her eyes alight with passion as she moaned his name.

His cock went rigid in moments, his breath hissing between clenched teeth. Gods, he needed her. He couldn't have her, not ever again. The knowledge made his gut churn, his self-loathing warring with his desire.

Grabbing for the bar of soap, he washed himself efficiently, but nothing would put a damper on his lust. Unquenchable fire burned in his veins, made his heart pound. He'd gone too long without. Not just sex, but *her*. He wanted her. In his bed, in his arms, in his life. He just couldn't have those things, whether he craved them or not.

Cursing, he slid his soapy hand down his stomach until he grasped his dick. He bit off a groan. Even though he knew it was foolish, he let her image form in his mind.

Every aspect of her was seared into his memory, and he was grateful for that. Her scent teased the edges of his consciousness, and he didn't even have to try to recall the flavor of her on his tongue. The Chloe in his thoughts smiled at him, pulled him to her for a hungry kiss. He couldn't hold back the groan this time as her slim fingers dropped to rub his cock.

He sucked in a breath, the hot water moving down his back like the stroke of her hand. A shudder passed through him, and his hips bucked, driving his dick into the ring of his fingers. He rolled his thumb over the head, squeezing and pulling at the shaft in rough motions that drove him right to the edge.

Days without her touch had done this to him, made him so desperate and needy he couldn't see straight. He held tight to the fantasy, where Chloe caressed him, whispered in his ear, bit the lobe and flicked her tongue over the captured flesh. Goose bumps rose on his skin, rippling down his limbs with the shower water. He tried to drag enough oxygen in to satisfy his starved lungs, to cool the fire in his blood, but there was no stopping now.

Pumping his cock hard, he let go of control. He always lost it with Chloe. A smile curved his lips, pleasure streaking through him, so hot and sweet it almost dropped him. He rotated his grip, ran his fingers along the underside of his dick, and imagined the wet warmth was her mouth moving on him, sucking him deep.

"Gods," he groaned.

The dream dragged him under, and he felt the hot spill of his come over his fingers. The orgasm just kept going as he pictured her lips and tongue on his cock, her eyes gleaming with wicked glee because she knew at that moment she owned him, could make him beg, and she liked the power. Final spurts made his cock jerk, and he shuddered, wanting to hold on to the ecstasy as long as possible.

"Merek." Her voice was so real, so precious, that he had to close his eyes. She wasn't there when he opened them. He knew she wouldn't be, but for a moment he'd wished with every scrap of his battered soul that she would be.

He choked, sagging against the wet tiles. How was he going to survive without her? It was acid corroding his veins knowing she'd never be his again. The people he wanted with him the most would never be with him again. Hell, even the damn cat would never pester him again. He'd never been so alone. Until he met them, it had never mattered to him.

So, he forced himself to remember soaring through the night air with Luca, circling to land on the top of a building where both Alex and Chloe were ripped to pieces by werewolf teeth and claws. He made himself recall the raw sound of Luca's sobs as he realized the woman he loved was lost to him forever. Merek knew that pain. With Laura, his parents, his childhood friend. Even then, it didn't stop him from wanting to drive straight to Seattle and get his people.

One thought came through crystal clear: he couldn't do it. Not to them, not to himself.

How many times did he have to fail them to learn that lesson? Over and over again, he'd failed them, failed himself, failed his own expectations. Some tiny part of him had begun to believe it could be different this time, to need that close human contact again. Some idiotic portion of his soul had reawakened at having people he couldn't read. People who mattered. Not because of work, or any other proximity he had no say in, but just *because.* Because he wanted them, because he craved the contact, because he *needed* them.

And they'd damn near died because of it. Again.

If Chloe had been with another Magickal, someone who could read her future enough to know when danger was coming for her, all of this might have been prevented. He couldn't quite smother the knife of jealousy, of possessiveness, that sliced through his gut. They were *his.* No one else would protect them as vigilantly as he did. He checked the thought. He hadn't done a very good job of protecting them, had he? Which was how he'd ended up in his current position.

Regret and pain and a longing so deep it made his hands tremble twisted inside him. He missed Chloe. He missed Alex. He missed being around them, talking to them, laughing with them. Everything felt empty, hollowed out with hurt.

He'd thought he'd feel less like a complete failure after they were safely away from Smith, after Smith was dead and could never harm them or anyone else again, but nothing had changed. It wasn't about Smith, was it? It wasn't even about this situation. It was about Merek, about how he couldn't handle the fact that his clairvoyance shut down with the people he loved. And he *loved* them. Gods, how he loved them. And they loved him back. He knew it as surely as he knew the sun would rise in the morning. Chloe had even said it.

The warmth that flooded his chest at the thought was so good it was almost painful. He could have them, if only he had the courage to reach out and take what they offered him. Love. A family. People to come home to, and not just an empty existence that consisted of his job and his bitterness.

The choice was his to make. Claiming them meant dealing with the fact that he could never see their future, and had to live day to day knowing that to lose them would rip the heart beating from his chest. But, hell, he already hurt so badly he could barely breathe, and he hadn't even lost them yet.

No, he planned to *throw them away.* He winced, but made himself face that reality. For a man who didn't lie to himself, he'd sold himself a lot of half-truths lately. The meager contact he would have offered Alex would have been an insult to a boy who'd become a son.

And Chloe deserved far better than he'd given her the past week. She'd kick his ass for not calling her, for avoiding her. For avoiding himself. For failing to be honest with her about loving her so much it was like a hammer blow to the heart. He knew she wouldn't blame him for all the other failures he'd seen in himself lately, and while he might never agree with her on that score, he knew she'd be hurt by *this* failure.

But going to her now to make things right, being honest, giving her everything, was a risk. Because he knew exactly how it would feel if he risked it all and lost again.

He'd been right—he couldn't do it. Not to them, not to himself. He couldn't walk away. To do so would be the biggest lie of all. The whole truth was he couldn't live without them, no matter how bad it scared him, no matter how much it could cost him in the end. Having them now was worth it.

Loving them was worth it.

17

Whatever had remained of boyhood was gone from Alex's eyes. A threshold had been crossed, and it couldn't be un-crossed. Far too early, the boy had become a man, the last of his childhood stripped away.

Chloe ached to see that knowledge in his gaze, but the pain was tempered by the understanding that events could have turned out so much worse than they had. She had survived and so had Alex. Even Tess, for all the pain she had to deal with, was alive and would recover someday. She had a life ahead of her, even if it wasn't the life she'd expected.

As Chloe and Millie stepped further into the wolf's hospital room, Chloe watched him hang up the phone, and pointedly didn't let herself think of the still absent Merek and Luca. Every day that passed with no word made her heart hurt.

Millie caught her hand, somehow sensing she needed the supportive gesture. It had been an eventful week since Chloe had been discharged. Ophelia and she were staying at her aunt's mansion in Upper Queen Anne for the time being, and Millie's bodyguard / chauffeur Philip insisted on driving Chloe anywhere she needed to go. All of it was more for her aunt's peace of mind than anything else. If this nightmare had proved anything to Chloe, it was that she was resilient enough to cope with whatever life threw at her.

"Excuse me." A nurse pushed past them both to check Alex's charts and draw a vial of his blood.

He gave the woman a tolerant stare while she stuck him. He'd had to deal with more needles in the last week than anyone should have to in a lifetime, but since he was the one person who had ever received Chloe's treatment for full moon madness, he'd become an instant science project. Desmodus Industries had offered Chloe her old position back, at twice the salary and research funds, so she was carefully monitoring everything the hospital was doing to Alex, but enough was enough. She was taking him home in the morning.

Ushering Millie into a chair beside the wolf's bed, she waited for Nurse Needle to take herself off. Alex brushed at his arm, the small puncture already fading to nothing. "From Desmodus intern to Desmodus lab rat."

"Please. We both know you only took that internship with me to be closer to your dad." Chloe crossed her arms on top of the bed railing, ignoring Alex's slight flinch at the mention of his father. "We need to talk."

"About what?" His voice clearly said he didn't care, which both worried her and made her want to shake him. It would take time, she knew, but she hated seeing him so shut down.

"The future, young man. Your future, to be precise," Millie snapped tartly. She plopped her purse in her lap and reclined in her chair. "What we're going to do with you."

He frowned at the older woman. "I don't understand."

Chloe opened her mouth to explain gently, but Millie beat her to speech. Her tone managed to be both kind and acerbic. "Your parents are both gone, and as far as we know, there are no other relatives to claim you."

Bleakness entered his gaze, and he focused on the wall across from him, cleared his throat. "No, there's no one."

"Okay." Chloe caught his hand in hers, squeezed until he looked at her. "I've already had Aunt Millie's lawyer start taking care of the paperwork so I can adopt you."

"You . . . What?" For the first time in days, she saw real emotion cross his face. Stunned was a good word for it. He blinked, shook his head. "You've been looking out for me the last few weeks, yeah, but adoption is permanent."

"Thanks for that news flash," she replied.

He snorted. "You know what I mean."

"Yeah, I do." And it hurt that he'd assumed after all they'd been through that she'd just let him be lost in the foster care system. The damage Ivan had done to this boy was inexcusable, making him believe he was so disposable. In his obsessed drive to assure that his son didn't die like his wife, Ivan had missed out on the only years he would have had with his child. So much ugliness and grief, and in the end it had all come to rest on Alex's doorstep.

"It's not really kosher for a non-wolf to adopt a wolf." His words were a protest, but he tightened his grip on her hand to an almost painful degree, his desperation so clear it made her want to pick him up and hug him like she had when he was a toddler.

"I'm your godmother. Your parents named me your guardian if anything should ever happen to them. And something happened to them." She tossed her head. "So, fuck 'kosher.' "

"Well, all right." His free hand lifted to rub his nose. "If you're sure."

"I'm one hundred percent sure." She nodded firmly, wrapping both her hands around his.

"What about Merek?"

She twitched her shoulders in a shrug, not meeting his eyes for the first time. "I don't know. He's off doing his cop thing, and I haven't seen or heard from him."

"He's called me a few times, just to check in."

"Ah." That piece of news just twisted the knife already lodged firmly in her heart. "Well, then. I'm guessing that means he's not part of a package deal for adoption. It's just you and me, kid. I'm sure he'll keep in touch with you, though."

Alex looked pained, but didn't reply, and Chloe was grateful for the silence. There really were no words to make this better. Nothing could.

The boy cleared his throat twice, glanced away, sighed and then managed to meet her eyes.

"Merek . . . ah . . . asked me to tell you that Smith was killed today. It's over." Alex tried for an encouraging smile, but didn't quite make it. "He'll be back home soon."

"Well, that's a relief." Millie spoke up; her hazel eyes had a steely glint that should have worried Chloe, but she was too deep in heartache to care.

Chloe knew Merek had contacted his partner, Alex, *and* Millie in the last week, but not her. That answered a final question, didn't it? She wanted to track the man down and beg him to give them another chance, but then wanted to beat herself for her own neediness. He knew better than anyone else except her aunt how damaged she was and how that made her reach for comfort in the middle of the night. He knew if he stuck around she'd turn clingy and pathetic.

He'd walked when he'd had the chance at a clean break, and she couldn't even blame him.

With his control issues, watching them be kidnapped and almost killed while he was shot and unable to do anything to save them would have been his very worst nightmare come true. Again.

If anyone understood that, it was her. Even with all she'd been through, she was still uneasy with the dark. She didn't think she'd ever conquer that. If Merek was there, it was bearable, but he wouldn't be ever again. The sooner she accepted that, the sooner she could get back to coping with the normalcy of her life.

It hurt. Gods, but it hurt worse than anything she could ever have imagined. She wanted to curl into a little ball and scream with the pain of it. If she had thought it would help, she might have done it, but it wouldn't. Nothing would. Like all the other tragedies in her life, she'd just have to endure. Someday it would get better. It might take years, but it *would* get better. If she didn't believe that, she might just collapse from the agony eating away at her soul.

Focusing on something else would help. She had Alex to distract her. Tess's recovery. Work, with its ongoing research. Even Millie and Philip and Ophelia would divert her. Surviving the nights alone in her bed would be her own cross to bear.

She offered Millie and Alex the best smile she could. "I'm going to head over and get my house ready for us. Alex will be released in the morning, and I think it's past time we both went home."

The house was pristine, Alex's room was ready for him, Ophelia had settled in like a queen, and Chloe was about to crawl the walls. She had to get out. Twelve hours of darkness and alone time stood between her and when she went to pick up her godson. She thought about using her research as an excuse and going down to the hospital to check in on Tess and him, but they'd both know something was wrong.

Because she was the biggest masochist on the planet, and because she needed some closure on her relationship with Merek, she put on a slinky dress and took a cab to Sanguine. The place where she'd met her warlock. It seemed a fitting place to say good-bye.

She called Alex and Tess on the way to say good night, then called Millie to let her know where she was headed just in case she was needed for something. Plus, she was going out alone, so it seemed like a good idea to inform someone.

Closing her cell phone, she slipped it into her evening bag and walked into the noise and music that was Sanguine. Dropping her purse on the bar, she slid onto a tall stool and crossed her legs. The place was just as she remembered it, dim lighting, scarred wooden bar, lots of Magickals dancing, drinking, and looking for some play. She nodded when the bartender approached. "What can I get you?"

Just to torture herself a little more, she met the other woman's gaze and asked, "Got anything with honey in it?"

The bartender tilted her head, considering. "I can do a Honnessey or a Honey Bee for you."

"What's the difference?" Not that Chloe cared. If it had alcohol and she could toast to her shattered heart, she was game. At the moment, she was more than ready to drown her sorrows. Tomorrow was soon enough for her to be strong and responsible and parental for Alex.

"One has Hennessey; the other has rum. Twist of lemon, little bit of honey." The bartender flashed a fanged grin. Vampire. "Pick your poison."

"I'll take the Honnessey." And, because Chloe really intended to earn her masochist stripes tonight, she said, "Put a little more honey in it than usual."

"Coming right up."

She dropped a twenty on the bar. "Thanks."

"No problem." The other woman scooped up the bill, went to the cash register, and brought back change. "I've seen that look before. Worn it a time or two myself."

Chloe's grin was weak, but at least she managed a smile at all. She tried to tell herself every day would get better, get easier, but she didn't think it would be that simple. She'd always been so careful in her relationships to not get in too deep, to not need too much. Now that she'd fallen and fallen hard, it was going to take a long time to recover. She couldn't even imagine a relationship after Merek. It made her stomach cramp to consider it.

The bartender slid a drink in front of her and then kindly left her to her misery. Closing her eyes, Chloe took the first sip, let the honey roll over her tongue along with the sharp bite of alcohol.

Gods, just the flavor of it warmed the pit of her belly, and still managed to make her insides ache with longing. She sighed, her breath ruffling the surface of the liquid. Taking a couple of deep chugs, she welcomed the burn. A final toast. To her great fall. It had hurt when she'd crash-landed, but she'd survive. She'd survived a lot lately, so she knew this wouldn't kill her. She'd pick up the pieces and move on, but for a long, long time this would be a gaping wound within her.

The chorus of voices in her head began to murmur. *Merek. merek. MEREK.*

As if she needed her clairaudience's reminder of why she was here. Ignoring the mental noise, she took the final swig of her drink and looked up to motion for the bartender. "Can I get another one?"

"Actually, she's just about to leave, so she doesn't need anything." Merek's sub-bass voice managed to cut through the din of music. "Can you close out her tab?"

The vampire shook her head, flashing a wary look at Merek. "That was her first drink, and she paid cash for it."

"Great. Thanks." He closed his fingers around Chloe's arm and tugged her off of her stool; the neon lights emphasized the angles of his face and the harshness of his expression. He didn't appear at all happy. "Come on, Chloe."

Looked like she wasn't going to avoid the Dear Jane talk. He'd just wanted to dump her in person instead of over the phone. She sighed and left a generous tip on the bar. "Thanks for the drink."

"Come back any time." A bit of sympathy shone in the other woman's gaze as she glanced between Chloe and Merek.

"I will." Though she knew she wouldn't. After tonight, she'd never be able to come back here. It would remind her too much of Merek, and after the closing discussion they were about to have, one more reminder of him would just be too much for her.

The bright streetlights outside illuminated his face better than the neon inside. He looked like hell. His eyes were red-rimmed and bloodshot, and though he appeared clean and healthy, his clothes were ripped and stained with things she didn't even want to identify. He looked like he hadn't shaved in days, and lines of exhaustion carved grooves beside his eyes and mouth.

He was the most beautiful thing she'd ever seen.

And he wasn't for her. Not anymore. She looked anywhere except at him as he escorted her to his car and helped her in. The moment he slid into the driver's seat, she rushed into speech. "Alex and Tess are doing well."

He cleared his throat. "I know. I called."

"Alex said you'd checked in on him." The words were stilted, painful. He hadn't called her, hadn't cared to find out if *she* was all right. So, why did he have to put her through this? The answer would splinter her into a million unrecognizable pieces, and after all the upheaval of these last weeks, she just wasn't brave enough to ask. It wasn't like him to be cruel, but he'd want to make sure it was okay to stay in touch with Alex. Her stomach clenched into a hard knot. That *was* something Merek would do—he was too good a man to lead her on or to abandon a boy who worshipped him.

He controlled the car with his characteristic quiet competence as he navigated the streets on the way to her house. "Alex said you're adopting him."

"Yeah." She stared out the windshield, but managed a small smile. "I sicced my Aunt Millie's evil lawyer on the All-Magickal Council to get it pushed through as soon as possible."

"The adoption people aren't going to know what hit them." Listening to him in the dark was so familiar, so sweet and good she wanted to cry. Instead, she straightened her spine and clenched her fingers around her evening bag.

"As long as I get what I want, they can have a little tailspin hissy fit over it."

He snorted. "Why am I not surprised?"

"I'm a Standish. Why would anyone be surprised?" A sigh of relief eased out of her when they pulled up to the curb in front of her house. Thank the gods. She could escape soon.

"Are you going to look at me?" His deep voice was low and strained.

She hummed in her throat because she had no idea how to answer that. The fact that he hadn't called her was like a spreading bruise inside her, so she chose silence over accusations or tears. How could they have been together for weeks yet he didn't care enough to check in with her? Selina or Alex or Millie or even the hospital staff would have told him she was alive, but that wasn't the same as talking to her and finding out how she was really *doing*.

Sucking in a deep breath, she focused on his hands on the steering wheel because she couldn't meet those gray eyes. "Okay, here it is. I'm adopting Alex, but I want you to feel comfortable being involved in his life. I know you love him, and he adores you, so even though this—" she waved a hand between them "—isn't going anywhere, I don't want you to think I'm going to try to keep you and Alex apart. I wouldn't do that."

"I know you wouldn't." He swallowed twice, his knuckles white as he gripped the wheel. "I guess . . . that answers all the questions I had then."

"Well . . . good. I'm glad we got that settled." She fumbled for her door handle, her belly twisting so hard she thought she might puke. That confirmed that, didn't it? Game over. All he wanted from her now was Alex. She was safe; his duty was done, so this thing between them was done, too. She tried to tell herself it was what she'd expected all along, that she was ready for the pain, but she was wrong. It was crippling, blinding.

"Settled . . . yeah." He turned off the car, let go of the wheel, got out, and came around to open her door for her. She leaped away from his helping hand and scurried along in front of him as he walked her up the steps to her door. The last thing she wanted was for him to touch her. She'd break down and just lose it all over him.

She straightened her shoulders, unlocked her front door, and tossed her purse on the small table in the entryway. Turning to face him, she stood in the open door so it was clear he wasn't invited in. They could finish this little chat outside. She just prayed her voice didn't shake when she spoke. "Was there anything else you needed before you left?"

There. That was good. Polite, calm. She could do this for Alex, no matter how it pained her.

"You," he said softly. The color of his eyes was the deep gray of the sky before a storm. "I need *you*. No matter how hard I try to run away from that fact, I can't escape it. I'm always going to need you." His voice was a grating rasp, and he set his hands on her shoulders, gripping so tight it hurt. "I fucked up, in so many ways, but I love you, Chloe, and I'm sorry I hurt you."

"You . . . you *love* me?" Somehow hearing him say the words was like taking a swift blow. It bowled her over, left her reeling. She'd been so *sure* he would never come for her. She was safe, and he could escape his nightmare. The end. A tear spilled over her lashes, and she dashed it away, a sob hitching her breath. "B-but you didn't call m-me. You c-called to check on Alex, but you didn't bother to do the s-same for me."

Gods, it sounded so needy and whiny. Pathetic. She closed her eyes. Tears continued streaking down her cheeks, and she fought hard to keep from totally breaking down.

"Don't cry, sweetheart. I know I totally fucked things up

between us." Merek eased her into his arms, cradled her against his broad chest. He tilted her head back, wiping the moisture from her cheeks with the pad of his thumb. "Please don't cry. I *wanted* to call you, but I couldn't."

A watery laugh huffed out of her. "Yeah, that's what I told myself, too, until Alex said you *were* calling him."

"That's not what I meant." He rested his forehead against hers, rocking her gently. She could see deep into his eyes, read every emotion there. He didn't try to hide anything from her. "I didn't mean I was physically unable to call you; I meant I had some personal shit to work through. A lot of personal shit."

She leaned back a little and searched his face, but even without the open expression, she'd have known. "Because you couldn't *see* to help us and save us from all the bad stuff."

A chuckle rumbled from him, and he kissed her temple. "You know me too well."

"That's not going to change, I don't think." She swallowed, wishing she didn't have to remind him, wishing she could just take what he said at face value, but she couldn't bear it if he walked away again. She had to know he'd stick it out even if it meant living with his worst fears every day. "You're not suddenly going to wake up tomorrow and be able to see our future. I don't even want you to."

"I know." He sighed, lifted his hand to cradle the back of her head and burrow his fingers into her hair. "That was the shit I was working through. Once I got my head on straight, I drove like a bat out of hell to get to you."

"So you're fine with it?"

"No, I'm not." His smile was rueful. "I'm never going to be, but I'm a lot less fine with walking away from you and Alex because I can't protect you like I want to be able to. I thought it would be better for you if I left, but I couldn't do it. I didn't want to. I want to be with you. I want to help you with the kid. I want all of it. I know it's a risk to love people, and there's always a chance something will take them from you, but I'll take that risk with you. I have to."

"I want all of that, too. I'm willing to take the risk." Letting out the breath she hadn't been aware she was holding, she cupped his face in her palms. His eyes closed, and he leaned into her touch, a fine tension she hadn't noticed before easing from his muscles. She mapped the lines of his face with her fingers. "I thought . . . I thought you might also have some doubts because"—the words caught in her throat, but she forced them out, needing to have everything clear between them—"because I need you too much, and since my mom died, I tend to hold on too tight to the people I love. I cling." She flushed, and she knew he'd see it in the bright beam of her porch light. Every light in the house was on. "I mean, you were bleeding out and all I could think was *don't leave me alone. Gods, I'm so sorry.*"

"Shh. No. None of that." He pulled in a slow breath, his gaze steady, his touch so tender it made tears prick her eyes again. "Sweetheart, did you ever think that of all the people in the world, Alex and I are two who could really use someone who holds on and refuses to let go?" He stroked her hair, her shoulders, her back. "I don't want to leave you alone, and even if that's all you were thinking when I was shot, you still managed to pull nine bullets out of me. You saved my life." He brushed his mouth over her lips, and she fisted her fingers in his shirt to keep him close. "Need me as much as I need you. Love me so much it feels like you can't even breathe. Hold on tight and never let me go."

A sob bubbled out of her, and pure joy broke through. Yes. That was what she wanted with him. Every day for the rest of her life, as long or short as that might be. "I love you, Merek. Everything about you. Dangerous job, control freak, and all. Even if that dangerous job takes you away from me, I will always be grateful for the time I had with you. I love you just the way you are, because you love me the same way, with all my baggage in tow."

"You're the best thing that's ever happened to me." He hauled her up on her tiptoes, pressing her flush against him, and slammed his mouth over hers.

A moan ripped loose from deep down inside her. She knotted her fingers in his hair and shoved her tongue between his lips. His hands cupped her ass, ground her against the hard arc of his erection. Her skin flashed hot and her sex went wet, her head spinning after days and days without him. Gods, she wanted him. Needed him, craved him, loved him.

She tugged him backward, pulling him with her inside the house. He didn't break the kiss as he shut the door and locked it, engaging the security spells. That made her smile against his lips, and then shove him against the closed door.

Jerking his shirt from his pants, she pushed it up until he had to release her mouth to get it over his head. He groaned when her hands skimmed over his chest, her fingers circling his small nipples. "I love your hands on me, sweetheart. I've missed you so fucking much."

"Good. I want you to miss me." She flicked her nail over one nipple, and he jerked and chuckled at the same time. Then he hissed out a breath when she licked the flat brown disc, sucking it between her teeth to nibble. Her fingertips toyed with the other nipple, rolling and pinching it until he groaned for her.

Then she used magic.

A hoarse cry wrenched from him, and he shuddered, his big hands biting into her ass. *"Fuck."*

She let his nipple loose, flicking her tongue over it to tease him. "We're getting to that."

He bent and scooped her into his arms, which made her squeak and grab for his shoulders. "We're a hell of lot closer than 'getting to that,' sweetheart. I haven't had you in days. You can play with me later." His teeth flashed in a white smile. "Much, much later."

"Hurry."

The room sped by as he moved toward her bedroom. He set her on the bed, and Ophelia uncurled from the end of the mattress, trotted over to them, and purred. Merek chuckled and scooped the cat against his chest, stroking her as he walked away. "Sorry, sugar. This is a human-only reunion."

He dropped her to the floor outside the bedroom and kicked the door shut as he came back to Chloe. She propped herself up on her elbows, watching him. Her breath caught when she noticed the puckered scars that now marred his torso. She sat up, brushing her fingers over them when he drew near, searching out all of them on his chest, side, and back. How close she'd come to losing him. Her throat closed at the thought.

"It didn't happen, sweetheart." He caught her hands, drew them to his lips to kiss. "I'm here. I'm not going anywhere."

She nodded. He was right. They'd had a lot of close calls lately, but they were still here. They just had to hold on as tight as they could for as long as they could. Starting now. She bent forward and flicked her tongue across a scar that sat just above waistband of his pants. She kissed her way across the taut skin and hard muscles of his lower abdomen.

"Chloe," he groaned, sliding his fingers into her hair when she worked his belt and fly open. Her body tightened with longing as she moved her hands over his flesh. She wanted to savor, but it had been too long.

Shoving his pants down, she waited for him to toe off his shoes and socks and step out of his jeans. She stuck her finger through a jagged hole in the heavy fabric. "Rough day?"

"Rough week." He chuckled and dropped to the bed beside her, pushing her flat and leaning up on one elbow to gaze down at her. He slid the pants from her grip and tossed them on the floor. "I'll tell you everything you want to know later. Right now, I need you."

She kicked off her heels, her heart thrumming in her chest at the look in his eyes. "Well, then. I'm all yours."

"Mine. Yes. I like that." He smiled, leaned forward, and brushed his lips over her collarbone. "I also like this dress. You look like a felony waiting to happen."

Shrugging delicately, she let the strap fall off one shoulder. "I clean up okay."

"You're beautiful." He reached for the zipper on the side and slid it down. She arched her back to help him drag the shiny garment over her head. His grin turned feral when he gazed at her bare breasts. "Beautiful . . . and mine."

"Mine," she whispered. She let her fingertips drift down his torso until she could swirl one around the head of his cock. He was wet with pre-cum, and she brought the pearly fluid to her mouth to taste.

His pupils expanded until only a thin rim of silver remained as he watched her. He stopped breathing for a moment, and then he sprang into action. He wrestled her panty hose and under-wear down her legs, and she was naked in seconds. He settled on top of her, his thighs shoving hers apart.

Wrapping her arms around him, she pushed her feet against the mattress, lifting herself in offering. He groaned, reached between them, grasped his cock, and rubbed it up and down her slit, circling the head on her clit. Moisture gushed from her sex, excitement coiling with each brush of his hot flesh against hers.

"Please, Merek," she gasped, shudders running through her body. "Inside me. I need you."

"I need you, too, sweetheart. Always." He guided himself to her entrance, pumping in one slow inch at a time. She wrapped her legs around his waist, thrusting her hips up hard to take all of him. Patience was beyond her.

They both groaned when he was seated deep within her pussy, stretching her channel. She cupped her hands on his strong jaw and urged him down to kiss her. She had to taste him, honey sweet and all Merek. Masculine and perfect and hers. Perfect *for* her. He licked her lips before shoving his tongue into her mouth. His hot, sensual rhythm matched the tempo he set with his hips, working his cock into her slick sex.

Magic flowed so easily between them, twining and melding together. Every movement brought a new wave of pleasure spells skating over their skin. Magic skipped and sizzled, pure carnal energy. Love.

"I love you," she moaned, sliding her hands over his shoulders and back, down to palm his ass and pull him tighter against her.

"Yes." His breath sighed out, and he plunged deeper into her pussy, harder. Faster. "Say it again, sweetheart. Don't ever stop."

When he ground his pelvis into her clit, she sobbed it. The words became a litany born from her soul. "I love you. I love you, Merek. I love you so much."

She arched beneath him, the hair on his chest scraping over her nipples. They tightened to points, and she sighed at how good he felt. He slowed down his thrusts, and she moaned a protest, but his hard penetration every time he entered her made tingles explode over her skin. He braced his arms straight out on either side of her, which changed the angle of his thrust and pushed him deeper between her thighs.

Gasping, she tightened her legs around his waist and tugged lightly at the hair on his chest. The smile he gave her was wicked, and he rolled his hips against her, sending a flood of magic right to the core of her. Her pussy flexed around him, and she sucked in a shocked breath. "Oh, *gods.*"

"I love you, Chloe." Harsh breaths bellowed in and out of his lungs. Sweat gleamed on his face and chest, and he shuddered over her. The way he clenched his jaw and groaned every time he pushed his cock into her sex told her how close he was to orgasm. As close as she was.

The intensity of the spells pouring over her sensitized skin made her writhe. Every inch of them that touched was electrified with it. Power. Pleasure.

He lowered himself until he could suck the tip of her breast into his mouth, his teeth and tongue working her nipple. Then he bit down, and she burst into a thousand pieces. Her pussy spasmed on his cock, her inner walls clamping down on him in strong pulses. He released her nipple with a moan, and he thrust hard and fast into her sex, riding her with fierce intent. His gray eyes sparked molten mercury, swirling with the energy racing back and forth between them.

She arched into him, sending a sizzle of magic down his skin. "Come for me, Merek. Now."

A shout erupted from him, and he froze over her, his cock buried deep. His fluids pumped into her, and he shuddered, his gaze locked with hers as they rode out the storm together. Then he sighed and sank down on her. She wrapped her arms and legs around him, cradling him close. They both shook with the aftereffects of their loving, hearts pounding against each other, sweat sliding down their heated skin.

"I love you, Chloe. Gods, how I love you." He crushed her to him, rolling them onto their sides, but staying deep inside her. Enough love to last ten lifetimes shone in his eyes. He stroked her hair back from her face, his voice and touch reverent. "Only you."

"I love you, too. Only you." She shook her head, tears shimmering in her eyes as she smiled at him. Only Merek had ever made her let down her guard enough to love, to need without fear or shame, to give everything. Her heart and body and soul. Only Merek could bring her through her worst nightmares and still make her feel safe, cherished, loved. Hopeful that their future would be far brighter than their pasts. Bright enough to keep the darkness at bay.

Only Merek.